The Way Back

The Way Back

Marilyn DeMars

iUniverse, Inc.
New York Lincoln Shanghai

The Way Back

All Rights Reserved © 2003 by Marilyn M. DeMars

No part of this book may be reproduced or transmitted in any form or by any means, graphic, electronic, or mechanical, including photocopying, recording, taping, or by any information storage retrieval system, without the written permission of the publisher.

iUniverse, Inc.

For information address:
iUniverse, Inc.
2021 Pine Lake Road, Suite 100
Lincoln, NE 68512
www.iuniverse.com

Author's photo

taken by Terry Bartle

Cover photo

taken by Marilyn DeMars

ISBN: 0-595-29172-4

Printed in the United States of America

To my husband, Dick…
who lights the stars in my sky

Acknowledgments

Thanks to my husband, Dick,
for his awesome editing help,
a few good pushes in the right direction,
and for loving this book as much as I do.

Thanks to my daughter, Terry,
for her endless support,
enthusiastic belief in this book,
and for one adventurous trip to the Isabella River.

Chapter 1

▼

The phone woke Jody Mitchell out of a sound sleep and sent her lunging across the bed toward the nightstand before even realizing what she was doing. She grabbed the receiver automatically. "Hello?"

"Jody." It was a man's voice she didn't recognize.

The green numbers of the digital clock glowed in the dark. 11:37 PM. She sat up amidst her rumpled blanket, voiceless, frightened, heart pounding.

"Jody, I know it's late, but it's important."

Though by now the guy sounded familiar, she still couldn't put a name on him. She blinked her eyes, ran a hand through her hair, tried to think, sharpen her wit, stay calm.

"Jody? Are you there?" the voice asked urgently.

For whoever this was and whatever it was about, there was a distinct sense of trouble. So far she felt the safest keeping silent.

"Jody," he said.

If only it were daytime instead of…

"It's Larry, your cousin Larry," the caller identified himself.

"Larry." Knowing him, being related to him, wasn't settling enough. Though he lived here in town, the two of them didn't communicate often, and his calling now at this hour was way too strange. "What's wrong?"

"I know it's late. Sorry. I'm at a bar in Myre and—"

"Myre?" she questioned.

"It's up north beyond Two Harbors. Glen and I have been camping near here. This is our last night in the area before heading home to Winona and we stopped in for a few beers. I wanted to call and tell you right away that I ran into Don."

Jody felt as though she'd just had the wind knocked out of her. "*Don?* You saw Don?"

"Yeah," Larry said in his own dismay. "About an hour ago. Glen and I were coming in as he was going out. Don and I were suddenly face to face. We just stood gawking at each other without saying anything for about a minute. Then finally I said, 'Is that you, Don?' He nodded and said, 'Hey, Larry.' I asked if this was where he'd been hiding out for eight years. He didn't answer. So then I go, 'Hey, man, why don't you come home? Because isn't it about time? Glen and I are starting back first thing in the morning. You can come with us. I'd really like you to. I really think you should.'"

"And?" Jody prompted.

"He wasn't for it."

"What'd he say? What'd he—"

"He gave me that look. You know, that look of his, told me to piss off, then he left."

Jody dropped back against her pillows, feeling numb from the super fast rise and fall of hope that Larry just took her through regarding her long-lost brother. How dispiriting that the first word ever of Don, since he'd left home in an angry rage eight years ago, should only come like another harsh good-bye.

"So what happened next, Larry?" she asked, eager for anything more he could give her. "Did you go after him?"

"Yeah, sure, I tried. Both me and Glen, we took off outside after him. But he was gone, disappeared just that fast."

"How could he? Surely you would've—"

"There was no sign of him anywhere, believe me, Jody. Nothing, no one on the street or parking lot, no car racing off. He was as gone as if he'd only been an illusion."

"Was he?" Disappointment made her challenge Larry's report.

"Your brother was real, Jody. That's why I'm calling. To let you know I saw him and spoke to him. After he took off I checked the phone book but he wasn't listed. I questioned people here in the bar, but it's like nobody knows nothin' or aren't sayin' if they do, know what I mean? I lost him. Sorry. I had him but I lost him. Don still wants to be lost, that's all I can make of it."

As always, Jody was left hanging between anger and hurt where her brother was concerned. "Stupid! This is just so stupid!" she said from her frustration. Only to add more softly, "How'd he look? Did he seem okay?"

"A little older, of course, otherwise pretty much the same as when any of us last saw him. Ornery. Still ornery. Sad. I thought his eyes looked sad. But I suppose it could've been from drinking. I could tell he'd been drinking, but he wasn't drunk."

"Did he ask about me?"

"No. Like I told you, Jody, he barely said anything before he split. But hey, he's right here in Minnesota. At least we know that much now."

"I'm glad for that," she said, trying to let it be enough.

"You okay?" Larry asked, as if he knew, over the phone, that there were tears welling into her eyes.

She stared into the darkness and aloneness of her room. "Not really. But I guess I have to be. How about you?"

He gave a short laugh. "Still in shock. I mean, figuring how long we've all been on the lookout for Don and then I go running smack into him in a remote little out-in-the-sticks place like this. Unbelievable."

Jody knew that if she'd been the one who had run into Don, he wouldn't have gotten away.

A sigh from Larry indicated his own regret. "I don't know if he actually lives around here or is just passing through like me and Glen. I wish, Jody, that I could stay longer and hopefully meet up with him again and get more out of him, but I can't. My schedule's really tight. Glen and I have to make it back to Winona by tomorrow night, because the day after I'm booked on a flight to New York for a week-long business trip. I recently got this big promotion and I can't—"

Jody understood his limits. "It's okay."

"I wish my news about Don could've been better, something more solid."

She deepened her breathing, trying to own up to the fact that the situation with Don might never get better. "Sometimes...I don't know...I just really feel like giving up on him."

"But you won't," Larry said.

A twitch of a smile slipped through Jody's despair. "You seem awfully certain about that."

"I am. Because even though I don't see you very often these days, little cousin, I know, like I've always known, that you're a girl with guts."

"Guts?" She grimaced at the concept.

"The kind that gets you what you want in life."

"So far I have nothing," she said.

"You're young," Larry denoted, as if his being a couple years older than she made him so much wiser. "Eventually you'll get what you want, just wait and see."

"Like my brother coming home?"

"Sure. Probably. That and a whole lot more."

"Because of my guts?"

"It's your power, kid. Use it. Whatever you want, you only have to go after."

"Just like that?"

"Just like that."

Jody pulled her pajamad knees up to her chest, drawing herself into a tight little huddle. She wished she was as confident as Larry. But the fact was, most of the time the way of the world seemed too big and difficult for her to mess with.

"You haven't forgotten, have you, Jody," her cousin continued, "how when you were ten you went after the neighborhood bully who stole your bike, fought him for it, and got it back all on your own."

"I remember," she said, amazed that Larry still did.

"You were one feisty little tomboy."

"Well, that was then and this is now. I'm no longer ten, nor anywhere near that brave."

"I'm just saying, Jody, to hang tough on whatever is important to you."

It took a moment for her brain to get the signal. "Like…you think I should come up there and look for Don?"

"I don't know. Maybe. Whatever."

"Because it sounds like that's what this call is about."

"Why don't you ask that feisty ten-year-old inside you what's important to her and what she wants to do about it?"

"Sure," Jody scoffed.

"Really," he said.

"Like, she's still here?"

"Isn't she?" Larry returned the question, making it seem like the answer.

"Myre," she verified his location.

"Yeah."

"I don't know, Larry." Her free hand tucked some of her dark hair behind one ear. She squiggled her toes against the sheets, blinked her brown eyes, felt a whole new wave of panic swelling inside her. "I just don't know."

"Yeah, well, it's a shock, that's for sure. Glen and I, we'll probably hang around here for another half hour or so then go back to our campsite. Got a lot of driving ahead of us tomorrow and need to get some sleep. If I should get anything more on Don, I'll call you back. Otherwise…hey, how about if you and I get together when I get back from New York?"

"Let's do that," she said.

"Okay, great, we will. Take care, Jody."

"You, too."

"Yeah. See ya."

"Thanks for calling. See ya, Larry."

Jody hung up, left her room, and walked down the hall past the doorways of the two other bedrooms. She felt more alone than ever now in the old family house, hearing that Don had been seen but still had such a hostile attitude toward coming back.

The steps creaked beneath her bare feet as she descended to the foyer. The banister wobbled when she took it, and her hand flinched at the instant reminder of its unstable condition. The foyer nightlight, on the side table near the front door, shone dimly into the living room. Jody strolled about aimlessly, her mind spinning with the news of Don.

It was hard, living with the agony of having a fugitive brother. She'd spent eight years of her young life hating how he'd taken off, but nonetheless forgiving him. Missing all they might have had together as brother and sister. Longing to reunite with him, but heartsick that might never happen. Worrying continually, praying for him to be okay. Myre…tonight he'd been spotted in a place called Myre.

She lifted a family portrait off a shelf and tilted it into the faint light. She studied the foursome. The mother, dad, brother, and sister. Everyone was smiling happily. But it was soon after that time that her mother had gotten sick and died from a swift, cruel illness. Jody'd been seven, Don twelve.

She picked up another picture off the end table beside the couch. It was of Don at age nineteen, the last picture taken of him before he'd left, a very solemn look on his handsome face. He hadn't been pleased that day, at her coming around the corner with her camera and catching him sitting on the front porch in his funk mood. He yelled at her for invading his privacy. And it left her wondering so many times after if she'd been one of his reason's for leaving home. Strange, how she both hated and cherished this photo. "I'm sorry," she whispered, setting it back on the table.

Jody was twenty-two now and Don twenty-seven. Unbelievable, how time passed. Unbelievable, how while she grew older and ought to be thinking about some sort of future for herself, she only seemed to be going around and around in hopeless circles connected to her past. She couldn't begin to imagine what Don might be doing with his life.

It was stuffy in the living room. She went to the side window, turned the lock, tried to lift it. Nothing. She gritted her teeth and tried again. Nothing.

"Stupid window!" She pounded the frame with the heel of her hand. Finally she managed to budge the window up a few inches.

The sweet night air drifted in through the scant opening, rewarding her effort. She inhaled deeply, gratifyingly. The breeze outside danced gently through her next-door neighbor's maple tree that hung part way over the property line fence, and moonlight sifted softly through the leaves.

Life wasn't easy for Jody, losing her mother so young, then her brother, then her dad only last year. When Fred Mitchell died, there'd been no way for Jody to get in touch with Don. Besides her aloneness and sadness, she agonized over and over how Don could disassociate himself like that from his family. Didn't he have a heart? Conscience? Didn't he ever think how much she needed him? She'd been left with a lot to handle all by herself, legal stuff, financial stuff, household stuff, emotional stuff. She needed him. He was her brother. He belonged home.

Suddenly hitting like a bolt of lightning, Jody felt the feisty ten-year-old come alive within her, deciding that she was going to go find Don and bring him back.

She flicked on the desk light just long enough to dial a number, then turned it back off. Standing in the dark, gazing out the window at the night, she waited for an answer.

On the third ring, a groggy voice snarled, "Yeah."

"Elliot, it's me. I can't sleep," she told the guy who owned the motel where she worked. He lived at the motel in room number one, adjoining the office. She could do this to him because he was more than just a boss. He was a good friend, her best friend.

"You woke me up to share that with me? Gee, thanks." The occasional gruffness that sprang from Elliot Treggor meant nothing. It was only his manly attempt to cover the teddy bear image he was stuck with.

"I won't be in tomorrow," she said. "I'm leaving town."

"What? Huh? What're you talking about? Jody? Wait a minute…gimme a chance to get my senses here, okay? Jeez."

She looked out the window again, allowing Elliot some time. Listening to the wispy rustle of leaves helped soothe her impatient wait.

When she figured Elliot was awake enough to handle it, she said, "I'm going to drive up to Myre to look for Don."

"You…you know where he is?" Elliot was now awake, but no less muddled.

"I got a phone call from my cousin Larry. He saw Don tonight in Myre."

"He did? Really?"

"They ran into each other accidentally."

"Amazing. And your cousin…he found out stuff? They talked?"

"Not much. Don didn't say much at all. He basically told Larry to piss off, and then he split."

"What is it with that brother of yours?"

"I don't know," she said dismally. "But I aim to find out soon as I find him."

"So you're—" Elliot interrupted himself with a moan. "Where the hell is Myre?"

"Somewhere up past Two Harbors. I've got to go, Elliot. In all these years I've never had a clue where Don might be. Now that I've got one, I've got to act on it. You can get by without me for a—"

"No. I mean, yeah, sure, the motel can manage without you, but no, you're not going off alone like that."

"I didn't call to have you try and talk me out of this, I just called to let you know that I'm going."

"Jody. No. Slow down." Elliot's words came faster and louder. "We'll talk about this in the morning."

"It's already morning. I'm leaving."

"No! I can't let you do that."

"Let?" She was partly amused, partly annoyed.

"You're a kid. You—"

"Right, I'm ten years old and madder'n hell."

"Huh?" There was no way he understood that.

"It's time Don came home."

"According to you."

"I'm going to go get him, Elliot," she said in a that's that tone.

"Look, Jody, you owe me more than a phone call in the middle of the night about this. Come to the motel, we'll have coffee and talk. At least promise me that before you take off, okay?"

"I have a lot to do and I—"

"Please."

"It won't do any good for me to—"

"Jody." His desperation reached the point of hers.

She blew a puff of air. "Okay."

"Good," he said, notably relieved. "Let's make it a few hours, like after we both get a little more sleep. Okay?"

"But, I—"

"App, app," he said as a reminder for her to slow down.

She agreed to the get together and hung up.

Still at the window, she took an endearing look at the house next door. There was a light in the kitchen. Matthew, who was eighty-five and often had trouble sleeping nights, was likely fixing his cure-all cup of warm milk. Jody hated warm milk but took some comfort of her own in simply finding that he, too, was up at this very same hour. She watched the shadowy figure move back and forth between the counter and stove several times before sitting down to the table. And then he was still except for the periodic lift of his cup.

When Jody's eyes eventually grew bleary from staring across the way at Matthew, she lifted her gaze upward to the open patch of black sky that stretched north in the promising direction of Myre.

Chapter 2

It was a beautiful summer morning. Sixty-four, low dew point, the rising sun slanting between trees and buildings like an affirmation of goodness. The Treggor Motel was ordinarily a twenty minute drive from Jody's house, though possibly fifteen as she drove today. The wind through her Reliant's open window ruffled her dark hair. An upbeat song played on the radio. Showered, dressed in jeans and a tee-shirt, and on her way to talk to Elliot, she felt really good despite not having slept more than three hours last night. After her late phone calls with Larry and Elliot, she'd curled up in a living room chair with an afghan over her and only dozed sporadically between her new and surging expectations of finding Don.

Three months ago, in the line of progress, the town of Winona completed a major redesigning of Highway 64. More lanes were added and unduly twists and bends eliminated, ultimately allowing the usual heavy east-west traffic to flow more smoothly and safely.

The Treggor Motel, unfortunately, was now left sitting back along the cropped off old stretch of Highway 64, out of sight and almost out of commission. It was a small motel, ten rooms in a row. Along with its decline in business, its appearance was slipping as well. Spreading weeds were choking the grass, windows were filmy, paint was peeling, and the front name sign hung faded and crooked. It was hard to figure Elliot Treggor's precise feelings toward the motel these days, because while he showed no desire for bringing it back to life again, neither was he willing to let it go.

He was in the office when Jody walked in, sitting on the stool behind the counter, sipping a mug of coffee. "Hey," he greeted her.

"Hey," she said, going directly over to inspect the register book that was lying open before him. "Nobody again last night," she observed, irked but not surprised.

Elliot cracked a laugh. "Yeah, we're on a roll…three days in a row without a guest." He was thirty-six, with slightly graying dark hair and a few extra pounds on his mere five six frame. He was funny, caring, sweet, and generous except for not having paid his employees in two weeks.

Jody pursed her mouth and slammed the register cover shut purposely hard. Having shared in the running of the Treggor as much as she had over the past two years, it pained her to watch it die. She knew it was painful for Elliot, too, even though his feelings about it always seemed to reel with more wisecracks than recovery tactics.

"You should be out there mowing the lawn," she said, motioning through the dingy front window.

"Yeah…I know…" he agreed lazily. "Tell you what, stay home from this trip you're carrying on about and I'll let you mow it."

"I'll mow it first, if you want me to," she said seriously to his kidding, "but then I'm definitely leaving for Myre."

Elliot poured coffee into the other mug and slid it across the counter toward her.

"No thanks," she said.

"But you like my coffee," he said.

She jingled her car keys. "I just came to hear what you have to say, then I'm going back home to pack. So…?"

Elliot took another drink from his mug. "So this trip, then that means you've actually got Don's address?"

Jody stilled her keys and rolled her eyes. "Not exactly."

"But you said Myre, your cousin saw him in Myre, wherever that is."

"I told you, it's somewhere up past Two Harbors. Larry saw Don there, yeah, but he wasn't sure if he actually lives there or was just traveling through."

"Great," Elliot said like a strike against hope.

"Larry would've stayed and tried to find him again, but he's scheduled to fly to New York on business tomorrow. I thought about this, Elliot. It's something I have to do. I have to go up there and find Don. I have to."

Elliot nodded skeptically. "And when you find him, if you do, then what?"

"I'll bring him back here with me."

"He knows your address, Jody. Why do you suppose, in all this time, that he's never come home on his own?"

"I don't know." She blinked to keep back the tears burning behind her eyes, and stuck her hands on her hips. "But that's what I'm going to find out."

"You've got money to make this trip? Elliot asked doubtingly. "With what I'm paying, or rather not paying you?"

"It won't cost that much. Gas for the car and—"

"I don't like it." Elliot slipped off the stool and came out from behind the counter, flapping his hands in the air as if he were shooing away her plan. "Your wanting to go off on your own like this to some unbeknownst place called Myre, looking for someone who obviously doesn't want to be found."

"I'll be okay," the ten-year-old within Jody argued the adult. "I'm determined. And determination makes one strong."

"It can also make one crazy. Jody, Jody, come on…" Elliot's caring reeked of warning, "don't do this." He stood before her, and in their sameness of height their eyes met straight on and earnestly.

"I'm not crazy," she said.

Elliot turned up a debatable grin. "You've never driven more than twenty miles outside of Winona."

"That doesn't mean I can't." She spun away from him and headed for the door.

"I'll see you when I get back."

Elliot caught her by the arm. "Whoa! I can't let you do this."

Jody gave him another moment, another choice. "Then go with me."

"You're kidding," he jeered. But in the next moment decided, "Okay, you're not kidding. But you are forgetting that I've got this motel to run."

She glanced from left to right at the small, inert office and gave a shrug. "What's to run?"

Elliot saw more. "We might get customers. I have to be here."

"Tom and Rose can watch it for you," she suggested of the Rissens, the married couple in their sixties who worked in short intermingled shifts with her and Elliot.

"I can't afford them full time," Elliot said.

"They'd probably baby sit the place for nothing if you asked them."

He chuckled at the truth of it. "Yeah, probably, but I can't ask."

"Then close the place down. Just close it down for a couple days."

Elliot held his head between his hands and moaned. "You've got all the answers, don't you?"

"No, not all of them."

"Jody, Jody…I'm the only one you've got looking out for you, and you know how much I care about you."

"I know," she said appreciatively.

"Therefore, I just can't let you—"

"I'm going! With or without you. So make up your mind, which will it be, Elliot." She started toward the door again.

"All right!" he barked.

Jody spun around and went back to throw her arms about his neck. "Thank you, Elliot! Thank you! This means the world to me! I love you!"

"Yeah, yeah," he said modestly, as if the force by which he was doing this hardly deserved any merit.

Jody was ecstatic that he was going and didn't mind that his heart wasn't as into it as hers. "Pack a bag and I'll—"

"Whoa!" He raised his hands in the air. "I thought this was going to be a quick trip…just a matter of going there, getting Don, and coming right back."

"Just in case," she reasoned. "We won't stay any longer than necessary, but we'll have a change of clothes along just in case."

Elliot gave in reluctantly. "Yeah…sure…okay…an extra pair of socks and a clean shirt, what the heck. So okay, uh, let's say I pick you up at seven tomorrow morning."

She narrowed her eyes at him. "We're going today. I'm driving."

"Tomorrow," he argued. "And I'm driving."

Jody offered a compromise. "You can drive, but we leave today."

Elliot chuckled at her shrewdness.

"I mean it," she said. "We're leaving today. It has to be today."

"Okay, okay. I'll pick you up at one."

"Ten."

"Noon."

"Ten-thirty."

"Eleven!" he said with the sound of finality.

"Okay." Jody simmered to the fact that he was at least going and a definite plan was in effect. "Think about mowing the lawn first," she said on her way out.

The door swung shut on an indistinguishable mumble from Elliot.

Matthew was in his front yard watering flowers and shrubs when Jody arrived home and pulled into her driveway. "Everything okay, Jody?" he called as she stepped out of her car.

"Yeah, sure, Matthew." She strolled toward the neighbor she dearly adored.

He was a tall, thin, slow-moving man who almost always wore an old red cardigan sweater and spoke with a chopped-up Jimmy-Stewart sort of drawl. "Well, uh...seeing you home at this time of day, it, uh...scared me a little."

Ever since Jody could remember, Matthew had been like a grandfather to her. She could not have loved a real grandfather more, had she ever known any. But there had never been one for her on either side of her family. Only Matthew.

"I came home to pack," she said cheerfully. "I'm going on a trip."

He turned off the hose to lend her his full attention. "Trip?"

"Yes," was all she could say about it. Though she was bursting to tell him about Don, she decided it best not to yet. Her brother meant as much to Matthew as he meant to her, and she didn't want him getting sadly disappointed if she failed to bring Don back.

"Be gone long?" he asked, as if he already missed her.

She shook her head and gave a smile. "I don't think so."

He swayed unsteadily. "Well, uh...I hope I'll, uh...still be here w-when you get back."

Jody took his arm. "Matthew, your daughter Ellen isn't coming for you for another two months. We've practically got the whole summer together before you move to Arizona. And—" she let up, all but spilling the news of Don, "I'm planning to bring you a very big surprise back from my trip."

"Surprise?" Childlike wonderment brightened his withered look of age. "Well, uh...what kind of surprise? Y'know...it...it's hard for someone my age to...to be surprised over anything anymore. It'd have to be pretty good, pretty big."

She'd put him on the edge now, and if bringing Don home didn't happen she'd surely have to come up with a satisfying alternative. But it had to be Don, it just had to be.

She reached to give Matthew a kiss on the cheek. "Gotta go. Take care. See you soon." She walked back to the driveway and across her yard.

"With the...the surprise," he called after her.

She looked back at him and smiled. "Definitely."

Chapter 3

▼

It was exactly eleven o'clock when Elliot got to Jody's house and rang the front doorbell. He was surprised that she wasn't waiting on the porch for him.

"Come in," she called from inside. "It's open."

When he pulled the screen door, it tipped into the catch of both his hands and scared the heck out of him. The top two hinges had come free of the framework, leaving the door scantily held by only the bottom hinge. He entered the house then turned to manually set the door back in place, like a bad joke waiting for the next person who opened it.

Jody came scurrying from the living room, passing him in the foyer and heading on through the dining room toward the kitchen.

"What have I told you about keeping your door locked?" he said to her fly through.

"I knew you'd be here any minute," she called from the kitchen, "and I had all this last minute stuff to do so I left it open."

"You might've warned me about the screen door."

"What?" she called.

More than the door thing, it bothered Elliot that he'd actually committed to going on this trip with her. It was like one minute he'd been telling her not to go and the next he was going with her. Crazy. Totally crazy.

Jody came back toting a green duffel bag. She dropped it on the floor by Elliot, observing him with a grin. "You look strange."

He chuckled out the side of his mouth. "Oh, I'm very strange. If I weren't I wouldn't be here right now."

"Forgot one more thing in my room," she said, spinning away again. "Be right back."

Elliot watched her run up the stairs. Strange, yes. Crazy, yes. This girl had that effect on him. Nobody could make him crazier than Jody could. And he knew, today more than ever, that the person responsible for making her crazy was her long-lost brother Don. Hopefully this trip would make some sane and meaningful sense out of everything. Elliot only wished he felt more confident than he did about going off to search for a guy who was staying away by choice, and who only maybe lived in the area called Myre, and who reacted to his cousin's surprise appearance by telling him to piss off. None of this felt right to Elliot...except, probably his agreeing to go with Jody rather than letting her go by herself.

She came thundering back down the steps, as excited as a child setting out for Disney World. She stuffed a rolled-up sweatshirt into her duffel, zipped it shut, swooped it up by the strap and slung it onto her shoulder. "That's it. Let's go."

Elliot went out ahead of her, handling the single-hinged screen door gingerly. "When did this happen?"

"Last week." She closed the inner door behind her and locked it.

Elliot guided the faulty screen door back into place.

"Elliot," she said as they left the porch together, "you did bring a bag, too, didn't you?"

"It's in the car. You should have told me about the door, Jody."

"Because...?" she razzed him.

Okay, he wasn't the world's greatest handyman and probably would've procrastinated over any attempt to fix it, but nevertheless, "I just would've liked to have known, that's all."

Jody's rusty old Reliant sat in the driveway ahead of his Skylark. "Don't you want to put it in the garage?" he asked her.

"No. I just want to go, Elliot. Let's just go." She jumped into the passenger side of his car, tossing her bag onto the back seat next to his.

He slipped in behind the wheel. "Are you sure, really sure, about this?"

"It'll be okay in the driveway, believe me," she said, buckling her seatbelt.

He buckled his own and started the engine. "I mean about going on this trip."

"Yes." Her answer was quick and easy and sure.

"Like, totally?" he asked once more before gearing into reverse.

Jody gave a loud, impatient sigh. "You're the one who doesn't seem sure."

"I'm not."

"Fine." In a one fast fluid movement she released her seatbelt and reached over the back of her seat for her duffel.

"No!" Elliot shouted. He grabbed the bag away from her and tossed it back. "Just simmer down, okay? I admit I'm not thrilled about going to Myre, but the fact is I'm going. I...I was just giving you a last chance to change your mind if you wanted to."

"I don't."

"Okay. Neither do I. Jeez."

He backed the car out of the driveway and into the street, sorry for having dampened the spirit of this joyous occasion. "Nice day, huh?" he said, trying to make up for it, dipping his head to view the blue, cloudless sky through the front windshield.

"Yes," she agreed halfheartedly, "except that it's already half over."

"But it's what we're doing with the second half that counts. We're on the way, Jody, toward finding your brother."

Refastening her seatbelt, she seemed notably trusting again. "Thanks, Elliot."

He gave her a sidelong look and caught her smiling. "Right. You couldn't have made this trip in that old clunk of yours."

"The Reliant's okay. Dad took good care of it."

Elliot laughed. "Yeah, I suppose he would have had to, in the hundred years or so that he owned it."

"It's old but it's good."

"Mine's better."

"Not much."

Elliot merged onto the highway that led out of Winona. "We're roughly looking at about three hundred miles ahead of us, Jody. That's just to Two Harbors. And as for Myre, it's not even on the map, because I looked. Did you know it's not on the map?"

When she didn't answer, he glanced over to see that she was into some intense staring out her window. Like, maybe she was trying to imagine what it would be like seeing her brother again after eight years. Or maybe she was worrying that they might not even find him.

Elliot offered her some reassurance that he really had to dig deep for. "It's going to be good, Jody."

"I know," she agreed weakly.

"How about some music?"

"Sure."

He turned on the car radio. Something soft and dreamy was playing. It was nice. He liked it, was enjoying it, until Jody reached forth and switched the station to rock.

"Hey!" he complained. "You really want me to drive that fast?"

She laughed. "One drives by speed limit not music."

With his fingers already rapping time upon the steering wheel, Elliot disagreed. "Tell my speedometer that."

She leaned over to look at the climbing gauge. Then she turned the radio back to the lite station and watched Elliot's speed mellow accordingly.

"It's a fact!" he insisted to the smutty little hiss he heard from her. "Do you know how many accidents are caused from drivers listening to rock 'n roll?"

"Whatever," she said blatantly.

"More than that," he confirmed.

"I mean, whatever gets us to Myre, I don't care. Drive thirty-five if you want to."

"Don't get smart, girlie. I keep up with the speed limit, I just don't go over it. Okay?"

"Whatever," she said again.

They stopped talking after that. And for a long while there was only the sound of the placid music competing weakly against the hum of tires over the pavement.

"Elevator music," Jody eventually made of it.

"Huh?" Elliot asked but then got it. "Come on, are you on this trip to listen to music or to get somewhere?"

It actually bothered him that she didn't have a snappy comeback to that and rather relented to letting him have his way. He owed her for the music choice, to which he paid her a very tender look and a promise he probably shouldn't have. "We'll get there and we'll find him, Jody. We will."

She nodded and gave him a smile so sweet that he almost turned the radio back to rock.

"I'm just not sure it'll be today," he said. "I mean, we'll probably have to lay over somewhere tonight and start out fresh again in the morning. Good idea, our packing bags."

"Oh, Elliot…" Jody said wistfully, "I can't wait to see Don. He's going to be so surprised."

"Yeah," Elliot agreed, though considered the word surprise in a broader sense.

"It's going to be so great."

"Jody, you gotta remember how Don reacted to your cousin Larry."

"I know. But I'm his sister."

"Sister. Right." Elliot could only hope that a sibling rated higher than a cousin. "I'm sure he'll be nicer to you."

* * * *

The afternoon went fast, as did their mileage. Heading into the far north of Minnesota, the roads became more and more thickly lined with tall pines, white birches, and fluttering aspens. Jody offered to do some driving, but Elliot told her no thanks, he was fine. Every so often they stopped for gas, food, a bathroom break, or just to get out of the car and walk around a bit.

So far the trip still seemed very unreal, very impossible to Elliot. Like, any minute now it would be morning and he'd wake up from the silly dream this was, caused by his eating too many Doritos the night before. But then gazing over at Jody, unreal and impossible as she was, he realized he wasn't all that anxious to wake up.

When they reached Duluth, the good-sized tourist's town on Lake Superior's western tip, Elliot suggested they get a place to stay the night. He said he knew of a particular moderate-priced motel up on the hill.

"You know of one?" she asked, as though maybe she shouldn't have asked.

Jody's reaction made him guilefully explain, "Not like you think. Vacations. I've spent a few vacations here. By myself. Years ago. I don't know, maybe the place I'm thinking of isn't even there anymore. We'll see."

Though they'd had a wide, breathtaking view of the great water on their highway approach, within the streets of downtown they could only catch scant glimpses of the lake between the aggregation of buildings.

"Wanna double up and save a buck?" Elliot asked.

Jody gave him a look. "Excuse me?"

"Share a room. I mean, since neither of us have the money to—"

"Okay."

"Okay? Just like that?" He felt slightly offended that she took it so innocently. "You're not the least bit worried about—"

"It's you and me, Elliot. You and me. What's to worry about?"

"Right," he said, unsure whether that was a compliment or a put down.

"Two beds," she insisted upon.

Elliot shook his finger at her. "Ah-ha...you were a little worried, weren't you?"

"You sound like you want me to be."

"Uh, be what?" He was suddenly having to focus tighter on his driving. Man, the traffic was conspiring. He'd had his signal on to move into the left lane so that he could make a left turn at the next intersection, but some bozo in a sports car zipped up along side him from out of nowhere and wrecked his chance. Elliot blasted his horn and got fingered in return.

"Worried," Jody said.

Elliot resented having to go a block farther now to turn. As if one extra block, after all the driving he'd already done that day, really mattered. Winning entry into the left lane this time, he relaxed enough to give Jody a quick look and the return of his attention. Except he didn't understand the look she was giving him. "Sorry. Did I miss something?"

"I was just assuring you that I wasn't worried, for one minute, about sharing a room with you."

"Oh." The light changed and Elliot turned onto a street that led uphill to where he figured the Skyline Motel to be.

Chapter 4

▼

Even though their room at the Skyline Motel was an economical, no frill basic, Jody rated it ten times better than the Treggor. Elliot, after giving it his professional once-over, only rolled his eyes and shrugged. The motel's best feature was how, from the front of it, Lake Superior could openly be seen down the hill beyond the colorful collection of rooftops. Unfortunately, the window of the room they were assigned faced a dismal back alley.

After freshening up they went out to get something to eat. They left the car at the motel and walked, finding a modest little restaurant two blocks away. Since it was past the usual dinner time, there weren't many customers and it was quiet. A seat-yourself place, Elliot did the honors of offering Jody his arm and escorting her to a table with a vinyl tablecloth and an unlit candle. He held her chair for her, took out his lighter and lit the candle, then picked up the menu and handed it to her. He was playing the gentleman bit to the hilt, which was corny, but nice.

"How come you carry a lighter when you don't even smoke?" she asked him.

"For lighting candles, of course," he said through a chuckle.

The waiter brought them water. Jody ordered a hamburger and a Coke. Elliot ordered meat loaf, mashed potatoes, green beans, a basket of bread sticks, a beer, and apple pie.

Later into their wait, Jody said, "I can't believe we're here."

Elliot gave the place a sweeping second look. "Hank's Haven, believe it."

She giggled. "No, I mean Duluth, on our way to finding Don."

"Oh. Yeah. I know. Unreal."

"What?" she questioned when his look upon her turned strangely unfamiliar.

"The candlelight, it becomes you."

"Candlelight? Elliot, in addition to this one little candle between us there are fifty million lights in the place."

"You counted?"

"A dozen, at least."

"But your face, catching that candle glow...I don't know...it...you look so...uh...good...older..."

She tilted her head sideways. "Like maybe thirty?"

"No, no," he said. "Maybe...about...twenty-three."

"Twenty-three?" she exclaimed to the nothingness of it. "I look all of one year older to you?"

"I know," he said, as if it were something spectacular. "Amazing, huh? A year older, a year wiser. Maybe, I don't know, a little more mature. Lovely, very lovely...enchanting...enticing...sexy. Yeah, that's it, I'd say the candlelight makes you look very sexy."

Jody reached across the table and punched him in the arm. "Shut up."

He grasped his arm and moaned with pretend pain. The couple across from them were staring.

"Shut up," she warned him in a whisper. "Do you want to get us thrown out of here?"

"You were the one who took a swing. You'd be the one to go, not me."

"You were harassing me."

"No, I was telling you nice things."

"You were purposely rubbing in the fact that I'm sitting here in jeans, tee-shirt, scraggly hair, drooped shoulders and dark circles under my eyes. You were making fun of that."

"I was trying to pay you a girlie compliment."

"Well, you're not very good at it."

"So what would you rather I say?"

"Nothing. I'd rather you say nothing." Jody reconsidered the blandness of that and teasingly suggested, "Okay, you could try saying how cool my Reeboks are."

Elliot bent down, lifted an edge of the tablecloth, and peeked at her shoes. "Very nice," he said, straightening back up with that smirky look of his. "Thrift shop?"

"They're broken in," she said. "That's what makes them so cool."

"You sure it's not all the holes and tears in them, like air-conditioning, that makes them cool?"

"There are no holes, no tears. A few crinkles and stains, but they—"

"Maybe if you put them up here in the candlelight, I'd see the true beauty of which you are speaking."

Starting to feel giddy and challenged, from the combined effects of being tired and being with Elliot, Jody was just starting to lift a Reebok foot up to the table top when their waiter returned.

"Is everything all right?" he asked.

"Fine," Elliot said as Jody quickly tucked her leg back under the table. "Wonderful candle. Gives a wonderful effect. We're really enjoying it."

"Good. I'm afraid we're out of apple pie, Sir."

"You don't have to be afraid," Elliot chuckled. "I'll take blueberry."

The waiter shook his head no.

"Lemon meringue?" Elliot asked.

The waiter smiled and nodded. Then to Jody, he said, "May I suggest you keep your feet on the floor, Miss."

Jody and Elliot snickered quietly as he walked away.

* * * *

It had grown darker and chillier outside by the time they left the restaurant. They were glad they had their jackets. Jody suggested they take a stroll. Elliot moaned and held his stomach, but then said okay if she promised to walk slowly.

They went three blocks beyond the restaurant, two more down the steep hill, and across the busy main street. Jody wanted to see the lake close up, and Elliot admitted he did too.

They passed several warehouse buildings, empty parking lots, grassy areas with benches, old-fashioned lamp posts, and variant little gift and snack shops closed for the day. Waves lapped noisily against the jagged embankment of rocks edging Superior's shoreline.

As they reached a sandy area near the water, Jody lit off into an excited run, shouting, "Isn't this awesome!"

"Awesome," she heard Elliot, behind her, cheer to a lesser degree.

Obscured as it was by the darkness, the ocean like water was nothing less of thrilling. The smell, the sound, the surging in, and the extending back out to its seemingly endless mystique was phenomenal.

"It's so big!" Jody exclaimed.

"A hundred and...and sixty miles across its...widest part," Elliot said in breathless gasps as he followed her.

When Jody jumped over a big piece of driftwood and slipped in the sand and fell, Elliot was there in an instant, dropping to his knees beside her. "You okay?"

Her answer was a helpless burst of laughter. After which she was instantly back on her feet and lending him a hand back up to his.

"Jeez, you gave me a scare," he said, clutching his chest.

"Sorry." She began dancing in a circle.

"You could say it like you mean it," he said.

Jody took off again, skipping down the beach, hands raised to the sky in praise. "Don't you just love Duluth, Elliot? It's gotta be the most awesome place in the whole world!"

He didn't answer until he caught up to her. Even then he stood quietly looking out over the dark, moon-sparkled water for a few minutes before speaking. "I haven't been here in years. But yeah, I agree, it's pretty awesome. So this is your first time here?"

"Second. I was here once when I was a kid. I loved it then and I love it now."

They stood side by side, equally smitten by Lake Superior and with no further want of the moment.

When Elliot suggested they sit down on the grounded tree limb lying in the sand behind them, Jody thought it was a good idea. As she sat she pulled her jacket shut tighter against the fine sprays of water coming off the lake.

"We can find a more protected spot," Elliot said, settling beside her and scrunching deeper into his own jacket.

"No, this is great." Though Jody was shivering, she was unwilling to distance herself any farther from the water. "So, you said you used to come here?"

"Years ago."

"Often?"

"Yeah, kind of."

"Why?"

Elliot laughed. "Vacations. Why the why?"

"You don't seem like the vacationing type."

"How about getaways? Do I seem more like the getaway type?"

"I don't know. What were you trying to get away from?"

He didn't answer, but Jody kept at him. "Did you bring women here? To the Skyline Motel?"

Elliot laughed nervously. "No. I told you before that I used to come here by myself. What kind of guy do you think I am?"

"You're bringing me here."

He sobered quickly. "You…yeah, you…"

"I don't know much about your past, Elliot. You never talk to me about it."

"You never ask."

"I'm asking now."

"Like what?"

"You know, your relationships with women. I mean, you've had them, relationships with women, haven't you? You must have, at your age. So tell me what were they—"

"You're beginning to sound like a jealous girlfriend."

Jody punched him in the side.

Elliot fell backwards off the log, surely more from playfulness than impact. Although for the way he then laid there totally motionless and silent, Jody got scared.

She swung her legs over the log and dropped down beside him, shaking him. "Elliot? Elliot!"

He popped his eyes open and laughed. "Gotcha!"

She'd been had. Deservingly so. "I shouldn't have hit you. I'm sorry. I was just goofing around."

He got to his feet and helped her to hers. "You pack quite a wallop. And twice in one night now. My injuries just may hamper my driving tomorrow, you know."

"I'll drive," she said.

"No, no, I'm fine." Elliot's recovery was quick.

Jody doubled her fist, threatening to hit him again.

Elliot held up his hands defensively. "Hey! That's enough! Jeez, no wonder your brother left home."

Their kidding around died on the spot. Jody walked away from him, feeling badly.

Elliot fast-stepped along side of her, slipping an arm around her shoulder. "Sorry. I didn't mean that. I have no idea why I said it. I...was just goofing around."

Goofing around was something they both did a little too much of sometimes. She looked at him with a half smile. "We'll call it even, okay? My punch, your punch."

"I can see that the one I gave you was harder than the one you gave me."

"I'm okay."

"Me too."

"I wasn't cruel to Don," Jody said as they strolled beside one another.

"I'm sure you weren't."

"I loved him."

"I know."

"I…suppose…sometimes…I irritated him."

"Guys don't leave home because of irritating little sisters," Elliot said.

"So why then?" she asked, feeling painfully unsettled. "Why do they?"

Elliot shrugged.

"Look at you," she said, stopping in place for a moment to do just that, "you kept your family ties, you're running your father's business."

"Only because he died and stuck me with it."

"Which has been how many years now?"

"Just because I'm still with it doesn't mean I like it."

"Then why are you still with that stupid motel if it's really not your passion?"

Though Elliot had no answer, no wisecrack, no laugh, no shrug, his eyes began to shimmer with something.

"So what is your passion?" Jody urged. "I mean, everybody has one and—"

"Let's not get away from the subject of this trip, which is Don, not me."

She sighed at the truth of it and started walking again. "You're probably thinking that it's *my* passion, finding him, bringing him home."

Elliot, walking beside her, overstated his response. "No, I would've never thought that."

"There are other important things in my life besides Don. It's just that in order to focus on them I first need to get some things settled with him, you know?"

"That brother of yours, he really means a lot to you, doesn't he?"

"Yes."

Elliot put his arm around her again. "We'll find him, Jody, we will," he said with the sound of a guarantee.

* * * *

It was good, getting back to their motel room. Quiet, cozy, warm and dry. Except it was kind of strange, Jody thought, how Elliot stopped just inside the door and stood there in place. His expression as he watched her turn down her bed covers seemed to imply that he might be having second thoughts about their sharing a room.

"What's wrong?" She gave him the chance to back out if he wanted.

"Nothing," he said.

When Jody took off her shoes and jacket and crawled into bed with her clothes on, Elliot did the same in the bed across from hers.

She clutched her covers up tight to her chin, feeling chilled through from the time they'd spent by the water. She would shower in the morning, but right now she only wanted to snuggle down deeply, get warm, and go to sleep.

Even with the light out, the room did not go completely dark. A flickering reddish glow shone through the papery window shade from the neon bar sign across the alley. Thoughts about tomorrow and their resumed search for Don stirred at her and kept her awake for a long time.

When Jody finally started to feel herself drifting off, she yawned, turned onto her side and took a last look over at Elliot. "Good-night," she whispered.

But he was already out and snoring softly. She closed her eyes, feeling a nice sort of comfort in listening to the sound and in having him near. "Thank you," she whispered.

CHAPTER 5

▼

Don Mitchell sat on the ground outside his cabin. With his back against a tree. By himself. In the dark. Gazing up at the stars. Still feeling horrendously shocked at having run into his cousin Larry last night.

It'd been a long time since he'd seen anyone from his family or his past. Which was fine, the way he'd come to prefer it. Until suddenly last night out of the blue that preference was blown. Larry appeared face to face with him, asking questions, laying blame, trying to set up his next move for him. Unbelievable, a chance meeting such as that, given the size and location of Myre. But Don had offered very few words to his cousin and had gotten out of there fast before he could mess with his mind any further.

Now, tonight, alone with his after thoughts, Don realized the full dire effect last night's brief incident managed to foist on him. Throughout his logging job today he'd felt a needling sort of strangeness consuming him. It took him most of the day to figure out what it meant. And when he did, it hit hard. He realized that maybe the tough, unyielding Don Mitchell was actually feeling sorry about things. Sorry. About last night. Possibly about everything.

His seeing Larry last night had bothered him all day. Enough that it distracted his attention away from his tree cutting at one point and nearly cost him a serious accident with his chain saw. The close call shook him up plenty, as did the harsh verbal lashing it drew from his foreman, Jim. As usual, Don's own hot temper bucked and he spat back some equally bad words at Jim, after which he almost took off right then and there from his job, just as he'd done last night from Larry and eight years ago from Winona. But he didn't. He stayed. And he worked double hard at controlling himself after that and concentrating better on his work. Thus he'd managed to hang in there till quitting time.

Before coming home tonight to his secluded little hideaway in the woods, he'd stopped off at the bar in Myre for a talk with Brad, the bartender, about Larry and Glen having been in there last night. He asked Brad if he knew whether the guys had truly left the area as they'd planned. Brad was able to make a pretty good assumption that they had. And then he'd additionally assured Don that for all the questions his cousin had asked about him last night, nobody in the place had given any actual answers. Knowing that brought a sense of relief to Don. He appreciated the fact that most folks who lived around there respected and guarded one another's privacy.

Sitting in the deep and silent dark, swigging from a bottle of vodka that he'd chosen instead of supper, Don reaffirmed his need for solitude. Even though he felt regretful about his current life, he knew that keeping to himself was still a necessity. That's just how it was. The way it had become and was destined to stay. He couldn't go back to his previous life if he wanted to. Not ever.

He'd messed up bad years ago in Winona. He'd said and done things he couldn't get over, couldn't fix, couldn't deal with in any other way but to leave. There'd been all those fights with his dad. About his education, his faltering reputation, his lack of direction. He'd never been able to do anything right in his dad's eyes. Not one solitary thing. It didn't help any either, Don's finding out that some of the guys he thought were his trustworthy good friends were actually doing armed robberies behind his back and using him for social cover. And there was Krista, the girl he'd loved and wanted to marry but who dumped him and turned to his best friend Rossi. At age nineteen, Don's life had literally fallen apart, and it had been just so much easier to run from it rather than trying to mend it.

He blinked at the tears starting to well in his eyes. The stars he was looking at became a misty blur. He was tired. Physically, mentally, and spiritually. Okay, maybe he'd weakened for a time today, but the vodka was helping and he was better now. He'd just needed a little recharging, that's all, toward reassuring himself that Don Mitchell was just as tough and unyielding as he'd always been. Right.

Chapter 6

▼

Elliot waited in the car for Jody the next morning. It was almost ten. They'd planned to be on the road by eight, but both of them had overlooked setting the alarm before crashing last night. For as worn out as all that driving had left him yesterday, Elliot had no problem sleeping in this morning. He might've still been sleeping if Jody hadn't woke up on her own, found how late it was, then brutally shook him awake.

He checked his watch again. For the rush she seemed to be in, her turn after his in the bathroom seemed to be taking forever. Or maybe it was just that he had gotten ready and packed and out of there in super fast time, once he'd been brutally awakened, kind as if he felt there'd been something immoral about having spent the night in a motel room with Jody. Ridiculous. Nothing happened, nothing could have, would have. This trip wasn't about them, it was about her brother. Those funny little twinges he sometimes got about her were nothing more than jangled nerves. She unjangled him the way any hyper active child would. Except, she wasn't exactly a child.

She finally came out, looking adorably perky, as if the extra couple of hours sleep she'd accidentally caught, had done her a world of good. Her brown eyes were bright with anticipation and her step was bouncy. Elliot was glad to see her so refreshed, because she'd pretty much been running in high gear ever since hearing about Don.

She tossed her bag onto the back seat and hopped into the front across from him. "How could you forget to set the alarm last night?" she asked, with an attitude that knocked points off looking perky.

"I suppose the same way that you'd forgot to," he dished it back to her.

They left Duluth by way of North Shore Drive, a narrow curving road closely following the edge of Lake Superior. Lending perfect balance to the beautiful open view of the water off one side of the road were steep, rugged embankments of rock, trees and wild flowers on the other. Seagulls flapped and soared in the air. The sun shone brightly and the sky was a clear blue. This venture was almost starting to feel more like a vacation than a search mission.

They would stop for breakfast in Two Harbors and inquire there about how exactly to find Myre. Elliot wondered who, if anyone, might possibly have heard of Myre.

* * * *

Time was really getting away from them. It was almost eleven-thirty when they finished having pancakes in a Two Harbors café. Elliot's need for help came down to the wire. He disliked the idea of having to seek verbal instructions instead of following a map, but since Myre wasn't on the map, he had no choice. Somewhere beyond here, where they were at right now, was all he had to go on. He needed more. Okay, so who should he ask? Who was less likely to burst out laughing at his asking about such a destination?

After carefully scanning everyone in the place, he eventually approached an old guy with a plaid shirt and suspenders seated at a table with two other old timers. "Ever hear of Myre?"

"What?" the man asked, frowning up at Elliot as though he was either hard of hearing or greatly puzzled.

"Myre," Elliot repeated. "Ever hear of it?"

"Yup," the man said.

"Know where it is?"

"Yup."

"Wanna tell me?"

"You don't know?"

"Do I sound like I know?" Elliot's voice shortened.

"Know where the Isabella River is?"

"No, that neither."

"Get off North Shore Drive at the next stop light," the man said, with his bent bony finger drawing it in the air, "and go due north seventy-five or eighty miles. Myre's up there. Near the river. But not quite as far as the river."

"There'll be a sign? You think there'll be a sign?"

"Yup, should be a little sign."

"How little?" Elliot asked, testing his credibility. "I mean, will we see it? Do you think we'll see it?"

"You're not from around here, are you?" the man gathered sympathetically.

"It's not on my map." Elliot still found that hard to imagine, hard to accept. "Are there any maps available that it might be on?"

"Nope."

"No. No, of course not. Why should I expect it to be on any map, this place we're looking for? What am I thinking?" Elliot smacked himself in the forehead.

Embarrassed and eager to leave, Jody paid the check and pushed him outside. "Relax, okay? I think we've got enough directions to go on."

Elliot wasn't so sure. It really bothered him, having no map, no preciseness. "We're going into the wilderness here, Jody. I don't know, I just don't know."

She was smiling and coaxing him on with those bewitching eyes of hers. "You act like you've never been on an adventure before."

He sighed heavily and pulled his keys out of his pocket.

"We'll find it," she said. "The man said it's up there."

"Up there," he granted sarcastically.

"There are roads, Elliot, real roads. What is your problem?"

"It's not on the map, that's my problem!"

"We should've gotten a much earlier start than this," Jody reminded him.

"Yes, dear," Elliot made like a henpecked husband.

"We're running two hours late."

"I know, dear."

"You dawdled way too long over your coffee in there."

"Yes, dear."

After one too many *yes, dears* Jody slugged him in the arm. "Want me to drive?" she asked as they reached the car.

"No, dear," Elliot said, then ducked when she threatened to hit him again.

"Stop that!" The game had tired, but she couldn't get out of it.

"Yes, d...*Jody*." Elliot, himself, had a hard time getting out of it. "Myre's not on the map, that's my problem. I happen to feel very insecure about driving to places that aren't even on a map."

Jody turned quiet. Elliot gave her a look, regretting his negativity. But she was expecting an awful lot here. For him, a Winona motel owner, to suddenly turn northern woodsman. To know precisely where he was going when the location of Myre seemed anything but precise.

He gave her another look, supposing that her wholeheartedly counting on him the way she did touched him as much as it scared him. And he knew that somehow he had to come through for her.

"Up there," he said, reaffirming their destination and trying to make like he really believed it was just that simple.

Chapter 7

▼

The thick national forest they were soon weaving through proved to be more scenic than threatening, and Jody was glad to hear Elliot admit it and begin to enjoy the view as much as she was.

"It's beautiful, really beautiful," he exclaimed.

"Of course it is," she said. "Did you ever see so many trees in all your life?"

"Never. But I suppose a blacktopped road, with a yellow center line and occasional sign posts, does insure that we're still linked to civilization. At least, I hope it does."

"We're still on the planet earth, Elliot."

"Earth," he said, ridiculing it with a goofy grin. "Maybe I'd be more apt to believe that if I weren't sitting next to an angel."

She swatted his shoulder.

"And yet," he added laughingly, "I doubt that real angels hit people."

After fifty some miles of picturesque forestry, the view started turning grim. Smooth, clearly marked roads transformed into narrow, primitive roads, winding even deeper into remote backwoods. Surely they were headed to nowhere and nothing, Jody was beginning to think. But though her confidence had started slipping, she was not yet ready to admit this trip might be a mistake.

Finally, thankfully, there came a small sign with an arrow pointing out a turn.

MYRE–26 MILES
ISABELLA RIVER–29 MILES

Nearly hidden by brush, it was frightening how they almost missed it. It was only by luck they hadn't.

"So far this trip is riding on more luck than sense," Elliot said.
Jody gave a quiet nod.

*　　*　　*　　*

When they reached Myre, they found the town's center consisted merely of a grocery store and a bar. The bar was no doubt the one where Larry had run into Don.

"There!" Jody pointed to it..

Elliot parked the Skylark. "Yeah, I can sure use a drink."

Though Jody, too, felt tense, as much from their long ride as to their nearness of finding Don, she wasn't sure that drinking was a good idea.

"What…no hitching rail?" Elliot quipped as they strode toward the bar with its old-west facade.

Across the road and beyond the grocery store were a scattering of five houses. Jody observed them longingly. "I wonder if Don lives in any of those."

"I doubt it," Elliot said.

They entered the bar, slightly blinded at first, going from sunlight to the dimness inside. It was the middle of the afternoon, no other customers, no TV going, no music. Dead quiet.

The bartender greeted them into his obvious slow day. "What can I do ya?"

Elliot squinted at him. "Huh?"

The bartender rephrased his question. "What can I get you?"

"Oh, uh…scotch on the rocks."

"Vodka sour," Jody said for herself, causing Elliot's eyebrows to rise. It was the only drink she was even halfway familiar with since turning twenty-one a year ago, and of which she'd only ever drunk a couple times at that and managed to tolerate. Anyway, now, it gave her a sense of sophistication having a specific drink name ready the moment the occasion called for one.

She and Elliot took stools at the mahogany bar. The bartender asked to see Jody's ID.

She went through the hassle of digging out her driver's license. "I've never been carded before."

"Because you've never ordered a drink in a bar before," Elliot said.

"I have so," she snapped.

The scruffy, middle-aged bartender compared her to her picture ID and nodded. "Unbelievable. Thought sure you were a teenager."

Elliot chuckled. "It's her spunky attitude. Some days I swear she's thirteen."

Before Jody could protest, the bartender was setting their drinks before them, no napkins. "Your license says you're from Winona. Gotta say I never heard of it."

"It's a hellova lot bigger than Myre," Elliot let him know.

"What are you doing in these parts?"

"Having a drink so far," Elliot said as he paid him.

Following a modest sip of her vodka sour, Jody more seriously disclosed their business, "We're looking for somebody. Don Mitchell. You know him?"

The bartender gave Elliot his change and poured himself a shot of something, stalling an answer, as if a simple yes or no was an enormously big decision for him.

"Do you?" she pressed.

He directed his look at Elliot. "You a cop?"

"Naw," Elliot said. Only to add whimsically, "A private investigator."

Jody moaned under her breath, shook her head and rolled her eyes.

"Well, uh…what's up?" The bartender was as cautious as he was curious.

"Nothing, nothing," Elliot said.

"Don't get many P.I.s around here."

Elliot gave a casual shrug. "Don Mitchell…we're just looking for Don Mitchell."

"What'd he do?"

"Nothing, nothing."

"So what do you want him for?"

"Well, we—"

"What led you here?"

They had come too far to not be any closer than this. Jody was losing patience with the game this was turning into. "Look, do you know him or not?"

The bartender chugged down his shot and poured himself another. Jody was just about to grab his arm and demand some straight answers from him when Elliot intervened and grabbed her by the arm first. Her weird-acting friend made a quirky signal to her with his eyes. Of which she guessed she'd seen enough P.I. movies to know meant follow his lead. She guessed the game was still on.

"Got a name?" Elliot questioned the drinking bartender.

"Brad."

"I'm Elliot, this is Jody."

They shook hands back and forth.

"Own the place?" Elliot asked.

"No, just work here."

"Don't imagine your drinks are free then, right?"

Brad grinned sheepishly.

"Let me buy you your next one, okay?" Elliot slapped more money onto the bar and did the honor of pouring Brad a refill from the bottle he'd been favoring.

Brad was happily surprised. "Thanks. Two more for the both of you?"

In unison, Jody said no as Elliot said yes.

They had some driving to do yet and Jody preferred it be done soberly. She gave Elliot a miffed look. And Elliot, in turn, gave her his P.I. look. And Brad served them another round.

Elliot got out more money. "Yeah, it's pretty up around this country," he said, as casually but slyly as any investigator would begin to work his suspect. "Lotsa trees. Lotsa real nice trees."

"Yeah," Brad agreed, "lotsa trees." He rang up Elliot's latest charge and brought him back his change.

Elliot left the remainder of his twenty on the counter, as if he were planning to keep the drinks coming.

Brad tipped his shot glass high and easy, as if it tasted better to Elliot's paying for it.

Meanwhile, Elliot nudged Jody and showed her how to play this safe. Secretly, on their side of the bar and out of Brad's view, he emptied some of his drink down into the spittoon near the foot rail. Amazed that there should even be a spittoon, Jody did the same with part of her drink then quickly raised her glass back up to a normal hand holding height.

They bluffed Brad the bartender along, buying him back-to-back shots while inconspicuously dumping their own drinks into spittoon. They worked Brad into a talkative mood, as per Elliot's intention, with a discussion that rambled from the weather, to the tourists, to the fishing in the Isabella River, and eventually to Don.

"Then you do know him," Elliot said.

Brad nodded openly. "Comes in now and then. And…so…how is it that you two know him?"

Jody started to say, "He's my br—"

"Our friend," Elliot said. "Just a friend, that's all. He, uh, invited us up to go fishing with him."

Brad was notably confused. "Ahh…so you're not an investigator."

"Yeah…yeah, I am," Elliot wasn't about to give that up, "but see, I'm not here on business. Just some R & R with our good buddy Don. Except…" he broke a quick laugh, "we lost the damn map he sent us on how to find his place. Stupid, huh? Jeez, I don't know where it went."

Brad's eyes were nearly shut. Holding to the bar for support, he didn't look good at all. Jody wondered how a bartender could lose track of his own drinks like that. He seemed close to passing out.

Elliot shoved a paper at him and stuck a pen in his right hand. "Map. Could you maybe just sketch out a little refresher map for us on how to get to Don's place? We'd appreciate it, Brad. And who knows, maybe we'll drop off a fish or two for you on our way back through here if we catch any."

Brad bought the map-for-fish deal. Looking dizzy and dazed, and holding the pen shakily, he managed to draw some lines and scribble some words just before his eyes rolled back in his head and he collapsed to a thud on the floor behind the counter.

Elliot took the paper, muttering disappointedly that the directions looked useless. But he was viewing it upside down.

When Jody turned it around, it looked better. The main road out of Myre and up to Junction 12, then left for a distance. A right at Avery's Corner, whatever that was, then a short line over to a box with Don's name in it.

"Looks like a grave," Elliot said.

Jody bopped him in the chest. "Why would you say such a thing?"

"Sorry." He slipped off his stool. "Let's go."

"What about him?" She motioned to the body on the floor. Though Brad was breathing and appeared to be all right, she hesitated leaving him like that.

"It's nap time. He did good. Let him rest. He'll be fine."

On their way out Elliot flipped the door sign over from *Open* to *Closed*.

"I guess I have to say you were pretty cool back there," Jody awarded him as they drove off in accordance with the map.

"Yeah…well…" he said matter of factly, "I knew the guy wasn't going to direct us to Don unless we loosened his tongue with booze. These out-in-the-sticks people, they really guard one another's privacy."

"Maybe you shouldn't have started out by saying you were a private investigator."

Elliot chuckled. "Hey, how often does that opportunity come along?"

She laughed as well. "You're crazy."

"The guy believed it. Can you believe that he believed it? You know, I almost believed it myself."

Crazy as the event had been, Jody was glad they'd acquired the information they needed. "I guess it was all those drinks you pushed onto him that did it."

"You probably noticed that I didn't have to push too hard."

"Can you believe anyone drinking like that on their job?"

"Thanks to me, huh," Elliot boasted proudly. "Though I suspect he had somewhat of a start before we arrived."

"What was that bottle he was drinking from?"

"Tequila."

"Ouch!"

"Hey, here's Junction 12." Elliot made the turn.

"I'm scared," Jody said, losing her bravery and kind of wishing now that she'd put as much vodka into herself as she had into the spittoon.

"It'll be fine." Elliot passed her a smile and a soothing tone of voice. "I'm right here with you."

Avery's Corner amounted to a one-pump gas station on a corner with the name Avery on a hand-painted sign. They made another turn there, getting down to the last couple marks on Brad's map. Elliot's driving became slower and slower on the road that was rutted and bumpy and gloomy within the closeness of trees. It was hard to imagine anyone wanting to live this secluded.

In accordance with the map, the road came to a dead end. And there off to one side, in a meager clearing, sat a small cabin that supposedly was Don's. Though it wasn't what you'd call pretty, it did have a rustic sort of charm. In fact, the dirt driveway before it, edged with a low picket fence and some yellow wild flowers, actually set it off with a little-house-in-the-woods storybook effect.

Jody remained in the car for a while. She couldn't believe they were here. She had to let it sink in. She wouldn't have expected to feel this nervous. She hated that she did. When she finally got up her nerve to get out and start forth, she made sure Elliot came with her.

"Right behind you," he said at her heels.

"Hello!" she called, going through the fence opening.

There was no answer.

"Hello!" she called again, rapping on the door to the house.

Nothing. No one.

She turned to Elliot. "Where is he? What if this isn't even his place?"

"It's his. According to the map, it's his. It's four-thirty. He must have a job. He's probably not off work yet. And you were worried about our getting a late start this morning."

"I can't stand this," Jody said.

Elliot motioned to the yard just right of the cabin. "Look, some lawn chairs over there. Come on, let's go sit and wait. He'll show up eventually."

"How do you know he will?"

He pulled her by the hand. "I'm not God, I don't know that he will. I'm just me, Elliot, and I can only presume that he will."

The closer they got to connecting with Don, the more delays there seemed to be. As Jody's tenseness grew, she could see that Elliot's did too. Though he didn't say much, he sat nervously socking the fist of one hand into the openness of his other hand.

Her irritability rose. "Planning to punch someone?"

"Me? No."

"The fist thing."

As if he'd been mindless to what he'd been doing, he looked at his hands, stilled them, and laid them in his lap. Next, however, he took to chopping the heel of his right shoe against the ground before him.

Waiting for Don was difficult enough for Jody, without her having to endure Elliot's fidgety mannerisms. For deviation, she made an inspecting gaze at all she could see from where she sat. Desolate as it was, this little place was notably well cared for. The cabin was painted brown with white trim. The driveway fence was neatly intact and matched the of brown of the cabin. The scatter of wildflowers along the fence were of a cheery, natural beauty, and the grass between the fence and the cabin was surprisingly thick and green. There was a birdhouse in a near tree, a rain barrel beside the house. The chairs they were sitting in, plus the little matching table between, were nicely crafted and seemed homemade.

Jody picked up the newspaper lying on the table. "Yesterday's date, Elliot. Yesterday's date! Don buys the newspaper! He's not a hermit!"

"You thought he might be?"

"Yeah, didn't you?"

"Yeah."

It was a long wait. It began to seem like forever that they'd been sitting there. At first the scene had been different and captivating. But after a while it became more like a boring isolation from the rest of the world.

"I couldn't live like this," Jody said, from having tried to imagine it. "Could you, Elliot? Elliot?" When she turned her head toward him, she found he'd dozed off. "Elliot!"

"W-what?" He jumped with a startle.

"Don't do that! Don't leave me alone like that!"

"Sorry." He straightened up in his chair and squinted at his watch. "What time is it? Where the hell is that guy? Jeez, seven o'clock. I'm hungry."

"Elliot, what if he's not home by dark?"

"He's a grown man, Jody, don't worry about him. *Really* hungry."

"Us, I'm thinking about us. We'll soon be sitting out here in the middle of nowhere in the dark. If he's not here by dark, let's go back into town to that bar."

"No!" Elliot said.

"But we can't just sit here and—"

"Jody, no! That's a place we'd best not ever show ourselves again. Sure we had a late breakfast, but no lunch. *I'm starving.*"

Jody gave an impatient huff, then simmered back.

Before much longer a car came down the road, into the driveway and parked next to Elliot's car. Someone got out but was half hidden behind some tree branches.

"Do you think it's him?" Jody asked hopefully.

"Good chance." Elliot said.

A slender young man came walking toward them. "What can I do ya?" he asked uneasily.

"He must hang with that bartender," Elliot whispered to Jody. "They talk alike."

Jody and Elliot stood up.

Chapter 8

▼

Don Mitchell stopped before getting too close to Jody and Elliot. Jody said nothing, waiting to see if he recognized her. She didn't want to have to tell him outright who she was. He stood there for a long couple of minutes, staring at his surprise guests as if he were trying to make something out of this but couldn't.

When Jody could no longer hold back, she shouted his name and ran to him. "Don! It's me, Jody!"

"I know," he said, catching her in his arms.

They hugged like a make up for eight lost years. Without reason or blame or expectation. As if there was only here and now. This moment. A family reunited.

"So you knew me right off?" Jody eventually asked.

"Not right off, no. But as soon as you started to speak, in that instant between your saying my name and your name, I knew."

She started crying with her closer observance of him now. "It's so good seeing you, Don."

"Can't be that good if it's making you cry." His own eyes shimmered through the grin he was giving her.

"I didn't know if I'd ever see you again," she said shakily. "But look at us…here we are, like a miracle."

"It's not a miracle, Jody." Don let go of her and gave a quick, self-conscience wipe to the corner of his right eye. "I know it was Larry who told you where I was."

"The fact that you two ran into each other like you did the other night, *that was the miracle.*"

Don tilted his head to one side. "Miracle? Or mistake?"

Jody took a deep breath, trying to steady herself against his indifference. "You consider it a mistake, an incident that led me to you?"

He shrugged sheepishly. "Okay, so tell me then exactly what, led by the miracle, are you doing here?"

"Doing?"

"What's your reason?"

"Reason?" It hurt that he had to ask, didn't know, didn't feel exactly as she did. "I'm your sister, that's my reason."

Her assertion got through to Don. He opened his arms for her again and said, "C'mere."

As they hugged a second time, even tighter, Don admitted, "I'm glad to see you, Jody. Really, I am."

It was wonderful. She didn't want to ever let go of her brother or this moment.

Yet it was just as great, on a lighter note, when he broke their embrace to laughingly suggest, "We could go inside, you know. Come on."

Jody motioned Elliot forth. "Don, this is Elliot."

Elliot offered a handshake, and Don took it, saying, "Hi."

"Nice to meet you, Don," Elliot said. Then added with a chuckle, "Finally."

Don led the way inside and turned on a light. The cabin was but one single room. A stove, refrigerator and sink were on one side. A couch, rocker and fireplace on the other. A small table, with two chairs, were in the center.

"I'd give you a tour," Don said with the sweep of his hand, "but I'm afraid this is it. You can see it all from right here."

Jody's gaze rounded the room with interest. When it returned to Don, she could see now, in the better light, how truly handsome he still was. Older yes, than eight years ago, but otherwise the same. Judgmental blue gray eyes. Quick grins, but guarded words. Casualness, with an edge of control. Hair as dark and thick as ever. Jeans, a long-sleeved denim shirt, and muddy work boots which he now bent down to take off and set aside.

"So what do you think?" he asked.

"Nice," she said.

"Yeah, nice," Elliot echoed.

A stretch of silence befell the cabin, whereas the three of them just stood there staring at one another. Eventually Don motioned for Jody and Elliot to sit down on the couch, and he backed himself into the rocker. Thus the three of them then sat staring wordlessly at one another.

"So what do you think?" Jody threw Don's own question back at him.

He shrugged. "About…?"

"About our being here."

Seeming as discomforted as if he'd been asked some sort of trick question, Don dropped eye contact with her, shifted himself in the rocker, didn't answer.

"You really haven't said much," she said.

Tapping his watch, Elliot surmised to her, "You guys have been together what, ten minutes? Maybe your brother's still trying to absorb the shock of it."

"We need to talk," she kept at Don.

Don rubbed his forehead as he met looks with her again. "Talk, sure, I know. But it's like, what? What am I really supposed to say, Jody, after all this time?"

"It better be a lot," she said.

"Maybe you should go first."

"Dad died last year."

Don said nothing. In fact, his overall reaction was a total blank.

"He wasn't sick or anything," Jody said. "A heart attack just up and struck him on his way to work one day. He…he didn't even have an accident with the car. He managed to pull over before he—"

"Guess that was Dad," Don said apathetically, "neat and tidy to the end."

Don's words struck even harsher than his silence. As Larry had warned her, he still had his infamous attitude. Jody had so hoped he'd drop it for her. She so badly wanted, needed, for them to be on the same level.

Don studied her with some obvious concern, or possibly regret. Then his voice warmed. "So you're alone now."

Jody nodded, hoping he'd automatically appoint himself as her savior.

But Elliot hastily beat him to it. "She's got me."

The look that came over Don made Jody defensively explain, "Besides my friend, Elliot's also my boss."

"What's your line, Elliot?" Don asked him.

Elliot cleared his throat and tried too hard to be funny. "You mean, as…as a boss or…or as a—"

"As your job, your work," Don said.

"Right." Elliot laughed nervously. "Motel. No, no…don't take that wrong," he added before Don could react one way or the other. "That is my work. I own the Treggor Motel in Winona. Treggor being my last name. Jody works for me, as do this couple Tom and Rose. Not much business. But the two of them, they're keeping an eye on the place so's I could make this trip with Jody."

Don nodded. "I'm sure Jody was grateful for that."

Elliot nodded also. "Yeah." Then immediately conscious of how it may have sounded, he tried to take it back. "Well, not that grateful, I assure you. I mean, we...your sister and me...we're just really good friends, that's all, and she and I would never—"

"Shut up," Jody said, giving him a punch. "Friends," she assured Don.

Though her brother seemed more disturbed over her hitting Elliot than anything else, he let it pass. "I suppose we should eat," he said, getting up from the rocker. "You probably haven't eaten since—"

"Only liquid," Elliot said, putting up his hands protectively when Jody spun toward him.

She didn't hit him this time. But she should have, for that mouth of his. Instead she covered his stupid remark with a better truth. "We sat waiting in your yard for over two hours," she told Don, "and yes, we're hungry."

Don went to the kitchen area and opened the cupboard above the stove. "I'll see what there is."

From where she was sitting, Jody could see a supply of canned goods on the shelves. She left the couch and crossed the small room. "I'll do it. You guys just sit and chat and I'll fix the food. Okay?"

Don was quick with an okay. He gave her a thankful bow and went back to rejoin Elliot.

Jody took three cans of chili out of the cupboard. *The can opener? Where is it?* She couldn't find it and was just about to ask Don when she found it in the unlikely place beside a box of cereal on a cupboard shelf. *It's supposed to be in the silverware drawer. Men!*

Elliot made conversation with Don by telling him about the sad dying status of his motel business. Don seemed interested and sympathetic.

When Elliot finally dropped the motel talk, he asked Don what kind of work he did.

"Logging," Don said.

"Right," Elliot caught himself. "I should have guessed as much, going with the territory. Good hard honest work, logging."

"Yeah, it is," Don said.

Jody saw him roll his shoulders back and around as though they ached from an arduous day. As the chili heated in the pan, she sliced up the remaining half of a loaf of French bread she found in a bag, tore off paper towel sheets to use for place mats on the coarse topped wooden table, and poured three glasses of milk.

"So…" Elliot chatted on to Don, "then you like it up here in the woodsy north? I know, I know," he snubbed his own question and answered it himself with a chuckle, "you wouldn't be here if you didn't."

Jody was glad the guys were conversing, but was even more glad when the meal was ready and she could call them to eat.

Don pulled the rocker over to the table for himself, allowing his guests the two regular chairs. Fingering an edge of the paper towel place mat beneath his bowl, as though the use would never have occurred him, he slipped Jody a fond smile of approval.

"Good…very good…" Elliot raved of his first spoonful of chili.

"Thanks," Jody said, hardly feeling she deserved any praise for what little effort the meal had taken.

The three of them were quiet as they ate. There were no more pressing statements or trivial small talk for the moment. Jody and Elliot were both travel fatigued and Don had no doubt put in a hard day's work.

Jody barely took her eyes off her brother during supper. She studied the way he lifted his spoon, his jaw movement as he chewed, his throat as he swallowed. She obsessively wondered, from second to second, what he was thinking, feeling, going to do next. So far she didn't have a very clear picture of what this detached life of his actually represented. And for sure he hadn't a clue about hers. But this was it, finally, here and now, despite the present awkward lull, their chance to become close again and make everything better.

After the meal, Don stood, stretched and said he was going outside for some fresh air. Jody hurried after him, panicked that he was going to take off on her again.

She was surprised that he was only right outside the cabin, just standing there. In his stocking feet, no less.

Don seemed equally surprised at her.

Then suddenly, amidst their checking one another out, they both burst into laughter.

"Hey, it's okay," Don said softly.

"I know," she said, accepting what was, though feeling some embarrassment. "I guess we're both pretty edgy."

Standing side by side, she and her brother stared into the approaching darkness around them. There was a spooky sort of silence. This was so desolate. Distant. A million miles away from the rest of the world.

"Krista married Rossi a few months after you left Winona," Jody thought she should tell him.

When Don didn't say anything, she added, "I'm sorry."

After a few moments he said, "I figured she would."

"She didn't even—"

"I don't want to talk about Krista," he said.

"Okay, let's talk about Myre. Is this really where you want to be, Don? In this unbeknownst place called Myre?"

"You don't like it," he gathered as much.

"I don't understand it. Or you."

Don drew a deep breath and let it out with a hard sigh. "You got me off guard here, Jody, showing up like you did. I still don't really know what to say to you."

"So far you haven't said much."

"I know."

"Especially about Dad."

There was a pause before he again said, "I know." He shrugged and waited for her to fill the next gap. When she didn't, he added, "People die, Jody."

"People?" It hurt her terribly that he took their dad's passing so casually.

Don hung his head. "Look, Jody, I've grown apart. I don't have a whole lot to say, about Dad or about anything."

"You live alone in the woods," she said with a snap in her voice. "You don't get a lot of practice talking, do you? Which, I suppose, is probably just exactly how you like it, right?"

"Right."

"Don, are you sorry I found you, that I'm here?"

He didn't answer one way or the other. But the shimmer of emotion in his eyes said a lot.

"I didn't know if you would be glad to see me or not," she went on, "but after hearing about your whereabouts from Larry, I had to come. I just had to."

"Yeah, I suppose you did. Larry…he didn't waste any time telling you, did he?"

"Should he have?" Jody asked, but didn't wait for an answer before adding, "Don, why are you hiding out like this?"

"I'm not hiding. This is my—"

"Eight years!" she said. "No word whatsoever from you in all that time. Don't you know what that did to Dad and me? What's wrong with you?"

"Maybe I'm still trying to figure that out," he confessed with a sad sort of mockery.

Out of questions, argument, and energy, Jody finally turned silent.

Don put his arm around her shoulder. "It's past nine. You're tired, we're all tired. We probably should get some sleep."

She agreed and went with him back inside the cabin.

They found Elliot asleep on the couch.

"I guess he's wiped out from all the driving he did in the last two days," Jody made of his bad manners.

"It's a long way from Winona," Don said knowingly.

"Well, we moteled it in Duluth last night, but yeah, a lot of driving."

Don flicked another look over at Elliot's sleeping body, then back at Jody. "You moteled it?"

"Not like you think," she said.

"Right." Don nodded, as though with his own fixed notion to that.

"He's my boss and my friend, that's all."

"Right," Don said. He pointed to the back of the cabin. "The bathroom's back there, as you already know, and—"

"Inside plumbing, which I was happy to find."

He pointed at a ladder leading up to a small, railed loft over one end of the downstairs. "You can sleep up there, Jody, in the bed."

"What about you? Where will you sleep?"

He went to a closet and came back with two blankets. He covered the sleeping-like-a-baby Elliot with one and dropped the other one on the bare wood floor for himself.

"I can't let you sleep on the floor," Jody said.

He smiled and laid himself down.

After using the bathroom, Jody climbed up to the loft, feeling totally exhausted and only slightly guilty for stealing Don's bed. The bed was the one and only piece of furniture in the loft, but it was enhanced by the cute little square window on the front wall and the beamed ceiling that slanted halfway down the two side walls.

Still in her clothes, she laid staring out the window for a while. She watched the sky darken to pitch black. She said a silent prayer of thanks for finding Don. Part of her felt peaceful, but another part still felt the nauseating fright she'd felt when Don got up from the supper table and went outside. She wished she trusted him. But they'd been separated for eight years and she knew she'd probably have to depend on something a lot more than wishes to keep them together now.

Thoughts of Kevin slipped in between her thoughts of Don. She had to tell her brother about her ex-boyfriend. Had to, because there was a baby involved. Don was family. If she couldn't talk to him about this, she couldn't talk to anyone. Not even Elliot. Kevin, and the baby, were her main reasons for finding Don and needing him so badly. Tomorrow they would talk about everything. She wished it were tomorrow right now.

After having waited long enough to feel sure that Don was asleep, Jody quietly sneaked back down the ladder. Tiptoeing carefully, she felt her way blindly across the black room to the couch.

"Elliot…" she whispered, shaking him gently. "Elliot…"

"Mmm…wha…?" he moaned.

"Shh…" she said.

"Jody…" He opened his eyes without really seeing. "What? What's wrong? Jeez, it's so dark in here."

"It's okay, Elliot," she said, keeping her voice down. "We're spending the night with Don. He's sleeping on the floor. Over near the table. Don't step on him if you get up in the night."

"No…no, I wouldn't think of it," he assured her.

"I'm sleeping in the loft."

"You mean…it's not really you here beside me?"

"Elliot, before I can go to sleep I need to know that—"

"You haven't been to sleep yet? What time is it?"

"—you'll keep one ear open for the door."

"Huh…?"

"The door. Don't let Don go out the door without our knowing. Okay?"

Elliot yawned and raised himself on one elbow. "If he's by the table, then he's closer to the door than I am."

"Elliot," she pleaded.

"He could escape pretty easily."

"Elliot," she pleaded as forcefully as she could in a whisper.

"Okay, okay. Just call me eagle-ear Elliot."

"Thanks." She left him and went back to the ladder, feeling much more certain that she'd be able to sleep now.

Chapter 9

▼

Lying there on his hard bed of the floor, Don only pretended to be asleep. Actually he'd heard the whole thing of Jody's coming down and talking to Elliot, and it made him very uneasy as to what the two of them might be up to. As if their surprise visit hadn't been astonishing enough, it seemed they had some sort of unreputable intent beyond just dropping in to say hello.

Given some time tonight, Don had eased into the fact that yeah, sure, okay, he was glad to see his kid sister again. But that was as far as it went with him. Whatever else Jody and Elliot might be concocting, he didn't like it, didn't want it. And yet, whatever it turned out to be, he knew it would be two against one.

Staring into the darkness of the cabin, his mind rambled restlessly. The disturbing scene of a few minutes ago worked at him like a puzzle he felt compelled to solve before morning. Though he wanted to get some sleep, he was too wired now over wondering about his sister and her sidekick. With the stress of it came his desire to drink. He considered sneaking across the floor to the cupboard below the sink and pulling out the half-full bottle of vodka that was there. But he didn't, figuring he'd probably get jumped by Elliot and punched out by Jody.

Larry...he hated that Larry discovered his whereabouts the other night and passed it on to Jody. Jody...he hated that she still looked up to him and expected something from him after all this time. Man, what was happening to his life all of a sudden. The new one, the private one, the supposedly safe one. Lately it had become pretty evident that he still wasn't far enough away from everything and everyone to be truly free of his past. He should never have come back to Minnesota once he'd left it. Big mistake. But things had seemed okay, up until now. Until suddenly running smack into his cousin like he had the other night. And now his sister and her weird friend dropping in on him out of the blue, with something shifty up their sleeves and between their words. Something that was already starting to make Don feel like a prisoner in his own house.

He changed his position on the floor, turning in the direction of Elliot on the couch. He knew Elliot was back to sleep because of the low, patterned rumbles of his snoring. Don covered his ears. Not against Elliot's snoring as much as against the vodka in the cupboard that kept calling him. He wanted so badly to respond to it, go to it, drink it. He could probably get up and move freely about the cabin now without Elliot hearing him. But Jody, in the loft, was no doubt still awake and monitoring. So he stayed in place, except for tossing back over to his other side toward the kitchen area.

Krista…along with everything else that was stirring rampantly in Don's head right now, he started thinking of her again as well. As if she were ever very far from his thoughts. By rights she was supposed to be far gone from his head by now. An ex-girlfriend exed by all the mistakes he'd made years ago. Double exed by the span of eight years. Triple exed by the official news he'd gotten tonight of her marrying Rossi. Yet Don knew that no matter how many drinks he ever had, or trees he cut, or distance between them, or husband she now had, he was never going to get over her.

He moaned faintly under his breath and rolled back onto his other side again, the side toward Elliot. He needed to concentrate on the here and now suspiciousness of his house guests. He had to carefully prepare himself for whatever this might come to be. And yet, that seemed so stupidly unnecessary. This was his territory. He had his rights. If he wanted to leave the cabin right now, no one could stop him. No one. If he wanted to do that. Which he didn't, but felt content knowing that he could. He tried to close his eyes, but they only popped right open again. Damn.

Elliot's continued snoring was the only sound in the otherwise silent cabin. Eventually Don tried listening to it, really listening, and focusing on it like the repetitious chant of someone meditating. After a while it actually started to have a soothing, hypnotic effect. Weird. But he was finally able to keep his eyes closed now, and his head began to clear to a nice sort of nothingness. The floor felt softer. His body lighter…drifting…drifting…

Chapter 10

When Jody went down the ladder early the next morning she found Don quietly puttering in the kitchen area.

"Hope I didn't wake you," he said, noticing her.

She smiled sleepily. "I smelled the coffee."

He nodded. "Mmm...one of life's greatest pleasures."

"And coffee is your morning ritual?"

"You bet."

Jody gestured at the shirt of his she'd confiscated from the loft last night, had slept in, and was still wearing now. It was big and comfy on her, hanging well past her thighs and hands. "Do you mind?" she asked, despite it being a little late for permission.

He gave her an amused second look. "No."

"It was on the floor up there. So I didn't think you'd mind if I—"

"It's okay," he said. "Did you sleep okay?"

"Yeah. You?"

"Fine."

Jody saw that Don had his work boots on. And then she realized that what he was doing at the counter was packing a bag lunch. "You're not going to work," she protested.

He laughed. "While some people go off on vacations with their boss, some have to work."

"This is no vacation," Jody let him know. She gazed across the cabin at Elliot Treggor, P.I., still sacked out on the couch. He was supposed to be helping her with this, not sleeping.

Don poured a mug of coffee for Jody and handed it to her. "Here. Nothing like a shot of caffeine to brighten your day."

She yawned, tucked some strands of hair behind her ear, and accepted the drink. She sipped it as he watched and smiled. Don was being really nice, except for his planning to go to work. "Please don't go," she said. "I just got here. We've got a lot to talk about."

"Jody, I have to." He finished his coffee and put the empty mug in the sink.

"I was counting on our having today together."

Don deepened his look at her. "You should have learned by now not to count on things so hard."

Her heart ached with fear and frustration. "Yeah, well, maybe that's you but it's not me."

He shook his head as if he was feeling equally frustrated with her and said in warning, "You're gonna get hurt."

"As if I haven't already," she said.

"Jody, I don't expect you to ever understand why I—"

"Don't give yourself all the credit for hurting people, Don. There are others who do it just as well as you."

His eyes narrowed with new concern. "What does that mean?"

"Nothing." She took another drink of coffee.

"I know I must have hurt you, leaving and staying away like I did. But who do you mean by others? Who else hurt you? Because it sounds like you're telling me that somebody else did." He pointed at Elliot. "Him?"

"No." There was Kevin, and there was the baby, but there was no time to get into any of that with Don now. "If you have to go to work, you have to. We'll talk when you have the time, impossible as that may sound."

"It's Friday. If you and your sidekick want to hang around, we'll have all weekend to talk."

"Hang around?"

"Jody…"

"Go!" she said, giving him the freedom he wanted.

Don took his lunch bag and keys off the counter, looking guilty, but not enough to stay. "Make yourself to home. I'll see you later. Okay?"

"Later," she scoffed.

"Tonight," he promised.

As Jody watched the cabin door close behind him, she felt a strange mixture of good-bad feelings.

Chapter 11

▼

Elliot woke up squinting at the daylight meeting him. He checked his watch. Couldn't believe he'd slept this late. On the couch. In Don Mitchell's cabin. Don…where was he? He didn't seem to be here. Had he gotten away? If so, Elliot was in big trouble.

Before he'd gotten any farther than sitting halfway up, Jody was standing over him, hands on hips, brown eyes expectant. She seemed upset, yes, but not angry, as Elliot would have imagined.

"I'm sorry for letting your brother escape," he apologized for failing guard duty.

"It's not your fault," she said.

"It's not?" He finished sitting all the way up, distrustful of how easy this was going.

"Don went to work."

"Oh."

"He said he'd see us tonight."

Elliot gave her a slanted look. "But you…you didn't believe him, did you?"

"Yes. No. I don't know." Her hands slipped off her hips, her shoulders dropped, and her dark eyes took on the look of an abandoned puppy.

Elliot got off the couch, straightened his twisted shirt and ran a hand through his rumpled hair. "He'll be back after work like he said, Jody. I'm sure he will."

She smiled hopefully. "You think so?"

He put more confidence into his smile than what he felt. "Yeah, I do. Hey, the coffee smells great."

- 53 -

Barefoot and looking elfin small in what was obviously one of Don's shirts, Jody went over to the kitchen counter and poured him a mug. "Want breakfast?"

"Sure."

"Oatmeal, toast or eggs?"

"Yeah," Elliot answered on his way to the bathroom.

"Which?" she called after him.

"All of the above."

Jody fixed him the works. Then she sat at the table with him as he ate, being remarkably quiet and patient. It was nice, though hardly meant to last. He'd just barely finished his breakfast when she rose from her chair, got a frantic look on her face, and started in on her next dilemma. "So what are we going to do around here all day while we wait for Don to come home?"

There was no rest with this girl. None. "I'll take you fishing," he offered.

"Fishing?" She scrinched her face.

Elliot supposed maybe it was something more to his interest than hers, but at least it was an idea over no idea at all. "We'll go find that Isabella River, what'dya say? It's supposedly only three miles from here. I spied a couple rods lying in the yard yesterday."

Jody was scouring the cabin for something better.

"I'll worm the hook for you," he said.

She was in her own little dream world, barely paying him any mind.

"I'll paddle the boat," he offered.

Suddenly Jody was bubbling over. "Oh, Elliot! That's it!"

He, too, felt a rush of excitement, figuring it must have been the paddling thing that finally won her over. But in the next moment he realized that wasn't it at all. Watching her, he could tell that her exuberance was definitely about something else. Something probably more feminine. His eyes followed the whimsical little dance she started doing about the cabin.

"I've got it! I've got it!" she sang.

For some reason, seeing her this happy made him very apprehensive.

"Elliot," she said, accidentally bumping into the rocker, "I figured out what we'll do. We'll give this place a spic and span cleaning for Don, then go buy groceries at that store in town, then cook a really good meal to have waiting for him when he comes home tonight."

Elliot tossed his hands in the air. "Wow! How come I didn't think of that? Marvelous idea. Marvelous! I'll whip up a cake for dessert. Not from scratch though. From a mix. Think that's okay? So which one, Pillsbury or Betty Crocker? Help me decide. Or Duncan Hines. How about Duncan Hines? Chocolate or white? Or how about yellow? Yeah, I think yellow. I really like yellow. Hopefully Don does, too. With chocolate frosting. I'm so excited over this idea! Just so excited!"

"Will you stop it!" Passing him on her way to the sink, Jody hauled off and slugged him in the arm.

Elliot rubbed the spot, mocking immense pain.

Jody didn't even look, didn't even consider that she might have really hurt him.

His eyes narrowed after this wild girl who felt she could deck him whenever she wanted to and get away with it. It was time to show her some spunk of his own. He sprung from his chair. Now she was looking.

As Elliot started toward her Jody caught his message, dodged around the table and ran outside screaming. Chasing after her, he roared like a wounded bear.

He caught her in the yard and play-wrestled her to the ground. Jody was strong and feisty for her size and had some surprisingly good moves of her own. She managed to get him into a head lock that almost made him say uncle. But when he broke loose, it only took him a second to pin her to the ground. "No more hitting, okay?" he said, trying to make it sound like her promise was the only chance she was going to have of being turned loose.

"Sorry," she apologized through a burst of giggles.

Laughter spilled from his as well. "You think you're one tough cookie, don't you?"

Jody proved just how tough she was by flouncing beneath him enough to get one hand free.

"Hey!" Elliot shouted.

She started to take a swing, but before her hand connected with him, he seized it. Gripping both her wrists, trying to still her writhing, Elliot suddenly realized the embarrassing position they were in. She was flat on her back and he was straddled on top of her.

Both stopped moving and stared wondrously into each other's eyes. Like, how could this happen? Like, what did happen? It wasn't what it looked like, that was for sure. An innocent little wrestling match, nothing more. Innocent. Right. Except that it scared the wits out of Elliot. And for sure now Jody was looking way too serious. They untangled themselves from one another and got up.

"Marble cake," Elliot said for the sake of filling the awkward silence. "I've decided on marble cake with marble frosting." He sucked in a tremendously deep breath and followed Jody back to the cabin.

Though he lagged a safe distance behind her, he kept a fascinated watch on the delightful little figure ahead of him. Bare legs walking briskly. Small hips shifting noticeably sexy through the free fall of Don's shirt. Dark hair in an uninhibited tousle. And attitude, all that attitude. *Jeez, she was cute*, he thought. *Really cute. Gotta watch it. Really gotta watch it..*

Chapter 12

Jody was well aware of what had almost just happened between her and Elliot. She felt bad. Responsible. The instigator. Even though she had her panties and bra on beneath the generous cover-up of Don's shirt, she supposed the look might've seemed a little suggestive. She hadn't meant to suggest anything to Elliot. That yard thing had only started out as innocent goofing around. They goofed around a lot in their relationship, she hitting him and him making a big deal out of it. But this time, when he chased her outside and play-wrestled her to the ground, it was different. A look came over him that she'd never seen before, at which point she'd looked at him every bit as strangely.

"I'll just go get dressed," she said, starting up the loft ladder in the cabin, "then we'll get busy."

"That was close," she heard Elliot mutter to himself as she climbed the steps.

Jody sat on the loft floor and looked down through the railing spindles at Elliot. He was sitting on the couch, bent over with his head buried in his hands, obviously disturbed about the yard incident. Well, she was disturbed too. She adored Elliot's friendship and no way wanted to knock the comfortable casualness of it off track.

Suddenly his head lifted out of his hands and he started turning his face upward toward the loft as if he sensed her looking down at him. Jody jumped back out of view, confused as to what was happening here.

As the day progressed, the two of them managed to relax and returned to their usual naturalness with one another. They grocery shopped at the one and only store in town, then came back to the cabin and cooked and cleaned like dutiful elves for their master.

When Don got home that night he was surprised and pleased with all they'd done. "Hey, all right! This is great. Thanks, you guys."

Jody felt that the most reward in it all was the fact that he even came home. And she didn't mind Elliot's smugly whispering to her, "I told you he'd come back."

The three of them sat at the table together again as they had the night before, paper towels for place mats beneath their plates. Jody served a chicken casserole, creamed corn, biscuits, watermelon wedges, and apple pie, not cake, for dessert. Don and Elliot complimented her cooking with nearly every bite they took. Plus Don further praised the going over they'd given his place.

"Elliot and I did it together," Jody proudly stated.

Elliot started choking on the water he was drinking. Don made a quick move to slap him on the back, but Elliot raised an I'm-okay hand while glaring at Jody.

She rephrased her sentence. "We shared the cleaning fifty-fifty."

"Though I appreciate your work," Don said, "it really wasn't necessary."

Jody's laugh, along with Elliot's dramatic head nodding, assured him otherwise.

"Okay, okay," Don reconsidered, laughing as well, "so maybe it was necessary."

"I suggest you consider letting your current housekeeper go," Elliot said.

"Like you think I have one?"

"Not a good one anyway."

"So hey, you guys want the job?" Though Don was grinning, he sounded serious.

"You couldn't afford us," Elliot said. Then he laid his fork down, actually took a pause from eating, and pondered the possibility. "But maybe we could work something out. With the Treggor dying, who knows."

"It's too bad about your motel," Don responded caringly. "Really, isn't there something you can do about it? Like, maybe you could—"

"Why didn't you ever come home or phone all this time?" Jody sprung an attack on her brother.

Don and Elliot flashed startled looks her way.

She didn't care. She'd lost patience to what she considered a waste of time. "I didn't come all the way from Winona to Myre to talk about Elliot's motel!"

"Maybe I did," Elliot said with a chuckle, obviously trying to lighten the intensity she created. But it didn't work. "Excuse me," he said secondly, leaving the table, "I think I'll step outside for some air."

Jody held her eyes on Don, awaiting his answer, not for one minute sorry she'd forced this matter into the open.

"This *is* my home," he said, "and I don't own a phone."

"Very funny."

"Fact."

"What do you know about facts?" She stood up, screeching back her chair and causing it to fall over on the floor.

Don left the rocker and set the chair upright. "Take it easy, okay?"

"I haven't taken one minute easy since you walked out on me and Dad eight years ago!" Her long suffering pushed behind her words.

"I'm sorry," the brother said.

"And that makes everything all right, I suppose, you're being sorry."

He shook his head slowly, looked away from her, then back. "Jody, making everything all right is something I gave up on a long time ago. Maybe you should have too."

Her eyes were already flooded with tears. And her heart was breaking for the millionth time over this issue. "How could you give up on your family like that? How could you think that we'd ever give up on you or stop missing you or worrying about you?"

"I'm sorry it was so hard on you, Jody. But I...I'm sure it was more like a relief to Dad."

"Relief? You think you did him some sort of justice by leaving? God, is that what you think?"

Don's eyes widened and shimmered as his voice exploded. "Yeah! For him and me both!"

Jody locked her hands onto her hips. "Well, you're wrong! Dad grieved for you after that as if you were dead."

"Jody...Jody...don't you think maybe it was easier for him to grieve a dead son than a bad son?"

It touched Jody, his saying that, thinking that, believing that. It slowed her down and made her less hard on Don for a moment. "You weren't that bad," she concluded. The slight smile he managed to give her was weighted with sadness. "I guess time sweetens the memory. But yeah, back then I was pretty bad. I worked my way into some wrong things I couldn't get out of, and I had to leave. I had no choice other than to leave, Jody. No choice."

"I can't believe that."

"You can't believe that?" His anger flared again and he pointed a gun-like finger at her. "You come all this distance, searching me down, just to stand there and tell me you think you know me better than I know myself?"

Jody raised her chin. "Yeah. Maybe."

"You're a kid. You don't know anything."

"I'm not a kid, I'm twenty-two."

"Whoa…" he ridiculed her.

"You were a kid when you left home."

"I was nineteen going on thirty."

"I try, I really try and feel and imagine how you could have done such a thing to your family, to yourself, but I can't. I just can't."

"Well, maybe you shouldn't try so hard to do that."

"Well, maybe I have to try and do something."

"Damn!" Don kicked the chair that had been Elliot's across the floor and into the wall. "I'm me and you're you! Don't expect that we're the same or anywhere near the same!"

Elliot came running back inside, checking them both over. "Kids! Kids! Hey, come on…"

"We're okay here," Jody said.

His interpretation was different. "Yeah, right. You sounded real okay from where I was outside. Like, I'd say this calls for a referee."

"We're not fighting," she said. "We're talking."

"Feels like fighting to me," Don said.

"Talking!"

"Fighting!"

Elliot made a shrill whistle through his teeth. Then in the quiet that followed, he said, "If this is what brothers and sisters are about, I'm glad I never had any. Jeez!"

He stood his chair upright and plunked himself down on it.

Jody stomped off to the bathroom, and Don slammed outside.

Chapter 13

▼

Sitting by himself in the befallen silence, Elliot felt good about having stopped the brother-sister fight and having brought temporary peace to the cabin. Except, before long it was the quiet that became oppressive.

He left his chair and went outside to look for Don. He was in the driveway leaning against the front of his car. "Jody's a little overwrought about all this, that's all," Elliot said, approaching him.

"A little?" Don stressed the understatement.

"Okay, immensely."

"What about me?" Don sounded off. "I mean, she's had some time to prepare for this visit, but it was just sprung on me out of the blue last night. I haven't exactly had much adjustment time."

"Then you're not counting those eight years?" Elliot couldn't resist the dig.

Don took out his keys and whipped open his car door. "I gotta get out of here."

"No! Wait! Wait!" Though Elliot managed to grab his arm he couldn't hold him.

"I don't have to listen to this crap," Don said, getting in behind the wheel and slamming the door shut behind him.

"This crap Jody wants to discuss with you is your life, man."

"My life is just fine the way it is," Don said through the open window. "What's past is past, I can't do much about that." He started the car.

Stomping his feet and grasping his head in frustration, Elliot turned in a circle. Then he stopped and looked at Don, pleading, "Jody will kill me if I let you take off like this. Put that on your conscience, if you have one."

Don backed out of the driveway, no doubt conscience free.

"I'm not exaggerating here!" Elliot shouted at him.

"I'm gonna be hanging out at the bar for a while," Don said at the last moment. "If you guys want to come join me, fine."

"Where? Which bar?" Elliot's heart skipped a beat.

"Myre. There's only one bar in Myre."

"Oh shit!" Elliot said.

Jody came running outside seconds too late. "How could you let him go?"

"Let him? Jeez! Like I was suppose to draw a gun on him or something?"

"Where'd he go? What'd he—"

"It's okay, it's okay," Elliot tried to convince her over his own doubt. "Don just feels like he needs some time to—"

"To what?"

Elliot recognized the turmoil of hurt and love and anger going on in Jody. He wanted to fix it. He really did. But he wasn't so sure that agreeing with her all the time was the way to do it. "Jody, look, maybe you should go a little easier on your brother, you know? I know how stressed you are, but he seems really stressed, too."

Her hands went onto her hips. "Where'd he go, Elliot?"

"I don't know."

"Where'd he go?"

Elliot sighed heavily. "That bar in Myre. He….he, uh…said we could come join him there if we wanted to. But I don't know, Jody…I mean, Brad the bartender might be there and—"

"We're going!" she stated. "Soon as I clean up the kitchen, we're going. Come help me, Elliot."

She started back to the house.

Elliot followed.

Chapter 14

▼

Taking a stool at the bar, Don greeted the stocky, gray-haired man tending it. "Hey, Andy."

"Hey, Don," Andy Nolan returned the greeting. "What'll you have? The usual?"

Don grinned and slapped his hand twice on the bar. "The usual times two."

Andy fixed the drink and set it before Don on a napkin. "Double vodka on the rocks. Bad day, huh?"

"You bartenders are born analysts, aren't you," Don commended him and took a needy drink from his glass. "Yeah, very bad."

"Sorry, Don," Andy offered his sympathy.

"But good for business, right?" Don tipped his glass again.

"I'd rather be pouring drinks for happy customers than sad ones."

"I'll be happy soon," Don promised. He finished his drink, then bounced the glass twice on the bar. "Hit me again."

Andy's eyes held a concerned warning. "Slow down, Don."

"Why? You just told me you'd rather serve happy customers than sad ones. So okay, come on, make me happy."

He started to rap his glass on the bar again. Andy gave in, snatched it away from him and made the refill.

"Thanks," Don said. He took but a mere sip this time to Andy's watching. "Slow…see…you don't have to worry about me."

Andy tapped a beer for a guy at the other end of the bar, took it to him, then returned to Don.

"I never touched my drink while your back was turned," Don assured him.

Andy Nolan was neither impressed nor amused. "I'm not your baby-sitter. I'm just a bartender trying to keep reasonable control here."

Don nodded, curbing his cockiness. "So where's Brad? Didn't you guys switch your Friday and Saturday nights a while back? Isn't this his night behind bar?"

"Looks like both Fridays and Saturdays are mine till Wylie hires a replacement. He fired Brad."

"What?" Don looked for a sign of a joke, but Andy was serious. "Fired? No, I don't believe it. Why?"

"You knew that Brad had a tendency to drink a little on the job, didn't you?"

"Yeah," Don said. "But...I mean...that was just who he was and he—"

"It was probably just a matter of time before it caught up with him. Or, I should say before Wylie caught up with him. Happened yesterday afternoon. Seems Brad had barely started his shift. Couple strangers came in. Some guy and a girl. Brad's only customers at the time. They got to talking. And drinking. All three of 'em."

"So Brad shouldn't be drinking and serving at the same time," Don reasoned, "but it's nothing new with him. He's always gotten away with it, handled it, before. What was different about this time?"

"This guy and this girl, it seems they practically poured the drinks down Brad's throat themselves."

"Right," Don began to make jest of it but stopped when he saw the truth of it in Andy's face.

"This guy and this girl," Andy continued, "they were high pressuring Brad to talk as well as to drink."

"Talk?"

"As a matter of fact, Don, they were grilling him about you."

Don had been in the process of lifting his drink, but he put it back down on the bar instead. "Me? Who would've been—Wait a minute! Okay, yeah, I think I know who they were." He took up his glass again, but rather than drinking from it he held it against forehead.

"You know them?" Andy was surprised.

Don swiveled his stool from side to side and moaned. "Oh, man...Brad obviously did a terrific job telling them about me, directing them to me, because that guy and that girl...they found my place just fine. Their names are Elliot and Jody. They're staying at my cabin."

"Oh. Well, that's a relief, your knowing them. Because you are saying that you do know them, right?"

Don sighed heavily.

"And it's true, about the guy being a private investigator?" Andy verified.

"What?" Don removed his glass from his forehead and drank from it. "Investigator? No. I mean, not that I know of. He owns a motel. Unless he was just shitting me about that."

Andy seemed bound on getting this straight. "So you don't actually seem to know a whole hell of a lot about him, do you?"

Don gulped down some more of his drink. "No, not really. But the girl…she's…well, I do know her."

"Ahh, the girl. It always comes down to the girl."

"She's my sister."

Andy's eyebrows arched. "Sister? You've got a sister? I suppose next you're going to tell me that you actually have a mother and a father, too."

Family matters was the last thing Don wanted to get into. But he did want to know more about Brad. "So exactly how did this lead to Brad's getting fired?"

"Wylie came late in the afternoon. The closed sign was on the door. He found Brad passed out on the floor. That was it. Soon as Brad was able to get up, Wylie kicked his ass out of here. He finished the shift himself and called me in for tonight."

Don stared into his drink, feeling like in a round about way this was his fault. "I'm sorry for what happened to Brad. I know he didn't always do right by his job, but he really didn't do all that badly either. Until yesterday, I guess. I'm sorry that my house guests are the ones who railroaded him. Damn!"

"Yeah," Andy agreed. "Anyway, Brad called me last night after he sobered up. Told me all this stuff over the phone. He was taking it pretty hard. Not sure what he's gonna do now. I told him I really didn't think he deserved what happened to him. He…well, he feels his only consolation is that if he ever meets up with that P.I. again he's sure as hell gonna give him what he deserves."

"Better start fixing me another drink," Don said.

Andy didn't move. "You know, there are other reasons, besides Brad's, that can get a bartender fired. One of them is serving irresponsible customers too fast."

"You're calling me irresponsible?" Don resented that desperation should be so mislabeled.

"I'm just warning you, for the second time, to slow down, that's all. For your own benefit as well as for mine."

Don lifted his glass, checking its contents. He still had a third of his drink left. "I suppose I can make this last for a while yet." He put down the money he owed and slipped off his stool. "I'm gonna go play the jukebox."

He carried the remainder of his drink with him and headed for the Wurlitzer in the corner. "Hey!" he shouted, drawing more annoyance than interest from the other customers. "How come nobody's feeding the music? It's like a morgue in here! Come on! It's Friday night! Let's party!"

Don stuck money into the jukebox, studied the selections and pressed the buttons to his choices.

"Hey, I remember you," a sweet, melodic voice suddenly spoke from beside him.

He turned and met the close look of a strikingly pretty blonde girl in a pink sweater and an ultra short skirt. *Whoa, baby.* He smiled gratefully for her company, though had to ask with a vagueness she was probably going to dislike, "Uh, am I suppose to remember you?"

She returned the smile as easily as if it were her second nature, and made some sort of sexy motion with her shoulders. "Yes. But evidently you don't. So I'll tell you."

"Thanks."

"You're the guy who turned down my personal invitation to go home with me a couple of Fridays ago."

Don slipped an arm around her and drew her close. "Well, I've gotten a lot smarter since then."

Her smile was a definite come-on. As were her hands reaching around behind him to grab a feel of his butt and her suggestively asking, "So…are you saying I can for sure look forward to closing time tonight?"

"You can look forward to right now," he said, "'cause now is when and where our good time begins. Wanna dance?"

She rocked her head to the beat of the music, and her golden hair flew. "You really liven up a place, Don."

"You know my name?" That baffled him more than anything else so far.

She nodded and did her shoulder thing again. "Of course. But I'm hoping to learn a whole lot more about you than just that tonight."

"Right. So…do I know *your* name?"

She laughed. Then sobered upon realizing he wasn't kidding.

Don grinned sheepishly. "Something with an S. Sharon?"

"Nope."

"Shelly."

"Nope."

"Sh….sh…Shirley."

"Three strikes and you're out. Lisa," she had to tell him.

"Aw, man…" Don slapped himself in the forehead. "But there is an S in it, right?"

"You promised me a dance," she reminded him, forgiving him and starting to gyrate her sexy body.

Don finished the last of his second double vodka, left the empty glass on top of the jukebox, and swept Lisa out on the dance floor. She was a knockout. How could he have forgotten being with her before?

"So tell me," he said amidst their vigorous workout to the Rolling Stone's classic *Satisfaction*, "exactly how…how much satisfaction have you and I had together?"

"Not this much." She bubbled with laughter and danced like blue fire.

Her laugh. It suddenly hit Don now as something he did remember about her. This girl, Lisa, her laugh sounded a lot like Krista's laugh. Hauntingly so. He supposed that's why he'd been infatuated with her on that night they'd supposedly met. Her laugh. It was the only thing that came back to him now about her or that night, the fact that her laugh reminded him so acutely of Krista's.

Don started feeling overwhelmingly unfair and dishonest about this. As if he were being unfaithful and wasn't even sure to whom…Krista, Lisa, or himself. He walked away from the dance and headed for the bar.

Lisa followed him, clearly offended and letting him know it with her hardened voice. "What are you doing! You can't just quit in the middle of a dance!"

Don slapped his hand twice on the bar.

Andy tried to ignore him. But when Don continued beating the bar, he finally fixed him another double vodka.

Don motioned at Lisa beside him. "Give her whatever she wants, I'm paying."

Lisa ordered a screwdriver in a tone clearly denoting that she considered it a poor trade-off from dancing. Don put down some money, left the bar with his drink, and headed for the back game room.

The girl tagged after him. "Hey! Where you going?"

He turned his head, telling her over his shoulder, "Outer Space!"

"What?" she shrieked.

Don entered the back room and set his drink on the glass top of the pinball machine entitled Outer Space. He dug some money out of his pocket and fed the slot. He took an eager turn. The ball shot up the track, around curves, through passages and bouncing off rubberbands. Bells dinged, lights flickered and the backboard score window tallied up his points.

Chapter 15

Jody added a sweatshirt over her shirt and jeans against the evening's chill, and she and Elliot started for town.

"Your brother was in some mood when he took off," Elliot warned her as he drove.

"So am I," Jody said.

They found Myre's bar quite different, on this a Friday night, than what it'd been Thursday afternoon. Jukebox music was loud and lively and it was crowded with good-timing people.

"I don't see him, good," Elliot assessed as they sorted their way through the crowd.

"What do you mean good?" Jody asked.

"Brad. I'm referring to Brad. He's not tending bar. It's some other guy. That's good. It probably means we'll live."

Jody didn't care one way or the other right now about Brad. She left Elliot ordering drinks at the bar and ventured on alone to find Don.

Mood. She'd show her brother a thing or two about mood. She had plenty of her own to use on him. But where was he? They'd seen his car outside. He had to be here.

A lumberjack sort of guy purposely got in her way. "Hi, doll. Lookin' for someone?"

"Yes," she said, all too urgently.

He laughed arrogantly. "Well, I'm someone."

Though Jody resented the stupid come-on, she didn't want to discourage any possible chance of someone helping her find her brother. "Don Mitchell. Do you know him? Have you seen him? Can you tell me where to find him?"

"What? Huh?" The guy motioned at his ears, pretending he could no longer hear her. Undoubtedly his clever little way of handling rejection. Then when some girl accidentally bumped into him from the other direction, he turned with delight and began working, what he considered to be his charm, on her. "Hi, doll. Lookin' for someone?"

Jody shoved her way past the both of them and continued on her way. She went through a doorway in the back, discovering a game room. There was an immediate sound change as she entered, likely from the carpeted floor and walls. Softened as the music and voices were within it, there was however the additional sound of pinball bells and video game sound effects. She spied Don playing pinball at the other end of the room and went toward him. A blonde girl was glued to his side.

"Hi," Jody said, interrupting both his game and his cuddling.

Don's surprised, glassy-eyed look spread into a big smile. "Hey…hi!"

Jody was no longer mad at him, nor felt like arguing. She was only glad she'd found him. "Sorry about before."

"Me too." He slipped an arm around her.

"Well, don't mind me," the blonde he'd broken away from complained.

"This is my sister," Don told her. "Jody, Lisa. Lisa, Jody."

"Sister?" His Lisa friend was obviously doubtful. "No guy ever gets approached by his sister in a bar."

Jody was only too eager to explain. "I'm here because we've got some making up to do. I've been kind of a long-lost sister for way too long, know what I mean?" She wrapped an arm around Don's waist. Then behind his back she winked an eye at the unhappy Lisa, vengefully contradicting the significance of sister.

"I'm outta here!" The blonde stuck her nose in the air and started away.

"Hey! Wait! Where ya goin'?" Don made a clumsy attempt to grab her, but missed and only managed to spill his drink down the front of himself. "Damn!" He wiped at his wet shirt, muttering, "What's with her?"

Jody shrugged innocently. "Maybe she's got a thing against sisters."

The next look coming over Don, as it remet with hers, indicated that he didn't really mind so much after all.

Elliot found them, and came carrying two glasses of beer. As he handed one to Jody, Don snatched the other away from him as if it were his, saying, "Thanks."

Elliot gave him a nasty look. "It's because I'm short, isn't it? You wouldn't have stolen my beer if I were taller, would you?"

Don laughed and returned his drink to him. "Here. I was only kidding. I'm drinking vodka. Of which I need a refill badly. Keep your eye on Jody. I'll be right back."

Elliot was amazed at Jody's just standing there. "You're letting him go?"

"I see something different in Don tonight."

Elliot chuckled. "His being drunk."

"No, it's a...a certain look in his eyes."

Elliot nodded. "The vodka."

"No, I mean, it's like he's trying to find me as much as I'm trying to find him."

"Well, congratulations, you've both succeeded."

Jody sighed at Elliot's shallowness. "Come on, let's try to find a booth out in the front area."

"Try being the operative word," Elliot said, following her through the crowd.

They luckily spied a booth that another couple were just leaving, and they dove into it before the vinyl seats had even cooled.

Jody stared at her glass of beer. "Why beer? Why'd you get me a beer, Elliot?" Thirsty as she was, she went ahead and drank some though clearly expressed her displeasure in it.

"You know, Jody," Elliot said, indicating some displeasure of his own, "there are a lot of times lately when it seems you're becoming more and more of an ordeal."

"Ordeal?" She wiped her mouth with the back of her hand and frowned at him. "What do you mean, ordeal?"

"When we got here, I asked you if you wanted a drink and you said yes."

"Drink. Right. Not a beer."

"Oh, pardon me, Miss Sloshoholic, for not getting you the right stuff, the hard stuff."

"You know I drink vodka sour."

"Not until yesterday, I didn't."

"And you can't remember that far?"

"You should've been more specific."

Jody fingered the rim of her glass. "A real drink has ice cubes."

Elliot laughed. "Ice cubes. You've really acquired a whole new world of sophistication in your young drinking life, haven't you."

Don found them and slipped into Jody's side of the booth beside her. It looked like he'd already drunk half of the drink he'd just bought.

"You want to make your sister happy?" Elliot challenged him.

Don laughed, flicking a dubious look between the two of them. "What do I have to do?"

"How about this?" Elliot two-fingered an ice cube out of Don's vodka and plopped it into Jody's beer. "Thank you."

"Elliot!" Jody shrieked.

Don flinched at the splash it made. "What do you call that?"

"Just something that seemed outrageously important to her," Elliot said, making it sound characteristically common. "It doesn't especially have to make any sense."

The event brought bursts of laughter out of all three of them. Which made the senselessness of it almost worthwhile. It pleased Jody, seeing Don so loosened, even if it was mostly due to his drinking. It was like, maybe now she and he could have a real talk without blowing up at each other.

She peered into Don's glass. "You said vodka, huh? That's what I drink normally."

He studied her deeply. "Aren't you kind of young to be drinking?"

"I'm twenty-two and legal."

Don laughed and slid his glass toward her.

She lifted it, took a small sip and made a face. "Eew…what's it mixed with?"

Don laughed again. "Just ice cubes, little sister."

She rubbed the taste of it off her mouth with her hand. "I drink mine with a mix."

He reclaimed his drink and took a long swallow.

Jody sipped some more of her beer, deciding maybe it wasn't so bad after all in comparison.

Before she could start a conversation with Don about his going back to Winona with her and Elliot, he opened up with, "You know, there's this other bartender, Brad, who used to work here but just got fired yesterday."

Elliot choked on his beer, coughed a couple times, then asked raspily, "Did you say Brad?"

Don nodded. "Yeah, seems the owner walked in and found him drunk and passed out on the floor behind the bar yesterday afternoon."

"Jeez!" Elliot responded with exaggerated surprise, slipping a nervous look at Jody.

"Story goes that two strangers, a guy and a girl, were asking him questions about me," Don continued. "Brad said the guy was a private investigator. Which made him real edgy. He said the couple, the guy and the girl, pressured him into drinking. And at the same time they pressured him into talking…you know, making him say stuff he really didn't want to say."

"Huh," Elliot faked some sympathy.

"Brad felt he'd been purposely set up. Hates himself for falling for it, but it seems he hates that P.I. a hellova lot more."

"I don't blame him," Elliot agreed.

"*Are* you a private investigator?" Don asked.

Elliot broke into a guilty laugh. "Me? No."

"But it was you two in here working Brad over about me, right?" Don said more as a fact than a question. He waited while Jody and Elliot exchanged quiet, uneasy looks.

Then Jody turned sideways, frowning at Don. "So what's your gripe here? That we located you, or that we got Brad into trouble?"

"Neither." Don smiled, easing off of the matter as soon as he got the truth about it. "I'm not going to worry about why you guys came to Myre or what you did to Brad. At least not right now. Not tonight. I'm in too good of a mood." He lifted his drink, his magic cure-all, and tipped some down zestfully.

"Maybe I should switch to vodka," Elliot considered, watching him enviously.

"Can we have a talk, Don?" Jody asked her brother, still facing him, still trying to draw so much more out of their togetherness than what she'd so far gotten.

"Isn't that what we've been having?" he said.

"You know the talk I mean."

Don propped his chin into his hand, grinning fondly and agreeably at her. "Yeah…sure…why not…let's talk."

This was it, her best chance yet of reaching him. "I want to know, haven't you ever thought about me over the years?"

The hard-driving beat of the next jukebox song started Don's head to bobbing and fingers tapping the table. "Yeah…sure…a lot, Jody."

"But you stayed away."

"Yeah." Thump, thump—thump, thump.

"You haven't wondered what's happened to me all this time? You don't want to know? Catch up?"

"Seems you've turned out okay." Thump, thump—thump, thump.

"On the surface, maybe," she said. "But I'm a mess inside. Elliot can vouch for that."

"A real mess," Elliot all-too-willingly vouched.

"Besides being worried sick over you," she divulged to Don, "and missing you, I've had to deal with Dad and then with losing Dad and now…well, I've decided to sell the house."

Her brother's attention to her was still obviously distracted by the music. She wasn't sure how much of what she was saying was really getting through to him.

"The house," she said, getting a little tired of trying to compete with the music. "The house was left jointly to the both of us and—"

"Do whatever you want with it, Jody," Don said. "If I have to sign something, I will. Just send it to me here and I will. Whatever you want, I want."

"I want you to come home! And don't tell me you are home. I mean real home, before its sold and gone forever, and…before Matthew moves away."

"Matthew?" Don was notably taken aback by the mention of him. "He's moving? Matthew's moving? How is he?"

"His house has become way too much for him to keep up all alone. His daughter Ellen, from Arizona, is coming for him in September. It would be nice for you and he to see each other again before he goes."

Don took only a small sip of vodka this time. Then, head down and serious, he seemed to disappear into some sort of private place in his mind. Jody waited him out, allowingly.

After a few minutes, he sprung up out of the booth, grinning with another happy attack and asking her, "Wanna dance?"

"Sure." She amazed herself at how readily she gave up on their talk and went out on the floor with him.

A soulful Mavericks song was playing. She and Don closed up to one another and began a slow, easy sway to the captivating music.

As they danced, Jody happened to notice that on the sidelines, watching and glowering at them, was that Lisa girl who'd earlier been with Don. For sure it appeared even more obvious now that she'd never bought the sister story. Jody was glad. She felt no remorse. She needed Don all to herself right now. And had him. And held tight to him.

"So what's this Elliot guy really about?" Don eventually got around to asking in a big-brother manner.

"My boss, my friend," Jody stated simply.

"He seems like more."

"I know. But he isn't." She looked into her brother's intoxicated eyes. "Don?"

"Yeah?"

"Please say you'll come home with us."

He smiled sweetly and genuinely, as if he were totally won over by her. "Okay."

"Really?" Excited as she became, she accidentally stepped on his foot. "Sorry."

"Ouch!" he said.

The two of them laughed.

Then Don solemnly verified, "Yeah, really, I'll go back with you guys."

They didn't talk anymore, but rather only gave themselves fully to the music and the dance.

CHAPTER 16
▼

Elliot sat by himself in the booth, watching Jody and Don dance, feeling good about how well the two of them were getting along now. There was a definite closeness and caring between the brother and sister that neither their eight year separation, nor the big temper flare-up they'd had earlier this evening, could obliterate. There was a bond, permanently instilled in their blood relation no matter what. He admired that. Envied it. Was beginning to feel a little downhearted that he didn't have a brother or sister of his own.

"Dance?" a voice suddenly intruded on his thoughts.

He looked to the side, finding a tempting solution to his aloneness leaning in at him and asking again, "Wanna dance?"

Elliot chuckled, like it was totally unbelievable that some girl he didn't even know should come asking. Or, for that matter, that he should hear himself declining with, "Oh...uh...no thanks."

"Oooh..." she cooed disappointedly. "Does that mean you're taken?"

"T-taken?"

"Committed to another girl?" Her voice cooled and her posture straightened. She was young, though not as young as Jody. Red hair curled around a pretty face, blue sweater, jeans, shapely body keeping time with the music.

"No," he said, breaking into another nervous laugh. Then just as quickly, he sobered and changed his answer to, "I mean, yeah."

The girl grinned. "Well, are you or aren't you?"

"W-what?" Elliot hated what she was doing to him. And yet it was like, what *was* she doing to him? Man, it'd been such a long time since he'd played the

- 75 -

boy-girl game. With anyone other than Jody, that is, if you could even count that.

Suddenly he was drawn back again to watching Jody dancing out there with her brother.

"Okay, I get it," the girl beside him reassessed.

Elliot returned his look to her. "Huh?"

She smiled, in a giving up sort of way, and motioned at the dance floor. "That kid out there with Don. She's the one you're committed to?"

"Committed." Elliot said the word with so much unexpected tenderness and honesty that he embarrassed himself. He may have even blushed some. "Yeah…maybe…I don't know…I guess you could say that."

"Nice." The girl beside him actually seemed to be offering her approval. Until she smugly added, "Isn't she's kind of young for you?"

Elliot rocked his head and rolled his eyes.

"Okay," the girl said, starting to dole out free advice, "so let's say the age thing doesn't really matter to you. But maybe what should matter to you is that she's out there dancing with a hunk who's a lot younger and better looking than you and—"

"Hey! Nobody wrote you a dear Abby letter here, did they?"

"Barbie. My name's Barbie."

"Okay, look, Barbie," he said, emphasizing the doll reference of her name and the fact that he'd had enough of her, "maybe what you should be doing is looking for Ken, instead of wasting your time on me."

"And maybe what you should be doing," she chided, "is giving a grown-up, real-life Barbie a shot instead of wasting your time on little Raggedy Ann out there."

"Jody," he clarified.

"Whatever," Barbie said in a huff and disappeared into the crowd.

Elliot appreciated being left alone again. He finished his beer, already deciding he'd order vodka the next time the waitress came around. He leaned back in his seat, listening to the music and resuming an enjoyable watch of Jody and Don dancing. Mostly of Jody. And he got to thinking more about the word committed. And the probable, scary fact that maybe he sort of was.

Chapter 17

▼

Everyone slept late Saturday morning. When they finally got up, one by one, in slow motion agony, each popped a couple of Tylenols, drank a glass of cold water, and savored a mug of hot coffee.

After her shower Jody felt considerably better. Enough to rave chipperly to the guys, "I had a really great time last night."

Recovery took longer for them. Elliot muttered something indistinguishable, while Don didn't attempt to speak at all. Jody was okay with that and gave them the space and time they needed to come around as well as she had.

From the groceries she and Elliot had bought the day before, she started preparing a brunch of hash browns, eggs and sausage. Though neither of the guys seemed anxious to eat, she imagined after their showers they'd be fully revived and starving.

She loved working in Don's tiny little kitchen area. Actually, today she loved everything. Smiling and humming to herself as she cooked, she was sure she'd never been happier in her whole life than she was right now. This trip to Myre turned out being totally successful in that Don had agreed to go back home with her and Elliot.

When the meal was ready, Elliot willingly came to sit at the table. But Don, last to shower, still wet-haired and unshaven, said he wasn't hungry and walked out the door.

Jody's good mood crashed.

She charged outside after her brother. "What's with you? Last night you were prince charming, today you're grumpy bear."

Don dropped into one of the lawn chairs. "Last night I was drinking."

She stood before him, hands on hips, forehead scrinched.

He squinted into the glaring sun. "Just leave me alone, Jody, okay?"

"No."

He moaned and shook his head carefully, as if it might fall off.

"Explain this change to me," she demanded.

"I told you last night that I—"

"You can only be pleasant when you're drinking?"

"Like you can only be pleasant when you're getting your own way?" he turned it back on her, shading his eyes with his hand as he looked at her. "About last night...I probably said some things I didn't mean."

"Like?"

"You know what."

"You're saying now that you're not coming back with us?"

"That's right."

"Why?"

"Because I've sobered up. And I'm not leaving here, Jody. That's why."

She swept out her arms at their surroundings. Beyond the small clearing encircling the cabin were trees, trees, and more trees. "What have you got here? A little shack of a place out in the middle of nowhere."

"What do I have in Winona?"

"Your past."

"Well...there you go," he agreed cynically.

"And me," she said. "You've got me there."

"I said no, Jody. It's been nice seeing you but—"

"I don't get it. I don't get you."

"I've got a life here. Just leave me alone."

"You've got shit here."

A shrewd grin slid over his face. "Yeah, well, it's my shit, okay?"

Jody fell to a loss of words. And to the sad conclusion that it might've been better if she'd never come looking so wholeheartedly for Don in the first place.

Though he spoke in a softer manner now, his words were still as rejecting. "Maybe you think it would be good for me to go back, but the truth is, Jody, I just don't think I can face it."

"How can you not face it?"

"It's easier not to."

"And just take the easiest way, by all means!" she said.

He closed his eyes. Against the sun. Against her.

Jody left Don sitting there and took off for a stroll across the width of the yard in front of the cabin. She followed the fence that edged the dirt driveway, admiring the yellow flowers adorning it. For as furious and frustrated as she was feeling over Don, she patiently held out every chance for him to change his mind.

She knew he was drinking a lot last night. But she thought she'd seen and heard something so genuinely caring in him despite it. She, too, had wound up drinking way more vodka sours than she was used to or ever should have indulged in. And maybe, because of that, she'd been more unfocused and mistaken about last night than she wanted to admit today.

When she returned to Don, he was sitting there staring at the ground and wouldn't look up.

"Don…" she said his name, but got no response.

She stood there quietly waiting.

"Don…?" she said again after a minute or so, this time more as a question.

His gaze lifted slowly. "Sorry," was all he gave her.

Chapter 18

▼

While Elliot sat eating alone at the table, he'd overheard most of Jody and Don's argument through the screen door. He guessed he wasn't as surprised as Jody was over Don's changing his mind about Winona since last night. He understood, a lot better than she did, how a guy's over indulgence in liquor can alter his actions, his words, and the very best of his intentions. Though he liked Don, and believed the guy really did have a place in his heart for his sister, he could've easily bet a million dollars that he'd end up acting like this today. It didn't make Elliot feel any better, being right about it. He was on Jody's side and wanted what she wanted. He felt bad that he couldn't seem to do enough to help her get it.

Except maybe to eat the food she'd prepared. He could do that. For her. No woman liked to cook food for a man only to have him refuse to eat it. Elliot would never do that to her. But he wasn't even halfway through his plateful when she came storming back into the cabin in a fit that caused his fork to stop midway to his mouth.

He gave her a minute, then he left the table and went over to where she stood by the loft ladder. "I thought Don seemed a little too easy last night," he said.

"I've got to get him home, Elliot."

"This is his home now, Jody."

"No, it's not!" Her dark eyes were sad and needy of something more than sensibility here.

Elliot gave her a hug.

Jody was quiet for all of two seconds, then she flared up again. "It's for Don's own good. If I could just get him there, I know he'd see that. Last night he was fine with the idea, today it's all off. I don't know what to do. What do I do now?"

Elliot didn't know either. And it killed him the way she looked at him so dependently. "Relax, Jody," he said in the way an adult spoke to an out-of-sorts child. "Just try and relax, okay?"

"I can't relax."

"Give the situation more time."

"I've given it eight years."

"I know," Elliot said, though sighed with the frustration of not knowing. He gave it his deepest and fastest thought. Think, think, think. Something, something, anything. "Jody, let's go home, you and me."

"I'm not going back without him," she stated.

Elliot supposed that if he was to help her at all, he'd better try harder to stay on the same level as she. "Okay, okay," he forced himself to agree, "we'll figure something out."

"Sure," she said dismally.

"We will." He patted her arm.

"Like what?"

"I don't know."

"You don't know, because there's nothing."

"There...there's something," Elliot said.

"What?"

"There's something, Jody, I promise you." Promise? Did he just hear himself promise her? Whoa!

"What could there possibly be," she questioned, "outside of...of kidnapping Don?"

"Shh..." Elliot held a finger to his lips. Her whimful and outrageous idea clicked impressionably with him. "Yeah," he said, nodding, grinning, falling in with it, "kidnapping."

Jody looked at him as if she thought he was crazy but was counting on him to be sane. "Really? We could do that?"

"Yeah. Sure. Why not."

"Kidnap Don?"

"Yeah. Sure. Why not," he repeated.

"How? I mean, how could we possibly do it?"

"Well, uh..." Elliot walked away from her, scratching his head, thinking, thinking. Ideas were coming fast and furious and jumbled, not yet in clear detail. "Leave it to me. At least most of it to me. Your part, Jody, will be to...uh...pack a bag of some of Don's clothes. Essentials. But don't drop a clue to him. I'll be back later."

"Where you going?" Jody was struck with instant panic.

"Shh..." he reminded her lowly. "It's all right, it's all right. I'll be back. For sure. Believe me, I'm not skipping out here. Jeez, you're so insecure. I need to do some shopping in connection with our plan and—"

"What plan?"

"The one I'm working on, okay? It hasn't completely gelled in my head yet. But it will. Trust me. That's all I can say right now. Meanwhile, you just pack. His stuff, your stuff, my stuff. And not a clue to Don, remember. I'll see you later."

She followed him to the door. "How much later?"

"I may have to go as far back as Two Harbors, maybe Duluth, to find—"

"Duluth?" she exclaimed, several octaves over a whisper.

"Shuu..." he reminded her. "Yeah, to find what I want. So it'll be a while. You gotta hang in there, Jody. Stay calm. Stay happy. Keep your brother happy and don't get into it with him anymore now, okay? Can you do that?"

She shrugged.

"Okay, good," Elliot settled for that.

He headed out to his car, passing Don in the yard. "I'm taking off for a while. Look out for your sister, will you?"

"Where you going?" Don asked, sounding almost as panicked as Jody had. "You're not ditching her here, are you?"

Elliot chuckled. "Not a bad idea. But no, I just...well, I uh...just need a...a break from her, know what I mean?"

Don's grin showed that he knew only too well.

"Okay, good. See ya later." Elliot got into his car and pulled out of the driveway.

CHAPTER 19

▼

Don needed more Tylenol. The two he'd taken earlier weren't doing the job. His head was still splitting. He got up from the lawn chair and looked toward the cabin. He dreaded going inside and facing Jody again. She was expecting way too much here. Creating all this pressure. Getting way too disappointed over his reactions. Trying to make him feel guilty.

By the time he went inside, Jody was starting to clear the table. Despite the tension between them, he made an effort to be nice. He gave her a thin smile as their looks met. "Hi."

"Hi," she said as simply.

"You okay?"

"Yeah. You?"

Though Don's appetite was zilch, he offered, "Maybe I'll eat something now."

He sat down to the untouched plate of food Jody'd left for him, trying to ignore the nausea he felt in just looking at it.

"It's cold," she said, watching him.

"That's okay."

He forked a bite of scrambled eggs, tolerating the soggy flat taste they'd acquired from sitting. It didn't sit well with his already queasy stomach. With each bite he fought the urge to throw up. Though he once caught a smug little grin on Jody's face, as though she were enjoying this to be his due punishment, it was actually she who saved him.

She came to the table with the coffeepot and poured some into his mug. "Here, this is probably the only good part left of the meal." Then she took away his plate, saying, "You don't have to eat this, Don. I'll make you some toast, if you'd like."

He lifted the mug. "Coffee's enough."

She nodded, scraped the cold food into the trash container and washed the plate at the sink.

Don sipped his coffee and watched Jody, trying to think of something to say that would make her feel better, help her understand his refusal to go to Winona. Why couldn't she just go home and leave him there alone with the life he'd made for himself? They were brother and sister, for crying out loud, not husband and wife. Why was she acting so possessive of him? They'd been apart for eight years. Had a nice little reunion now. And that was that.

As if she felt him studying her, criticizing her, Jody suddenly stopped what she was doing at the sink and spun around to him. "You're my brother, you know."

"I know," he admitted as much.

"You didn't know it for eight years," she reminded him.

"I knew it Jody. I just couldn't...I couldn't help the way things changed for me."

"Living by yourself in the woods isn't exactly a change for the better, is it?"

"Not to you, maybe, but it is for me. Why can't you just accept that, Jody?"

"You're the only family I've got. I don't have anyone in the world closer to me than you to talk to or—"

"You've got Elliot."

"He's not my brother. He's not my family. I need you to help me with—"

Don got up from the table. "I don't want to get into this with you again, Jody. If you've got things to talk to me about, while you're here, fine, I'll listen. And I'll help in any way that I can. But if all you want to do is argue about my going or not going back to Winona, forget it. You've totally lost me on that."

Jody's look was uncompromising. And when her hands went onto her hips, that did it. Don started for the door.

"Where you going?" she lashed out at him.

"Well, not to Winona, that's for sure."

"But you're not...you're not going to—"

"I'll be in the yard," he said as the screen door banged shut behind him.

He strolled about, holding his head that still hurt, realizing he forgot the Tylenol when he was inside. Winona, Winona...he had to protect himself from Winona. For so many reasons. Krista was at the top of the list.

He stopped at the fence and gazed down the narrow rugged road that ran two miles to the highway. He wondered where Elliot really went. He'd claimed he needed a break from Jody. Don supposed he believed him, and yet there was something more, something suspicious.

Last night had been fun, the three of them at the bar. Drinking had certainly loosened everyone up, and for sure had made Jody and Elliot less threatening for the while. Don liked his vodka, and usually used it as either an enhancer toward feeling something or a numbing toward feeling nothing. But then there were his dry days, like today. When the clear reality of his wasted life stared him harshly in the face and he just tried choking it down without any booze whatsoever. Brave. Strong. Self-pitying. Stupid. Whatever. It was hard to rate himself accurately anymore. While Jody was feeling like she'd lost him, what she really didn't know was that he'd pretty much lost himself.

He glanced back at the cabin. He wasn't about to go inside again for his forgotten Tylenol, no matter how bad his head throbbed. It wasn't worth another confrontation with Jody. He'd just go sit in a lawn chair and hopefully escape his pain and misery and sister behind closed eyes. He crossed the yard, not especially proud of his chicken-shit resolution. Like he'd been proud of anything in a long while. Or like it mattered. Because it didn't. Nothing did anymore. Nothing.

CHAPTER 20

Through the window over the sink, Jody was able to keep her eye on Don while she finished the dishes. She was glad when he stopped wandering around the yard and settled into a chair. Hopefully he would stay there for a long enough time now to give her the opportunity to rummage his things and secretly pack a collection of his clothes and personal items.

She went to the closet and chest of drawers at the back of the cabin and started in. Luckily she found two duffel bags on the closet shelf that she could use. Perfect, she'd fill them both. She worked fast and kept a careful eye out in case Don happened to suddenly come walking in.

Poor Don. He had no idea of the plan against him that was in the making. So far Jody herself didn't know the details. Elliot had only told her to pack. Though she trusted Elliot, and this plan he said he was devising, she really had to wonder just how much of it he'd actually perfected yet. Jody knew the main object was to take Don home with them, but for as resistant as Don was being, she couldn't imagine how they were going to accomplish that.

When she joined her brother in the yard some twenty minutes later and asked how he was doing he opened his eyes unappreciatively and scowled, "Great."

"I finished the dishes and cleaned up the kitchen."

"You didn't have to. I would've done it later."

"You didn't even eat. No fair having to do dishes when you didn't even eat."

"Did you eat?" he asked.

"Some," she said. Then laughingly added, "Elliot eats enough for everyone."

She drew a smile out of Don. "Yeah, I guess. So where do you think he went?"

Jody shrugged and sat down in the other chair. "He doesn't tell me everything."

"But you were surprised that he even left, weren't you? I know I was."

She sighed and changed the subject. "It is kind of pretty out here."

"Nothing else like it," Don said.

Jody found herself liking the up-north environment more and more. After some serious tree gazing at the thick assortment around them, she zeroed in on the lawn furniture. "Did you, by any chance, make these pieces?"

"Yeah."

"Really?"

"Really," Don said as if it were no big deal.

"You're very good at it."

"It's kind of a thing with me, building stuff. I also made the birdhouse, the fence, and the bed frame in the loft. That little shed behind the house is my shop. Not much space in there, but it serves the purpose. I have a fair assortment of tools, a small but serviceable workbench, and lots of time to putter."

"What else do you do with your spare time besides putter?"

He grinned, shook his head, and turned out his hands.

"Don't you get lonely out here?" she asked.

"Doesn't everybody, at times, no matter where they live?"

Jody felt a direct aim. "I guess so."

"So does Elliot keep you from getting lonely?"

"No," she replied super quick. Then added with a giggle, "Yeah sort of."

"Sort of?" Don pressed.

"He's a good friend, that's all."

"He is a little old for you."

"Friend," she repeated.

Don kept at her. "So don't tell me a pretty girl like you doesn't have a regular boyfriend her own age. Do you?"

Jody left her chair, and him, and strolled across the yard to the flowers by the fence. There was Kevin, and the baby she'd had by him. But she couldn't just jump into that topic right here and now. "These are beautiful," she said, stooping to admire the yellow blossoms, touch them, sniff them. Uncomfortable with the boyfriend question, she ignored Don for a while.

When she turned around again, it was to ask him in fairness, "Do you have a girlfriend?"

"No." Don got out of his chair, seeming equally uneasy and invaded. He stuck his hands in his pockets and looked away from her. "So where do you think Elliot could've gone?"

Jody shrugged. "He gets restless."

Don resumed eye contact with her. "You don't think he went back to Winona and left you here, do you?"

Jody didn't find that funny.

"Sorry," Don said. "It's just that Elliot...he's the kind of a person who seems really hard to figure."

Jody let Don know, by the raise of her eyebrows, that he'd just described himself as well. And he admitted to it by way of a quick, guilty laugh.

The sun had long disappeared and the afternoon sky had become a murky gray. The temperature had fallen and the wind ceased to an almost eerie calm.

"Sure looks like rain," Don said. "Hope Elliot will be all right, wherever the heck he went."

Jody had no doubts about it. "He will. He's got windshield wipers."

She hadn't expected that it would sound so humorous, but for some reason it sent her and Don into a frenzy of laughter. At the very same time the sky disbursed a downpour. They ran for the cabin, getting unavoidably wet.

Don turned on a light then came back to stand beside her in the doorway. Together they watched the sheeting rain. Sharing the simple enthrallment made Jody feel like they were truly brother and sister again, that they'd found a definite link between their past and their present. She could tell that Don felt it too. They stood there without speaking, just watching it rain for a long time.

Eventually Jody left the door to go sit in the rocker, and Don took to the couch.

"I love the sound of rain," she said, rocking.

"Yeah, me too," he said, head back, eyes closed.

"And the smell of it."

"Yeah, the smell," he agreed.

"Remember how when we were kids we used to love running outside in the rain, throwing out our arms and dancing and splashing around in it? Mom used to have a fit."

"You were a baby then. How can you remember?"

"Seven. I was seven. I remember. I remember Mom standing in the doorway, calling at us to come in the house, scolding us, warning us that we'd catch our death. And then...she'd just sort of give up for a time and watch us and smile.

She loved us a lot. Wanted to protect us. Keep us safe. But it was only water. Only rain water. And…it was she who turned out being the unsafe one."

"She wasn't sick too long before…" Don stopped midsentence and shook his head.

"When she died," Jody continued, "Dad didn't seem to care as much one way or the other if we went outside in the rain or not. And…I guess…neither did we."

"After Mom was gone, all three of us stopped caring about a lot of things."

Jody sighed softly. "Life got hard, really hard after that."

"Yeah."

"So much of our childhood seemed to just stop."

Don opened his eyes and gave her a somber look. "Kids have to grow up, Jody."

"At seven and twelve?"

"We got an early start."

"Then why is it that sometimes…sometimes I still don't feel grown up, even now?"

Don teasingly verified, "You're saying that you want to go outside right now and run around in the rain."

"No. I'm saying that when you left home—"

"Oh, Jody, not that again," his voice hardened.

"—my life seemed to stop. You were my big brother. I had no one to follow after, or look up to anymore."

"But you made it. You made it just fine. You're okay. Don't dwell on the past."

Jody didn't feel okay. She felt like her life was hanging in pieces. Hundreds of pieces. Millions. Dangling, incomplete transitions from one difficult phase to another and another and another. She needed to find a oneness with which to tie it all together, keep it all together. Surely a big brother was meant to be that. Right now might've been a good time to pour her heart out to him about Kevin and everything, except that Don disappeared behind his closed eyes again and she decided to hold off and wait for Elliot's plan. When she got Don home to Winona, that would be the time and the place to talk about stuff with him, because then, for sure, they'd be a family again.

Chapter 21

▼

It was seven-thirty and still raining hard when Elliot returned to the cabin. He came charging inside, wet and laughing, carrying a grocery bag and two pizza boxes. "You guys eat yet? I hope not, because I brought two gigantic pizzas with everything on them and—"

"Including rain," Jody said with a laugh, popping out of the rocker to help him.

She took the bag from him, peeking into it. From it she pulled out a smaller bag, a bakery bag, and opened it. "Cookies?"

"Dessert," he said, setting the pizza boxes onto the counter.

"Six dozen?" she teasingly estimated.

"Two and a half," he said. Then added with a sheepish grin, "Actually there were three dozen to begin with, but I narrowed it down on the ride back."

Jody pulled two bottles out of the larger bag and held them up, giving Elliot a disapproving look.

"Vodka," he said.

"I can see that, but why would—"

He grabbed the bottles away from her, cagily giving her one of his P.I. signals. "Yeah, yeah, I bought these, seeing as how we all ended up having such a blast on the stuff last night."

"So you also got Sprite or something like that for me to mix mine with, right?" Jody asked.

"Whoops. I never thought of that. Sorry, Jody. Guess you'll have to drink like a man tonight."

She scrinched her face at the thought of vodka straight. Or for that matter at the idea of any of them indulging again so soon.

"You can handle it, trust me," Elliot assured her enthusiastically. Then turning his back to Don, he winked an eye at her and whispered, "Trust me…it's gonna be a great evening."

Elliot took off his wet jacket, hung it over the back of a chair, and glanced around. "It's cozy in here, you know? Real cozy. Good to be home. Let's party!"

Jody heated the pizzas in the oven, then the three of them sat at the table and ate, drank, and talked as the heavy rain continued outside. There was no thunder, no lightning, just the sound of the steady falling rain and the scent of soaked earth drifting in through the screen door. Though this was undeniably turning into a meaningful evening together, it bothered Jody that she couldn't yet see any sort of actual plan taking shape.

Later, when Don had gone off to the bathroom, she leaned toward Elliot and quietly questioned, "What kind of plan is this? You promised me a plan, Elliot!"

"Yeah, yeah, we're already into it. Remember how easy going Don got last night when he was drinking?"

Jody huffed. "You think that after a few more drinks here we're going to be able to reconvince him to go to Winona with us?"

"Shh…yeah, sort of."

"By then won't you be too out of commission to drive or me to care?"

Elliot shook his head no. "Remember what we did to Brad the bartender?"

"Faked our drinking while getting him sloshed?"

"Right. If we're careful we can do the same to Don now."

"He doesn't have a spittoon on the floor."

"Whenever we get the chance," Elliot jumped up, "like now," and took both his and her glasses to the sink, "we'll exchange our vodka for water." He dumped their drinks down the drain and refilled the glasses from the faucet. "Here," he said, handing a glass of pretend vodka back to her, "this should go down a little easier."

Jody was impressed. Except with, "What if we do manage to get Don to go with us? What about when he sobers up and finds out he's half way to Winona? He'll kill us!"

"Not with these on, he won't." Elliot slipped a pair of handcuffs out of his pants pocket. "Had a bitch of a time finding a place that sold these."

Jody's eyes widened. "Where *did* you find them?"

"There are places that sell official police equipment. It just took me some scouting around before tracking one down."

"And just anybody can go in and—"

"I'm not just anybody," he professed with a devilish laugh.

As Don came out of the bathroom, Elliot ducked his plan's phase 2 out of sight in the nick of time.

It was an interesting evening from Jody and Elliot's standpoint, the two of them playing off Don's increasingly laggard condition while they themselves faked their own inebriation. To cover their ploy they kept up a steady, distracting conversation on just about everything and anything they could think of.

Amidst his having a good time, it was certain that Don had absolutely no idea he was being set up. But by two in the morning, he was wearing down to the point of scarcely being able to keep his eyes open and was slipping farther and farther down in his chair.

Jody stood up, pretending that a whim of an idea just now struck her. "So what do you say we go for a drive? Get out of here for awhile? Come on!"

"I think…" Don said, then paused, then continued, "I'm beyond driving."

"Elliot's not," she said. "Are you, Elliot?"

Elliot stood up, wavering enough to fit with all the drinking he'd supposedly been doing. He turned an imaginary steering wheel in the air. "I think I can handle it."

"Like you haven't done enough driving, after…" Don seemed to lose his train of thought for a moment, "after…wherever the heck it was that you were all day."

"Naw, I'm fine," Elliot said. "I could drive forever."

Don still pondered it. "I don't know…"

"Don't be a party pooper," Jody told him.

"I'm not."

"You're sounding like it."

Don motioned outside. "It's just that…it's still raining out there."

"Elliot's car has windshield wipers," she reminded him, thus got him to laughing and onto his feet.

Don stumbled over to the door for a closer look at the weather. And Jody, behind his back, whispered to Elliot, "The clothes, the clothes…"

"Where are they?" he asked.

She gestured that the bags were behind one end of the couch with a blanket draped over them.

"Well," Elliot said loudly, with a crisp clap of his hands for emphasis, "guess maybe we'd all better take a potty break before leaving. Me first."

Jody went second.

When it was Don's turn, he claimed he was fine. The snag in their plan made Jody panic. Now how would Elliot sneak out the suitcases?

But Elliot, in his crafty P.I. character, simply pointed to the bathroom and ordered Don, "Go now or forever hold your pees!"

Don staggered off good-naturedly.

Elliot grabbed all the duffels, plus the bag of cookies, and hurried out with them before Don returned.

Jody waited for her brother. They put on their jackets, then huddled together under the additional cover of a blanket and ran out to Elliot's car.

"This is crazy," Don said from the back seat as they drove off. "Where we going?"

The rain, in the headlights, sparkled like silver glitter. "I don't know," Elliot said casually over his shoulder to him. "Just around."

Jody was as scared as she was excited to their being under way, but faked a calmness in hope of calming Don. "Don't you just love riding in the car in the rain."

"It's crazy," he insisted. But after that he became quietly acceptant.

The car bumped and rocked along the rough road. The rain drummed fast and noisily upon the roof. Washing and clearing beneath the windshield wipers.

The next time Jody glanced around at Don she found him slumped over and asleep. "He's out of it," she told Elliot.

He pulled the handcuffs out of his pocket and gave them to her.

She held them. Stared at them. Felt really saddened by them. "I sure didn't want it to have to be this way."

Elliot gave her an understanding look. "You were desperate to get your brother home. He wasn't cooperative and you needed a desperate measure. The cuffs are it."

"He's going to hate me."

"Would you rather have him hate you and be home, or like you and be in Myre?'

Jody sighed.

Elliot laughed lowly. "Well, maybe when he gets done hating you he'll find it in his heart to like you."

"I hope so."

To be on the safe side, they drove a little while longer before pulling off the road and stopping. Elliot got out of the car, opened the back door and leaned partly in. To none of the sleeping Don's awareness, he cuffed his hands together before him. Then as added insurance, he also used a chain and padlock to fasten, with some slack, the handcuffs to the side armrest.

"How long do you think he'll sleep?" Jody asked, as Elliot returned to the driver's seat.

"A few hours, if we're lucky."

They drove off again.

"Aren't you getting tired?" she asked.

Elliot chuckled nervously. "I can't afford to get tired."

"What about when Don wakes up? Aren't you worried about that?"

"No."

"I am."

"Me too," Elliot changed his mind.

Chapter 22

Don slept way longer than either Jody or Elliot would have imagined he would. Jody dozed some herself. And Elliot kept driving, wanting to cover as much distance as possible before all hell broke loose.

The breaking moment came at 8:00 AM, just entering St. Paul.

"What the hell is this?" Don roared from the back seat.

Jody jumped with a startle and looked back at her brother. He was sitting up straighter and struggling against the cuffed restraint he found himself in. No longer subdued under the influence, he was sober and freaking out. And she was scared.

"What the hell is this?" He thrust his foot against the back of Elliot's seat.

"Ouch!" Elliot felt it.

Don kicked the seat again. "Get these cuffs off of me! What is this? Where are we?" He watched for recognition in the fast-moving scenery out his window and didn't like what he saw. "Damn you two!"

Jody kept turned to him as far as her seatbelt would allow. "It was the only way, Don. We had to do it. Don't be mad."

"Don't be mad?" He yanked uselessly at the cuffs.

"This is as much your fault as ours."

"Mine?" His eyes glared, voice snarled. "How do you figure that? Just how do you figure that?"

"Because I needed you to come home and you said no."

"My eyes are shot," Elliot said. "And I'm hungry. What say we stop for some breakfast. That is," He looked in the rearview mirror, "if you can behave like a nice little prisoner, Don. Can you?"

"Or what?" Don leaned forth to the extent that he was able. "Brad said he thought you were a cop or an investigator or something. Are you? Am I under arrest here? What's the deal? What's going on, Elliot? Why are you—"

"Please!" Elliot said. "One question at a time."

"Elliot's not a cop or a P.I.," Jody told Don. "He just wants to help me get you home."

"By kidnapping me?" Don clattered his cuffs together. "You don't think this is just a little bit against the law?"

Elliot exited the freeway and pulled into a SuperAmerica station. He got out of the car and went to open the gas cap, which was on the same side of the car as Don. While he stood pumping into the tank, Don jeered at him through the window and rapped his cuffs against the glass.

"If you're thinking that that sort of behavior will award you your freedom, you're sadly mistaken," Elliot assured him. "Niceness rates much higher with me."

Don fell back into his seat.

From the gas station, they cruised around in search of a restaurant. Jody and Elliot both at the same time spotted a small, inviting looking one set back from the main road. They pulled into the parking lot and past a sign that read,

Welcome To Wright's
You've Made The Wright Choice

"Oh, cute," Jody said with girlish delight, and Elliot chuckled.

"I can run, you know," Don flared up again. "Soon as you unfasten me from the door, I can run with cuffs on."

Elliot lost it. "Why would you want to? Doesn't it mean anything to you, seeing how much this means to your sister?" He got out of the front, slammed the door, and opened the back. "Besides, I'm chaining your feet together before we go into the restaurant."

"Like hell you are!" Despite Don's protest he found that there was actually nothing he could do about it.

With the second piece of chain he had, Elliot fastened Don's ankles together. Only when that was secure did he undo the other chain that linked Don's handcuffs to the door behind Jody.

"Maybe we should just get take-out," Jody suggested to Elliot.

"No. We all need to stretch our legs some, even your brother."

"See how much you can stretch your legs with a piece of chain fastened around them," Don sounded off.

Jody felt more sad than embarrassed as she and Elliot assisted their prisoner into the restaurant. There was only one other customer in the place, plus one waitress and a peering-out-from-the-back cook.

"Don't worry," Elliot addressed their obvious concern, "he's not harmful. Only to himself. Slight mental problem. He, uh…has these little fits. We're taking him to his clinic appointment right now."

"On Sunday?" the waitress questioned.

Elliot had no doubt lost track of what day it was. He cleared his throat and stammered, "Yeah…yeah…it's a real nice clinic…they're open Sundays."

The three of them sat onto stools at the counter, Don in the middle. The waitress handed out menus. Jody laid Don's open for him.

Soon Don was slipping off his stool and stating in a low voice to Elliot that he needed to go to the rest room.

Elliot, the good cop that he was, stayed with his man. "Order us something tasty," he told Jody, starting toward the men's room with Don. "With lots of coffee. And a couple Tylenols for your brother."

"Thoughtful SOB, aren't you," Don scoffed.

"Yes. Thank you."

"Then take these cuffs off of me."

"Not quite that thoughtful."

Jody smiled sheepishly at the waitress and placed three cheese omelet orders, hoping their story about Don was believable enough so that no one called 911.

The guys returned. And as of yet there was no sound of approaching sirens.

When the food came, it was difficult for Don to eat with handcuffs on. Fork in his right hand, but having to lift both hands up together with each bite, the jangle and clang of metal as he maneuvered. The waitress, the cook and the other customer down the way, all watched with fixed fascination.

When they'd finished eating, and the check came, Elliot found he couldn't pay. He said he thought he had more money left than he did, but he didn't, and he searched his pockets frantically. "Jeez, it's been going fast. I'm five bucks short. Jody, can you help me out?"

She gave him what she had, which was only three. She'd stupidly left her checkbook at home in Winona, and evidently so had Elliot.

Elliot solicited Don's help. "We still need two more. How about it?"

Don raised himself enough so that Elliot could pull his wallet out of his hip pocket.

With all three contributions, the check was met.

"A tip…aren't you going to leave a tip?" Don asked smartly as Elliot started returning his wallet.

"Oh, right." Elliot fished two dollars more out of Don's money for that. Then keeping the wallet a moment longer, he chuckled and helped himself to yet another two bills. "You're a very generous tipper, Don."

Don shook his head and muttered to himself.

The three of them left the restaurant. It was good getting outside again.

"You must be wiped out, Elliot," Jody said as she and he closely escorted Don back to the car. "I don't know how you've kept going as long as you have. Why don't you let me drive from here on?" She'd gone to the ladies room, washed her face, brushed her hair and was feeling quite refreshed now.

"No," he said. "I'm fine with it. Besides, the freeway entanglement from here on gets pretty wild."

"I'm a good driver."

"Defensive?"

"I'm good."

"That's not enough." He guided Don into the back seat, refastened his handcuffs to the armrest, and they were soon on their way again, himself driving.

"I packed some of your things," Jody informed Don as they rode. "Elliot put them in the trunk."

"Thanks," he said sarcastically. "All that drinking last night, it was part of the set-up, right?"

Though Jody couldn't bring herself to say it, Elliot seemed delighted to glance over his shoulder at Don and take credit. "Right. Neat idea, huh?"

"And that ride you wanted to go for in the rain, how come you two weren't as smashed as me?"

Gloating proudly over his scheme, Elliot explained, "Jody and I were dumping our vodka down the sink whenever we had the chance and refilling our glasses with water. Times we didn't get a chance to do that, we'd just drink especially slow." He paused to laugh about it. "You never got wise to any of that, did you?"

Don exhausted a heavy sigh. "Where'd you get the handcuffs?"

"A very interesting shop in Duluth."

"So that's where you went when you took off claiming you desperately needed a break away from Jody?"

"You said you desperately needed a break from me?" Jody confronted Elliot.

Elliot gave her an embarrassed look. "I never said desperately. Anyway, it was just a cover-up so's I could go find the cuffs. And hey, mission accomplished."

"Congratulations," Don scowled. Then he closed his eyes and dropped his head to one side, as if to tune out anything further.

* * * *

When they got to Red Wing, Elliot said all the driving he'd done was finally getting to him and he just had to stop and catch at least an hour's sleep before driving any farther. He left the highway and pulled into a rest stop area along the Mississippi River.

"An hour, just an hour…" he said, getting out of the car and heading over to a shady spot of grass along the river bank.

Jody, still sitting in the car with Don, called to him, "Hey! What are we suppose to do?"

"I don't know…" he answered weakly, already stretched out and sounding half asleep. "Wait…just wait…I'll be okay after a few winks…just a few…winks…"

She turned to look at Don behind her. He was left in her keep and she was helpless to their standstill. She glanced around at all she could see from her window view. Throughout the rest stop grounds were benches, trees and walk paths. Back across from the parking lot entrance were narrow streets with old, but well-kept, homes. Everything was so neat, clean and sedate. "Nice little town, Red Wing," she made of it.

Don said nothing.

"Remember your good friend Neil?" she asked him.

"I try not to," he grumbled. "Why mention him all of a sudden?"

"Well, he moved from Winona to here some time ago. He and his wife and two kids. He bought a service station somewhere along Second Street."

"You don't say."

"You and he used to be friends."

"Used to."

"How would you like to look him up and say hello, as long as we're here?" Jody suggested, excited with her idea.

"No," Don said.

"You need to get more in touch with your past, Don."

"No, I don't."

The key was still in the ignition. In a fast decisive move she slipped over behind the wheel and started the engine.

The pressure valve blew off of Don's sulking and he yelled at her. "What the hell are you doing?"

Elliot was totally out of it and unaware of Jody's driving the car out of the parking lot. "We'll be back before he misses us," she said. "You can't come this close to Neil without saying hello to him."

"Jody, I told you no!"

"About the handcuffs, we'll just tell him it's part of a joke or something."

It didn't take her long to find Neil's Service. Second Street was a block off Main Street, and the station was readily visible on a corner. She pulled into the lot and parked in the space along side the building.

Jody took the padlock key off the dashboard so that she could at least free Don from his attachment to the door.

"I'm not getting out," he insisted when she opened the back door to him.

"Of course you are," she said. "Neil will probably get a kick out of this."

"Jody, no!" Despite his protest, Jody's prodding somehow got him out of the back seat.

They were still there by the car when Neil, in greasy coveralls and remarkable good timing, came outside. The husky, mustached guy's reaction to seeing them was pure shock. He stood in place for a couple minutes, just staring at them. Then suddenly he came walking fast toward them.

"Neil, hi—" Jody began, "remember us? We were passing through and Don wanted to say hello to you before we—"

She had not yet completed her opening statement when Neil balled a tight fist and rammed it hard into Don's stomach. Then he left without ever saying a word.

Jody caught Don as he doubled over. "What was that for? What's with him?"

"I told you I didn't want to see him." Don clutched himself with his cuffed hands.

"Are you okay?" she cried.

His answer was a groan.

"You knew he'd punch you?" she asked, helping her brother back into the back seat of the car.

"No. More like I thought he'd kill me."

"Why?"

"Just get us out of here!"

"Why would he hit you?"

"Drive!"

"He didn't even ask about the handcuffs." Jody jumped into the front seat behind the wheel. Within seconds she had the car peeling rubber out of the lot.

Don moaned as he was thrown to one side.

"Should I take you to a hospital or something?" Jody offered, making nervous glances at him in the rear view mirror.

"No!" Don said.

"I'm sorry. Really sorry." She regretted her judgment, was confused at its outcome.

Elliot was on his feet pacing the river bank when she returned with the Skylark and the prisoner. He was a crazy man, meeting them. "Where the hell were you? Jody, I've been out of my mind worrying about—" He stopped ranting when he realized she and Don hadn't exactly been on a joy ride.

He helped Jody out of the front seat of the car, listening to her hyper explanation. Then he opened the back door and helped Don out. "I knew I shouldn't have allowed myself to sleep. Jeez, how ya doin', man?"

Don gave a sarcastic, "Great."

"Damn!" Elliot said. "I should never have trusted Jody with you."

"I didn't mean to cause so much trouble," Jody pleaded.

Elliot ignored her for Don. "Look, if I take the cuffs and chain off you now, will you promise not to flee? After all, Don, we've come a long way here and it'd be really stupid to run out on such an endeavor at this stage of the game."

"Game?" Don questioned the term.

"What do you say?"

When Don held forth his cuffed hands as his answer, Elliot freed him, wrists and ankles both.

Jody threw her arms around her brother apologetically. But her hug only made him flinch with pain.

"Oh, Don, I'm sorry," she cried.

He looked away, shaking his head.

The three of them walked over to the river and sat down on the embankment. No one said anything more. They just sat there quietly staring at the moving water.

Chapter 23

Despite what felt like an incredible slowing of time, the entire afternoon still managed to slip away. It had been okay, actually kind of nice, Don admitted to himself in his head…he, Jody and Elliot just sitting there watching the river so peacefully. Nobody talking. Or fighting. Nobody in handcuffs.

Don had expected there would eventually be more questions about the Neil incident, but he was surprised when it turned out being Elliot, rather than Jody, who started them up again.

"I'd really like to know why a guy would haul off and punch you the first time he sees you in years."

Don felt like saying back to him, Yeah, and I'd like to know why you consider it okay to handcuff and kidnap someone.

As if Elliot were reading him, he added, "Hey, I never hit you."

Don shifted his look from him to Jody. Her big brown eyes expressed just as much eagerness for the Neil story. Don pulled a blade of grass out of the lawn and played with it in his hands.

"You owe us an explanation about Neil," she urged him.

Don's long silence broke. "Owe?"

"I was there when he hit you," she said, "which gives me the right to know the reason behind it."

Don was amazed at how his sister felt she had so many rights where he was concerned. He shook his head unwillingly.

"Okay, okay," Elliot said, "we took the cuffs off of you, Don, so what say we just talk things over like three rational adults now."

Don gave a curt laugh. "Like your taking the cuffs off me automatically erases the fact that you put them on me?"

He watched Elliot and Jody exchange quiet looks, then he closed his eyes and massaged the tenderness of his stomach. His gut still ached, but not as bad as before. It just seemed so unbelievable, how he'd ever gotten into any of this. And maybe even more unbelievable, thinking there had to be a way out.

When he again met looks with Elliot and Jody, it was like they were the judge and jury and he was standing trial. They weren't going to let up on him. "Back when Neil and Angie lived in Winona, and I did too," he began.

"Yeah…?" Jody prompted the instant he paused to take a breath.

"Well, they were married young, you know, and—"

"And?" Jody said.

"This was after Krista and I broke up. Neil…he, uh…came home from work early one day and caught me and Angie in bed together."

"Whoa, that'd get a guy riled all right," Elliot sided with Neil.

Jody slugged him in the arm. "Shut up."

Don rocked his head at the circus these two were, but continued. "I was into my clothes and out the door before Neil could really react. But then he came running out of the house after me, yelling that if he ever laid eyes on me again he'd kill me."

"That's when you took off from Winona," Jody assumed.

Don nodded. "It was kind of like the last straw."

"The other straws being other guys' wives?" Elliot guessed.

"No. No other wives. Just…other stuff."

"Such as?" Elliot pressed.

Don hated getting into this, but he knew because of the Neil incident it was already too late. He was into it and that was that. "Such as going along with whatever crap came my way, as if I never had any common sense of my own."

Elliot, sitting Indian style, teetered back and forth as he reversed the crossing of his legs. "Exactly what kind of crap are we talking about?"

Don couldn't believe how Elliot and Jody were opening him up. It was like one more sly trick of theirs he'd fallen for. And it was like now that he'd started, he had to finish. "Junior high it was classroom disruption, property damage, attitude, fights. High school more of the same but worse, including alcohol and drugs. Never finished high school, as you remember, Jody. Couldn't hang in there. The more Dad hollered and screamed at me, the more I rebelled."

"I never heard him holler and scream at you," she said, as if she actually regretted the idea of having missed out on something.

Don gave her the hard truth. "You were his little angel, me his holy terror. Dad was careful in dealing with me so's none of the bad overlapped onto you."

"I don't believe that," she said.

"He and I had a lot of talks, a lot of arguments, you didn't know about, Jody. That doesn't mean they didn't exist."

"So you dropped out of school," Elliot coaxed the story along. "Then what?"

Don's gaze drifted back and forth between the river and his listeners. "Couldn't find a job that suited me, or I suited it. I had these friends who...well, they were, uh...pulling robberies. I...I didn't have a part in any of that myself. In fact, I hadn't the slightest idea what they were doing when we weren't together. But because I knew them, when they got arrested I got in hot water just the same."

"You weren't at all aware of what your friends were doing," Elliot verified.

This was really becoming more and more like a trial. First the handcuffs, now the trial. Don shook his head no, half expecting to be told he'd have to answer out loud for the records.

Jody frowned. "Then why would you get in trouble for it?"

"Come on," Don said, "you've never heard the expression you are who you know? Well, that was me, I got labeled with it. My friends got caught and sent to prison and I got brought down for having known them. Dad, well, he thought I should've been locked up right along with them. And Krista, she—"

"Dad never would've thought that," Jody argued.

Don gave her a guileless look. "I didn't do anything except know those guys. I didn't approve of their chosen profession. I even tried to talk them out of it, once I found out about it. But I couldn't. I failed them. I also failed my father. And...probably half the town of Winona." He held his head between his hands and moaned. "You were so young back then, Jody. Most of this was way beyond you."

"I just can't believe Dad would've condemned you for what your stupid friends did." Jody's eyes shimmered with held back tears.

Her having been so young and protected back then, Don knew she surely had to have had a whole different, lighter, perspective of the problem between him and their dad. Surely, now, he didn't want to darken the image of their father to her by saying too much. He rubbed the tension in his head and tried giving the matter careful thought ahead of words.

Having to go easy on this for his sister's benefit, he tried summing it up at this point simply by saying, "Dad saw what he saw, thought what he thought, Jody, and that's just how it was."

"But if you weren't guilty of anything except having some lousy friends. He would never have—"

"My lousy friends gave me a bad reputation, you know? Like I said, I got labeled. They got prison, I got labeled. Not only by Dad. But try to get a job after that. Or make new friends. Or hold onto your old friends. Or onto your own good grace. I was in a downward spiral I couldn't stop. Everything I did seemed to turn out wrong. Everything."

"At nineteen?" Elliot's reaction seemed torn between sympathetic and disbelief.

Don continued. "When I couldn't stand myself any longer, or facing people who couldn't stand me, I left. It was the only choice I had."

"Mostly it was about Krista, right?" Jody asked as if she knew.

Don didn't answer.

She nodded and concluded on her own, "So then you went to Myre."

Don stared at the river. At the piece of driftwood being swept along by the current. Jody and Elliot were the current, he was the driftwood. Lost to his grounds, taken by force. "Not right off," he said about Myre. "I bummed around other parts of Minnesota for a while. Then went to Mexico, L.A., Seattle. Only been in Myre the past year and a half."

"Like maybe you were working your way back home without really realizing it," Elliot gathered.

"No," Don replied with quick certainty. "I had no intention of going home. Ever."

"Well, that's changed now, thanks to Jody," Elliot said just as surely.

"Jody may have changed where I am," Don fended, "but not how I feel. Which is…the only way I can really keep my head straight about my life today is to leave my past behind."

He hated the way Jody was studying him. It seemed she had all these big expectations of him that he was never going to be able to meet. And it made him a little sorry, yes, but he'd spent too long a time building a protective wall around himself to let her, or anyone else, come tearing it down now.

Don pulled himself to his feet and went to lean against the trunk of a tree. He could hardly believe that Elliot and Jody would just turn around and take him all the way back to Myre now. Yet he could hardly believe, either, that they'd still want to forcibly take him on to Winona after everything he'd told them. It felt like there was no rightful place for him anywhere in the world.

Chapter 24

Sitting there in the grass, in yet another befallen silence, Jody realized this wasn't working. She'd only been fooling herself, thinking that she and Don were on their way to reassembling their sibling relationship. Even though he'd been freed of the handcuffs, and had started talking more, his contributions thus far were mostly cold and forced. He was still in a place where he didn't want to be, and that made her sad and sorry. She gave Elliot a needy look.

Her boss friend slid closer to her and whispered, "It's not easy for him, Jody. Or for you either. I think this is probably just going to take some time."

It was hard for her to be patient, to believe that more time would be beneficial. She turned her gaze back to the river. The Mississippi was so beautiful, its continuous flow so smooth and easy, yet strong and directed. She envied it, wishing her life was doing as well.

"Anybody else besides me hungry?" Don left his place against the tree and pointed to someone pushing a hotdog cart back along the walk path. "My treat, of course."

Jody and Elliot welcomed the idea and went with him.

Don paid for everyone's hotdogs, chips and sodas, which they carried back to the riverbank to eat. And without anymore actual conversation about anything particular, they pretty much just sat there quietly eating and watching the river.

After they'd finished eating, Elliot stretched and yawned and made a new evaluation. "Know what I think? I think all of us are seriously done in and Winona is beginning to seem way too big of an effort to reach anymore today."

Jody disagreed, though not without a yawn of her own mixing into her words. "It's not that far…we'll make it…we've just hung out here a little too long, that's all…it's made us more tired than rested."

"Yeah, maybe," Elliot wearily agreed. He got to his feet and gave her a hand to hers. "Let's go."

Don also stood, saying, "You two have had it for sure. How about I drive the rest of the way while you sleep."

Elliot chuckled at the offer. "And wake up to find we're back in Myre?"

"I'll drive to Winona," he promised.

"Sorry, man. Jody can drive if she wants to now, but not you."

As the three of them walked to the parking lot, Don crumpled his empty papers and dunked them hard into a trash barrel. "You know, Elliot, I can take off any time I please now and you'd never catch me. Car or no car."

Elliot rattled the handcuffs in the air.

"I'm not drunk and passed out," Don said. "You couldn't begin to clamp them things on me if you tried."

Elliot lost it with him. "Fine! Then go! Just go!"

Jody's heart sank, fearing that Don might do just that. Even Elliot, she noticed, didn't look quite as courageous about this as he'd sounded. He gave her the car keys when they reached the Skylark. And Don came up behind them, still with them, like the answer to her silent prayer.

Elliot dove into the back seat of the car, desperate to lie down and close his eyes. Jody got behind the wheel, and Don into the front passenger seat. They started on the final lap of their trip, Elliot's elevator music playing languidly from the radio.

With frequent sidelong glances at Don, Jody mostly found him quiet, solemn, feet against the dashboard, watching the passing scenery out his side window.

The one time she did catch him looking back at her, it disturbed her. "What? Why are you looking at me that way?"

"Twenty-two?" he verified, as if he were still having trouble believing her age.

"Yeah, what'd you think after all this time?"

"Somehow, I guess, that you'd still be that scrawny little fourteen-year old kid."

"She's long gone." While Jody just barely held the speed limit, other cars zoomed past her and around her like nothing. She didn't care. Tired as she was, she was handling this as carefully as she could.

"I missed most of your teenage years," Don said, actually sounding regretful. "What were they like for you, Jody?"

It was her chance to tell him. She blurted the answer bitterly, "I never got over losing my big brother, that's how they were for me."

"You had Dad."

"I didn't have you."

"Jody…" Don paused with a sigh. "I never meant for it to seem like I was deserting you."

"Then you shouldn't have left!"

"I had to."

"Well, then maybe I had to feel deserted," she fended sharply.

"Let's not talk anymore," he said.

"You're really not very good at it anyway, are you, talking?"

"It's too difficult right now. I'm tired, you're tired, and—"

"Fine!" She reached forth to switch the radio station to rock.

The sudden blast of it through the rear speakers jolted Elliot awake. "Jeez!"

Jody lowered the volume but kept her music choice, needing its energetic lift to fill in where conversation died.

Winona finally came as a welcomed sight to Jody. It was a nice town, a small town that had grown vastly over the years. Her hometown, of which she'd never been so far away from until her upstate trip to Myre. She felt comforted to be back. It would be nice if Don felt the same. She gave him a look. Surely he had to be having some emotions too. But if he did, he kept them hidden behind his stubborn, brooding silence.

She parked Elliot's car in the driveway behind her Reliant. Everyone got out. Don slowly started toward the house. Jody and Elliot held back a minute, watching him cross the front lawn.

He went up the steps to the porch. Stopped. Then walked back and forth the length of it, running his hand along the top of the spindle railing. Stopped again. There certainly had to be a lot of things going on in his head at this point. Things he wasn't sharing with anyone, that was for sure. He pulled the screen door, jumping with a startle as it tipped crookedly in his catch.

Jody muffled a laugh, and Elliot related to the happening with, "Jeez!"

As they joined Don on the porch, Jody apologized. "Sorry. I should've warned you about the door."

She started to get out her key, but Don showed her that he had his own. It touched her, his still having a key to the house after all this time. For sure it was a good sign. She gave him the go-ahead signal.

He stuck his key in the lock of the inner door and turned it. The sound of the click seemed like a personal welcome home greeting to him from the house. Jody and Elliot followed him inside. Elliot guided the screen door back into place.

Don stood stiffly in one spot at first. Then after a few moments he started walking around. Jody and Elliot waited in the foyer as he wandered through the whole downstairs by himself. He seemed interested and emotionally affected. Though he still wasn't saying anything, there was a shimmer in his eyes when he returned to the them.

"I guess we're all pretty wiped out," Jody made of the three of them standing there quiet and drooping. "Elliot, you're staying the night."

He gave her a tired smiled. "Thanks."

"Even thought it's still light outside, what say we just crash. Unless anybody wants something to eat first."

She didn't. Don shook his head no. And Elliot's yawn indicated that even he was more eager to sleep than eat.

The three of them started up the stairs, Don first. He grasped the railing but let go the instant it wobbled beneath his hand.

"Sorry," Jody apologized for not warning him.

Don didn't have to be shown which bedroom was his. He went directly to it and dropped onto the bed. Jody gave Elliot the room that'd been her dad's, then proceeded on down the hall to her own room.

The lights went out.

The house was still.

Don was home.

CHAPTER 25

▼

Elliot was in no hurry whatsoever to go to his own place of residence the next morning, which was the Treggor Motel. He was more interested in hanging around the Mitchells' house. Besides, in addition to inviting him to stay over last night, Jody'd promised him breakfast.

He went out to the car to fetch everyone's duffel bags. Funny, how no one had even thought of bringing them in last night. Some trip it'd been to Myre and back. And surprisingly successful, their managing to bring Don home, thanks to the brilliant kidnapping plan. Elliot felt good about the outcome, though probably not half as good as Jody did.

He lugged all four bags upstairs in one trip and dropped them in the hall. Don came out of his room, rubbing his eyes.

"Morning," Elliot greeted him. "Here's your stuff. I just got it from the car."

Don mumbled something unclearly, as though he were not yet completely awake, picked up one of his bags and took it with him into the bathroom.

"You're welcome," Elliot said.

Jody came out of her room dressed in jeans, a yellow blouse, hair in a ponytail, and a top-of-the-morning smile on her face. "Hi."

Elliot met her with adorned pleasure. "I didn't know you were up yet."

Her smile turned to puzzlement and she blinked her brown eyes at him. "You didn't hear my shower running a little while ago?"

"No. I...I just woke up a few minutes ago and went out to the car for the bags and—"

"Thanks." She stepped around them, heading for the stairs.

"Jody..."

She paused on the second step and looked back. "What?"

Elliot shrugged, suddenly feeling like an awkward schoolboy with nothing worthy enough to say to a girl as cute as she. He smiled stupidly.

"What?" she asked again.

"I…uh…was just wondering what you thought so far? About Don's being home?"

"I don't know. I mean, I haven't even seen him yet this morning."

"I have," Elliot said.

"And?" she asked.

Elliot chuckled. "Let's give him till after breakfast to judge."

"Right. Of which I'd better get started." She continued down the steps.

"What are we having?" Elliot called after her.

"Like it matters?" she said, with a crude little giggle trailing behind her trip to the kitchen.

True. No, the menu didn't really matter to Elliot. He could eat, and take pleasure from, almost any food. Jody well knew that and never ceased to rub it in. Yet, he supposed he hoped it would be pancakes with maple syrup and lots of butter.

Don wasn't too long in the bathroom. And then it was Elliot's turn. As he showered and shaved, he realized how amazingly good he was feeling about being here in the Mitchell house with the brother-sister duo. It felt like he was part of a family. It was nice.

Chapter 26

▼

Jody was enjoying making breakfast. It was a large kitchen. Of course any kitchen would seem large compared to Don's little cabin setup. Despite its size, this kitchen was farmhouse cozy down to its red-checked window valances, painted cupboards, Windsor chairs around an oval table, rag rugs at the sink and back door, and an actual kerosene lamp on one of the wallpapered walls.

She'd slept well, the sun was shining brightly through the east window, there was plenty of orange juice in the fridge and the pancake batter was turning out with just the right amount of lumps. The whole world seemed wonderfully perfect to her right now. Except, maybe, for the annoying kitchen faucet that sprayed a little shot of water sideways each time she used it. But Don could fix that. She'd already seen how capable he was with tools at his cabin, plus working with them was something he obviously liked.

She gazed out the side window at Matthew's house. She couldn't wait to show him the surprise she'd brought back, which was Don. It would surely be a grand reunion between the two of them.

When Don came downstairs and into the kitchen, he notably lacked her enthusiasm. Though he flicked Jody a slight smile as they said good-morning to one another, he was quiet and self-contained. He sat down at the table to watch her work. And as she continued with the breakfast preparations, she fought the urge to press for a conversation with him right now, thinking that they would have a better time to talk later.

By the time Elliot came down, Jody had the food ready and waiting. The three of them sat around the table. Matching dishes and real place mats were a far cry from Myre. She caught Don's grin as he smoothed a hand along the edge of the flowered fabric beneath his place setting.

"Man…" Elliot moaned, stretching his arms up and out and back before he dug in. "I think we all slept like zombies last night."

"I didn't think zombies slept," Jody said. "I thought they just moped around."

"Yeah, well…" He cut and forked a piece of his heavily buttered and syruped pancakes, "I just meant we were all dazed…dead-like…that's the point I was making. Don't be so literal." As he tasted his first mouthful, he told her, "Good pancakes, very good."

Jody watched Don closely, trying to determine his exact moment to moment feelings about everything. She wondered if he liked the pancakes. He didn't say. She couldn't tell. At least he was eating them. She wondered if he'd slept all right last night. In his own room. After eight years. Following their long trip from Myre. He still looked tired. And downhearted. She wished he'd talk more.

Elliot, on the other hand, never seemed to stop. "Your car appears okay out there, Jody."

"Why wouldn't it be?" she said blankly.

He chuckled. "I mean, nobody stole it or battered it."

"It's a good neighborhood, Elliot. I never worry about leaving it out of the garage."

"Right." Elliot ended that subject and began another. "So Don, what've you got in mind to do on your first day back in Winona?"

"Probably catch a bus back to Myre," he answered.

Elliot took it jokingly and started adding to it. "You really think Jody will let—

Ouch!" he said to the kick she gave him under the table.

Jody decided it was better to be quiet and pretend everything was great, rather than say too much and find out it wasn't. To her lead, the rest of the breakfast was finished in the safety of silence. It delighted her immensely, that Don devoured equally as many pancakes as Elliot.

When her brother finished eating, he took a refill of coffee with him, left the table, and went out the back door, opening it carefully lest it be as hazardous as the front one. The door was fine, but he would find the second step in poor condition.

Jody upped from her place at the table, urging Elliot, "Come on, let's go pick some tomatoes."

"Which, in translation, means let's go keep an eye on your wayward brother, right?"

It was her dagger look, more than anything, that got him off his chair and going with her.

Don was sitting on the top step, just outside the door, sipping his coffee and rapping the heel of one shoe against the rotting second step that he'd already found.

"Don't do that," Jody warned, as she and Elliot gingerly descended past him. "It won't take much more."

"Just testing it's condition," he said.

Elliot told him, "One good huff and puff might very well flatten this entire house."

"It's gotten pretty run down, hasn't it," Don concluded from what he'd seen so far.

"I'm hardly a carpenter," Jody claimed.

"There are carpenters for hire," Don suggested.

"Not on what I make at the motel," she said.

"Which is zero at the present," Elliot verified.

"Sad," Don said.

"It is," she agreed.

"Very sad," Elliot added.

Jody thought it almost seemed like the opportune time to get into a serious discussion with Don, except that Elliot pulled her by the hand and motioned at the tomato plants in the far corner of the yard to where they were supposed to be going.

She gave Don a to-be-continued look and went with Elliot.

"You're not giving him enough time," her boss friend advised her when they got beyond Don's range of hearing.

"I gave him through breakfast," she said.

"Don't rush him. I can see that you—"

"We need to talk. Don and I need to talk. I didn't bring my brother all the way back here to just sit on the steps and daydream."

"Maybe that's what he needs though, right now. He's home. Be glad he's home, Jody. Let things sink in for him. This wasn't his idea to come back. He was forced, and I'm sure it's been a jolt to his system."

Jody glanced back at the house, at Don sitting on the steps.

"Just stop pushing him every chance you get," Elliot said.

"You're saying I'm a pushy person?"

Elliot chuckled.

Jody bopped him in the arm. "Let's pick tomatoes."

Chapter 27

▼

Don sat on the steps, watching Jody and Elliot across the yard from him, who, amidst their tomato picking, seemed to be keeping a close eye on him as well. He still couldn't believe he'd been manipulated into coming to Winona. He didn't want to be here. How could this have happened? How could he have let it? Well, he wasn't staying long, that was for sure. Jody could pout all she wanted and Elliot could keep his damn handcuffs to himself. Enough was enough. He'd made the trip back with them. But that was it. Ask no more. Expect no more. Demand no more. He had nothing to give. Nothing. Didn't they already know that by now?

Last night, walking into his old bedroom that he'd been away from for eight years, had been strange. The strangest thing about it was how he'd unexpectedly felt an immediate sort of comfort in it. Unless, of course, it was just that he'd been so terribly exhausted that any place other than Elliot's car would've seemed exceptionally comforting. He didn't know. Wasn't sure. Except that this morning, when he woke up in his old bed, his old room, it still had the same strange, welcoming effect on him.

He set his empty coffee mug behind him, then bent forth over his knees to further inspect the second step. He ran a hand over the decaying wood. If Jody brought him back here to fix things, she was in for disappointment. His being her brother, and having grown up in this house, and being here now for an ultra short visit, didn't, by his book, automatically make him the person for the job.

He suddenly sensed that someone else was watching him other than Jody and Elliot, someone off to the side. When he turned his head to check, he found it was Matthew just over the fence.

"Is that…really you, Don…?" The elderly neighbor stood squinting at him, as if he didn't quite trust his eyes.

Don left the steps. "Yeah, Matthew, it's me."

The two of them walked to meet where the dividing fence ended. The red sweater Matthew had on seemed to be the man's main source of vibrancy over the otherwise older, slower, more sallowed look he'd acquired since Don had last seen him.

"I…I don't believe this. I just…I…just don't believe this…" Matthew stuttered through a tearful smile.

They hugged one another, and Don felt the thin frailty of his neighbor. Lost years came into a painful account he wouldn't have expected. "It's good to see you, Matthew."

"I…I never thought I'd, uh…see you again, Don…" Matthew backed out of Don's arms in order to get a better, fuller, second look at him.

"I never thought I'd be back, Matthew. I can't believe that I am."

"Well…w-what happened? W-whatever got you here then?"

Don pointed to Jody and Elliot, who were, by then, finished with their tomato picking. "They did it, those two. They teamed up and did this to me." Don's explanation ended on a helpless laugh.

Matthew laughed as well and lifted his hands in praise. "Bless them. God, bless them."

Jody came hurrying across the yard, bursting with joy. "How do you like the surprise I brought you, Matthew? This is it! Don!"

Happy tears glistened in his hollowed eyes. "I love it. It's the…nicest s-surprise I, uh…ever received."

While Jody proudly took credit, Don hung his head taking none at all. It was strictly her idea. Hers. Achieved by her stubborn urgency, nagging force, and faithful sidekick Elliot.

And yet, Matthew seemed to prefer accrediting Don the most by way of how he wrapped his arms around him again and this time let go of a few emotional sobs against his shoulder. "Thank you, Don…" his voice quivered. "Th-thank you for…for coming home."

Don didn't really consider himself to be home. At least not in the sense that Matthew and Jody thought.

The disturbed look he was getting from Jody right then was as if she were reading his mind, didn't like it, and was already protesting it.

Shit, he thought, watching his sister's hands go onto her hips.

Chapter 28

As Elliot came carrying tomatoes, Jody introduced him to her neighbor. "This is Matthew, my honorary grandfather. Matthew, this is Elliot. He went with me to find Don. He owns the motel I work at."

Though he couldn't do a hand shake because of the tomatoes he was holding, Elliot exclaimed enthusiastically, "Matthew, I've heard a lot of good stuff about you from Jody."

"And Elliot..." Matthew said fondly, "I want to commend you."

Elliot's eyebrows arched. "Oh, yeah? For what?"

"For being a part of finally getting our boy Don home again."

"Hey, no problem," Elliot boasted, flicking a back-and-forth look between the brother and sister. "Well, not too much of a problem."

Jody took two tomatoes out of Elliot's collection and gave them to Matthew.

He was happy to have them. Looking them over in his hands, he told her, "These early tomatoes...they d-did real well, didn't they.

"And there's plenty enough of them to share," Jody said.

"Thank you.

"You're welcome. I'm going to invite you over to dinner with us one night soon, Matthew."

"Okay. T-hat'd be nice." He started toward his house with his tomatoes. "See ya later, Don."

Don gave a silent nod.

"Bye, Matt," Elliot called after him. Then to Jody and Don, he said, "I'd better get out to the motel now and see what's happening. Or," he chuckled, "what's not happening. See ya later, okay?" He turned the remaining tomatoes over to Jody.

"Wait…here…" She handed him back a couple for himself.

"Thanks."

She walked him to his car. "So you're okay with my not coming in to work today?"

He motioned at Don. "You've got all the work you can handle right here."

He slipped into the driver's seat, set his tomatoes over onto the passenger seat, then turned back to give her a solemn look through the open window. "Jody, I'm really glad I was part of all this. I can see now, more than ever, how important it was for you to get Don home."

She took a deep breath and smiled appreciatively. "Thanks, Elliot. I couldn't have done it without you."

He returned the smile. "We do make quite a team, don't we."

"I've never assisted a P.I. before."

He laughed. "I've never been a P.I. before."

"You did good."

"So did you."

"Together we accomplished our mission."

Elliot turned the ignition. "Jody, take as much time off from the motel as you need now. I mean it. And…I'll talk to you later."

"Later." She stepped aside and watched him back his car out of the driveway. Then she went into the house, put her tomatoes on the kitchen table, looked for Don and found him in the living room using the desk phone.

"Yeah, I'll wait," he was saying to someone. When he noticed Jody, he explained, "Work. I'm calling my work."

She puttered about the room, plumping the accent pillows on the plaid couch, picking dead leaves off the philodendron plant in the corner, straightening the large wall painting of a farm scene. How her dad had loved that picture. And how often, over all the years it had hung there, it had required adjusting. Somehow the hook had never been properly centered. Maybe Don would fix it. *Why was he calling his work?* she wondered.

After waiting on hold for several minutes, Don finally began a conversation with presumably his boss. "I won't be in today. No. Well, I'm sorry, but I just couldn't call before this. I know it's Monday. No. No, I'm not sick. Jim…Jim, could you just listen here? I'm in Winona. Well, it's where I'm from. It's my home town. I've got sort of a family emergency here. My kid sister needs me for a while."

Nearby and listening, Jody got goose bumps hearing him say that. It made her feel special, like maybe the trip actually did mean something to him after all. Yes! She was only sorry that it was creating a problem with his job, his boss.

"I don't know…yeah, maybe," Don went on answering questions over the phone. "I think Lyle can handle it okay. Yeah, I'm sure he can till I get back. Yeah…yeah, he's worked it a few times. I don't know, Jim. I doubt I'll get back there by Wednesday. But for sure by Thursday."

Thursday? Just when Jody had started relaxing about Don, panic struck again. No! That was nowhere near enough time for her and Don to have together. How could he possibly think it was?

As soon as he finished on the phone, she planted her hands onto her hips and confronted him. "How can you do that? Say you'll be back there by Thursday? After all Elliot and I went through to get you here."

"Maybe you'd like to handcuff me again," he said, putting his wrists together and offering them forth.

"I thought by now—"

"You thought what by now?" Don asked, as if he couldn't imagine and didn't care.

"How does one get through to you? Because I'm finding it really difficult. Is this the sort of thing Dad used to have to contend with with you?"

"You're a lot like him, you know that, Jody. Pushy, demanding, always trying to get inside my head."

"We both loved you a lot, that I do know was the same."

"Loved an image of what you thought I should be." Don flipped his hands into the air. "Image."

It hurt how he had her and this and everything so wrong. "You were never an image to me, Don. You were always real."

"If I'm so real to you," he said smartly, "then you'll realize I have a real job and a real life I need to get back to."

They stared at one other from separate grounds but mutual pain.

"I think you've forgotten what's real," she said.

"And maybe you've never known." Without a twinge of guilt, he spelled out his deal to her. "Okay, so you got me here. Twenty-four hours. I'm giving you twenty-four hours, Jody, that I'll help with whatever it is I'm suppose to help you with, then I'm gone."

He left the living room, and Jody stood there feeling befuddled, unfinished, unsatisfied. None of this was going right. Not since that very short while in the kitchen first thing this morning, when she'd met the new day with so much hope and glorious expectation simply due to the fact that her brother was home again. She realized now that he was but he wasn't.

She sank down onto the desk chair with disappointment. She checked the clock, estimating that Elliot would be at the motel by now. Needing to talk to him, she picked up the phone and dialed.

"Treggor Motel," he answered professionally on the first ring.

"Elliot," she began.

"Jody. I just this minute got here." He laughed and joked at what her call might possibly be about, "The prisoner escaped, right?"

"Tomorrow. He's going tomorrow."

"Tomorrow?" Elliot turned serious.

"What am I going to do, Elliot?"

Silence.

"I expected a much bigger chance than this with him."

Silence.

"Elliot!" she said. "Are you there?"

"You never give a guy a chance to think, do you? Yeah, I'm here. Where would I have gone? Jeez."

"Sorry."

"I'm really trying to think here, Jody. But I don't know, I just feel so used up from getting any more ideas. It was hard, really hard, coming up with one to get Don back here, you know?"

"I know."

"And now you're saying we have to come up with a plan to keep him here?"

"I know."

"Talk to him. That's all you can do now, Jody. He's there, at the house, and you can talk to him on a much better level there than you could at Myre. So, just talk."

"But if he's planning to leave in a couple days I can't—"

"Jody, Jody!" Elliot interrupted. "You're wasting valuable time, talking to me. Your brother, go talk to your brother. Be glad you've at least got this much time with him. Make good use of it, okay?"

She sighed. "I guess so."

"Good girl. I'll talk to you later."

Don was nowhere in the house. But when Jody heard a power mower going by the windows, she ran out the front door to find he was cutting the grass.

"You don't need to do that!" she shouted over the noise of the motor.

"Somebody does!" he shouted back. "It's a mile high!"

She sank against the porch railing, shaking her head in frustration. What did he think he was doing, mowing the grass, when there was so little time?

On his next swipe back he made a request. "Jody! Make some iced tea, will you?"

"Iced tea…iced tea…he wants iced tea…" she sputtered to herself, going back into the house and through to the kitchen. "Sure, Don…whatever's more important to you, Don…surely not me. Mowing grass seems to be your priority after all these years. Okay…fine…whatever. If you think that's why I wanted you home, to mow the grass, you're one stupid brother. But maybe it's kind of stupid of me, also, because I'm going to make the stupid ice tea for you even though I don't want to."

By the time she'd mixed up a pitcher of tea and ice cubes, Jody had simmered considerably. Deciding she might as well be doing something more worthy than waiting around for her brother to have some spare time, she busied herself with washing the breakfast dishes. Getting Don home had definitely been the easy part, as compared to keeping him there and trying to communicate with him.

Ten minutes later the brother came in, slouched and sweating and needing a break. Jody motioned to the pitcher and empty glass beside it on the table. He poured himself a drink and chugged most of it down in a single tipping.

"Don, why are you doing the lawn?" Though Jody spoke softly, there was a definite edge behind it.

"It needed it." He finished his tea and poured some more.

"What about what I need?"

"Get yourself a glass," he said, holding up the pitcher with his other hand. "This is really good, Jody. Thanks for making it."

"I don't need tea," she said. "I need us to have a worthwhile talk. Are you almost finished with the lawn?"

"Well, yeah…but…" He set the pitcher down and wiped his shirt sleeve across his damp brow. "Matthew came out to the fence, said I was doing a good job and asked if I'd come do his lawn for him when I get through with ours."

"What?" Jody couldn't believe it. "He's got some boy that does his. Why would he—"

"I guess the kid is gone on vacation."

"Don, what about us? We need to talk."

"Yeah, later, we will."

Though there seemed to be a promise in his voice and in his look, Jody wasn't sure it was the kind of promise you could trust. She watched him finish his second tea. Then soon he was back outside mowing again.

When Jody saw Don starting on Matthew's lawn, she went next door to sit with Matthew on his back steps. The two of them watched the back and forth of Don's mowing as if it were some kind of phenomenal production.

"I can hardly take my eyes off him," Matthew said.

"He disappears when you do," Jody complained.

"W-what…?" the neighbor asked.

"He looks good, doesn't he," she said, changing her words and raising her voice against the noise of the mower.

"He looks very good," Matthew agreed. Then turning a closer look on her, he added, "You're the one who…who doesn't look so good, Jody."

"Me? I'm fine."

"You've got a…a very long face." He trailed a light finger tip down the length of one of her cheeks as proof. "Aren't you happy that Don's home?"

"Happy? Yeah. It's just that he's not staying long, Matthew. I hate that he's not staying long."

"Some time is better than…than no time, I'd say."

Matthew seemed content with the moment. Why couldn't she be the same with that? She forced a smile, trying to see as he did.

"W-where you going?" he asked when she suddenly jumped up.

"Be right back," she said, taking off for home.

A few minutes later Jody returned with the pitcher of remaining iced tea and three glasses. She poured Matthew and herself each some then signaled to Don that it was there for him whenever he wanted another break.

She sat back down onto the step beside Matthew, relaxing her focus only upon here and now. A feeling of closeness and trust set in, toward Matthew, toward Don, toward the moment itself. And she was amazed that it should happen not by trying so hard to make it happen, but rather just by letting it happen.

She sipped her tea, feeling better now than she had a while ago. She smiled, feeling as if she'd fallen under some sort of magical influence. Glancing sideways at Matthew, she supposed that yes, she had.

Chapter 29

"So how was your vacation?" Tom Rissen got around to asking when Elliot finally came to a standstill in the motel office later that morning.

The first thing Elliot had done upon getting back was drop his duffel in his room, which was right off the office, look through the stack of mail, answer Jody's frantic phone call, return a dreaded phone call to an impatient creditor, and take an inspective walk around the outside grounds. Lastly, he'd come back inside to restlessly pace about the office while Tom sat on the stool watching.

It felt really hard for him to settle down. But trying now, he leaned against the counter, gave a long sigh, and set Tom straight as to, "It wasn't a vacation, it was business."

"Oh." The white-haired, loyal employee he'd left in charge for a few days looked seriously concerned. "Pertaining to the Treggor?"

"No, no," Elliot was quick to say. "Jody's business. She...she needed my help with something."

"Oh." Tom's concern didn't lessen, it only switched tracks. "She's a nice girl. Hope everything turned out okay."

Elliot nodded. "It will, given a little more time."

"Young girl alone like that, I wouldn't doubt she'd need someone's help now and then."

"Yeah, well, most of the time that someone's me. But now that her brother's home, I imagine it's going to be him." He turned the register book around to look at. "Is this what I think it is?"

Tom laughed proudly. "Yes. We had a guest while you were gone."

"How about that!" Elliot cheered. "Not that six or seven guests wouldn't have been better, but I'm totally impressed that there was at least one."

"And to boot, next day, after he'd gone Rose went in to change the linens and clean the room and found a ten dollar tip he'd left for her on the dresser."

Elliot was amazed, yet not amazed, because Rose was, after all, an amazing and deserving person. "I'm sure she treated our guest elegantly."

"Tom nodded. "The man asked for a bucket of ice the night he checked in and Rose brought it to him."

Elliot gazed across the office at the boxy-looking machine in the corner. "But our ice maker hasn't worked in months. How'd she—"

"Rose hopped in the car and made a quick trip over to our house. Dumped both ice cube trays into a bucket and was back in less than ten minutes."

Elliot grinned sheepishly. "That was very commendable of Rose, but she shouldn't have had to do that. I…I keep meaning to get the ice maker repaired."

"One guest," Tom said, stressing both the importance and the simplicity of it. "We felt like we owed him the world."

Elliot understood, and agreed with a nod.

"You look exhausted," Tom observed.

"I am. Jody's business, that I helped her with, it wasn't so easy."

"I can stick around longer if you want to take some more time to—"

"No, I'm fine, thanks. You can leave now, Tom. I'll take over."

On his way to the door, Tom paused to look back. "It's good having you home, Elliot."

Elliot smiled. "Thanks. I'll settle up with you and Rose for putting in the extra time."

Tom shooed a hand at him. "It's not a problem."

But paying his employees *was* a problem. One Elliot hadn't been handling honorably for some time. "Tom," he said hesitantly.

"Yeah?" Tom waited.

"Tell me…if you were me, owner of the Treggor, what would you do with it?"

It took some time for Tom to answer. "I don't know."

Elliot chuckled. "Yeah, same here. Well, I guess good minds think alike."

Tom said good-night and left. Elliot was alone. With his motel. No present guests. No present employees. Just him and the whole pitiful joke this place was becoming.

He looked at the register book again. At the number of entries for the last few months. Not enough. Not anywhere near enough to keep the place going. And yet, Elliot didn't have the courage to get rid of it. He slammed the register cover shut hard, which was usually Jody's way of expressing her frustration with it. It worked. The outlet felt good. He slammed it a few more times.

Then stuffing his hands into his pants pockets, Elliot strolled across the office to stand at the front window. Staring out at nothing, he gave a long, forlorn sigh. Certainly he'd felt more alive on his Myre venture with Jody and her brother than he ever had here. Reminiscing the trip and all its catastrophes made him smile sadly for missing it. Maybe he'd been more cut out to be a P.I. than a motel owner.

He was glad he'd helped bring Jody and Don together. They had a good chance now of being a family again. Elliot had no family. Only this pitiful, dying motel.

Suddenly the quiet of his melancholy was disrupted by the sound of a car. But was it real? Yes. Maybe. He blinked at the sight of a car pulling into the lot and stopping. A man got out and came toward the office. A guest? Another guest? His mind snapped back to the credence of here and now and the not-so-dead-yet Treggor Motel.

The man entered the office, saw Elliot, and smiled pleasantly.

Before Elliot could quote the room rates or hand him a pen to sign the register, the guy asked, "Can you direct me to 300 Laughten Place? It's a tall business building that's supposedly just off Highway 64 somewhere. I think I'm a little lost, made a wrong turn accidentally and—"

"Yes," Elliot said, covering his disappointment with a quick laugh.

The man's look turned to puzzlement.

Elliot pointed out the window to the left. "Go back that way. When you come to the fork in the road, go right and get yourself back onto the highway. Go about two more miles down 64 and take Exit 28."

"Thanks," the man said and left.

Elliot went to the counter and gave the register book cover several more hard slams.

Chapter 30

▼

Jody phoned Elliot again later that afternoon.

"Treggor Motel," he answered.

"Elliot—" she began, only to be interrupted by a shuffling sound on his end of the line.

Amidst the distraction, Elliot told her, "I'm busy at the moment. I'll call you back."

Click.

"Busy?" She hung up and stood in the kitchen in silent dismay. Since when was Elliot ever too busy with the motel to talk to her?

Feeling doubly brushed off, she returned to the back screen door to look out at Don napping on the freshly mowed grass. He didn't have time to talk to her either. He'd said they would talk later, but after he did their lawn and then Matthew's lawn he laid down and fell asleep. Elliot had told her to call anytime, but then he hung up on her. She tried to practice Matthew's wise advice of earlier, of living in the moment. But she hated the moment. She felt alone, rejected, frustrated. She tucked her hair behind her ears and sighed.

What was the good in having Don home? she thought. Nothing was getting accomplished here. There was so little time and he was wasting it. Then too, maybe she'd ruined their chance of having a worthy talk tonight by having asked company to supper. But no, if Don was going to make bus arrangements back to Myre already tomorrow she had done right in asking Matthew to come eat with them. And if Matthew was coming, then Elliot might as well come.

Lying on his stomach, one arm folded beneath his head for a pillow, Don was no doubt cool, calm and content in the shade of the big elm tree. But as far as

Jody was concerned, he was missing the whole point of his coming home. Because it sure wasn't in his mowing the grass, or taking a nap in the yard, or already making plans for returning to Myre. It was in accepting his place in this family. Which was being a brother to her and an assistant keeper of this house.

Matthew was still sitting on his back steps, watching over Don like some sort of guardian angel. It seemed to be enough for him, just to observe and to be. Jody admired his simplicity but still had trouble finding it herself. Maybe when she got to be eighty-five life would be simpler for her too. Right now, it just wasn't.

When the phone rang she grabbed it on the first ring.

It was Elliot, apologetic and excited both at the same time. "Sorry to cut you off like that, Jody, but I had a guest here."

"A guest?" she exclaimed.

He laughed. "Yeah, can you believe it?"

"Barely."

"A businessman, with luggage and everything, who wasn't just lost and asking directions."

"Lost?"

"He'd just arrived when you called. A guy stopped in earlier, but was only lost and seeking directions. This one stayed, he really stayed. But it's okay, we can talk now. He's snugly checked into number six."

"How long is he staying?"

"One night."

"One night?" Jody was not impressed.

"You don't think one is better than none?"

"Yeah, sure, great, Elliot."

"Okay, okay..." he said, realizing that she had something more pressing to speak of. "How are things there?"

"Terrible."

"Your talk's not going well with Don?"

"What talk? First he mowed the lawn. Then he mowed Matthew's lawn. Now he's taking a nap on the lawn."

"So what do you want from me?" Elliot asked.

Jody thought about it. "I don't know. Something. Think of something."

"Like I'm made of ideas."

"Elliot..." she pleaded.

"Way I see it, maybe Don just needs more time to deal with all of this."

"Then why is he going back to Myre so soon?"

"Yeah, I know," Elliot sympathized.

"I wanted this to be so much more."

"Hey, we tried, Jody. We really tried."

"Why can't he try?"

"It's not like we can handcuff him to your house, you know."

"I know." Jody played with the phone cord, twisting it one way and then the other, gazing back out at the body on the lawn. "Elliot, I asked Matthew to supper tonight, so you may as well come too."

"Gee thanks, I like how you put that."

"Six-thirty."

"Sure, okay. I'll see you then. Wait! With a guest in number six, I can't just lock up and leave. If I can get Tom or Rose to come mind the office then I'll be there. But if I—"

"Elliot, be here!" she ordered him.

"I do have other responsibilities," he reminded her.

"I know. Sorry. I'm just really upset. Plus…"

"Plus?" Elliot asked when she paused there.

"I guess I've forgotten what it's like for the Treggor to have guests."

He laughed. "Me too. What timing, huh? Look, I'll do my best for supper, Jody. I'll see what I can work out. Meanwhile, hang in there, okay?"

She took her car and went for groceries, stopping at the bank first to transfer some money from her savings to checking. She left Don a note in the kitchen, in case he missed her and wondered where she'd disappeared to. Though she really rather doubted that her being gone would cause him any alarm.

When she returned an hour later with her arms full of brown bags, he was, to her surprise, in the house, rested, cleaned up and glad to see her.

"Hi." He took the bags from her and set them onto the counter.

"Hi." She was instantly respirited.

When Jody began the meal preparations, Don offered to make the salad and actually proved to be quite good at it. Working on the meal together turned into the most fun and meaningful thing they'd shared since his homecoming.

Matthew came over at six-thirty and the three of them waited from then on in the living room for Elliot.

When Elliot showed up, twenty minutes late, Jody and he greeted one another in the foyer with yelps and hugs and some dancing up and down to the delight of the Treggor having acquired a guest.

"Can you believe it, can you believe it?" he said over and over ecstatically.

"No," she said amid her giggles.

"Neither can I. There'd been one with Tom and Rose the other night, and now this one. That's two, Jody. Two." His excited jittering continued on into the living room.

"Congratulations," Don told him, clearly amused at the guy's delirium.

"Thanks," Elliot said, then noticed Matthew's presence. "Matthew, how've you been since this morning? I like your shirt, very nice shirt." He sniffed the air. "Boy, something sure smells good. Spaghetti? Is it spaghetti? Jody, did you make spaghetti? She makes the best spaghetti sauce. The absolute best."

To the surprised looks he was receiving from Don and Matthew, Elliot did an about switch to down play his familiarity to Jody's cooking. "Well, uh…I've tasted her spaghetti sauce once. Or so. Only once or so. But enough to know it's the best. Don, you did a great job on the lawn out there, just great. I noticed it on my way in. Really great."

"Maybe you'd like some lemonade," Jody offered, ready to leave the room and go get him some, hoping it might calm him down.

But he took a deep breath, smiled, and said, "I thought I came here to eat."

The four of them went into the dining room to begin their meal.

"You used your own tomatoes in this, I presume," Don said to Jody as he spooned some of the thick red sauce onto his plate of spaghetti. And then after his first taste, he exclaimed, "It's great!"

"I totally agree," Matthew said. "Ellen always says I…I shouldn't eat spicy foods at…at my age. But I, uh…don't know why…as it n-never seems to do me any harm."

"Don't become hen-picked out there in Arizona, Matthew," Don advised him. "You've been your own man for a long time."

"No…no…I don't intend to." Matthew ate another forkful of food then continued talking. "You know…I…I've spent a whole lot more time with the Mitchells over the…the years than my, uh…own family. And I'm going to…to hate leaving you behind. Especially since y-you just got back, Don."

Jody watched Don shift uneasily on his chair, as if he didn't know what to say to that. And so she said it for him, "He's leaving tomorrow. Or Wednesday for sure."

"So soon?" Matthew reacted as if the gift he'd only just received was suddenly being snatched away from him. Which, in a way, it was.

"I've got a job to get back to," Don said.

"Yeah, right, a job," Jody verified in a cool monotone.

Over his plate of rapidly-disappearing spaghetti, Elliot looked up to ask, "So Don, when you going to be back for another little visit?"

Saying nothing, Don flashed Elliot an appalled look.

"Probably eight years," Jody had the answer.

Don gave her the same look he'd given Elliot.

"Sure would be nice if you could stay longer," Matthew told him.

Breaking his piece of garlic bread in half, Don said, "A lot of things that would be nice also happen to be impossible."

Jody wiped her mouth with her napkin and eagerly explained to Matthew, "The word impossible meaning cop out."

"A person can't cop out on something he never promised in the first place," Don maintained.

"And," she kept on, "promise never comes when you're already seeing everything as impossible."

Matthew changed the subject. "Remember how when you were kids, Jody and Don, and you...you used to come over to my house for hot cocoa in the winter? Oh, I knew...I knew your dad kept cocoa mix at your house too...but you seemed...seemed to prefer having it at mine a lot of the time. Remember?"

Jody's disposition easily sweetened to the memory. "Yeah, Matthew."

Watched and waited upon for his response, Don nodded and also told Matthew, "Yeah, I remember."

"It must have been very special," Elliot said enviously.

"Lydia, my wife, was there then," Matthew rounded out the picture to him. "And I...I think she was what made it so...s-special for the kids...their having lost their mother."

"Lydia was special all right," Jody recalled, "but you've always been equally special, Matthew."

He smiled, accepting the honor from her as well as a respective nod from Don.

* * * *

After dessert, which had been chocolate pudding with Cool Whip, Don and Mattrew went into the living room to spend some time together and Elliot helped Jody with the dishes.

"Dinner went very well," Elliot said, drying to her washing. "I'd say very very well."

Jody wasn't so sure. "The food? Or the conversation?"

"Well..."

"He's so difficult. I didn't think he would be."

"Don? Or Matthew?" Elliot joked.

"He's here in Winona now, thanks to our hard efforts. Why does he have to turn right around and go back so soon?" She rinsed a soapy plate under the hot water faucet and set it into the draining rack.

Elliot took the plate with one hand, while his other hand snapped his dishtowel in the air. "Soon as I'm off K.P. duty I'm outta here. And hopefully Matthew soon will be, too, so you can have Don all to yourself."

"Sure," Jody scoffed.

"Hey now, no more of that pouty stuff. Just give it your best shot with him, that's all you can do, Jody. All right?"

She turned up a half smile.

"Good girl." Elliot dipped his finger into the dishwater, collected a clump of suds and tapped it onto the tip of her nose.

Chapter 31

After Elliot and Matthew had both left, Jody went into the living room and attacked Don with, "You can't leave tomorrow!"

He reacted with pure astonishment. "*Can't?*"

"Shouldn't," she tried a softer approach.

The two of them stood staring uneasily at one another. Like, it was their time to talk but it wasn't going to be easy.

Don shrugged and shook his head. "I don't know, Jody, what I'm suppose to say or do here. I know you have some sort of expectation of what my coming back here is suppose to represent, but I still don't know what that is or—"

"You're my brother and I need you here," she summed it up.

He sighed. "Come on, Jody, brothers and sisters grow up and go their separate ways. That's life. You've gotten along without me all this time and—"

"I haven't gotten along. Not very well anyway. It's been hard. And it's going to be getting a lot harder."

"What do you mean?"

"Stay and you'll see."

He narrowed his eyes distrustfully.

Jody planted hers hands on her hips. "Why is it so hard for you to accept some family responsibility here?"

"I detached myself eight years ago. Doesn't that speak for itself?"

"You're here now."

"Yeah, I'm here now," his voice rose, "because I was drunkened, handcuffed, chained and transported in my sleep!"

Jody went to sit on the couch. But Don was right there after her, grabbing her roughly by the arms and yanking her immediately back up. Though he looked more deeply into her eyes now than he had thus far, he still wasn't seeing her any more clearly. "What do you want from me, Jody. What the hell is it you want from me?"

Maybe nothing, she reconsidered now for the way this was going. Not if he was going to be so heartless and crude. Not if he was going to remain some stranger to her rather than the brother she had counted on him to be. Still, she supposed she did owe it to herself, as well as to him, to keep trying at this her last opportunity. She looked as equally deep into his eyes. "I never got over your leaving."

"So you've told me," he said.

"Besides my trying to deal with that, I also had to deal with Dad's on-going depression over losing Mom and then his depression over you and—"

"I can't believe he ever missed me."

"He did. We did. Every day. Unending. It was hell, wondering where you were, if you were okay."

"I'm sorry."

"Eight years. Weren't you ever sorry before right now this minute? Didn't you ever wonder about us?"

Don hung his head and turned away.

"Couldn't you have kept at least some contact with us?" she said to his back. "An occasional phone call? Or letter? Then losing Dad last year, that was really hard. It was like, one day he was here and the next he wasn't. I wasn't even able to notify you about it. How do you think I felt, burying our father without your being here, without your even knowing about it?"

"I'm sorry," Don said, slowly turning back to her.

"It's been hard. Real hard."

"I'm sure it has."

"I want to sell the house."

"I know. You told me. It's probably for the best."

"I saw a realtor, but there's a lot of involvement to it. There are a lot of things in poor condition around here, and he thought I—"

"Like what?" It seemed as if Don was actually, maybe, finally starting to become a little drawn in. He smiled slightly, admitting, "Okay, I've noticed a few."

"The roof is bad, some of the water pipes need to be replaced, one window and two light fixtures are broken, the railing to second floor is wobbly, the front screen door needs rehinging, the bathroom needs painting, one back step is rotted, the living room and dining room carpeting needs cleaning…" She paused to breathe. "And there's a whole lot more that I can't even remember. I'm suppose to make a list."

"Give the list to whoever buys the house," Don blatantly suggested.

"It doesn't work that way. The realtor said it would be better if I did these things around here first, before even putting it on the market. I. Me. Alone. Without his even knowing that I had a brother. Without *my* even knowing if I still did." She paused again. Then, "Besides the house situation, my job's likely going down the drain as per the Treggor dying. And Matthew's leaving. How can I face up to Matthew's leaving? He's always been there for me and now he'll be going away. And I don't know what I'm going to do after the house sells and I no longer work for Elliot. What will I do? Where will I go? It's like I don't have a future."

When she stopped listing, Don coldly asked, "Is that it? Everything?"

His smartness zapped her like the crack of a whip. Tears came as she emitted one more last thing. "On top of everything else I…I had this fight with my…my friend Kevin." She hadn't intended to mention Kevin yet, at this time, but she needed to use everything she could to win Don's support. And it was, in fact, the boyfriend subject that worked the best on him.

His look mellowed and he opened his arms to her. "C'mere."

Though she wanted words, affirmative words, surely a hug was worth a thousand of them. Her brother held her, rocked her, soothed her. As if at last he was finally beginning to know what family ties were all about.

However, after just a few moments he backed away from her as if he were suddenly catching himself from becoming all too human. "That's a lot to dump on me, Jody."

She was more hurt than ever now. He'd fooled her good. His moment of tenderness had meant nothing.

"Dumped on?" she said. "That's what you think I'm doing to you?"

He rolled his eyes, looked away, then back. "I care about you, Jody, but I can't commit. Not to the house. Not to my sister. Not to anyone. I'm sorry. It's the way I am, the way I've become."

"Fine!" she said, giving up. "Who needs you!" She ran off through the house, feeling a strange, nice sort of relief in letting her hurt turn into anger. It actually seemed to make her feel stronger and braver. If he could be tough and heartless, so could she.

She came to a stop in the dark kitchen. In her new sense of toughness, she regretted having ever looked Don up and brought him home in the first place. It was a stupid mistake. He was nothing but a hero fantasy she'd held on to from her childhood all those years. In reality he had no time or concern for her now that they were together again. He only cared about breaking free and taking off again.

The sound of a car starting up suddenly jolted Jody's attention. It sounded close. It sounded like her car. She rushed through the dining room and into the front foyer, where she swept open the door just in time to see Don backing her Reliant out of the driveway. She spun back to the side table where she'd left her purse, finding that her keys were indeed gone.

She phoned Elliot, feeling at least grateful to have him to turn to. Except when he came onto the line she became totally unglued and could barely speak coherently.

Without even getting the details clear, he said he'd be right over. Tom was still at the motel and could mind the office a while longer.

On his return to the house, Jody eagerly let him in and threw herself into his arms. "Elliot, thanks for coming back. He's gone. I tried talking to him, but he doesn't care about anything. And now he's taken off with my car."

Elliot held her, patted her. "You tried, Jody. That's all you could do. Hey, you've still got me, if that's any consolation. You know you've always got me."

"I know."

"I'm here for you."

"I know."

Elliot pulled a Kleenex out of his pocket and gave it to her. Then suggested, "Hey, let's go sit out on the front porch. What'dya say? It's a beautiful evening out there, and what else have either of us got to do, huh?"

He pulled the two wicker chairs together, and they sat side by side in them with their feet propped over onto the railing. The sweet scent of freshly cut grass drifted up from the lawn. It was quiet except for an occasional car passing down the street.

"We have our limits, you know, Jody," Elliot said of the Don issue.

Jody nodded but wasn't as sure as he was that they'd reached them.

"And," Elliot added carefully, "I guess maybe Don does, too."

They hadn't talked much or sat there long before Don, to their surprise, returned. He passed Elliot's car at the curb and drove Jody's car up into the driveway.

He walked across the yard and came up the porch steps, looking equally surprised at finding Elliot was back.

Elliot dropped his feet off the railing, straightened in his chair and spoke first. "Hey, Don. Jody thought maybe you were on your way back to Myre."

Don laughed, shook his head, and held up a bottle. It was vodka, no bag. "This, I just went to buy this."

"Are you an alcoholic?" Elliot boldly asked him.

"Are you a P.I.?" Don asked him back.

"Fair," Elliot said, dropping it there.

Don crossed the porch, passing behind Elliot's and Jody's chairs and coming around to sit on the part of railing where there was a pillar for him to lean against. He opened the vodka and took a drink.

There was so much to be said, but Jody felt discouraged from making another useless start. Don slugged away at his vodka. She watched him slugging away at it, while Elliot hummed some silly little tune.

A half hour later everyone's attention perked at the soft-sounded motion of two people coming down the main sidewalk. The couple was holding hands amidst their slow stroll. The street light revealed them as Rossi and Krista Glennon. They stopped before the Mitchell house and stood staring at it, as if wondering if that could truly be Don sitting on the porch railing.

"Don?" the big guy with a short-cropped beard called over.

Don said nothing.

Rossi turned in and came cutting across the lawn for closer proof. "I'll be damned!"

Krista, keeping to his side, seemed equally fascinated. "Don. It's been a long time. How are you?"

Sitting there on the railing, still saying nothing, Don looked down at the both of them. Mostly at Krista.

"So when did you get back?" Rossi asked him. "This is great, really great, seeing you. Man, what a surprise."

Don was wordless. Purposely and rudely wordless. Though Jody understood the reason behind it, she surely would have thought it had expired by now. Rossi and Krista knew, as well as she did, where Don's mood was coming from and thus were as equally affected.

Jody got up from her chair and stepped forth to the railing in an effort to smooth the moment. "Hi, you two. What a perfect night for a walk."

The couple brightened at her friendliness and returned their hellos to her.

"It's also a nice evening to sit on the porch," she added, "which is what we've been doing. I'd like you to meet my boss and good friend, Elliot Treggor. Elliot," she motioned him forward, "this is Rossi and Krista Glennon. They live just a few houses down the block."

Elliot reached over the railing to shake hands with each of them. "Hi. Nice to meet you. Yeah, I'd say you've got a perfect night for a walk. Mosquitoes aren't bad. Lots of stars in the sky."

Jody didn't give the Glennons any explanation as to why Don was back home. Nor did she tell them that he was intending to leave tomorrow. Just getting past this one awkward moment seemed to be enough for everyone to handle.

Chapter 32

Don couldn't take his eyes off Krista. Even though it felt like they might burn right out of their sockets if he kept looking at her the way he was. It didn't much matter to him, either, that Rossi was standing right there beside her, seeing what he was doing. Don couldn't help relishing the sight of her. It was like a make up for all he'd missed in eight years. Something he deserved, though he supposed he wasn't sure if it was a reward or a punishment. Either way, it was proving for sure that she was still something to him. Something.

He wondered how Krista's heart was reacting right now. And if, in fact, he still meant anything, to her. If only she knew how many dreams he'd had of her over the years. If only she knew how sorry he was that things didn't work out between them way back then. If only she knew him as the person he was today and could forgive him for the past. If only she knew how much he was aching over her this very moment.

"Yeah, it's a nice night," Rossi finally said in response to Elliot's weather observation.

The weather wasn't so nice in Don's estimation. Way too sultry. Although maybe it was actually Krista, and not the weather, that was inflaming his blood. He continued taking her in as visually as he could, despite the darkness, despite her husband. She was like a drink more satisfying than his vodka. Like the one and only real fix he really needed, but couldn't have.

Her hair looked black in the night, but he knew the lustrous red highlights the sun could bring out of it. He knew her soft, sweet feminine nature. The way her smile melted right through you. Her favorite music. Color. Food. Her winsome laugh. Her touch. And the way it felt to touch her. He knew every sensuous curve of her body. He knew way more about Krista than one guy ought to know about another guy's wife. Rossi's wife.

"I just can't believe you're here." Rossi's voice jolted Don out of his smoldering computations like a splash of cold water.

More like you don't want to believe it, you SOB, Don thought to himself.

And then like another cold wake-up splash, he realized that everyone was staring at him, expecting him to say something, to make a polite verbal acknowledgment of Rossi's and Krista's presence. But he didn't feel polite. And he sure didn't have any words. Maintaining his stubborn silence, he rather only took another swallow of vodka.

"So how long you staying?" Rossi nevertheless tried drawing him out. "Or are you home for good now?"

Don gave him a go-to-hell look, left the railing, crossed the porch and retreated into the house, not bothering to set the broken screen door back in place behind him.

He took the inside steps two at a time. And felt a grand sense of relief, reaching his bedroom and closing the door on the world. Man, what had he gotten into here, coming back to Winona with Jody? How could he have let it happen? And what was going to happen from here?

He took another drink of vodka.

And another.

In the darkness of his room, he went to stand at the window. Moonlight softly bathed over his face like a sweet angel kiss. He closed his eyes and took comfort in it. But, he thought, if only it were a Myre moon rather than a Winona moon. He missed his cabin, his privacy, his safety distance from all of this.

He thought about the earlier evening, of Jody's listing her needs for wanting him there. Amidst them had been some sort of boyfriend problem, but mainly her problems seemed to pertain to the house. Though he felt sympathetic to her problems, he had his own. And there was no one to help him with his but himself. And the best way for him to do that was to go back to Myre. Sorry, Jody.

A few more drinks of vodka helped condition him for sleep. If he couldn't put himself back in Myre right this moment, he could at least put himself to sleep. He was warm. Unbearably warm. Hot. It never got this hot in Myre. He took off his shoes and pants and shirt, and in his underwear laid down against the smooth, cool bed sheets.

Turning away from him made it easier for her to admit, "There's some personal baggage in my life, sure. Like everybody has some, right?"

Elliot rolled his eyes and nodded in a so-so manner.

"I just have this stuff I need to discuss with my brother. But how am I ever suppose to do that when he makes it so difficult?"

"Stuff?" Elliot sounded rejected. "That you can't talk to me about?"

"Don's my family. My only family. My stuff...it's family sort of stuff, you know?" She refaced Elliot, surprised at the shimmer in his eyes. "You're my best friend, Elliot, but this is like stuff I need to tell him first and then I can tell you. Okay?"

He let her off with a another shrug and an automatic smile. Then he proceeded to dish out the best advice he had. "Like I told you before, Jody, you've just got to give your brother more time."

"Time is something I don't have because he's going to take off again. I need a plan to keep him here longer so that we can get things worked out between us. You've got to help me, Elliot. I need a plan."

of her body. He knew way more about Krista than one guy ought to know about another guy's wife. Rossi's wife.

"I just can't believe you're here." Rossi's voice jolted Don out of his smoldering computations like a splash of cold water.

More like you don't want to believe it, you SOB, Don thought to himself.

And then like another cold wake-up splash, he realized that everyone was staring at him, expecting him to say something, to make a polite verbal acknowledgment of Rossi's and Krista's presence. But he didn't feel polite. And he sure didn't have any words. Maintaining his stubborn silence, he rather only took another swallow of vodka.

"So how long you staying?" Rossi nevertheless tried drawing him out. "Or are you home for good now?"

Don gave him a go-to-hell look, left the railing, crossed the porch and retreated into the house, not bothering to set the broken screen door back in place behind him.

He took the inside steps two at a time. And felt a grand sense of relief, reaching his bedroom and closing the door on the world. Man, what had he gotten into here, coming back to Winona with Jody? How could he have let it happen? And what was going to happen from here?

He took another drink of vodka.

And another.

In the darkness of his room, he went to stand at the window. Moonlight softly bathed over his face like a sweet angel kiss. He closed his eyes and took comfort in it. But, he thought, if only it were a Myre moon rather than a Winona moon. He missed his cabin, his privacy, his safety distance from all of this.

He thought about the earlier evening, of Jody's listing her needs for wanting him there. Amidst them had been some sort of boyfriend problem, but mainly her problems seemed to pertain to the house. Though he felt sympathetic to her problems, he had his own. And there was no one to help him with his but himself. And the best way for him to do that was to go back to Myre. Sorry, Jody.

A few more drinks of vodka helped condition him for sleep. If he couldn't put himself back in Myre right this moment, he could at least put himself to sleep. He was warm. Unbearably warm. Hot. It never got this hot in Myre. He took off his shoes and pants and shirt, and in his underwear laid down against the smooth, cool bed sheets.

Chapter 33

An awkward silence befell Don's leaving the porch that no one knew how to amend. Not even Jody. Especially not Jody. She stood beside Elliot at the railing, trembling, close to crying. Partly because she was angry at Don, and partly because she felt sorry for him.

Rossi and Krista said good-night, walked out to the main sidewalk, and headed home.

Elliot gave a sigh of relief to his and Jody's being alone.

"Don and Rossi used to be best friends," she said.

He chuckled. "Yeah, I could see that."

"Really, they were," Jody said seriously. "And Krista, well, she was once Don's girl."

Elliot nodded and took a guess. "Until Rossi stole her away from him."

"Not exactly. Krista left Don. Then, and only then, did she start seeing Rossi. Don thinks Rossi stole her, but the truth is that he'd already lost her."

Elliot sorrowfully gazed at the door where Don had made his dramatic departure. "Rough."

"He was crushed. He was only nineteen and had lost at love. I guess Krista knew what she was doing, but I don't think Don ever did. The breakup, it had this really heavy effect on him."

"So Rossi, he wasn't one of those gangsters Don knew?"

"No. He was separate. Totally separate. A totally good guy. He and Don knew each other from way back when they were kids. Like I said, they were best friends. But after high school, Rossi got busier with college and Don sort of got busy with these other guys."

"He should've followed his best friend on to college."

"Don didn't even finish high school. Remember?"

"Oh, yeah, that's right. Too bad."

"You know what's really too bad?" Jody said. "The fact that he's probably leaving tomorrow."

"Yeah."

"We need a new plan, Elliot."

"Yeah."

"A plan," she repeated more urgently.

"You think I'm made of plans?"

The way Elliot grasped his head and massaged it made Jody realize that he was just as disturbed over this as she was. "What can we do, Elliot? There's got to be something we can do."

"I'm thinking, I'm thinking, okay?" He walked to the other end of the porch.

Jody sat on the railing, watching Elliot, counting on him to come up with something. "There's just not enough time, if he goes back to Myre tomorrow."

"I know."

"Elliot, it's almost tomorrow already."

"Jody..." he said her name on a sigh as he came back to her. He stood close, looking like he had a solution.

She waited hopefully, holding eye contact with him as a means of trying to draw his idea out of him.

But all he had to say was, "Jody, I really hate seeing you this upset."

"Then make me happy," she said.

He put his hands on her shoulders and smiled.

Jody needed more than that. She slipped off the railing and away from his endearment. "Why is Don acting like this? Why?"

"You mean toward you or toward Rossi's wife?"

She stuck her hands on her hips. "It's hard for him, I know. But it's hard for all of us. Life is hard. Trying to run from it doesn't work. I want him to face things and get over things and go on from there."

"Why do I get the feeling," Elliot said from studying her, "that you've been trying to escape from facing something yourself?"

"What do you mean?" she asked. Elliot knew nothing of the baby but was almost acting like he did. It made her nervous.

He shrugged and backed down from it. "I don't know. I guess just that sometimes I get this feeling there's more to Jody Mitchell than meets the eye."

Turning away from him made it easier for her to admit, "There's some personal baggage in my life, sure. Like everybody has some, right?"

Elliot rolled his eyes and nodded in a so-so manner.

"I just have this stuff I need to discuss with my brother. But how am I ever suppose to do that when he makes it so difficult?"

"Stuff?" Elliot sounded rejected. "That you can't talk to me about?"

"Don's my family. My only family. My stuff…it's family sort of stuff, you know?" She refaced Elliot, surprised at the shimmer in his eyes. "You're my best friend, Elliot, but this is like stuff I need to tell him first and then I can tell you. Okay?"

He let her off with a another shrug and an automatic smile. Then he proceeded to dish out the best advice he had. "Like I told you before, Jody, you've just got to give your brother more time."

"Time is something I don't have because he's going to take off again. I need a plan to keep him here longer so that we can get things worked out between us. You've got to help me, Elliot. I need a plan."

Chapter 34

Elliot's mind was going a zillion miles a minute. Jody could do this to him like nothing or nobody else could. Think. Think. He hadn't better let her down. "What about your keys?"

She blinked dumbfoundedly. "Keys?"

"Your car keys. Did you get them back from Don?"

"No. Unless he—"

Elliot followed her inside. Her keys were lying there beside her purse on the entrance table. Yes. Good. She picked them up and clutched them to her chest.

"Hide 'em," he said.

She started looking for a place.

"His wallet," Elliot whispered. "If we can get Don's wallet away from him now we're okay. I mean, no car, no money, no I.D....he can't possibly go anywhere, right?" Elliot glanced up the staircase. "Think he's asleep yet?"

"I don't know," Jody said.

"Go try for the wallet. I'll wait here."

"Me?" she wailed.

Though Elliot felt inwardly amused at her for maybe just a couple seconds, he was careful not to show it and rather kept the seriousness of his plan in tact. "Yeah, you. Hey, in case he's not fully asleep, he'd really wonder what I was doing in his room, wouldn't he? But you...you could make up something logical because it's your house."

"Right." She started up the steps slowly. Midway, she paused, turned, and looked back down at him. "Don't go."

"I'll be right here," he assured her.

As Elliot stood waiting in the foyer, he realized how much his involvement with this brother situation was growing. Or was it more his involvement with Jody that was growing? He felt strangely good. Which meant he felt good in a very strange way. Which he didn't really understand, except that he knew it was nice. Sort of. Along with being scary. He rubbed his hands together. Took a deep breath. Anxiously watched the stairs for her return.

When Jody came back down minutes later she excitedly expressed how it had been no problem getting Don's wallet. He'd appeared to be asleep, and his jeans were hanging over a chair, and thus she'd gotten in and out of the room in no time.

Elliot snatched the wallet away from her, opened it and removed the contents.

"What are you doing?" she asked.

"Counting the money. We'll witness the amount together so's no one will get accused of shorting him later."

"I trust you, Elliot."

"It didn't sound like it a second ago."

"I just didn't know what you were doing, that's all."

"I wasn't stealing his money, that's for sure."

"I know, I'm sorry."

He counted it outwardly in his hands so that she could double check it at the same time. "Two hundred, seventy-three. Wow, the guy's loaded. Let's see…yeah, driver's license is here. Okay. Good. Jody, I'm taking Don's wallet with me. Because if you honestly don't have it in your possession, he can't wrangle it away from you, right?"

"Elliot," she began with childlike fear.

"What?"

"You're leaving? You're not staying? I thought you'd stay the night so you could help me deal with Don in the morning."

"Me?" He laughed at the outrageousness. "You gotta be kidding."

"But, Elliot—"

"Shh…" He held a finger to his lips. "I'm taking the wallet and leaving. You're going to be fine, Jody. You know how to handle him. You really do."

"He's going to be a crazy man in the morning."

Elliot held the doorknob, hesitating to the needy look in her dark eyes. "Come on, you wanted a plan to help buy you more time with him. This was all I could come up with."

Her bottom lip curled. "Guess it's better than nothing."

"Is that a thank you? Or what?"

"Elliot," she said, with her pout turning into a smile, "what would I do without you?"

"I don't know. But you just may get to find out if Don decides to kill me over this stunt."

"He won't. He likes you. Even with all the stuff you've pulled on him, I know he likes you."

"Yeah…well…in spite of everything he's done, I like him too. I mean, hey, he's your brother." Elliot turned the doorknob.

"Elliot?" Jody's neediness stopped him again.

"What?" he asked, easily enslaved.

She took his arm. "I want you to know that…you're like a…a very special brother to me, too."

"Brother," he repeated the word as if it were an honor he didn't quite deserve. Or want. For there had been many times when his thoughts of this girl had been far from brotherly. Times he was sure Jody was unaware of. Times, he supposed, that had only ever been quick, fleeting and totally irrational. He smiled. And nodded. And wondered how many brothers a girl needed anyway?

Jeez. Elliot suddenly remembered that he had a customer in number six and had to get back to mind the motel so that Tom could go home. He kissed Jody's forehead, told her good-night, and left.

Chapter 35

Jody locked the door behind Elliot, wandered into the living room, over to the side window, and gazed across at Matthew's house. It was completely dark. Which meant he was sleeping. Good. It gave her a sense of calmness and readiness toward her own sleep.

She went upstairs. Without turning on a light, she walked across her bedroom to the front window, pulled the curtain aside, leaned against the window frame, and stood looking down upon the yard, street, sidewalk. She rethought the whole evening with mixed emotions. Why did Don have to be so complicated? So resistant to everyone and everything? Why didn't his being home make him happy?

Elliot kept telling her she should give him more time. He even devised another plan to forcefully make Don stay so that there would be more time. Jody was appreciative of that. Of Elliot's wacky nature that always came through with something wild and far fetched but nevertheless helpful. She was so lucky to have him. She honestly wondered where she'd be with any of this right now if it weren't for him. Her progress with Don would obviously not have come as far as it had.

Elliot was a very special friend. She and he had grown pretty close over the two years they'd known each other, worked together. And closer yet in the last few days. It was easy to talk to him. Jody felt like she could talk to him about anything. Well, almost anything. Except for the Kevin and baby issue, which was something she had to tell her own brother about first. Tomorrow. She'd tell Don tomorrow, then she'd tell Elliot.

Jody went to the bathroom to wash her face, brush her teeth and put on her pajamas. On her way back to her room, she stopped for a minute in the hall and listened to the silence. When she closed her eyes, she was seven and Don was twelve. Her big brother was teasing her about something. He was laughing and she was squealing and they were chasing each other about in the upstairs hallway. Their mother was warning them to be careful so they didn't accidentally fall down the steps. Their mother loved them so much, wanted to keep them safe, was always trying to protect them. And then it was she herself who wound up getting sick and dying. No one had been able to protect her enough.

Jody opened her eyes to here and now and continued to her room. She laid down on her bed, yearning to talk to Don about their shared childhood every bit as much as the Kevin issue. They only had each other left to share that part of their past. And she had such a passionate need to reconnect with him about it. Didn't he ever feel that way, have the need to look back, far back to even before his teenage problems?

Staring at the ceiling, that was softly illuminated with bluish-white moonlight, Jody delicately rubbed her hands across her stomach and thought about Kevin's baby she'd had and had given up. It hurt, like an ongoing sin she couldn't forgive herself for.

She prayed in a tearful whisper, "Thank you, God, that Don's home. Please forgive me for the wrong I've done. And let Don forgive me also."

Chapter 36

"Okay, where is it?" Don came charging out the back door the next morning to where Jody was sitting on the steps.

"Where's what?" she asked blankly, chin in hand.

He went past her, skipping the bad step, down to the sidewalk where he turned to face her squarely. "You know what!"

She batted her eyes at him.

"My wallet!" he shouted.

"I don't have it."

"Then where is it? Come on, Jody, where the hell's my wallet?"

She could see how mad he was. It frightened her some. But she shrugged innocently, as if she knew nothing.

It didn't take Don long to figure it out. "Elliot! Elliot has it!" He stamped his foot and clenched his fists. "You're wearing me down here, Jody. You're really wearing me down."

"Me? What've I got to—"

"Yeah, right, like you're off the hook because Elliot has it. Like you're not in cahoots with him or anything."

Jody stood up, and from the bottom step glared back at Don with her own breaking anger. "Don't our efforts tell you anything?"

"Just that you're both crazy."

"Desperate! How about desperate?"

"Exactly what I'm feeling right now. Come on—" He grabbed her by the wrist on his way back up the steps and took her with him into the house.

"Where? What?" Though she put up resistance, he forced her along.

"Get your car keys," he said.

"Let me go!" she protested on their way through the kitchen. "You can't treat me this way!"

"Me treat you? That's a joke. The keys, where are they, Jody? Because I didn't find them in your purse."

"You don't have the right to keep going into my purse," she said, as he pulled her through the dining room.

"Like you had the right to take my wallet? And kidnap me from Myre?"

By the time they reached the front foyer, Don's urgency had worked its full effect on her. *Okay*, she thought, *give him the keys. What's the use? Let him leave if that's what he wants.*

Free of his grip, she dropped to her knees and slid her hand beneath the side table, feeling for the keys she'd hidden there last night. She retracted them easily and stood back up.

Don stood angry and impatient, all but grabbing the keys out of her hand. Jody hesitated giving them to him, knowing that the moment he got them he'd be gone, wallet or no wallet. Somehow he'd get himself back to Myre with her car, because he was desperate enough to do it. But he still didn't know about the biggest desperation in her life, and now it seemed likely he never would.

As if the keys weighed twenty pounds, she slowly lifted them toward Don.

"Keep 'em," he said and gave her a shove toward the front door. "You drive."

They went out to the Reliant. Jody got in behind the wheel and Don into the passenger seat.

"I don't want to do this," she said.

"Start the engine," he ordered her.

She sat there doing nothing.

Don raised his voice. "Let's go!"

She started the car. "So where are we going?"

"Drive!" he said.

She backed out into the street. "You're going to make me drive you all the way back to Myre, aren't you? You're making me go with for spite, aren't you? Kind of like now I'm the prisoner."

When they got to the corner and he instructed her to go left, it became clear that Don's aim was a lot worse than Myre.

"Take me to Elliot's motel!" he said in the tone of a death threat.

Chapter 37

Sitting behind the counter in the motel office, Elliot looked up with surprise when the brother-sister duo walked in. He could tell right off, by their faces, that this wasn't a social visit. "Jody! Surely you can't be coming in to work after you—"

"No," Don said, "she brought me here to work on you!" There was no pleasantry whatsoever in the guy's voice, look or manner as he came storming across the office and around the counter.

Elliot jumped off the stool and put up his hands defensively. "Now wait a minute, wait a minute!"

Don stopped. Checked his watch. "Okay, one minute. That's all you've got to fork over my wallet, including its contents."

Elliot exchanged a tense look with Jody. His smart plan had gone awry and he had no back up. Nor did she. He sure didn't want to give Don the go-ahead to leave town, but neither did he want to get the crap kicked out of him. He wished now that he'd used the handcuff technique on him again instead of the wallet taking one. He'd feel a lot safer right now if this guy's temperament was under some form of restriction.

"Time's up!" Don said.

As the madman lunged forward, Elliot jolted backward. But it turned out that Don had been going for the file cabinets, not him. In a destructive rampage he pulled out one drawer after another, ransacking and flinging things out of them right and left in search of his wallet.

It blew Elliot's mind, watching valuable paperwork being thrown about to land like so much litter on the floor. "Don! Don! Why don't you just simmer down here!"

"I'll simmer down when I get my wallet back and a bus ticket to Myre."

Don next took on the wooden cupboard that stood with the file cabinets along the wall behind the counter. He opened its doors and drawers and from them dumped and scattered trays of envelopes, pens, stamps, paper clips, everything.

"Stop it!" Jody screamed at him.

"You want me to call 911?" Elliot threatened him.

Don encouraged the call. "Fine. Like who'd be in the most trouble here, you for stealing my wallet or me for looking for it?"

"Did I say I had it?" Elliot said. He'd had enough of this game and was almost ready to give Don his damn wallet. "You're wrecking this place! You're really wrecking it!" He ducked as Don recklessly hurled a handful of papers at him.

An assortment of blue, yellow and white documents sailed through the air.

At that exact same time, the office door opened and a stately-looking man in a three-piece suit walked in on the disaster.

Elliot's heart sank at the appearance of the guest from number six, standing there in dismay. How, he wondered miserably, could this Don situation have gotten so out of control? How could good intentions have gone so wrong? So far the wallet-taking plan had done more harm than good. And now, probably, Jody would be expecting him to come up with yet another plan to try and save her brother from himself. Well, maybe his next plan should be to personally set Don on his way back to Myre.

"Inventory," Jody said to the guest in a pitiful attempt to justify what was going on. She scooped up a handful of debris off the floor, looking far more ridiculous than professional. "Five of these, Elliot. There are five number ten envelopes and—"

"He's a thief!" Don said, maliciously expressing his own version of the truth to the puzzled Treggor guest. "This guy here, who you probably assumed was trustworthy when you checked in, has taken my wallet and I'm looking for it. Maybe you'd better check to see if you still have yours."

The man in the suit stood frozen in place. As if he distrusted all three of them and whatever next might possibly erupt on the scene. As if his life hung only by his own careful assessment of the moment.

"Okay, this isn't an inventory," Jody changed her story. "It's…it's…"

"A crime," Don said.

"No, it's not," she told the frozen man in the suit. "The truth is…what's going on here is a family matter. It's really kind of hard to explain, but see, Mr. Treggor is only trying to help with—"

Don fired an open box of paper clips against the wall, and hundreds of small silver pieces exploded off into all directions.

"It's…been nice…" the guest said, walking backwards to the door. He felt behind himself for the doorknob, opened it, then turned and made a run for his car.

"Hey!" Elliot snapped out of his stupor and into a harsh realization ten seconds too late. "He didn't pay! He took off without paying!"

At the sound of the car ripping out of the gravely front lot, Elliot lowered himself remorsefully onto the stool. He was now as angry with himself as he was with Don.

Jody reached across the counter to touch his arm comfortingly.

Elliot hoped she wouldn't ask why he hadn't collected the money from the guest upon registration in the first place. Because he himself didn't know how he'd been so negligent. All he could say was, "That's probably why the guy came in here now, before leaving, to pay for his room. Except then he got scared off from the ruckus he walked in on. Thanks to Don."

Leaning against an emptied-out file cabinet, Don looked at Elliot as if he maybe actually regretted what happened. Until he demanded, "Hand it over!"

In a beaten sort of surrender, Elliot raised himself enough to draw Don's wallet out of his back pants pocket.

Don took it, looking amazed at where it had been all along. He opened it.

"Everything's there," Elliot assured him.

"What's the nightly rate here?" Don asked.

Elliot gave a quick, sardonic laugh. "You're crazy if you think I'd rent a room to you after this."

"How much?" Don said.

Elliot shrugged. "I guess I shouldn't be prejudice. Forty-two dollars."

Don held out two twenties and two ones. "For the room I just caused you to lose."

When Elliot made no motion to take it, Don threw it onto the counter.

"Now what?" Jody asked her brother. "Good-bye and maybe I'll see you again some time? Say in another eight years or so?"

Don shook his head, as if he were having the same trouble getting through to her as she was to him. "You don't get it, do you? I've got a job and—"

"No you don't get it!" She planted her hands on her hips.

"We'll keep in touch," he said. "We'll work something out, Jody."

"That's not good enough."

Mocking her, Don stuck his hands on his hips as well, telling her, "*You're* not good enough, you know that! You're a silly kid who thinks she has to find answers for every single, solitary thing in life. Well, I'm not one of your answers, Jody, so quit trying to make me out to be."

Jody joined Elliot behind the counter. But she certainly wasn't looking for his comfort, because when he tried putting an arm around her shoulder she stubbornly shrugged out of it and moved to the other end of the counter. It was as if she suddenly wanted, needed, her own space. As if whatever she was getting ready to divulge, she had to do it solely on her own.

Something a whole lot more serious than Don's wallet or his choice of dwellings seemed about to break. Though Elliot couldn't begin to imagine what, the look in Jody's eyes was really scaring him.

Chapter 38

Jody took a deep, steadying breath. The moment had come. There wasn't going to be another time, a better time. This was it.

"Okay, what's this really about?" Don seemed worn down and ready to listen. "It's something more than the fix-it list you sounded off about last night, isn't it?"

She nodded.

He turned out his hands and shrugged. "What?"

He was going back to Myre, she had to tell him now. She swallowed hard first. "It's about my baby."

"Baby?" Elliot exclaimed.

"You're pregnant?" Don gasped.

Jody's eyes filled with tears. "No...I'm not...but I was."

Don and Elliot exchanged concerned looks.

Then looking back at her, the brother questioned, "You were pregnant? Were? Like, you had a miscarriage? Lost a baby? What?"

"No miscarriage," she said. "But I did lose it."

Don shook his head. "What does that mean?"

"Sounds like abortion to me," Elliot said.

A tear trickled down Jody's cheek and she wiped it with the back of her hand. "I had a baby when I was sixteen. Dad made me give it up for adoption."

The guys were wordless and awestruck. And in the time Jody gave them to absorb the shock, the Treggor office became like a dismal, silent aftermath of a bad storm. Two storms, Don's wallet and Jody's baby.

She looked at her brother from the bottom of her heart. "You don't know how difficult it's been, not having you here to talk to about this."

He nodded, sighed heavily, stared back at her, said nothing.

"Say something," she urged him.

Nothing.

Jody looked to Elliot, who just shrugged and also said nothing.

Don stepped forth to the counter, found Jody's purse beneath a mess of papers, opened it and took out her car keys.

"No!" Jody screamed.

Don charged out of the office.

Jody started after him, but Elliot grabbed her. She fought him, but he was stronger than she'd ever known him to be and she couldn't break free. "We've got to stop him! He's getting away!"

"Jody, no!" Elliot said.

"He's got his wallet and the car and he's leaving and—"

"Let him go, Jody! Just let him go! Jeez!"

"What are you saying? How can you—What if it—" Suddenly she felt way more drained than angry and she weakened in Elliot's arms.

"You have to let him go," Elliot verified, this time in a voice more softly. We've done everything we could to get Don here and keep him here. It didn't work. It's not something he wants, Jody, and you just can't make it be."

"But he—"

"No. Stop it. No more. You've got to give this up. Please. Enough is enough."

Stilled in his embrace, Jody knew that she'd run out of arguments.

"Jody," Elliot's voice was but a whisper, "I'm sorry about your having a kid and being forced to give her up. That's a lot of weight for anyone's heart to carry around. I just...I just wished you would've felt free to talk to me about it. I know I'm not family, but I consider myself a good friend and—"

"You are. You are a good friend, Elliot. The best. It was stupid of me to think that Don was the only one I could talk to about this when I had you right here all along. I'm sorry, Elliot. Big misjudgment."

He gave her a forgiving smile and took her hand. "Come on, I'll drive you home."

"I could stay here and help you," she offered.

He shook his head no, took her outside to his car, opened the passenger side and motioned her in. "You'll be better off at home right now."

"Alone," she verified.

"Yeah. I can't leave the motel for long. I'll just drop you off and get right back. You'll be okay. You have to be okay now, Jody, because things are the way they are and the time has come for you to face that. You and I, we'll talk more later. I promise."

* * * *

Jody felt lost and sad and terribly alone in the house by herself. After crying her eyes out, she wandered from room to room, sat for a long spell in a living room chair, drank a glass of orange juice, nibbled a piece of cheese, and took repeated looks out the front door. Don's leaving became a fact. He was gone. That was it. Nothing she'd been able to say or do had kept him. Life was hard. And she had to grow up and become harder right along with it.

Jody was curled up and dozing lightly in the easy chair that afternoon when the sound of a key in the front door startled her. The door opened. Don came through the foyer and into the living room, looking every bit as beaten and weary as she. She stood to his approach.

"Oh, Jody," he said, coming to take her into his arms.

"You're back," she said, holding tight to him for proof of his realness.

"Yeah, I'm back. I started for Myre like I couldn't get there fast enough. But as I drove, I did a lot of thinking about all you went through to get me here. And about your having a baby and having to give it up. I finally realized how desperately you needed me and how…how stubbornly resistant I've been. I'm sorry for having been so insensitive, Jody."

"You're back," was still all that she could say.

"Well, hey," he reasoned, "we're brother and sister, right?"

She looked up at him with a teary-eyed smile.

In the next moment, Don was going to the desk with an urgent need to make a phone call. Jody stayed near, listening with surprise as he spoke to his boss in Myre.

"Yeah, I know I told you I'd be back by tomorrow," he was saying, "but now it looks like I won't. I know that…yeah, right. I know. Look, Jim, it can't be helped. It's my sister and—Yeah, I said sister. She needs my help here and I've got to stay. I don't know how long it'll take. Fine! Fine! Then screw the job! Send me what I've got coming. 834 Burgess Street, Winona."

Though Jody was glad Don was staying, she was sorry for what it was costing him.

Her brother's head was down, and he was rubbing it with his free hand while continuing his phone conversation. "Yeah…yeah…I appreciate that. Right. I will. Thanks, Jim. Good-bye."

When he hung up, he turned around to face Jody. "Well, that's that."

"You quit your job," she confirmed apologetically.

He nodded, making like he didn't care so much. "It was a tossup between me quitting and Jim firing me, and I guess you could say we came to a mutual agreement. But hey, that's behind me now. I have this new job now of putting both this house and my sister back in shape."

Now that she had what she wanted, it didn't seem quite enough. "Your job…in Myre…I didn't want that you should…I mean, I didn't expect you to—"

"It's okay," he said. "Jody, I can't be in two places at once, can I? And I can't expect them to hold my job indefinitely, can I? Jim got a little riled, then I got a little riled, and…now it's settled."

"Don, I'm sorry."

He nodded, smiled, and came to put an arm around her shoulder. "How about something to eat. I'm hungry. Aren't you?"

They went to the kitchen together. Because of all the craziness that morning, any serious thoughts of lunchtime had pretty much been ignored by both of them until now.

Don stayed near, not helping any but rather just watching Jody make the sandwiches. Out of his own inner thoughts, he eventually assumed, "That Kevin you mentioned last night, so he's the baby's father?"

Jody dropped the mustard. "K-Kevin?"

Don retrieved the yellow plastic bottle from the floor and handed it back to her. "The guy you told me you had a fight with is the father of—"

"No," she lied. "It…it happened long before Kevin."

"Oh," Don said, with a look that seemed to be seeing right through her.

But she'd told him enough for now. It was too hard to tell him everything right off. Later she would, after he'd adjusted to this much. Meanwhile, she padded her lie, "It's just that when I told Kevin about the baby and everything, he…well, he didn't want to see me anymore after that and…and that's when we broke up."

She paused, nervously expecting Don to have another ready question. But he didn't and she was relieved for the moment.

They took their bologna sandwiches and cans of Coke out onto the back steps. It was shady there that time of day and the yard was a nicely coiffured view from yesterday's mowing.

"I can't believe I made such a mess of Elliot's motel office," Don said as they ate.

"I can't believe he and I stole your wallet," she said.

Before they knew it the two of them were laughing about it all.

When Don finished his sandwich, he turned serious and started in again on his notions about Kevin. "So this guy, who broke up with you because he didn't like something you did, he doesn't have a single glitch in his own past?"

Jody hated that they were back to Kevin. "I don't know. I only know that he didn't like mine."

"Why would you have even told him about the baby in the first place?"

"Why do you think?" she snapped.

Don's face was blank. "I don't know. I'm asking."

"Because I thought I should be honest and open to him. No secrets, you know?"

Don nodded and supposed so with a sigh. "So tell me about the baby's father."

Honest and open. The words Jody had just used stuck in her conscience. She sipped some Coke. Sure, she wanted Don to know about her baby, but she didn't want to talk about the baby's father. The fact that Kevin was the father was something she still wasn't ready to divulge.

"It was some guy," she tried making light of it. "Other than Kevin. Just some guy back then."

"Some guy? That's all you can say of him?" Don tipped his head, giving her a dubious look.

Jody broke the crust off of what was left of her sandwich and tossed the pieces out for the birds.

Don was grilling her to say a lot more beyond what she already had or was willingly able to. But he'd become interested and involved with her life now, which was what she'd wanted, wasn't it? And she supposed his asking all this stuff was a good sign, not bad, wasn't it? Except, she still had this need to protect Kevin. Or maybe to protect herself and the real mess of the matter that she'd made even beyond having had the baby and given it away.

She gave Don just a little more information. "I was with this boy who, well, he was eighteen, and I was fifteen and innocent and trusting and dumb, really dumb."

"No." Don gently disallowed her put down, "don't say that. I don't think you were ever dumb."

"Dumb!" she repeated, far more knowingly to the matter than he.

"I wish I'd have been here for you back then," Don said with heavy regret. "God, I wish I'd have been here. I would have seen the punk for what he was before any of that ever happened and would have told him where to go."

Jody didn't doubt that he would have been the rescuing big brother, had he been living here then. He was trying very hard to be as much now.

"When I learned I was pregnant," she continued, "and told this...this guy, he got real mad. And when I told Dad he got real mad. I felt like such a bad person, Don."

"I know the feeling," Don said.

"Dad made arrangements for me to go stay with Aunt Marlo in L.A. I finished my sophomore year of high school out there, had the baby, gave up the baby, then came home all neat and tidy and respectable again. Dad simply told people that I'd been away on an extended vacation."

"Vacation." Don moaned at the term.

Jody stared distantly ahead, as if she might miraculously see all the way to California. "Somewhere out there is a...a little six-year old girl who doesn't know I'm her mother. And never will."

"Girl," Don said the word ever so carefully, as if were fragile and might break in the air. "Bet she looks just like you. Your daughter, my niece. Damn." He set his empty Coke can on a step and stood up on the sidewalk before her. "So what are we going to do, Jody? Go look for this kid? Try and get her back? Where do we start?" He sounded eagerly ready to take on the whole world if necessary.

She reached for his hand. "No. No, we can't do that. We can't do anything about her. It's a done deal. I only have to learn to live with it. And in order for me to do that, I needed to tell you about it."

He leaned down to her, with his new brotherly conviction. "I'm sorry for what you went through. And that I wasn't here for you. I'll do whatever I can to help you now, Jody."

"I didn't want to give my baby away," she said with a choke in her voice and tears welling into her eyes again.

"But you couldn't tell Dad that, could you?" Don seemed to know and understand only too well.

"No. I was a kid. He made arrangements that I had to abide by."

"He always knew best and everyone had to follow suit or else."

"You chose the or else."

"Yeah, well, I pushed him to the limit first. Maybe he wasn't always so right about a lot of stuff, but neither was I. Maybe it's taken me eight years to figure that out."

"I wish you'd have taken me with you."

Though Don looked at her with some serious consideration at first, he was soon laughing at how it might have been. "My fourteen-year old little sister, hitting the road to nowhere with me? Yeah…I don't know…maybe I *should* have taken you."

"Was it hard for you, seeing Krista again last night?" Jody caught him completely off guard when she abruptly changed subjects.

"No." He dropped eye contact with her, as if that made it easier for him to lie.

"The fact that she's married to Rossi?"

"I'm fine with her and Rossi being married. They deserve each other."

"Oh…." she said teasingly, "you sound so tough."

"I am."

"Really?"

"Really."

"Okay, so maybe you can teach me to be tough."

Don remet looks with her and grinned. "Maybe."

Chapter 39

While Jody spent the rest of the afternoon doing things like laundry and dusting and watering plants, Don roamed about the house making a preliminary investigation of all the repairs that were needed. There were a lot. And they now became his responsibility.

By evening he was both physically and mentally depleted. He knew Jody was feeling the same, for how she'd fallen asleep watching TV in the living room. Eventually he got up from his own dozing in the recliner and strolled to the kitchen. He took an apple from the bowl on the table and headed out the back door to get some fresh air.

It was dark and cool and peaceful outside. He walked as far as the tomato plants, where he stopped and stood in place to gaze up at the stars and the crescent moon. He still couldn't believe the unexpected turn his life had taken. It was scary, finding out how badly he'd been needed here. Scarier yet, thinking that he probably would never have returned to Winona if Jody hadn't come and forced him like she had. It was also pretty scary how he'd thought he knew exactly what he wanted and what he was doing until she got a hold of him and worked him over. Life had become confusing and complicated for him all over again now, only after his long-suffering efforts had finally managed to help him simplify it. Was it so much to ask for, he wondered, a simple life? Or was it possible that the real essence of simplicity meant accepting life's complications?

On his way back to the house, chomping on his apple, he spied the shadowy figure of Matthew sitting out on the dark steps of his own house next door and it startled him at first. "Matthew…"

"Evenin', Don…" the neighbor called over.

Don walked to the fence. "What are you doing sitting out here this time of night?"

"W-well you…you got a better idea of what I, uh, should be doing?"

Don laughed. "No."

"How's Jody?"

"She's okay."

"I don't know, Don…" Matthew said indifferently, "lately it just…just seems like so much of the time she's carrying the weight of the world on those young shoulders of hers."

Don wondered how much Matthew actually knew about her. Bits and pieces, or everything? "She's okay," he said again.

"Maybe not entirely."

"Maybe not," Don agreed. "But I'm here now to try and fix that."

"You're a good brother, Don."

Don laughed lightly. "Well, I guess it's good to know that at least a couple people still believe in me, you and Jody."

"I take it you've decided to, uh…to stay awhile. You were going this morning…and now you…you're s-still here."

Don stretched, yawned and gave a long sigh. "Yeah, I'm staying. For now. There seems to be quite a few things around this old house that need my attention."

"Well, I'm glad to see that you…you still believe in yourself."

Don supposed that he, himself, hadn't really seen it that way until just now. And now that he did, he guessed it didn't feel half bad.

"It's just…darn good having you around again, boy," Matthew's voice quivered. "Jody's s-surprise of…of bringing you home has been just about the biggest and best surprise of…of my whole life."

"It's pretty good being here, Matthew," Don admitted.

"You look tired."

"I am."

"B-better hit the hay."

"Yeah. Think I will. You too, Matthew." He said good-night and went inside the house.

As he entered the kitchen, the phone rang and he answered it.

It was Elliot. "Don! What the hell! I thought you'd left!"

"I did. But now I'm back."

"Man…Jeez…well, that's good. I'm glad. Just a teeny bit surprised, that's all. How'd that happen?"

"I did some pretty serious thinking, which turned me around."

"Bet Jody's happy."

"I guess she is."

"What's she up to? Can I talk to her?"

"She's asleep on the couch."

"Oh," Elliot said. "Well, don't bother her."

"You sure?"

"Yeah. Let her rest. I imagine she's wiped out after the kind of day it's been. Man, she sure shocked the heck out of you and me today with her baby news, huh?"

"You really didn't know abut the baby till today?" Don verified, still feeling skeptical about that.

"Today was the first I heard of it, right along with you, I swear," Elliot responded. "I have to say though that I sort of had this feeling for a long time that something really deep was bothering her. Something deeper than her obsession over finding you and haulin' your ass back here."

"She's a pretty emotional girl," Don concluded.

"Tell me about it," Elliot said.

Don laughed, ran his free hand through his hair, shut his eyes for a moment, then turned away from the wall to find his sister standing in the doorway to the dining room.

Chapter 40

"Who is it?" Jody asked, squinting at the shock of bright kitchen light she'd walked into. She shuffled groggily across the floor toward Don. "Who's calling so late?"

"It's only ten o'clock, sleepyhead." He handed her the receiver. "Here. "It's Elliot."

She took the phone reluctantly. It was never going to be the same between Elliot and her now that he knew about the baby. It would be awkward. Uncomfortable. Difficult to know what to say to each other. She tried to prepare herself.

Don was ready to take the phone back. "You don't have to talk if you don't want to."

She shook her head no, forced her bravery, and said, "Hi, Elliot."

"Jody." There was a sound of relief in his voice, for hearing hers. "I haven't been able to quit thinking about you since this morning."

"My story was a real shocker, huh?"

"It was. But I've recovered. How are you?"

"I'm much better now than I was this morning."

"Good. So Don's back and he came back on his own. That's a good sign, Jody."

"I know," she agreed.

"I suppose you and he talked about stuff."

"Yes."

"And it was good?"

"Yes."

"You and I...we have to talk more too, Jody."

- 164 -

"Not now."

"No, not now. I was just calling to see how you were, not knowing that Don was back. You should've called me about him. I would've liked to have heard that he—"

"I'm sorry. I should have."

"Anyway, besides my calling to check on you, I was calling to tell you that we've acquired another guest here at the motel. Two actually. A couple. Been married a month. I put them in the honeymoon room."

"We have one?" She scrinched her face in doubt.

"Number nine. It has the best bedspread and drapes. Plus the mattress dips in the center."

"Oh, Elliot," Jody said in a burst of giggles.

"That's better. You sound much better."

"I'm okay."

"Yeah, I know you are," he said softly. "Look, Jody, I know you've got your brother there for you now, and I'm real glad about that, but I want you to know that I'm always here for you too."

"I know. Thanks, Elliot."

"I mean it."

"I know."

"And…"

"And what?" she asked.

"Could you come in to work tomorrow? I mean, if you can't, if you're not up to it, just say, I'll understand. The mess Don made, well, I started on the stuff in front of the counter, but the rest, behind it, I don't know. I just can't seem to get going on that."

Jody glanced around at Don, who was still in the kitchen, getting himself a glass of milk. Maybe she could trust leaving him alone now. He seemed serious about staying and working on the house. In fact, he'd given up his job in Myre for it. She could probably allow herself some time away from him to go help Elliot. "Okay, yes, I'll come in tomorrow," she told her boss.

She caught Don smiling, as if he were pleased to hear that she was planning to do something ordinary.

"Good," Elliot responded. "And Jody…"

"What?"

"Bring some of those good doughnuts from O'Ruskee's Bakery, okay?"

"Okay, Elliot."

"Good-night, Jody."

"Good-night, Elliot.

Chapter 41

"I got to hold my baby once," Jody told Don the next morning as they sat at the kitchen table, finished with breakfast but having second cups of coffee. There was a sweet-sad ache in her heart as she spoke of the brief, precious moment that occurred amidst her tragedy.

"That must have really been hard," Don said compassionately.

Jody smiled at the delicate picture coming to her mind. "She was tiny. And pink. With lots of dark hair. Her tiny little fingers curled around one of mine. Can you believe it, a brand new baby grasping hold of your finger? I held her, talked to her, then kissed her good-bye, all within ten minutes. Ten minutes I had my baby. That was it."

"Oh, Jody," Don said.

"I didn't want to sign the papers. Or let her go. Up until the very last I—"

"How could Dad have put you through that?"

She shook her head and lowered her eyes shamefully. "It wasn't just him. How could I have put myself through that? To have let everything happen like it did? I was young, but I think I was old enough to have been more responsible."

"As to your boyfriend? Or to Dad?"

"He wasn't my boyfriend, he was just some guy."

"So much for being responsible."

"Yeah, I guess," she agreed sadly. "And now I can't stop hating myself over it. How do I do that? Tell me how to do that."

Don stood up from his chair, stuck his hands in his pants pockets and glanced out the window over the sink. "You toughen up. Somewhere along the line you just learn to toughen up and turn your back on stuff you can't do anything about."

"And that makes it stop hurting? The toughness?"

When he looked back at her, she saw that his eyes were a lot softer than his words and she told him, "You really don't seem so tough to me."

His quick smile gave him away even more. "Well, I used to be, till you dragged me back here and turned me into a wimp."

"You're not a wimp either. What are you, Don? What's the real you like, that you're trying so hard to hide?"

He shook his head and sighed. "I don't know, Jody. I guess maybe I'm still a creature from my past. I mean, I guess everyone's got stuff from their past following them, haunting them, right?"

"But you went away and turned your back on your stuff."

"I tried. And I was doing pretty well until you and your sidekick showed up and—"

"Kidnapped you?"

"While you were so desperate to get me home, you know, I was just as desperate to stay away."

"You could've told the people at that restaurant were we ate that you were being kidnapped, but you didn't."

He laughed. "Like my word, a mental patient, against Dr. Elliot's word."

"If the police came they would have checked things out."

"And you and Elliot would have been in deep trouble. Maybe I didn't want to get my sister into trouble with the law. Anyway, I thought we were talking about your problems here, not mine."

Jody left the table and went to stand beside him. "You're one of my problems, Don."

"I shouldn't be, no."

"I want you to be all right. And then I'll be all right."

"Don't base your well being on mine, Jody. Please, don't do that. Your baby incident—"

"You've already helped me with that, advising me to be tough."

He looked at her with regret. "Maybe that was a little harsh. You're too cute to be tough."

"Don, your being home means everything to me. It's helping me, our talking about stuff. And I'm thinking that if it's helping me so much already, then maybe it can help you too."

He gave a short laugh. "You think I need help?"

"Yes. I'm your sister. I want you to know that I'll talk to you and listen to you about your stuff as well."

"You don't mean..." He dipped his head and arched his eyebrows, "all the stuff I've been trying so hard to forget."

"Maybe talking is better than forgetting. I know I feel much better, having talked to you about my stuff."

"That's you, Jody, not me."

"I want to know what's been going on with you all these years."

"I work. Eat. Sleep. And...well...that's about it."

"You never got over Krista, did you?"

"That was a long time ago."

"It was the other night. Plus she's the main reason you left Winona, isn't she? Not your problems with your criminal friends. Or with Dad. Or with the bad reputation you'd acquired here. Krista. Only Krista."

"Let's get back to you," he said. "What about the baby's father?"

"I told you."

"Right. Some guy. Come on, Jody, give me more than that. I want to get this whole thing straight about your baby."

She swallowed hard.

"Didn't your giving the baby away bother him, the father, any?" Don pressed.

"He...he thought I had an abortion. It was what he, this guy, wanted, for me to have an abortion. So I told him I did. I let him believe that I did."

"But the hospital, when the baby was born didn't they need to know who the—"

"I told them I didn't know who the father was."

"Oh, Jody," Don said, slowly shaking his head.

As they stood there talking, Jody became distracted by the view out the window. At the scene of Matthew, next door, running fresh water into his bird bath. "I don't want him to go."

Don also looked out at him. "Things change, Jody. Life's full of changes."

"Yeah," Jody agreed sadly.

"How about the change of me being here?"

She smiled for that.

"You know, if I'm going to stay I'll have to arrange to get some more of my clothes and stuff from my cabin."

Jody's eyes widened. "If you go to Myre you won't come back."

"Hey, come on, I—"

"You won't! I know you won't!"

"I wouldn't go back on my word to you, Jody, any more than I'd drive all the way up there, grab some stuff, and drive all the way back here. I'll contact a friend of mine to box up some of my stuff and send it to me."

"Really?" Jody brightened.

"I'm staying, okay? Really."

"Because there's a lot to do around here, right?"

"That's right."

"There's money of Dad's in the bank, which is now in my name, to use for whatever repairs the house may need."

Don nodded. "I'll give everything a tighter look today and make an official list. Maybe we'll find that our house problems are a lot easier to fix than our personal problems."

"Yeah, maybe." She gave him a smile then left for the motel.

* * * *

Even though she and Elliot had talked on the phone last night and it had been good, it was nevertheless difficult for Jody, walking into the Treggor today. She resisted eye contact with him as she joined him behind the counter.

"Don't do this to me, Jody," he said.

"Do what?"

"Turn awkward and embarrassed around me just because I know about—"

She took her routine look at the register book. "My car made some weird noises on the way over here."

"You're insulting me here, Jody."

"Because my car acted up?"

"Because you won't look at me."

"Sorry," she apologized, eyes still down.

"Jody," he said.

"It was kind of a pinging sound."

"I'm insulted because I thought we were closer friends than this."

"Only when I went over forty."

"Jody, stop it. Look at me."

She wouldn't, couldn't.

Elliot pulled the register away from her. "So you've got a past. A regrettable past. So I know about it now. But I'm still here for you, can't you see that? No. No, you can't because you're refusing to. Look at me, Jody!"

She needed to be comfortable with Elliot again. And he with her, she knew, for how he clasped his hand over hers coaxingly.

When she finally did brave a look at him, she found it really wasn't as difficult as she'd imagined. The warm smile he was giving her helped her relax.

After they hugged, and were perfectly okay with one another again, there was a lot of work to be done. Elliot had already cleaned up the floor in the front of the office, so that it wouldn't scare off a new guest who might happen in. But on the floor behind the counter, sight unseen, still lay the aftermath of Don's tantrum.

"Well, here goes." Jody swooped up a handful of papers to sort.

Elliot moaned at the mess. "I know, ain't it somethin'?" And then his next concern was, "Jody, where's the donuts? Did you bring the donuts? The coffee's made and I thought we'd start with a coffee break first off. You did bring the—"

She motioned to the white bakery bag she'd set on the counter with her purse upon first walking in.

"You're a doll." He picked up the bag and looked inside. "An absolute doll."

She made a careful shuffle through the clutter on the floor. "Save your praises for if and when I ever make any order out of all this."

Elliot was already biting into one of O'Ruskee's famous old-fashion donuts. It's not that I couldn't do this myself, it's just that I figured you could probably do it better. And faster. You mind?"

"You're the boss."

Deciding the best way to handle the job was to sit amidst it, Jody cleared an area on the floor with the sweep of her foot and sat down.

Elliot, with his doughnut in hand, squatted to face her. "You know, I'm not mad at Don for doing this. I should be, but I'm not. I figure the outcome made it worthwhile. It drove out the truth of why you wanted him home so badly. And it must be a relief for you to finally share your baby story with him. You needed to do that, Jody. And I don't think you need to worry about his taking off anymore. He decided to come back on his own. It's pretty clear how much he cares about you. You two, you're closer than ever because of the truth now, right?"

The truth of the matter was that Jody's whole truth still had a ways to go. The dose she'd given Elliot and Don had only been part of the truth. The rest, the other truths that she was still holding back about Kevin, would have to come later.

She tucked her hair behind her ears and began sorting papers into categories.

Elliot stood again and poured two mugs of coffee from the coffee maker on the counter. "Rose is coming in later to do the cleaning of rooms nine and six.

And Tom's working the evening so I can take you and Don out to dinner. I mean, if you guys would like that."

"Sure. Thanks. We would. That's nice." She took the coffee and doughnut he handed her.

"I like your brother," he said.

"I know."

"He's okay."

"Yeah."

"A little crazy, but okay."

"He thinks the same of you, Elliot."

"How about that, me and your brother having mutual feelings about one another."

Jody giggled. "I'm glad."

"Me too." Elliot chuckled as he sat onto the stool and took a second doughnut out of the bag. "I'd hate to stay enemies with him. He throws a mean handful of paper clips."

Chapter 42

"What 'cha doin'?" Matthew asked, peering through the Mitchells' back screen door later that morning.

Don looked up from the paperwork he was involved with at the kitchen table, glad for the interruption. "Come on in, Matthew." He fanned his face with one of the papers. Another hot day. It never got this hot in Myre.

The neighbor entered on a slow shuffle, looking warm but placid. "Seen you out in the yard earlier, walking around the house and, uh....looking upward. Oh, I know...I know I'm a nosy old man...but I'm, uh...here to...to admit that you've got me m-mighty curious."

Don smiled and pushed out a chair for him. "Have a seat."

"Thanks." Bending stiffly, he sat down across from Don and tried to finagle an upside down look at what he was writing.

Don turned the top page around for him. "Part of me is trying to make a list of all the house repairs needed—"

"And the other part?" Matthew questioned teasingly.

"Is wondering what the hell I'm even doing here in Winona."

"W-why doesn't the...the one half of you tell t-the other half that you're making a list?"

Don grinned but answered seriously, "You know, Matthew, it's one thing to argue with another person about something, but when you start arguing with yourself—"

"Been doin' it for years," the neighbor consoled him.

"Want a Coke?" Don asked, getting up.

"Sounds good."

When Don got back from the refrigerator with the drinks, Matthew tapped the list with his finger, denoting, "Looks like a lot of work."

Don retook his chair. "It's what has to be done to make selling the house easier, so the realtor says."

Matthew nodded. "Jody told me the two of you are selling it."

"Yeah, it's what she wants."

"And you? What do you want?"

"I only want to help her get what she wants."

Matthew drank some Coke and arched his eyebrows. "Well, everything's been a…a bit much for her to handle, I know. I don't blame her…for…for wanting a little more freedom in her young life."

"Freedom," Don said, followed by a forlorn sigh. "Now there's a word that's not all it's cracked up to be."

"Nothing wrong with the word freedom," Matthew differed. "Maybe the preciseness of it just needs to, uh…fit the individual."

Don studied him fondly. "You always have this special way of seeing things, don't you."

"A person's seen a whole lot, time he gets my age. Ain't much use if you can't share some of…of the acquired w-wisdom with others."

Don grinned, wiping perspiration off his forehead with his shirtsleeve. "So okay then, tell me how you see this, a whole new roof or just a patch-up job?"

Matthew rubbed his chin in thought. "Well, uh…let's see…I do believe your roof's going on…sixteen years now. Near the expected life of a roof in the Midwest, I'd say."

Don was amazed at his neighbor's knowledge of the Mitchells' roof.

Matthew continued his data, "I know because there was a…a big wind storm in the spring of…let's see…uh, nine years ago last spring. Your dad had some repairs done to the roof because of it and he…he mentioned at that time that the roof was s-seven years old then."

Don fingered the rim of his Coke can, remembering something of his own from that time. "Nine years ago Joel, Max and Warren got sent up for robbery and—"

"More for beating the heck out of that…that poor gas station attendant and leaving him near dead than for the mere two hundred they got off him," Matthew stated.

"Yeah," Don said softly. Then tightening his expression, he added a fact of his own. "A lot of people thought I should've been locked up right along with them."

"I didn't. And you weren't. Because y-you had nothing to do with that robbery or the violence."

"Thanks." Don eased into a smile.

"Not guilty is not guilty."

"Not exactly. My innocence still left a dark cloud hanging over me."

"They were a few years older than you, those boys. How'd you…you even get mixed up with them in the first place?"

"I don't know. I really wasn't all that in with them. I just sort of knew them casually, or thought I did at the time. Which, I guess, I found out I really didn't."

Matthew laid his hand on Don's. "It was so unfair. You were a good boy, Don. Y-you weren't like those friends you sort of knew. Given more time, I bet you might'a influenced them over to your track."

Don laughed. "Or they might'a influenced me onto theirs."

"I don't believe that."

"Too bad you never had this talk with my dad."

"Don't think I didn't."

"You actually *did*?"

"I did, I surely did."

Don shrugged. "Anyway, he saw me as bad and his mind was unbending."

"I…I'm sorry, Don, that Fred had things so…so wrong about you."

"My whole life changed because of what my friends did, you know? Guys I liked and believed in. I was so stupid and blind to what they were up to behind my back."

"You can't be blamed for being blind."

Don gave a sardonic laugh.

"You learned some hard lessons in your youth, didn't you, boy," Matthew concluded sympathetically.

"I'm still trying to learn," Don said.

The old man's expression crinkled teasingly. "Well, uh…that's good…that's good, because to stop would mean you're dead."

Don got up from the table, deciding, "Let's make it a new roof for the Mitchell house."

"And I…I'll be right glad to help." Matthew, in slow motion, also rose from the table.

Don gave him a worried look. "No way am I letting you on that roof."

"No, no…" Matthew clarified, "I…I only meant I'd go along and…help pick out t-the color and…and the grade…if you'd want me to."

Don breathed easier. "Absolutely." He accepted Matthew's offer with a smile and a handshake.

*   *   *   *

Elliot's choice for dinner that night turned out being Quincy's Bar and Grill. He picked Don and Jody up at seven-thirty, in a very joyous mood.

"I'm glad your invite was casual," Don told him as they walked across the parking lot to Quincy's back door, "because when Jody packed my clothes before leaving Myre she missed throwing in my tux."

Elliot laughed. "And mine's currently at the cleaners."

Though Don and Elliot wore jeans and tee-shirts, Jody had specially primped for the evening. She wore a flowered dress of a soft flowing fabric, dangle earrings and, Don thought, she'd done a little something different with her make-up. He told her she looked great.

Though Elliot paid her no actual compliment, his eyes barely left her.

"Any more customers at the Treggor?" Don asked, as the three of them slid into a booth, he and Jody across from Elliot.

"No," Elliot said, opening his menu. "But Jody put the office back in good shape again."

"Sorry for the mess I made," Don apologized.

"Forgotten," Elliot said. "So what do you guys want? The burgers and fries here are out of this world, if you want my recommendation."

"Burger and fries," Don decided without opening a menu of his own.

"Me too," Jody said.

"You won't be sorry." Elliot closed his menu and pushed it aside. This time as his attention settled back on Jody, he found the words to go with it. "You're a knockout in that dress, you know."

She blushed and smiled cutely at him. And then for awhile the two of them became engrossed in sending eye messages back and forth across the table at each other.

Don felt socially left out, but didn't mind. The notable infatuation going on between Jody and Elliot was okay by him. He liked Elliot. Even though the guy was older, he considered him all right for his sister. Except for the kidnapping and wallet taking, he was kind, caring, and funny. He was tolerant to Jody's idiosyncrasies, and Lord knows, he had plenty of his own. The two made quite a pair.

"You should see Don's list," Jody told Elliot when they got around to talking again. "He has this list of all the things he's going to fix on the house."

"I understand you're quite the handyman." Elliot's eyes left Jody to acknowledge Don briefly.

"Well, we'll see," was the best Don could say for himself. "Just wish I had my own tools though."

"Dad's are in the basement," Jody said.

He nodded, he knew. He'd spent a long time sorting through them just that morning. But instead of zeroing in on what he was going to specifically need for his repair jobs, he'd gotten lost in examining each and every implement individually. His remembrance of how special those tools had been to his dad added even more sorrow to what he was already feeling.

In Don's early teens, before he'd turned so rebellious and indifferent, his dad had taught him a lot about tools and making things and fixing things. The two of them, father and son, had been so together on tools, and love and values back then. But that time had been regrettably short.

"I want you to know," Elliot said, breaking into Don's personal thoughts, "that I'll be glad to help you guys with whatever I can on the house."

"Thanks," Don accepted the offer. But when he looked across at the guy who made it, he found Elliot to be still far more taken up by Jody than by any home improvements.

Chapter 43

The hamburgers were huge, with shredded lettuce, a slice of tomato, a slice of onion and a sesame seed bun. The French fries were thick and golden and uniquely seasoned. Jody, Elliot and Don all ordered margaritas as their before, during and after-meal drinks. It was Jody's first time having this drink, and she found it delectably better than vodka sour. Even though it included tequila, it was icy and tangy and went down as pleasantly as lemonade.

Besides the food and drinks being so great, she was having a wonderful time in general. A four-piece country band began playing loud and lively later into the evening, doing well-known songs that inspired sing-a-longs. She, Elliot and Don were a happy, carefree threesome. Forgetting their problems. Tapping their feet under the table. Singing off key. Laughing continually over everything and nothing.

The atmosphere dimmed however when Don bumped Jody's arm and motioned to someone across from them. "Hey, who's the guy staring at you?"

She turned to look. It was Kevin, sitting alone in a booth. He sent her a little wave. She felt like she was going to die.

"What's wrong?" Don asked, observing her reaction. "Who is he?"

Jody wriggled in her tight seat against the wall. "Let's go. Please. Let's just go, all right?" She tried standing up, but there wasn't enough space. She nudged at Don, but he wasn't moving.

"It's Kevin, isn't it?" he guessed.

"Kevin? Who's Kevin?" Elliot asked excitedly.

"The guy with the eagle eyes over there." Don motioned to him again. "You didn't know about Kevin? Jody's boyfriend who, when he heard about the baby, dumped her?"

"No...I didn't know she...she was seeing anyone." Elliot's gaze returned to Jody, as if he were suddenly now, because of this, seeing her as someone totally different. "I didn't know you'd been seeing someone."

"Thanks a lot, Don," she told her brother resentfully.

"Your ex-boyfriend's got his nerve," Don said, "sitting there gawking at you so smugly after what he did to you."

"It's okay, it's okay," she urged him to drop it.

"No, it's not okay! Want me to go say something to him? I will. I'm gonna!"

"No." Now it was Jody stopping Don from getting up. She wanted him to leave the booth, yes, but not to go badger Kevin. "He's history, okay? Let's go home."

"If he's history, why is this bothering you so much?" Don insisted.

"It's not. I mean, what's bothering me about this is that it's bothering you."

Don was fired and ready to fight. "I can handle this."

"No."

"Jody, you wanted me back in your life to help you with things, and it sure seems that he—"

"No!" she said.

"Maybe you should let Don help you with this," Elliot advised her.

"There is no this," she said. "And I don't need help. I just need to get out of here."

Don and Elliot exchanged considering looks.

"Please," she said to the both of them, with tears welling into her eyes.

She wasn't sure if it was the please or the tears that did it, but the guys finally slid out of the booth, out of her way.

Elliot left the check money, and the three of them headed for Quincy's back door.

Before they got there, Don stopped for one last look at Kevin.

"Come on," Jody said anxiously.

"You guys go ahead. There's something I have to do."

Don started in the direction of Kevin, but Jody grabbed him by the arm. "No! Don't do that! Please!"

"Sorry, I have to."

"You'll just make things worse," she cried.

He narrowed his eyes at her. "What do you mean worse?"

Jody bravely took a chance on letting go of him, turned, and went out the door to the parking lot.

Elliot followed.

And thankfully Don did also.

The three of them got into the Skylark.

Jody, sitting in front with Elliot, felt upset and undeserving of his coolness. "Are you mad at me?" she asked.

Without saying anything, he started the car.

She glanced around at her brother in the back seat. "Thanks for not starting something with Kevin."

Don said nothing.

She hated the quietness in the car as they swung out of the parking lot. Like she could really help what happened back there, Kevin's being there and her getting upset over it. "I'm sorry for spoiling the evening, okay?"

Neither of the guys spoke.

"Please don't be mad about this," she pleaded.

The only other sound within the car, other than her own voice, was the click, click, clicking of Elliot's turn signals until he completed his turn at the corner.

"Look," Jody said, feeling like she was merely talking to herself, "Kevin was my problem, and I knew the best way of dealing with him was simply to leave. Don't hold that against me. Don't make me feel guilty. You guys are really making me feel guilty here, you know that?"

"How come you never mentioned this Kevin character to me before?" Elliot asked, as if that one single thought had been burning in his mind ever since learning of him.

Don leaned forth from the back seat. "Jody, how come you felt such a need to run off from Kevin like that? So the guy's in the same restaurant as you, big deal. You said he was history. You could've just ignored him."

Maybe it wasn't so good, the guys starting to talk to her again. Not if it meant they were going to badger her like this. "Because," she began in answer to both of them, "because there's more to Kevin than what I told you."

"More?" Don asked. "What? Like what?"

Elliot, just as intrigued, gave her a sidelong look.

She twisted her hands in her lap. "He...Kevin...he's the baby's father."

Don came still further forward, practically into the front seat. "Kevin? But you said—"

"I know. I lied. I said Kevin wasn't the father, but now I'm saying he is. It's just...it's been really hard for me to admit all this at once, you know?"

Elliot braked sharply when he suddenly came up too close to the car ahead of him. Everyone jolted forward then snapped back.

"So," Don worked at furthering the facts, "he's the original one? The one who wanted you to get an abortion? Didn't that show he didn't give a damn about you? Why would you have ever wanted to get reinvolved with him again now? I don't get it. How could you be so dumb?"

After three margaritas, plus the stressfulness of seeing Kevin, plus her getting into it with the guys, Jody's head was spinning. At the next stop sign, on an impulse, she opened her door, jumped out of the car and took off running.

"Talk about dumb!" she heard Elliot blame Don.

"Jody!" Don shouted after her. "I'm sorry! Don't do this! Come back!"

The guys were out of the car and coming after her in the darkness, both calling to her in what sounded like a mixture of anger and panic.

Jody kept going. Fleeing seemed like her only means of escaping the Kevin issue. Her breath shortened to gasps as she ran through one dark yard after another. In addition to sorting through scratchy bushes, stumbling over obscure lawn furniture, and climbing over unexpected fences, a couple of fierce, barking dogs leaped out at her from the ends of their chains and almost stopped her heart.

She knew the guys weren't far behind. She pushed herself to stay ahead of them. She didn't want to get into anything more about Kevin tonight and be subjected to any more of their disapproval.

"Jody!" Don's voice rang out again. "Come on! This isn't funny! You didn't like how Elliot and I were acting…but hey, look at how you're acting! Like a baby!"

Baby. Why did he have to say baby? It was what all of this was about, what was hurting her so badly and giving her such difficulty explaining. She wished both Kevin and the baby were still her own private secrets and that she had never told them to Elliot and Don. Because right now she wasn't feeling any better for doing so, only worse.

Chapter 44

"Jody! Jody!" Don repeatedly called his sister's name as he and Elliot searched for her. Though his outward feelings were projecting anger, deep inside he was sickly relating this incident to a similar one of years ago.

Jody was four, he was nine. The family was on a picnic. After eating, Don went for a walk along the beach, picking up rocks for his collection. He didn't know his little sister had tagged after him until she said something from behind him. He turned sharply, telling her she had no right to follow him. Despite the tears that came quickly to her big dark eyes, he yelled at her to get lost. She turned and ran off. He hadn't meant it literally, about her getting lost. He'd only meant for her to get away from him, to go back to their parents at the picnic table. But when Don eventually returned to them, he was shocked that she wasn't with them.

"She went to catch up to you a half hour ago," his father said.

"How could you lose her?" his mother cried.

Don dropped the six precious rocks from his hands and turned in all directions, trying to make a good guess as to where his little sister might've gone. There was a woodsy area back in a ways from the beach. He ran as fast as he could toward it, shouting her name. "Jody! Jody!"

He found her there, in a thick enclosure of trees, picking wild flowers. He grabbed her into his arms, thankful she was all right, feeling horribly guilty for having told her to get lost. He was feeling the same way right now about Jody. Responsible this time, as well, for his little sister's taking off. He was so sorry, so worried, so scared.

When something rustled in the bushes near Don, he stopped, listened and waited. Then just as the something started to break through the thick leafy hedge to his side, he sprung forth making a grab for it.

"Elliot!" He let go the instant he found it wasn't Jody.

"I thought you were over that way further!" Elliot snarled.

"I was!" he snarled back. "But I'm not just staying in one place, you know."

"Stay on your course, just stay on your course!"

"Course?" Don questioned.

"We each have our own course, okay?"

"We're both looking for Jody, right?" Don stressed the point of the matter.

"I'm the back yards, you're the front, so we don't miss her."

Don exhausted a heavy sigh. "Okay, so this is the side yard, who covers the sides?"

"Front half of a side is yours, back half, like this, is mine," Elliot stated as if it were a written rule.

"Well, excuse me for infringing on your course," Don said.

"Gotta have a system, that's all."

Don huffed. "Right, like I'm not familiar with some of your systems." He headed off toward the front, shaking his head and muttering some cuss words.

"Thank you," Elliot called after him.

Chapter 45

▼

Jody was wearing down. She felt like she'd run a mile, though it had most likely only been a couple blocks. She needed to stop and catch her breath. She took a moment near some garbage cans, where it seemed darkest, safest.

The thing about Kevin, she thought as she rested, was that there was still even more to the matter, beyond what she'd told Elliot and Don tonight. Though she'd made a worthy start toward being open and honest with them about this, it was difficult, complicated, painful, and, as of yet, incomplete.

She held her head, wishing it would stop spinning, aching, thinking. If only she could push a delete button and make the whole Kevin issue disappear.

Suddenly popping out of nowhere, someone seized her from behind. She screamed, kicked and fought against the force, fearing that other than just Elliot or Don it might be some maniac killer or rapist.

Her struggle was useless and quickly overpowered.

There was a familiar jangle.

Hard metal bracelets hit, clasped and locked over her one wrist, then the other. Handcuffs. It was either Elliot or a cop.

As she was taken into the alley beneath a light post, she was not altogether relieved seeing that it was Elliot.

Don came rushing out of the shadows, surprised at seeing her captivity, her means of captivity. "Idiot!" he scolded her. "You little idiot!"

"Glad I grabbed the cuffs out of the glove compartment," Elliot boasted.

"What's with you?" Don continued at Jody.

"I was upset!" She yanked at the handcuffs, testing their proficiency. But they were every bit as steadfast on her as they'd been on her brother a few days ago.

"You don't think Elliot and I weren't upset when you took off on us like that?"

She knew now that her running away had not accomplished anything. "I'm sorry. I shouldn't have done it. I don't know why I did. Maybe it was the margaritas."

"It was Kevin!" Don said assuredly. "How could he freak you out like that? How could you let him affect you in the slightest anymore?"

"Maybe she really cares about him," Elliot suggested.

"You guys don't understand!" Jody jiggled the cuffs again, stamping her feet as she did. "Get me out of these! Let me go!"

"Not till you simmer down," Don said. "Good idea, bringing those cuffs," he commended Elliot.

"I know." Elliot swelled proudly.

"Kind of like having a cop for a friend."

"10-4," Elliot responded.

Jody leaned against the corner of a garage. "I feel like I have to throw up. You've gotta free my hands."

Staying wise of her, Don said, "You don't need your hands to throw up. Just bend over."

She gave a swift kick to the garage instead.

"Feel better?" Elliot asked her.

"Terrific," she said.

"Good, then let's go."

The guys marched her out to the main sidewalk and back to the car. Their treating her like a criminal was morally unjust. She hated Elliot. And Don. And Kevin. And the evening. And herself. And these stupid handcuffs.

Elliot opened the front passenger door. Don gave Jody a shove that landed her hard into the seat.

"Aren't you going to take these cuffs off me now?" she asked Elliot as he slipped into the driver's seat.

"It's up to my partner," he said, still playing cops.

Jody looked over her shoulder.

Don, in the back seat, shook his head with a cruel glint of pleasure. "See how you like it."

They drove off, with Jody still in restraint.

She stared down at her bound hands in the lap of her flowered dress. Not only were the handcuffs offsetting its prettiness, but there was a tear in the skirt where she'd caught it on a sharp edge of fence. Though the dress was new, it had hung in her closet a month before this her first wearing of it. She had saved it for a special occasion. How sadly mistaken she'd been, having ever thought this might be it.

She hated what this night had turned into. Thanks to Kevin's having been at Quincy's. Thanks to her reaction toward his being there. Thanks to her bright idea of running off like she had. And thanks to Elliot and Don's chasing her down like they had. She reconsidered the last part, Elliot and Don's coming after her, truly knowing she shouldn't be mad about that. She knew she ought to be grateful that they cared so much about her. She shuddered at the thought of something far worse having happened to her other than being toted home in a pair of handcuffs by these two.

By the time they pulled up to the curbing before her house, Jody was feeling considerably calmer. Things didn't seem nearly so drastic now as they had a while ago. And she felt sincerely apologetic. "I'm sorry. For spoiling the night. I just want you guys to…to know that I'm very sorry."

Elliot took the cuffs off of her and stuck them into the glove compartment.

Don got out of the back of the car and opened the front door for her. "Come on, let's call it a day."

Chapter 46

▼

As the brother-sister duo walked up the dark sidewalk to their house, Elliot, in lingering confusion, laid his head forth onto the steering wheel. He remained sitting there after Don and Jody went inside, waiting for something about this latest escapade to ring more clearly in his mind. But it didn't.

Every time he thought he knew Jody inside out and backwards she threw a new curve at him. It was unsettling. So damn unsettling. This Kevin joker really bothered him. Especially since tonight was the first he'd ever heard of him, seen of him. Especially since the guy was the father of Jody's baby, and had originally advised her to get rid of it. He didn't blame Don for wanting to confront the guy before leaving Quincy's. He'd felt like doing the same. And yet, what could either of them have possibly said to Kevin to make things any better? Probably nothing.

Elliot could only shake his head in puzzlement at how this evening had started out so light and frivolous and wound up so crazy. It had gone from pleasant and fun to strange and stressful in almost no time. Jody was good at taking you for rides like that. *Jeez.* And it left him wondering, now, how much more important stuff she might be withholding about her secretive little life that one day, in her own sweet time, she'd use to knock him for another loop.

This girl was too much, just too much for a guy like him to be getting so worked up over. Maybe he ought to be thinking about protecting himself from her while he still could. Maybe it was already too late.

He was tired. Really tired. Drinking made him tired. Running through all those yards made him tired. Plowing through bushes made him tired. The intricacy of Jody made him tired.

He straightened up in his seat, giving a last wondrous look at the Mitchell house before leaving. He had to go home now, though he actually didn't want to and wasn't sure what that psychologically denoted. It seemed he barely understood himself anymore, let alone Jody or her brother.

In a fit of frustration Elliot smacked his hands hard against the steering wheel, unmindful that they would hit the horn.

The blast shocked him back into clear consciousness.

He shifted into gear and drove off.

CHAPTER 47

▼

In the two hours Jody had been at the Treggor Motel the next morning, she'd done nothing more than sit behind the counter pondering whether or not she should turn around and go back home to be with Don.

Elliot stood near, also at the counter, writing out checks in payment of bills. Well aware of her mood, her latest dilemma, he finally advised, "Jody, just go ahead and do whatever it is you think you should do about your brother, okay?"

She sighed ahead of saying, "He was going to start work on the house today and could probably use my help."

"Then go home."

"It's just that I don't want to be in his way."

"Then don't go home."

She sighed again. "I'm just not sure which is the most important right now. My brother or my job."

Elliot gave a quick laugh. "Job? What job?"

"I don't want to make any more mistakes with Don." Jody looked sideways at him, adding, "Or with you."

"I told you..." he said, between licking envelope flaps, "you needn't have come in at all today...since you'd...gotten the files back in order."

"I know. But I wasn't sure I should spend the day hanging around Don either. Like, maybe I should give him his space."

"Space?" Elliot spurted another laugh. "You kidnap him all the way down here from Myre just to give him his space?"

"You know what I mean."

"No, I'm not sure I do. After last night, Jody, I gotta say that knowing what you mean has become more difficult than ever."

"I don't want to crowd him."

"That Kevin stuff was pretty confusing."

"Don's not used to being crowded."

"I'm sorry about the handcuffs last night," Elliot said.

"I have to be careful with him."

"You really scared us, taking off like that."

"What if Don takes off again?" It suddenly came crashingly clear to Jody how very much that still worried her.

"You still think he might?"

"I don't know. Yeah, I guess." She gave Elliot a needy look, drawing on him for understanding, comfort, solution.

He shook his head, and in his own estimation said, "No, I don't think he would now, Jody. I really don't think Don would leave, after everything that's happened. But if he did, after all this, then I'd just say the hell with him."

She slid the register book over in front of herself. For something to do she spun it in around in circles. When she tired of that she drummed her fingers upon it. Then she flipped the cover up and down, making loud slaps. "Sure Don's home and agreed to work on the house, and sure he's listened to a lot of my problems, but I still feel as uneasy as if this were only a dream and he—"

"Go home, Jody," Elliot ordered her, rescuing the register book away from her. "Take a few days, a few weeks, whatever. If we get swamped here, I'll call you. You know I will. Meanwhile, go be with your brother."

She smiled gratefully for the sake of decision. "I think I should."

He returned the smile. "I know."

She slipped off the stool in her yellow skirt and blouse outfit, facing Elliot directly. "Thanks."

"Sure," he said.

She passed between him and the file cabinets and started across the office to the door. Before going out, she turned and gave him a last look and another, "Thanks."

He nodded and waved her off.

On her drive home Jody felt perfectly sure that this was the right thing for her to do, to spend as much time as she possibly could with Don, helping him, talking with him, just being together with him. Togetherness was, after all, the basis of their reunion.

She parked her car in the driveway and hurried into the house.

Moments later, and much slower, she returned to the front porch. Don wasn't there. Why wasn't he? Where could he be? Did it mean he was on his way back to Myre?

Though the porch was shaded and cool, Jody stood there feeling wilted. She picked her blouse away from the places it was sticking to her skin. She shifted her look up and down both directions of the street. Maybe Don still didn't want to be here and she couldn't make him stay. She had to accept the fact that there was nothing more she could say or do.

After a few minutes she backed up to one of the wicker chairs and sat down. She picked up a section of newspaper off the floor and fanned her face with it. Her skin burned as if she had a temperature. Maybe she did. Maybe she was making herself physically sick by obsessing over her need to bring more reason into her life. Maybe there was no reason or sense to be had out of her past, present or future. Maybe Don had already learned as much about his own life and had made peace with it in Myre. Maybe she, too, had to leave Winona in order to do that. Maybe she shouldn't have left the motel. If she was still there with Elliot, she wouldn't have found out that Don was gone.

A car coming down the street looked like Matthew's. Except that he hardly ever drove anymore, so how could it be? Jody ran errands and shopped for him occasionally, as did his nephew who lived fairly close by. She couldn't remember the last time she'd seen Matthew's car out of his garage. Yet, this car now pulling up into his driveway was most definitely his.

She left her chair and went to the end of the porch toward Matthew's lot. Her neighbor was getting out of the car's passenger side, and it was Don getting out of the driver's side. The two of them were engaged in a steady flow of talk and laughter and didn't notice her right away.

When Matthew did see her, he reacted with alarm. "Jody! Why aren't you at...at your job?"

Don came around the car, looking up at her on the porch with the same concern. "Hey, what's wrong? You come home sick? You don't look real good."

"I'm fine," she said evenly, trying not to let neither her anger nor her relief show. "Elliot didn't need me at the Treggor. I thought I'd see what I could help with here."

"That's what I've been doing," Matthew said, seeming years younger for his involvement. "Been offering my...my services to Don."

"Mainly the use of his car," Don explained, opening the trunk.

The guys carried boxes and bags over to the front porch steps of the Mitchell house.

"Be careful, Matthew," Jody fussed at him.

"I will...I will..." he said.

Following their first trip, he and Don went back to the car for more.

"What is all this stuff?" Jody asked, already rooting through some of it on her own.

Don called out a partial inventory, "Plaster, paint, nails, pieces of pipe, new light fixtures, switches..."

From a bag that was plain and did not have Menard's on it, she withdrew a twelve pack of beer and held it up.

"Matthew's idea," Don said.

Jody gave Matthew an off sided look.

"Wh-what can I say..." he played along, "I'm a party animal."

The three of them shared a round of laughter.

When the car trunk had been emptied, Matthew climbed the Mitchells' steps and seated himself in one of the wicker chairs, seeming more than a little done in. Don handed him a beer, which he accepted gratefully, popped the top and took a thirsty swallow. Jody declined Don's offer of a beer but took the chair next to Matthew. Don straddled the railing, enjoying his brew.

"I didn't know where you were when I got home and you weren't here," Jody told her brother.

He didn't apologize for scaring her. He probably didn't even realize that he had. He just went on to say that so far he'd paid for everything out of his own pocket, but when the roofing material got delivered tomorrow he would have to pay for that out of the money their dad had left.

Jody listened quietly, still wishing she had a better feeling about all this.

Soon Don was observing her as if something was now starting to bother him, too. "So why are you home from work this time of day?"

"I told you, there was nothing to do there and I thought there might be something I could help you with here."

"You weren't just checking up on me?" he asked in a way that was hard to tell whether he was amused or annoyed.

Is this what they were going to be doing to one another now? Jody wondered. Staring, hovering, constantly trying to figure the other one out? She shifted guiltily in her chair.

Just as she was about to try and explain herself and her expectations, Don went off into a whole different conversation with Matthew. Something or other in reference to that one bad step in the back and then Matthew's mentioning that he might have a board just the right size in his garage.

Their renewed relationship, Don and Matthew's, had already become easy and automatic. They were devoted close buddies, the two of them, planning these home improvement strategies together, shopping together, drinking beer together.

Enviously trying to fit in, Jody offered, "So, Matthew, do you want me to go get that board from your garage?"

Neither of the guys even heard her, and by then were discussing the roof.

Jody got up from her chair. "I'm going to go change clothes," she announced, in case anyone might possibly notice her leaving.

"Wait!" Don said, stopping her just before she went inside.

She was surprised at having drawn his attention. Even more so for the way he was circling his finger in the air like a signal for her to turn around.

Feeling silly, with no idea as to what this request was about, she nevertheless made a full model-like turn under his and Matthew's watch.

A wide grin spread across Don's face. "Nice. I just wanted to say that you look really nice in that outfit, Jody."

"Always did like yellow..." Matthew also commended.

A nice yellow outfit? They were complimenting her clothes when all she cared about was qualifying for an actual part in their guy stuff?

"Nice, but you're right about changing," Don said. "I mean, you'll definitely want to put on something a little less nice if you're going to be painting and hammering and helping me out around here."

All right! This was exactly the acceptance Jody'd wanted. Yes! She carefully opened the tipped screen door, then set it back into place behind her.

"That door's first on my list," Don strongly proclaimed.

"Good," she said from the other side of it, then hurried upstairs for an old shirt and a pair of jeans.

*   *   *   *

After the front screen door had been rehinged, the afternoon progressed to the ripping out of the rotted back step. Matthew brought his board over, which was indeed the perfect thickness and width. Only the length needed to be trimmed. In addition to putting in the new step, Don reinforced the others with more well-placed nails. Then Jody undertook the job of painting, not only the new step, but the entire set of four.

Don left her working on that project while he went to take care of the water pipe replacement in the basement. Though their jobs were in separate places from one another, there was a definite sense of togetherness developing out of their shared commitment to fixing up the house.

By the time Jody finished the steps and went downstairs to check on Don's progress, she found that he, also, was nearly done. Paint spattered, rewardedly tired, and full of happy satisfaction, she watched her brother, trying to determine if he was feeling as good as she was. "Accomplishment is wonderful, isn't it?" she appraised it.

"Just a…little more…" he said, giving the wrench a final tug against the new pipe fitting that led to the laundry tubs, "and…no more wet drips…across the floor."

It was there. She saw it. Notable pride amidst the exertion in Don's face. Like an artist toiling over a difficult, but worthy, masterpiece. Careful, loving preciseness down to the final stroke. And then, at last, finished with a smile of gratification.

He turned the main valve back on and allowed Jody the honor of making the first actual test.

She turned the faucet.

Watched.

Listened.

Waited.

As the water gushed into the tub and the pipes remained dry, she let out an exuberant cheer, "You did it, Don! You did it!"

"Of course. That's what I'm here for, aren't I, to fix things?"

"But how do you know how to do all this stuff?"

"Who said I did?" His laugh implied that his skill came merely by chance. But Jody accredited it to much more than that.

They did the clean up together. There was gook from the old pipes to be swept off the floor, assorted scraps to be gathered and trashed, and their dad's tools to be returned to the workbench.

Before they left the basement Jody gave Don's job a final check. No leakage from the pipe, absolutely no leakage.

From there Don went to inspect her paint job of the back steps. The new board, plus the entire rise, done in battleship gray. He thoroughly approved and raved as happily over her achievement as she had over his.

"What's next?" she asked as they walked back around the outside of the house to the front.

He followed her up the porch steps. "Nothing more for tonight."

Jody opened and closed the fixed screen door several times, testing it with pure pleasure. "Amazing, just amazing."

Don laughed and followed her inside. "I need a beer."

When they got to the kitchen, Jody took one out of the refrigerator for him and a Coke for herself. They sat down to the kitchen table, both hit with the full impact of all they'd done. Also, with how late it was. Their busy afternoon had lapsed far into evening without their ever really noticing until now.

"I can't believe it's eight forty-five," Jody exclaimed. "Supper…we haven't even had supper yet. You must be starved. I'll make something. I—"

"Whoa!" Don stopped her. "Don't make anything. We'll send out for pizza."

Great, it was her favorite food anyway. She looked up Domino's phone number, and he called in the order.

A half hour later, just as they started in on their large pepperoni with extra cheese, Elliot dropped by. He let himself in the front door and came through the house to the kitchen, raving, "Screen door's fixed! Great! But you're still not locking it, are you?"

Jody gave him a plate and told him to help himself to some pizza. Don got him a beer.

"Screen door, major accomplishment," Elliot made of their day.

"Besides the front door, we did the back steps and the basement water pipes," Jody established. "What have you been doing all day?"

"Not much," he admitted sheepishly.

"Any customers?"

His laugh was his answer. But then he said, "I would have been here to help you guys, except that neither Tom nor Rose were available to cover the office so I had to stay. As if my being there actually turned out necessary."

"What do you think would help the Treggor?" Don asked, as if believing a simple solution was in the waiting.

Chomping a mouthful of pizza, Elliot rolled his eyes and scoffed, "A fire…maybe a nice…big…blazing fire. A mercy killing."

Don was serious. "How about some advertising? Have you ever done any advertising?"

Elliot shook his head no and took another bite of pizza.

Jody had offered enough motel suggestions to Elliot over the time to know it was a going nowhere subject. She yawned and rested her head into her hand.

"Maybe you could give it a try," Don coaxed him.

"Advertising wouldn't do it," Elliot said.

"What would?"

"I don't know."

"Don't you care?" Don asked disapprovingly.

"Care?" Elliot stopped eating and gave him a *dah* look. "Would I keep struggling, like I do, to keep that motel going for my dad, if I really didn't care?"

Jody grew tense, watching Elliot's disposition go from lighthearted, to mildly bothered, to greatly bothered, to highly agitated.

"But your dad's gone, right?" Don verified.

Elliot shifted uneasily on his chair and gave Don a piercing look. "Yeah, he's gone. But I'm trying to keep the Treggor going for him, okay?"

"Why?" Don asked.

Elliot laughed sarcastically. "Why? Because he asked me to. Because it was the last thing he asked me to do. It was what he wanted."

"What do *you* want?"

Elliot shot up from the table. "I want you to quit asking me all these stupid-ass questions, that's what I want." He left the kitchen.

Jody hurried after him. "Wait. Don't get mad. Don didn't mean to badger you. Elliot, come back."

He ended up in the living room, plunking himself into an easy chair. Like he wanted to be alone, despite the fact that he was in someone else's home.

Jody had never seen him this upset before, over the motel or anything. She stood near. Watching. Feeling sorry. Feeling obligated to try and make him feel better. "It's okay, Elliot, your hanging in there with the Treggor. I'll come in to work tomorrow and—"

"Work?" He lifted a dejected look at her. "There is no work at the Treggor. The most work we've had there in months was over the havoc Don created with the files. No, you're better off here, Jody. As…as a plumber's helper, or whatever it is you do."

Don sauntered into the room with a remorseful look on his face. "Hey, I'm sorry, Elliot."

"No, I am," Elliot blamed himself. "I don't usually lose it like this."

"It's just that I'd really like to help," Don said.

Elliot reminded him, "We dragged you down here to help Jody, not me."

Don took a sip of the beer he'd brought with him and studied Elliot further. "So who do you have to help you?"

Becoming his witty self again, Elliot straightened taller in his chair and responded, "I've got an uncle in South Philly. Maybe Jody and I could take the cuffs out there and kidnap him back here to save the Treggor."

"The Treggor's going to be fine," Jody assured him.

"With or without my uncle?"

"It's going to pick up again, you'll see."

The phone rang and Jody went to answer it at the desk. "Hello?"

The line was open but no one spoke.

"Hello, is anyone there?" she asked.

Click. Then a dial tone.

She turned back to the guys with a shrug. "Whoever it was hung up. Must've been a wrong number."

Elliot got to his feet. "I gotta go."

"There's lots of beer and pizza left," Don tempted him.

"No...no..." He started for the door.

"Please, Elliot," Jody said even more temptingly.

He made a last-minute pivot. "Okay."

Everyone laughed and returned to the kitchen in a better mood.

When the phone rang again, Don answered the one on the wall beside the cupboard. It was not a wrong number this time, as he turned his back to Jody and Elliot and became secretly engrossed in a low conversation with whomever the caller was.

Jody and Elliot exchanged looks across the table.

"My guess is Krista," she whispered.

Elliot nodded. "The married one who stopped by here with her husband the other night?"

"Yes." Jody wished she could hear at least a part of what Don was saying, but his secretive voice from the other side of the kitchen was hardly audible.

When he hung up and rejoined her and Elliot at the table, he gave no explanation. Jody didn't ask. She knew.

* * * *

It was eleven-thirty when Elliot left. Jody cleared away the empty pizza box, crumbs and beer cans. Don stood about restlessly, as if he were waiting for the opportune chance to say something.

When she finished her task and became still, he told her, "I'm going out."

"Out?" she questioned.

"Yeah."

"Where?"

"Just out."

"Want me to go with?"

"No."

He walked through the house and went out the front.

As the door closed behind him, Jody was right there to peek out the window. She watched him reach the main sidewalk and turn left. He was headed in the direction of the Glennons. She couldn't believe he was doing this. That he was purposely opening himself up to more heartache.

She went to sit down on the couch and await his return.

Chapter 48

Don knocked softly on the front door of another big old house just down the street. The Glennons' place, where he'd spent a lot of his childhood days with Rossi. Now Rossi's parents had moved into a retirement complex and left the house to him and his wife. Rossi and Krista...it was still hard to believe those two were married.

He stood in the scant light sifting through the window curtains onto the porch. Thinking. Yet trying not to think. Suddenly he realized, like a harsh awakening, that he shouldn't be there, didn't need this, had better leave. As he was starting to turn away, the lock snapped and the door opened.

Krista appeared, wearing a long, billowy, blue-print gown. "Hi," was all she had to say to make him stay and believe that this might be okay.

Don stepped inside and followed her through the foyer to the living room. It'd been so long since he'd been in this house. Or, for that matter, alone with Krista. He really wasn't sure what he was doing there now, except that on the phone she denoted having a reason for them to meet and he was curious enough to come find out if there actually could be one.

The one small table lamp burning was enough to pick up the red in her hair and the mystique in her eyes when she looked back at him.

"Sit down," she said.

Don didn't want to sit. He preferred standing. He had to be careful not to get too cozy, too trusting.

Krista sat into an easy chair. Though her winsome smile seemed intentional of trying to put him at ease, it was actually doing the opposite. "I told you on the phone, Rossi's not home."

"And I'm suppose to care whether or not he is?" Don asked harshly.

"You're really uncomfortable, aren't you?"

Hands in his pockets, shoulders stiff, weight shifting from foot to foot, he claimed, "I'm fine. How are you?"

"Fine."

From the unbreaking once-over he was still giving her, he nodded and said, "You look fine."

"Don, we have to talk."

"About what?"

"Us, you and me."

"Sounds interesting."

"Please sit down," Krista said.

Since he was starting to feel rather weak in the knees anyway, he took the chair across from her.

"I debated all evening about calling you," she said. "Then when Rossi left, well, I just did. Your sister answered the first time and I was…well, I know it was rude, but I said nothing and hung up."

"So that was you," he verified.

"I was glad when you answered the next time."

He narrowed his eyes at her. "What is it, Krista? Why are you doing this? Why this sneaking around? What do you want from me?"

She worked her smile on him again. "This isn't exactly sneaking, is it, your being right here in this house?"

"Your not disclosing yourself when Jody answered the phone? Your inviting me here, with Rossi being gone?" While Don considered it very sneaky, he knew he was, at the same time, feeling helplessly drawn in.

"Rossi's working. Anyway, he wouldn't care about your being here."

Don raised his eyebrows dubiously.

"We both want to talk to you and see more of you now that you're back in Winona," Krista continued. "Maybe what I want to talk to you about should just be separate, and prior, to Rossi's talk, that's all."

Don leaned forward in his chair. "What could Rossi possibly have to talk to me about?"

"He wants to resume his friendship with you," Krista stated.

Don gave a sardonic laugh. "Resume? Then that's like admitting that it actually had ended."

"Maybe it was just on hiatus," she said. "Don't turn things around. You've been away for eight years, you know, and—"

"You kept track?"

She seemed to loose her concentration for a moment before saying, "Let's get back to what I called you over here for."

Don got out of his chair, feeling a lot more secure standing and thus better able to charge Krista with, "Your asking me here this time of night, looking like you do in that…that seductive gown and…and the lights down low…yeah, I'd say that…that you definietly have something in mind."

Krista also stood. Her pretty face hardened and her hands swished the sides of her gown. "This caftan is hardly what you'd call seductive. And as for the lighting, I can easily alter that if it's giving you the wrong message."

She went around the room flicking on every lamp and fixture that there was.

"All right, all right—" Don followed her, feeling foolishly responsible for sending her into a frenzy. "Stop it. Krista, stop it."

She continued into the dining room, turning on all the lights there.

"Krista!" He kept after her. Sorry he'd misread her. Sorry his mind still worked the way it did where she was concerned. Sorry he'd foolishly come there.

The chandelier over the table shone with its collection of candle-like bulbs. Plus there was the antique lamp by the window. And the China cabinet display light. And the gooseneck lamp on the desk, which she aimed outward at the room. She'd gotten them all, and the excessive brightness seemed as satisfying to her as it was unnerving to him.

"Okay, I'm sorry if I misinterpreted this," he apologized, squinting through the room's glare at her.

"If?" she said, standing by the desk. "Like you're not really sure that you did misinterpret it?"

"I…I just don't understand why you—"

"I told you, I asked you here for a talk. *Talk*, something you never did understand about our relationship and obviously still don't."

He gave a sheepish grin and shrugged. "Never have been much of a talker."

"That's what I'm saying. It's probably the main reason you and I never did work out."

"Because we didn't talk enough? Come on, what about—"

"Don't even go there," she warned him. "I certainly don't want to talk about that."

Don nodded smartly. "Rossi…he's a good talker, isn't he?"

Krista said nothing.

Don slowly started edging his way around the table toward her. "How about the saying, actions speak louder than words?"

She didn't move. It was like she was frozen in place, as much by his approach as by the look in his eye.

"Krista?" Don said her name like a soft question.

Krista, the believer in talk, momentarily had no words.

"So how are Rossi's actions?" Don asked.

She didn't answer. Don took her quietness as a go-ahead for him to make his next move. He put his arms around her, pulled her tightly against himself and kissed her. His action began rather roughly and insistently, per chance she would resist him. But when she actually seemed responsive, he loosened his hold of her.

Krista used that very opportunity to break away from him and slap him hard across the face.

His eyes watered, more from a hurt ego than the actual sting. "You didn't want me to kiss you?"

Her grating look indicated no. As did her wiping her mouth with the back of her hand.

"Because..." Don reasoned, "it...it really seemed like you were enjoying it there for a moment."

"Why would I enjoy a kiss you forced onto me out of a sick, sad lust that you—"

"Don't make me out to be so wrong here. Don't think you can make me believe that you called me over here to talk when you know damn well I've never been a talker."

"I was hoping you'd at least listen to me talk."

"So far you haven't said much."

"So far you haven't given me much of a chance. I wanted to tell you that I hope we can still be friends and—"

"You've gotta be kidding," Don said.

"You're afraid of friendship?"

"There's still something more between us than that, Krista. Don't tell me you don't feel it."

Without looking him straight in the eye, she answered, "No, I don't."

"I don't believe you. I'm sure you don't even believe yourself. Krista, come on, I—"

"That's your problem, Don, you go around assuming things, the wrong things, without ever accepting reality." Her gaze, as equally harsh as the surrounding lights, remet with his. "You're limited to seeing only what your dream world allows you to see."

"Dream world." Though he was angered and insulted by the term she used, he supposed it was somewhat accurate. Though he hated admitting it, even to himself, he knew he'd come here tonight halfway thinking he had a chance of getting her back. But how wrong he'd been. How stupidly wrong. Which was way more reality than he cared to face. "Don't you know what this is doing to me, Krista? Being here? Seeing you?"

She brushed past Don, went around the dining room table, and headed back into the living room. He stood by himself for a minute, then followed her.

They retook their chairs across from one another. All of the lights stayed on. This meeting was for sure a mistake, on her part for asking, his part for showing up. No doubt for Krista it came down to a big disappointment from what she expected, but for Don it was like a painful twist of the knife that was still in his side.

"I would've thought you'd changed by now," she eventually said.

"Oh, I've done a lot of changing," he said.

"I don't see it. Not one bit. That grabbing me and kissing me is the old you. Hot, reckless passion as your answer to everything. You've learned nothing about deeper needs, or reasoning, or truth."

Don turned up a protective grin. "You mean like the truth being that you were my girl until Rossi stepped in?"

"That's your distorted truth, not the real truth," she argued. "I couldn't handle sharing the kind of life you were setting yourself up for, Don, you know that. So I stepped out of it."

"The kind of life?" He gave a protective laugh. "I was just fine, wasn't I, till my friends got in trouble? You never believed that I was innocent, that I knew nothing about what they were involved with, did you? Do you know how much that hurt, having the girl I loved not believe in me? Trust me?"

"I didn't have a choice."

"What do you mean, you didn't have a choice?"

"People were talking and—"

"People? And you listened to them rather than to me?"

"I fell out of love, or whatever it was I thought we had together."

He nodded bitterly. "I was a good guy. I always told you the truth, Krista. You could've trusted me. You should've trusted me."

She nodded as acridly. "And where does trust get you? You obviously trusted in those so-called friends of yours, and where did that get you?"

"It got me shit. A whole lot of shit I didn't deserve."

"Which wrecked your life."

"They didn't wreck my life. You did. I thought you loved me as much as I loved you."

"I...I'm not so sure now, Don."

"About what? My feelings or yours?"

"You were only nineteen. You definitely had some growing up to do."

"Rossi and you were both two years older than me. And I guess two years, plus the fact that he had no criminal friends, made the whole fucking difference, right?" Don shot out of his chair and started to leave. But then he stopped in the doorway to the foyer and looked back. He hadn't meant to lose it like that. But no amount of regret could take it back now.

"I told you," Krista began firmly, "Rossi was no where in the picture yet when you and I broke up."

"Right," Don said.

"He never took advantage of our breakup or—"

"Right," Don said.

"He and I never went out until a couple months after you and I were over. A couple months. He didn't steal me away from you. He didn't. Please understand that and believe it once and for all."

Don clung to his own version of the truth over hers. Because he knew what he knew, and because it had been fixed as such in his mind for too long to be any different.

Krista held a pitying look on him. He hated that. He'd much rather have her angry at him than feeling sorry for him.

"Don," she said, speaking way too softly to be trusted, "I want you to accept what was and what is. Please don't turn away from Rossi's attempts to be friends with you again. You and he go back long before me. I don't want to stand in the way of that."

In the way? If only she knew, Don thought, how much she stood in the way of his whole life. He dropped eye contact with her, lowering his look to the floor, shaking his head slowly, dreamily, like the admitted dreamer he truly was.

"Don?" she said.

So okay, he was thinking, even if Rossi didn't exactly steal her from him, the fact remained that Rossi had her now and he didn't.

"Don?" she beckoned. When he still didn't answer, she lost patience and snarled, "When are you going to grow up?"

Don snapped out of his personal thoughts and back into the here and now of the matter. "That was no kid that kissed you a minute ago," he said, realizing too late how very much he did, in fact, sound just exactly like a whining child.

"Get over the past," she urged him. "It's gone. If you don't start adapting to the here and now of your life, then it too will soon be gone and what will you have?"

"What do you have, Krista?" he dished it back at her, not especially seeing that she had so much.

She left her chair and came toward him, seeming more than eager to evaluate it for him. "I have Rossi. And this great old house. And love. And maturity. And security. And come February, we're expecting our first baby."

It felt like brakes screeching and scraping in Don's head, bringing his mind to a deadening stop. He couldn't say anything or do anything but stare at her.

"Did you hear me?" she eventually asked.

Yes, he'd heard her, he just wasn't computing well.

"Don, say something," she kept at him.

"Congratulations," he finally managed to tell her.

"Thanks." She studied him, as if not yet totally satisfied with him, or this, or anything. "The only thing missing for me, Don, is your approval, your friendship, your own personal welfare."

He stuffed his hands into his pants pockets and turned back into the foyer, leaving her with, "Sorry, can't have everything."

"Don! Don, wait!" she called after him.

He left the Glennon house without another glance back, trying to convince himself that he didn't care, didn't hurt. He hit the main sidewalk, nearly running, and headed down the block.

Jody had been sleeping on the couch but wakened when he got home.

"Are you okay?" she asked, jumping up and blinking at him.

"No."

"Krista?" she asked carefully.

He didn't answer. Didn't need to. Surely it was written all over his stupid face, for the way Jody was looking at him.

Except that wasn't enough for her and she pressed with, "But that ended a long time ago, didn't it?"

He turned away from her, saying in a slightly choked voice, "Go to bed, Jody."

"You shouldn't have gone over there."

"I'm tired, really tired."

"What happened? Tell me what happened."

"We talked. It's definitely over. That's it. I mean, if I didn't know it before, I sure as hell know it now."

"But, you're not okay with that?"
"Just tired."
"You going to bed?"
"In a while."
"So what are you going to—"
"Jody," he started to raise his voice, then lowered it, "I don't feel like talking. I'm pretty talked out right now. I need some time alone, okay?"

After his sister had gone upstairs, Don wandered out to the kitchen for one last beer. But he opened the refrigerator to find there was none left. They'd drunk it all earlier, he and Elliot.

After drinking a glass of water, he strolled back to the living room, turning out lights as he went.

Of all the things Krista had said to him that night, what stayed most hauntingly in his mind was her asking him what he would have for himself if he didn't start adapting to the present. Its affect was like a rude awakening. Like maybe he'd carried around a heavy heart for way too long. Like maybe his coming back to Winona was, in one respect, like a closure to his past, and in another respect like receiving a key to a whole new future for himself. He probably owed Jody and Elliot some real gratitude for kidnapping him and forcing all this onto him.

He smiled at the sudden, satisfying perception he'd made out of tonight and started up the stairs for his room.

Chapter 49

The new roofing shingles arrived and were stacked in the driveway. Gray, the same color as before, except a tinge lighter.

Jody followed Don about as he checked out the delivery, jotted down configurations, and walked around the yard looking up at the housetop from every possible angle. Because the roof had some ultra steep peaks, working on it was going to be risky. Don claimed that though he'd had a fair amount of shingling experience, no roof had ever professed to be as much of a challenge to him as this one.

To his spending long periods of time on the ground studying it and analyzing it, Jody suggested that maybe he should continue on with some more of the smaller jobs first. "Let the roofing job wait a while. It'll keep. Get to it later, when you're positively ready for it."

He laughingly lowered his gaze from the roof to her. "Like I'm really going to be more ready to go up there next week than this week."

"Yeah, maybe," she said, adding a quick laugh of her own. "I'd say it's worth the wait just to find out, wouldn't you? Besides, I think the loose stairway railing is more a priority."

"Plus that broken window in the back," he noted.

"And that squeaky cupboard door in the kitchen," she said.

"Squeaky cupboard door?" Don slipped his list out of his pocket and checked it. "It's not on here. I guess I missed that."

Jody scrinched her face. "Next to the stove, very annoying."

"Okay, let's go have a look." He started for the back door, deciding, "I'll get to the roof when I get to the roof."

"Good enough," she said, following him.

* * * *

After reworking the repair list and moving the roof to the bottom of it, all the other jobs, one by one, proceeded to get done. Jody stayed at Don's side, helping and enjoying every minute of their working together. The stereo was always near and loud, lending a lively rock 'n roll soundtrack to whatever project they were doing. Elliot was at the house as often as possible, generously donating his assistance and, per usual, his humor.

On the day that Don and Jody toiled over fixing the loose banister of the stairway leading up from the front entrance, Elliot took on the chore of cleaning the living room and dining room carpet by himself. He was in an especially good mood. He, who usually preferred elevator music, had Jody crank up her type of music loud enough for him to hear over the roar of the rented Power Mite, and then added a bouncy little dance step to his back and forth machine operation across the floor. His antics continually kept stealing Don and Jody's attention off their own work, sending them into fits of laughter.

Later that morning, as the three of them took a break on the shady front porch, Don told Elliot, "When we finish the house maybe we can put some effort into the Treggor. You know, perk it up some."

Elliot laughed. Not so much as he didn't appreciate Don's good intentions, but more as though he considered them totally useless. "The only perk it could use would be having 64 rerouted back in front of it."

It frustrated Don that he wasn't able to lend Elliot as much help as Elliot was lending him. Jody saw it and understood it, because she shared the same frustration.

"Thanks anyway," Elliot said.

"It's just that once I get going, I really get going," Don explained why his aspirations for the house improvements were spilling over into an interest in doing something for the motel.

"Me too," Jody said enthusiastically.

Ongoing drums and guitars from the music inside the house sounded through the screen door. Elliot wiped his perspiring brow and plopped into a wicker chair. "Don't waste your time on the Treggor," he told the both of them.

"Maybe fixing it up wouldn't be a waste," she said.

"Just thinking about it is a waste," he insisted.

"So what is going to happen to the Treggor?" Don couldn't let it go.

"I don't know." Elliot closed his eyes, seeming more engrossed, at the moment, with tapping his hand against his knee in time to the heavy rock beat.

Jody and Don exchanged disappointed glances at the hopelessness of getting through to him. Sometimes, Jody thought, it was almost as if Elliot wanted the motel to fail. As if maybe that would be the one and only way he would ever be able to justify his stepping free and clear of it. If that was the case, it surely wouldn't be much longer at the rate it was going.

As if she didn't already have her hands full, watching and trying to second guess her brother most of the time, she'd now pretty much undertaken the same task with Elliot. Though it seemed eminently necessary, her hovering over the welfare of these two guys, it was by no means easy and imposed a wearing effect on her.

Suddenly seeking a lighter side to herself and to the moment, Jody playfully knocked Elliot's feet off their propped position on the railing. As his body jolted forth to the shock of it, and his eyes blinked open, she made a fast getaway off the porch.

Within seconds he was out of his chair, down the steps and running across the front lawn after her, shouting, "Now you're gonna get it!"

He caught her next to the driveway, took her by the waist and started tickling her relentlessly. She fought, screamed and giggled, begging him to stop. When he finally did, she went limp in his arms and it took her several minutes to catch her breath.

"Never..turn...your back...on this one...." Elliot, in his own breathlessness, proclaimed to the world. "Or...close your eyes...in her presence. She has this...this real...wicked...sense of humor."

Though he was no longer tickling her, he kept a tight hold of her. And as he went on and on complaining about her behavior, he was grinning at her. And behind his grin, there seemed to be something else. Something beyond their usual goofing around. Though Jody didn't quite understand it, she really didn't mind the warm fluttery feeling it was causing in her heart. And she realized she was giving Elliot a look that he didn't quite seem to be understanding either.

When they separated and started back to the porch, Don's curious looks met them.

"I think I found your sister's weakness," Elliot said. "At last, a way I can get back at her when she does stuff to me. Tickle the daylights out of her."

Jody huffed. "Nothing I would ever do to you deserves what you just did to me."

"But the possibility that you might nevertheless get it just the same might stop you, right?" he warned.

Don shook his head and laughed at them. "I don't know about you two, I just don't know."

Elliot was first to get back to work. When the sound of his Power Mite from the living room, combined with the upped music from the hall, carried out onto the porch so loudly that Don and Jody could no longer hear each other talk, they too went back inside to their project.

*   *   *   *

When Don's final paycheck from his Myre logging job arrived in the mail one day, he took time away from working on the house to shop for a few more things he needed. Though Jody had packed a lot of his clothes for him, prior to the kidnapping, and his friend Lyle had recently sent him a box of additional stuff from his cabin, he mainly found he needed some new underwear. Now that Jody was doing his laundry, he realized the bad condition his was in. He also splurged and took Jody and Elliot out to dinner and a movie one evening. Whether it was working together or relaxing together, they were definitely becoming a very close threesome.

One morning, when the right time had finally come for Don to tackle the roof, Elliot unfortunately got tied up at the Treggor with another guest and couldn't make it over. But he promised to be there as soon as he could.

Don started the job alone. He borrowed an extra length ladder out of Matthew's garage, which made the highest areas of the roof more readily accessible than they would've been from his dad's shorter ladder. Matthew brought a lawn chair into the side yard to situate himself for watching.

Jody had her paint job to finish in the bathroom before she could assist with the roofing. Though Don had already made it strongly clear that he didn't want her up on the roof, she knew she would find some way of helping with it.

As she sat on the floor, painting the section of wall beneath the pedestal sink with apricot mist, she began hearing an exchange of voices calling back and forth to one another. One was Don's, amidst his hammering just outside and above her, and the other was indistinguishable, but familiar, from the ground. She laid her brush sideways across the paint can and went to the window to look.

It was Rossi. Standing on the lawn. Head tilted back. Voice projecting upward. "I told you, Don, I work nights and I'm free days. I'd really like to help you here."

Though it sounded good to Jody, her brother responded to him, "I'm fine! I can manage!"

Stubborn. Stupid. Jody didn't know how he could reject an offer like that.

Then Don must have dropped his hammer, because there was a thud and a scuttling sound all the way down the roof.

Rossi laughingly jumped out of the way as it pounced to the ground. "I hope that wasn't intentionally aimed at me."

He retrieved the hammer. Then he came up the ladder with it, also shouldering a stack of shingles, and greeted Jody in the window as he passed her.

She stayed put, unable to see the roof above her, but listening for all she could. She heard Don tell Rossi thanks. But Rossi didn't go back down. He stayed. It seemed that besides Don's hammer he'd also brought up one for himself, along with some nails, and thus began working.

Don exploded. "I told you, I can manage just fine!"

"I'm sure you can!" Rossi said. "But maybe you can manage even finer with someone helping you!"

"Yeah and maybe not. Get off the roof, Rossi!"

"No!" Hammer, hammer, hammer, hammer.

"Damn it, Rossi, get down!"

"No!" Hammer, hammer, hammer, hammer.

Fearing their getting into a fight on the roof, Jody left her painting and raced downstairs and outside to where Matthew was sitting. She put back her head, squinting up through the sun glare at Don and Rossi. They were no longer bickering. Braced to the roof, just a short distance apart from one another, both were now only intently involved with shingling as if there were no longer a problem between them. She breathed a sigh of relief and exchanged a smile with Matthew.

"Better make some uh, lemonade for the boys, Jody..." he suggested. "Don't think they oughta drink any beer while they...they do roofing."

She made another glance up at them before leaving the yard. "I'm just so glad Don has some help. I'm just so glad seeing him and Rossi working together like this." She started for the house. "Be right back, Matthew. I'll make that lemonade."

Chapter 50

▼

Don was surprised how after a while associating with Rossi began to feel almost natural, almost pleasurable, almost like old times. He began to realize how much he'd missed him, how senseless and too long his grudge against him may have lasted.

"It's good having you home," Rossi said amidst their duel hammering.

Though Don was feeling better about Rossi's presence, he wasn't yet ready to talk to the guy.

"I was starting to wonder if we'd ever see you again," Rossi continued one sidedly.

Don said nothing.

"I couldn't believe it, seeing you there on the porch that night Krista and I came by. It was like seeing a ghost."

Don wished that if Rossi had come up there to help him he'd do just that and not prattle so much.

"Krista's glad you're back too, Don."

"I don't want to discuss Krista," Don said.

"Who's discussing?"

"You."

"I only mentioned that she's as glad as I am that you're back."

"Fine. I'm glad everyone's glad."

"She said the two of you had a talk."

"Yeah. It was late. Real late. You were at work."

No response from Rossi made Don feel ashamed for having purposely implied that the event had been something that it hadn't. "Rossi?" he began, in an attempt to apologize.

Rossi kept working. Hammer, hammer, hammer, hammer.

"Nothing happened," Don said, which he guessed only made it sound worse.

Rossi kept working. Hammer, hammer, hammer, hammer.

Trying to get on the better side of this, Don told him, "Congratulations, by the way, on your upcoming baby."

"*Baby?*" Rossi's hammer stopped in mid air.

Don felt sick. And sorry. Like maybe Rossi hadn't known about the baby yet, and there was no way now to retract the news. He wished Rossi would put his hammer down. It was scary, the way he was glaring at him and holding it up in the air like that.

"Our secret..." Rossi said.

"What?" Don asked, even though he'd heard him clearly.

Rossi finally lowered his hammer to the roof. "It was our secret, mine and Krista's. We'd planned to keep her pregnancy a secret for a while because she'd had a couple miscarriages and...*how the hell did you know?*"

This was precisely why Don hadn't wanted to talk about Krista with him in the first place. Especially on a rooftop. He looked at the distance to the ground, then back at Rossi, who was anxiously awaiting an answer.

Rossi was definitely more interested in talking now than in shingling. "So you and my wife are already into telling secrets behind my back? Is that it, Don?"

"Secrets? N-no."

"The baby was a secret."

"W-well, she...Krista...she told me about the baby because she wanted me to know how happy you and she are with your lives."

"Is that right?" Rossi said.

"Yeah."

"And what was it about you that seemed to make her feel she had to prove to you how damn happy she is with me?"

Don knew he'd made another communication mistake with Rossi. He hadn't wanted to talk to him in the first place, and now that he was, he was saying all the wrong stuff. Before Don could think of anything right to say, Rossi was edging his way off the roof and climbing back down the ladder.

Chapter 51

Carrying a tray with a pitcher of lemonade and four glasses, Jody came outside just in time to see Rossi taking the ladder away from the house and lowering it recklessly to the ground. "Rossi!" she screamed at him. "What are you doing?"

The bearded guy headed out of the yard, saying, "Seems your brother likes being high and mighty, so let him just stay the hell up there!"

Jody put down the tray and went running after him. She caught up with him on the front sidewalk. "Rossi! Rossi! Come back! What? What's wrong? I can't raise that ladder and neither can Matthew. Whatever happened between you and Don, you've got to put the ladder back for him. You've just got to put the ladder back!"

He kept going. Stubborn. Ornery. He was the exact same type as Don.

"Rossi! Rossi!" She grasped the side of his shirt and at least caused him to slow down.

He grumbled something she couldn't make out.

"Please!" she begged him. "Please!"

He stopped.

"Please?" she asked more mildly.

He gave in and went back with her.

He was just about to raise the monstrous ladder, when he and Jody did a double-take for seeing Don in the side yard having a lemonade with Matthew.

"Anyone else?" Matthew offered drinks to them.

"How did—?" Jody started to ask.

"The small ladder was still propped against the lower back side of the roof," Don explained how he got down.

Everyone burst into laughter. And Don and Rossi quenched whatever they'd been so riled about a moment ago.

*   *   *   *

The roofing job progressed smoothly and rapidly over the next few days. As did Don and Rossi's friendship. They were soon back to being somewhere near the good buddies that they'd been before so much had gotten in the way. Before Rossi had gotten so busy at college, and Don's other friends had turned out to be so bad, and Krista had changed her mind about who she loved.

Elliot came over whenever he could and put in many long hard hours atop the house with the guys. Matthew watched. And Jody made lemonade.

One evening, after Don and Jody had had supper and were playing a game of checkers on the front porch, Ralph Remeer, the realtor Jody had talked with a couple months ago, came back for an update on the house. He was a fatherly sort of older man, who wore his wire-rimmed glasses halfway down his nose and looked at you over the top of them. He was pleased to meet Don and expressed how glad he was that Jody now had the help and support she needed. He toured the house inside and out, impressed with the improvements being done.

Along with his endearing personality, Remeer was, without doubt, a capable businessman. "As I told Jody a while back," he said to Don, "this is too great a house to sell short. With some effort here and there to put it in tip-top shape, it will easily up the value. You'll get back much more than what you put into it. And at least...well, you're lucky it has vinyl siding and doesn't require an over all painting."

"Yeah, lucky," Don agreed and gave a thankful sigh. Then he estimated to Remeer, "I'd say another couple weeks or so and we should have all the work around here completed."

Remeer opened up his notebook and looked down through his glasses to check his calendar. "Let's see...how about if we set a date? How about August tenth? I'll order the For Sale sign to be put up at that time and bring the contract by for you to sign."

"Sounds good," Jody said.

"Sounds good," Don echoed.

Remeer shook hands with the brother and sister, told them to keep up the good work, take care, and he'd see them August tenth.

After Remeer had left, Elliot happened by. He'd been there that morning, helping with the shingling, but in the afternoon had left to handle some business back at the motel. "Looking good," he said, standing in the yard, gazing up at the latest section of roofing put on that day.

Then he joined Jody and Don on the front porch to have a beer with Don, while Jody had a Coke, and watch the darkness close in. None of them were very talkative. But sharing the quiet was nicely satisfying. Elliot and Jody occupied the wicker chairs, and Don sat on the floor with his back against the inner wall.

The peaceful setting broke at nine o'clock however when the surprise of Kevin came up the walk toward the house.

"Kevin!" Jody shot out of her chair as though a pin had suddenly jabbed her from behind.

Elliot's foot accidentally knocked over an empty beer can, and it made a loud tinny sound as it toppled across the wood floor.

Don straightened up guardedly.

The visitor stopped on the middle step, eyes wary of his reception. "Hi."

"What do you want?" Don asked him.

Jody started forth, saying, "I'll take care of this."

Don jumped to his feet and blocked her way. "Not while I'm around."

"My brother," she explained to Kevin of the wall that stood between them.

Kevin had to lean sideways in order to see her.

"So what do you want?" Don asked him, as if whatever it was couldn't be warranted.

Elliot accidentally knocked over another empty can as he got out of his chair.

"Can't you be careful?" Jody blared at Elliot out of the anger she felt toward Don.

"Sorry." Stepping slowly and carefully, Elliot proceeded forth to get a closer look at Kevin.

"A friend," Jody, from behind Don, explained Elliot to Kevin.

"I came to talk to you, Jody," Kevin said, as if he were the solution, rather than the cause, to this matter.

Don continued shielding Jody from him. "Talk? You've got your nerve thinking my sister would ever want to talk to you again after the way you treated her."

"Treated her?"

Poor Kevin, Jody regretted. He had no idea what he'd come up against.

"I need to talk to him!" she said, trying to step around Don.

But her brother spread his arms out and back, managing to keep her right were she was. "So do I. I want to know how he can stand there so smug after what he did to you."

"I did to her?" Kevin protested.

"Don't make it sound like you're the victim," Don said.

Kevin's wary eyes widened still more. "Victim? What are you talking about here? Look, I just came over to—"

"You've got no reason to be here!" Don told him. "So leave! Before this gets ugly!"

Elliot laid a hand to Don's shoulder, suggesting, "Maybe we'd better just let the two of them have their talk."

Don jerked away from him. "Maybe you'd better just shut the hell up and stay out of this, Elliot!"

Elliot nodded and took a step backwards.

Don glanced back at Jody. "Go in the house. I'll get rid of Kevin."

"There's a law against murder," Elliot cautioned him.

"I'm not going in the house," Jody told Don. "You go in the house."

Still standing on the middle step, as though he were glued to it, Kevin chanced asking Don, "What have you got against Jody and me talking?"

"Jody's been through enough, that's what."

"I know," Kevin agreed. "And I thought it would probably help, my coming over here to tell her I forgive her for what she did to me."

"Forgive her? Why you—" Don made a lunge for him. Though Kevin was fast off the steps and out of his grasp, Don caught him again more securely.

"Don!" Jody screamed at her brother. "Elliot, stop him!" she secondly screamed at Elliot.

"What do you think you're doing!" Kevin said, as Don swung him around by his arm.

"Why don't you take a guess!" Don said ahead of shoving him to the ground.

By this time, Kevin was ready to fight back. When Don attempted to kick him, Kevin grabbed his foot, twisted it and brought him to the ground as well.

The two of them wrestled in the grass. A tangle of arms, legs, fists, gasps and groans.

Elliot ran out to them. "Come on, you guys! This won't solve anything! Don! Don, let him go!"

By drawing his right knee up to his chest, Kevin managed to brace his foot against Don's chest and keep him back. But Don still had Kevin's left arm, which he continued twisting and pulling.

While Jody tugged at Don from one angle, Elliot worked at freeing Kevin from the other. It was only when Jody viciously pulled Don's hair that she was able to make him let go of Kevin.

Kevin took off running down the street. Don was furious that he got away.

"It's okay," Jody said, trying to calm her brother despite her dislike for him right now.

"It's not okay with me." He sat there for a few minutes, rubbing his scalp. Then as he got up off the ground, looking in the direction Kevin had fled, he threatened, "I'm not through with him yet."

"You've got it wrong about him," Jody said.

"Maybe you've got it wrong. Any guy who—"

"Because I told you wrong," she said.

Don's look made a quick return to her. "Like he didn't get you pregnant and then—"

"Yes. But he wasn't as crude about it as I made him out to be."

"Like telling you to get an abortion wasn't crude?" Don verified.

"It wasn't that way."

"Then what the hell way was it?" Don's voice rose with impatience.

"Why don't you just shut up and listen to me?" she said.

"I will when you start telling the truth about all of this."

"Most of it has been true."

"Most? Like your truth rates a four out of five stars?"

"Hey, hey!" Elliot intervened.

Don took him as a new consideration, a possible new angle, new truth. "So where were you when all this was happening in Jody's life?"

"Me?" Elliot exclaimed. "I never even knew Jody back then. I've told you, she's only been working for me a couple years. We never knew each other before that."

Jody sat down in the cool dark grass. This was it, the time had come for her to be completely honest. No more half truths. "Kevin didn't tell me to get an abortion," she began.

Though she refrained from looking directly back up at Don and Elliot, standing over her, she could feel their quiet, puzzled expressions. "Yes, I got pregnant with Kevin's baby," she continued, "but I...I never told him, at the time, like I said I did. He never told me to get an abortion back then because he never even knew I was pregnant."

"What?" Don was trying to get this but not exactly managing it.

"Because," she said, still without looking at either of the guys, "by the time I found out I was pregnant Kevin had already made plans to go live with his dad out east and go to college there. Realizing I wasn't that important to him after all, I didn't think I should hold him back from his plans by springing my pregnancy on him. I was sure he wouldn't want me or the baby. And since Dad wouldn't allow me to keep the baby and raise it myself, I…I didn't see any point in telling Kevin. He never knew about the baby until just recently."

"Why didn't you tell me all this stuff straight out to begin with?" Don was more disturbed than ever.

"Because…" She lifted her gaze slowly, until her eyes met the searing disappointment in his. "Because the truth…it…was difficult for me."

"Difficult," he said, as if the word carried no validation.

"It was just easier to—"

"Jody," Don began then stopped, shook his head and turned away.

She stayed sitting in the grass. Because she felt safer there. And better able to finish explaining from there. "Kevin returned to Winona a while back, called me and started asking me out again. I don't know why I went, under the circumstances, but I did. As far as Kevin was concerned, he just thought of us as old friends. I tried to see us that way, too. No harm, seeing an old friend, right? Except then I began thinking how much I owed him the truth. So I finally told him about the baby, his baby, for the first time, and how I'd given it away behind his back."

"Rough trip," Elliot concluded.

Jody nodded. "That's when Kevin and I had a major blowup. He flipped out over my telling him."

"Wonder why?" Don wised off.

"That's why I've been in so much misery. For what I did to him, not what he did to me. Get it?"

"I'm trying," Don said.

"It was the worst thing of my life, giving my baby away. But having to admit to Kevin that I gave his baby away, that he didn't even know about or have any decision about, well, it's doubled my guilt, and I…I just haven't been able to live with it very well. It's why I've need you so much, Don."

"Me? Like you needed my reassurance that lying is perfectly all right?"

"Hey, Don—" Elliot cautioned him.

"Please don't be mad at me," Jody pleaded to her brother. "Because that's it now, the whole truth about Kevin and the baby."

"You're sure?" he asked, still with an edge in his voice.

She started crying. "Yes…that's it…everything."

Don gave a curt laugh, as if to let her know he had little reason for ever believing her again about anything.

Feeling only too eager to get this over with, Jody concluded, "After I told Kevin about the baby, he said he had a lot of thinking to do. I was scared as to what that might lead to. Scared as to meeting with him again, talking with him again. And then there he was, at Quincy's that night. I didn't know what was going to happen."

"Well, he came here tonight to tell you that he forgave you," Elliot pointed out.

While that meant a lot to Jody, what she really needed right now was Don's forgiveness and understanding. But while she sat there waiting and hoping for it, she got nothing. No special word. No special look. Nothing.

Eventually Don just walked off toward the house, shaking his head in that way of his and muttering to himself.

Elliot helped Jody to her feet, consoling her, "You were pretty young back then."

She sighed. "Young and dumb. I wish I could go back, Elliot. To change things. And if I couldn't change everything, I at least wish I had kept my little girl."

"I know, I know." He wrapped his arms around her.

After Elliot left, Jody went inside the house looking for Don. She found him in the living room, sitting behind the desk.

"I'm sorry," she said, crossing the room to him.

He looked up, saying nothing.

She stood opposite the desk from him. "For my mistakes with Kevin. But mostly, Don, for lying to you like I did."

"You gave me a lot of variations."

"I know. Because it was…it was really hard for me to come out with everything all at once."

He rolled a pencil between his hands while studying her. "You went all the way up to Myre, found me, and drug me home, only to lie to me?"

"I planned to tell you everything eventually. I just couldn't do it all at once. Please try and understand. I need you to understand, Don."

"That's everything now?"

"Yes."

"What about Kevin?"

"He knows everything too now."

"I mean, what about how I just treated him? I was pounding the guy when actually I should've been offering him my sympathy. How could you have not told him you were carrying his baby? And then to have given it away without his ever knowing about it?"

"Don't you think I've asked myself these things a million times? When Kevin came back to town, and we started seeing each other again off and on, I knew then I had to tell him. I knew he had the right to know. Even though it was too late to do anything about it. He didn't take it well. He went really crazy over it."

"Do you blame him?"

"I couldn't believe it mattered so much to him," Jody said. "But it did. I did a terrible thing to him, as if it wasn't bad enough what I did to myself or to our baby. I'm sick over this, Don. How can I feel better? How can I ever feel better?"

Though her brother was more gentle and patient with her now than he'd been out on the front lawn earlier, he was not yet totally accepting. "Truth…you just seemed like such a preacher of truth, Jody."

"I am," she insisted. "I really am."

"It's taken you long enough to get your truth straight."

"Because it's been painful, trying to get all this out to you. I wanted to say everything all at once, right away, but I couldn't. I wanted the truth between Kevin and me, and I wanted the truth between us, you and me, Don. That's what I've been working toward, what I've finally now accomplished."

"Truth…" he said dreamily, as though with a sad, breaking revelation of his own. He stood up and came around the desk to her. "Want my truth?"

"I thought I had it."

"Not all of it."

She gave him a go-ahead look.

"Truth is, Jody, I'm really sorry for taking off from here eight years ago. It was a mistake over all my mistakes. The one I had the most trouble living with, admitting to. At the time I…I thought Dad was totally unfair about a lot of stuff. I wanted his approval, I guess, way ahead of ever learning how to earn it. But it wasn't there. It just never was. And it didn't look like it ever would be, could be."

"He loved you for you," Jody said. "It was never anything you had to earn."

Don shook his head in disagreement. "Love and approval are two separate things. I guess I know that he loved me. But he never approved of me or my friends or just about anything I ever did."

"Well, look where your friends wound up," Jody reasoned.

"They weren't always like that. Joel, Max and Warren. I knew this…this other side of them, the better side of them."

"Dad was worried about you."

"Worried? Or overly judgmental?"

"*You're* a judgmental person," Jody said.

It brought a slight grin out of Don. "Please don't tell me I'm like him."

"Well…" she began.

"He was a hard man, Jody. After Mom died he came down on me about everything. Everything. It almost felt like since she was gone he put all his focus on me, had to make up for losing her by really trying to make something of me. He just had all these expectations of me that I couldn't live up to. I was only continual disappointment to him and—"

"No. No, you weren't. Don't say that."

"You and I knew opposite sides of Dad."

"You're saying that his sending me away to get rid of my baby like it never happened was the softer side of him?"

"No," Don said with somber realization.

"I saw both sides of him. Both."

"Yeah, okay, I guess you did. But I still pretty much only saw the one.

"So you left."

"By nineteen I was pretty much only seeing one side of myself as well. And didn't like it. Couldn't seem to change it. Didn't know what else to do, but leave. I'd lost Rossi to his time-consuming college studies, three friends of mine to prison, Dad's respect, endless jobs that didn't work out…and Krista. I'd had it, really had it. I…I just had to leave, get away from everything."

"Including me?" she asked.

He smiled fondly at her and shook his head no. "You were probably the one good thing I had here."

"But not enough to keep you."

"I had to find a new life for myself."

"Which turned out better?"

He didn't answer. Which seemed, to her, like a no.

"I wish I'd have found you a long time ago," she said.

"I wish I'd have found myself a long time ago," he admitted. Then with a quick laugh, he added, "I hope I still can."

"Sometimes you have to go backwards, rather than ahead, to do that."

"Thus you drug me back to Winona."

She smiled admittedly. Then sighed ahead of saying, "Dad had his hands full with us after Mom died. I think he was only a single parent doing his best."

"Yeah, I suppose," Don agreed.

"Even in spite of how he handled my baby situation, I knew he loved me. And despite the differences you and he had, I knew he loved you, too. Isn't that really the main thing?"

"I guess," Don said. "He was our dad, no matter what, wasn't he? And despite our differences, I do regret the grief I caused him. Wish I could tell him that, but it's kind of late now, right?" A sad sort of smile mixed into the hopelessness of his words. "Talk about truth, huh?"

"I'm glad we had this talk, Don."

He nodded. "Guess there's a weird sort of satisfaction in 'fessing up, huh?"

"Yeah, weird."

"Maybe there's still hope for us, you and me, Jody."

"As for being a family again?"

"A family, yeah. You, me and Elliot."

To the surprise of his including Elliot, she brightly assumed, "So you're no longer mad that we, he and I, kidnapped you from Myre?"

"Well…" Don contemplated.

"Tell me honestly, Don, would you have ever come back here under your own free will?"

"Truth?"

"Yes."

"No, I don't suppose I ever would have."

Though it hurt, hearing him say so, it justified the kidnapping all the more. "Then I'm glad Elliot and I forced you back here."

Don gave a slow nod. "If that's what it took, then that's what it took. Jody, it's too late for me to tell Dad I'm sorry for taking off like I did. But I can tell you. I'm sorry. I'm just really sorry."

She hugged him tightly. "Welcome home, Don."

Chapter 52

▼

"I owe you an apology," Jody was on the kitchen phone telling Elliot early the next morning when Don came downstairs. She motioned to her brother that the coffee on the counter had been made.

"You don't owe me anything," Elliot said, from the motel.

"Yes, I do. You're a special friend, Elliot, and I hadn't been totally open and honest with you."

Watching Don pour his mug of coffee, Jody knew that he was listening to her end of the phone conversation. And probably wondering, though not for the first time, what exactly was going on between her and Elliot. Most of the time she herself wondered.

"What's past is past," Elliot allowed her. "You don't owe me anything from that, Jody."

"Then you're not mad about—"

"I'm not mad about anything."

It made her smile. "Really? That's nice."

"I'm a nice guy."

"You are," she agreed. "I'll come out there later and we'll talk, okay?"

"Sure. I'll be here, sitting on my stool in the silent boring trend of the Treggor Motel. I really wouldn't mind a little talk."

"Maybe this afternoon, Elliot. How about this afternoon?"

"Okay," he said.

"Okay," she said.

"Good-morning," Don greeted her as she hung up and turned around to him. "Everything all right?"

"I'm working on it."

"Good." Curious as he seemed, he wasn't pushing.

She started across the kitchen. "So what do you want for breakfast? I'm sorry I'm running late here, but I got involved on the phone."

"Don't worry about it. Coffee's enough. Jody, look, there's really nothing around here for you to help with today, so if you want to go to the Treggor, just go."

She had a statement to make, which she certainly thought her brother would've well known by now. Her hands went onto her hips as she gave him a straight look. "If you and Rossi are going to be on the roof, I wouldn't think of being away."

"We'll be okay, whether you're here or not," he assured her.

"I worry when you're up there."

"Don't. Rossi and I are climbers from way back, we had a tree house together in his yard when we were kids."

A rap came at the back door and Rossi called, "Hey, Don! Ready to go?"

After one more swallow of coffee, Don dumped the rest in the sink.

Jody followed him to the door. "You didn't have breakfast yet. I know I'm late with it, but just give me a minute. Just—"

"It's okay, it's okay," Don said. "I'll take an early break. What do you say to a few pancakes around nine, if you're really planning to be home?"

"You got it." She went outside with him.

"Good-morning, you two," Rossi said to them.

"Good-morning, you one," Don said back.

"Is this the day you finally join us up top?" Rossi, grinning through his dark beard, teased Jody.

Every day he routinely asked her the same thing, and every day she routinely responded, "Yeah, maybe."

Then Don, always taking them seriously, would routinely flare up, "Hey, she's strictly ground supervisor and that's it!"

Jody and Rossi exchanged a quick laugh and a high five behind his back for having riled him once again.

As she helped the guys gather their supplies, and watched them raise the ladder, Jody supposed she was, after all, relieved at Don's ongoing refusal to let her join them on the roof. Joking or otherwise. Because truthfully, she was nervous enough seeing them climb up the rungs, without actually doing it herself. She was quite satisfied being ground supervisor.

"911!" Rossi, straddling a peek edge, was suddenly shouting down to her.

Her heart skipped a beat. "What happened?" she called back.

"Nothing. Yet. Just want you to remember that number. In case." He was laughing at the same time as he was nailing a shingle.

From his work spot near Rossi, Don also shouted down to her, "Forget 911! All you'll need to know is where the shovel and plastic bags are. If either or both of us fall off of here, that's all you'll need to clean up the mess."

"Oooh, you guys!" Jody spluttered. Though she liked kidding around with them, this was gross and made her stomach queasy.

She sat down in the grass, afraid to watch them, afraid not to watch them. She compromised by putting her hands over her eyes and peeking up at them only through the little slits between her fingers, as one did at a horror movie.

Don's and Rossi's attention soon settled strictly on their hammering and off of her. She was glad. The last thing she wanted was to be a hazardous distraction to them. She wanted to be there, needed to be there, but her main concern was that they concentrate safely on what they were doing.

It was touching how the shingling project brought Don and Rossi together. She wondered how or if they would have ever made it through their barrier had there not been a specific incident, such as the roofing, to promote it. With her hands off her eyes, she braved a full open glimpse at the two of them. It was great, seeing them work together, talk together, laugh together. If only it wasn't taking place so high up.

She lowered her gaze to the yard, off toward the back, deciding she didn't have to keep vigil over the guys every single second. Her thoughts switched to Elliot. Of how frequently he, too, was there helping with the roof as well as with other repair jobs. Though Don was always very appreciative of him, he was careful not to keep Elliot from his motel responsibilities too often or for too long at a time.

Elliot's response to that was always something like, "Thanks for worrying about the motel, but don't. I worry enough for both of us, okay? Besides, my sitting there behind the office counter doesn't necessarily promote any more business than my not sitting there. And anyway, Tom likes being left in charge."

Jody smiled with her thoughts of Elliot. She wondered if he ever smiled, thinking of her. While he was currently minding the Treggor, and Don and Rossi were hammering in the high heavens, she was sitting in the grass daydreaming, not being much help to anyone or anything, lest it be the thinker of good thoughts.

When she noticed a patch of clover beside her, she started sorting through it with her fingers. It was kind of fun. Something to busy herself with. However, her casual search in the grass soon became a diligent one. Until it was no longer a game, but rather an absolute necessity for her to find a four-leaf clover. Because after all, anyone could certainly use a little good luck in their life, right?

The roof hammering stopped the instant she let out a scream.

"What happened?" Don frantically called down to her.

"I found a four leaf clover!" She jumped to her feet, holding it up to the guys as if they'd be able to see it at that distance. "It's good luck! It means I'm going to have good luck!"

"You maybe, but not us!" Don straightened back from the edge he'd hung over. "That outburst nearly cost us a fall!"

"Sorry," Jody said.

"Sorry, she says," he mimicked her smartly.

Rossi played out the drama. "Yeah, she pulls something like that and probably doesn't even have those plastic bags ready yet."

"I got excited because I haven't found one of these in a long time," she explained.

Don and Rossi resumed their hammering, as if her treasure meant nothing to them.

It mean a lot to her. It was special. She spun the clover between her fingers, wondering what might possibly come from it. Maybe that was her good luck, already used up, the guys not falling off the roof from the startle she'd caused them. But then again, maybe there'd be something more personally directed just to her. She kissed the clover and placed it preciously into her shirt pocket.

* * * *

The whole morning had been cloudy and cool with the threat of rain. Shortly after twelve o'clock noon the wetness began as a drizzle, allowing the guys just enough time to wind up that day's work and clear off the roof before it turned into a downpour. Rossi went home and Don switched to some of the remaining inside jobs.

Matthew came over to the Mitchells' house through the rain. Jody met him at the back door, set his umbrella on the rug to drip dry, and motioned him on in to where Don was working.

The neighbor entered the dining room with a curious look up at Don, who was standing on a chair. "Well…what are you up to there, boy?"

"Fixing the kitchen sink," Don quipped, actually tightening the base screw to the new ceiling fixture he'd just installed.

Matthew was staring oddly at him. "W-what…?"

Don stepped down off the chair. "Just kidding, Matthew."

"Oh…" the elderly man drawled, "well I was w-wondering why the kitchen sink would be up there. I mean…this is the dining room."

Don laughed. "Okay, okay, you got me back. So how are you, Matthew, and what are you doing out on a day like this?"

"I'm fine…and there's nothing wrong with the day. It's just that I've, uh…just been worried about you kids."

"Me and Jody?" Don sat down on the chair, straddling it backwards.

"We're fine, Matthew," Jody, standing in the kitchen doorway, told him.

"Y-you didn't look or…or sound so fine last night," Matthew said. "I saw your…your ruckus out on the front lawn. I was…just getting up to…to change channels on my TV when—"

"You really should have remote, Matthew," Jody said.

"—when I saw the fighting," he finished saying.

"It was a misunderstanding," Don explained.

"Oh…uh-huh…I see." Matthew looked from one of them to the other. "You're okay then? Everything's okay today?"

Tapping his screwdriver on the back of the chair, Don smiled reassuringly. "Yeah."

"Everything's cool, Matthew," Jody assured him. "Sorry that we caused you concern." She hated to leave almost as soon as he'd come over, but she'd already decided to go see Elliot. Pulling on her jacket, she explained, "I was just on my way out to the motel."

"Drive careful…" Matthew told her, in a way that a grandfather would look out for his granddaughter, "with that rain c-coming down the way it is."

"I will," she promised, cherishing the endearment.

Chapter 53

Because Don recognized that Matthew was restless and in need of something to do, he was not surprised to hear him ask, "Mind if I hang around a while?"

"Might put you to work," Don warned him, knowing that was just exactly what the guy wanted to hear.

"That'd be fine…" Matthew said. "W-where do I start?"

From the dining room, Don next went to replace the light fixture in the front foyer.

Matthew followed, asking, "So how do you like being back home?"

Don climbed up on the chair he'd brought with and started to carefully unscrew the cracked and chipped glass shade. "Well, Matthew, I'll tell you, it's really made me face the truth about some things."

"Have you faced the one yet about…about how and why your dad changed so drastically after your mom died?"

Don dropped a curious look on him. "I'm not sure."

The neighbor continued in his chatty drawl, "Because maybe you should, Don…if you don't mind my saying. It was what turned him so callous, you know…his losing her. And I…I think you should understand that. And allow that. Underneath Fred was just so…so scared of raising two kids alone. S-scared of whether or not he could handle it…or anything…without her."

"You knew him pretty well, didn't you?" Don remained on the chair, though ceased from working.

"Well, yeah…I did." The strain in Matthew's voice implied that it hadn't been especially easy. "It bothered me, y'know…to see the…the way he became so unfairly hard on you kids."

"He was pretty tough most of the time."

"I know. He...he shouldn't have had to be like that. Don't guess he actually saw it himself though."

Don's hands reached back up to the light fixture. He couldn't blame his dad any more than he blamed himself for the rocky father-son relationship they'd had. "I was hard on him too, Matthew. I never helped him much. Mostly I did things that riled him."

"Well...your mom's passing, bless her soul, left a sad mark all way around in this household."

"I have learned that Jody had a rougher time back then than what I would've imagined." Don removed the old fixture from its bracket and handed it down to Matthew.

Matthew set it on the floor then handed up the new one directly out of its box. "A quiet one...just a quiet little one."

"Jody?" Don exclaimed with surprise.

"'Course she did tell me about the baby."

"You knew about the baby?"

Matthew nodded and smiled fondly. "She always told me things. But I...I mean she was more quiet when it came to dealing with your dad. Not like you were, Don...with your raging arguments and loud vile words. Your s-storming out of the house and...and screeching off with your car. She was quiet. What your dad said to Jody went. Whether she liked it or not. She idolized your spirit, and—"

"Oh, come on," Don doubted it.

"She did...she did. She often told me she wished she was more like you."

Don shook his head against it. "Stupid wish."

"Maybe...maybe, but her thinking about it was w-what helped keep her going all the time you were gone...all the time she missed you so much...waited for you to come home."

Don supposed the Myre kidnapping made more sense to him now, Jody's desperation finally kicking up enough spirit to get her what she wanted...him. The wonderment of his sister made him smile just as fondly over her as Matthew had. "So you know about the handcuffs then?"

"Handcuffs?" Matthew obviously didn't.

Don got down off his chair, ready to share the story. "Let me tell you about the handcuffs, Matthew."

Chapter 54

▼

The rain had turned into a real drencher. Coming down hard and furiously, as if it would never stop. Flares of lightning. Cracks of thunder. Elliot watched for Jody out the Treggor office window, worrying about her driving through such a storm, yet selfishly worrying even more that she might not attempt the trip at all.

It was nerve wracking, standing there watching and waiting like that. With his two-sided worry. And the slowness of time. Seeking a diversion, he left the window, went around behind the counter, and took out a deck of cards.

It wasn't that Elliot's mind was ever off Jody, that he hadn't heard her car pull into the motel lot, but more that the thunderstorm pretty well covered all other sounds. It therefore startled him when the office door suddenly burst open and she came scurrying inside. She was safe and okay, but as soaked as if she'd walked rather than driven there.

His game of solitaire ended the moment he saw her. "Hey, look at you! You look like a drowned rat! Mouse, a drowned mouse!"

"Wow! Do you know what it's like out there?" She seemed more happy than distressed, taking off her jacket, shaking the rain from it, water still dripping from her hair and down her sweet face.

"Must be horrid. I was really worried about you, Jody."

"Horrid?" Her dark eyes sparkled with vivacity. "No, Elliot, it's great!"

He shook his head at her. Only a crazy person would call a storm like this great. But after all, this was Jody.

She stepped out of her wet shoes, wasn't wearing socks. Barefoot, jeans, and a pink-checked blouse, she stood there with a look that make Elliot realize how very young she was in comparison to his age thirty-six.

She turned back to observe the weather through the front window, exclaiming, "I love the rain."

He could only halfway agree. "Rain, yeah, but Jody, this is—"

"Blinding lightning. Shattering thunder. Pounding rain." She waved her hands ecstatically as she spoke. "It's absolutely electrifying out there. I love it! It's the kind of storm that stirs up your soul and puts you one on one with nature."

Elliot felt like he was watching an actress in a dramatic theatrical performance. And he was almost taken in by the staging of it, until Jody looked around at him with a real look, checking his real reaction.

"Don't you think so, Elliot?" she asked. "About the storm and you and nature?"

"I...uh..." The humorous side of it got him, making him laugh, making him not sure.

"I'll take you for a ride. Come on!" She was ready to go again.

"No, thanks. You'd better get dry. I'll get you a towel. A real towel."

Since the office bathroom only had paper towels on a holder, he went around the counter and crossed the floor to the side door leading to his own private room. He went to his bathroom and yanked a clean towel off the wall bar. Then turning back, he found Jody had come into his room and was looking around.

"I've never been in here before," she said, curiously scanning it.

"No, I know." Elliot stood revealed, embarrassed, wishing at least that his bed was made. He swooped up a dirty shirt off the floor and some scattered socks from here and there.

Jody kept moving and observing. "Of all the time I worked here, I've never ever seen your room."

"I know." Elliot balled his shirt and his socks together and shot them into the bathroom.

"Oh, I'd seen you go in and out of here lots of times," Jody said, "only ever catching a mere glimpse through the doorway, that's all." Her inspection roamed from the dresser, to the bed, to the desk at the window, to the tall bookcase full of books. "Elliot, I didn't know you read."

He laughed stiffly. "Motel management requirement, you have to know how to read."

"Books, I mean read books. Wow, look at all of these." She stood reading off titles, fingering edges.

"Well, what else would I be doing with my spare time? I mean, besides tracking down wayward brothers." He finally handed over the towel he'd gotten for her.

As Jody rubbed the blue terrycloth against her hair and face, Elliot stood watching with fascination. God, she was cute. Really cute. Wet hair and barefoot cute. But something more. Something that—

She stopped what she was doing and broke into a giggle. "What? Why are you looking at me that way?"

"It's just…" He shrugged, shook his head, wasn't sure he wanted to tell her. Then, okay, he decided he would. "You look very, uh…sexy…doing that."

"Rubbing my hair with a towel?" she exclaimed. "Sexy? Come on, Elliot, just what kind of books are we into here anyway?"

"Airplanes, actually. Mostly stuff about airplanes."

"Oh, well, that explains it." She fired the damp towel back at him.

He tossed it behind him into the bathroom to land wherever. And then a strange sort of twinge began flittering through him, like a warning that he was feeling something a lot more here than he really ought to be. "Let's go," he said, walking past her and heading out of the room.

She stayed where she was. "Elliot, are you uncomfortable with my being in here?"

He paused in the open doorway. "No. Yes."

"Which?" She waited for him to decide.

He was nervous. Really nervous. Because of her. Without any words or jokes for a come back, he stared at the floor.

"Elliot, it's me Jody, remember?" she said innocently.

He took a deep breath and slowly lifted his gaze back at her. "I know it's you. And you're a girl and I'm a guy and it's raining out and we're all alone here and—"

"So?" She sounded as ready to take him on as she had the storm. "Are you saying that you think something might happen?"

He smiled uncomfortably. "That towel thing…it just got to me a little, that's all." He proceeded through the doorway and into the office.

"Elliot," she said, following him now, "don't do this to me."

"Do what?" He went behind the counter and took up his unfinished game of solitaire.

"Act funny."

"That's me, funny Elliot."

"Are you attracted to me? Or what?" She came around the counter to him. "Because I'm beginning to get these weird messages from you lately."

"Messages?" he questioned, guilty as he was.

"Are you, Elliot? Is that why you're acting strange?"

The cards he had only just picked up went flipping out of his hands into the air. "Me? I'm old enough to be your…your big brother."

"I have a big brother."

"Right, you do. Well, some people have two."

"Will you get serious?"

He swallowed hard. "Serious?"

"Yes. Because I came here to talk to you about Kevin, remember?"

"Kevin. Yeah. Right. I did kind of forget that. I'm glad you reminded me." He hated her switching tracks like that, even though the one they'd been on had been scaring the hell out of him. Serious. Yeah. Okay. He gave her his utmost serious look to indicate his readiness for the Kevin talk.

"I did a terrible thing to him, Elliot, and I…I've been having this really hard time living with that. What I've finally learned, though, is that the biggest help comes from talking about it."

His heartbeat returned to normal. His palms dried. He re-established himself to the real role he played in Jody's life, her friend. He gave her a smile A serious smile. "I'm here for you, Jody. Let's talk."

The rain continued. Streaming down the front window, drumming on the roof, creating a closed-in-away-from-the-rest-of-the-world sort of atmosphere. The hurricane lamp on the end of the counter lent a warm, cozy glow to an otherwise bleak office.

Elliot took a bottle of white wine out of the cupboard and two stemmed glasses that had been in there forever waiting for an occasion. The discussion of Kevin could definitely be considered an occasion. Though not especially a joyous one, certainly a drinking one.

Chapter 55

I wish I'd have talked to you about Kevin and the baby long before this," Jody concluded an hour later, feeling wonderfully unburdened and peaceful.

"So do I," Elliot said.

He'd been a good listener and had come through it just as compassionately as she'd hoped he would.

Sitting on the edge of the counter, legs dangling and swinging slightly, Jody gave a sigh of satisfaction. "I don't know what it might have been like for me to have gone on and on keeping all this inside myself. I just feel this big relief now for having talked to you and to Don."

Leaning against the file cabinet opposite her, Elliot gave a slow nod. "The way it should be."

"Can you forgive me for my past?" she asked him.

"Yeah. Sure. Can you forgive yourself?"

"I don't know."

"I hope you can."

"I guess that's important."

"It is. You have to do it, Jody."

She frowned.

"You can," he assured her.

"Do you really think so?"

It would have been Elliot's typical place to laugh and comically say something like no, I'm lying actually. But he didn't. He only smiled tenderly and said, "Yeah, really."

"How about you now, Elliot?" she asked.

"Me now? What?" He did react a little silly on that one, grinning and drawing back in exaggerated shock.

She finished her glass of wine, deciding she liked wine now a lot better than either vodka or margaritas, and set the empty glass on the counter. "Anything you want to confess up from your past?"

"I...well...I..." He set his empty glass atop the file cabinet. "Yeah, uh, all right. I've never mentioned to you that I was married."

"You were married?" she exclaimed.

"It was a long time ago. The divorce was bitter and painful and I've pretty much tried keeping the memory of it crammed back into the far closet of my mind."

"Oh, Elliot." Jody felt honored that he was sharing it with her now, and she wanted to be just as compassionate to him as he'd been to her. Looking at him deeply, she reached over and laid her hand on his arm. "A divorce. Wow. Your idea or hers?"

"Hers and the boyfriend she ran off with."

"Any kids?"

"No."

"Oh, Elliot." She saw him so differently now. Someone beyond managing a dead motel, having a messy bedroom and reading lots of books.

"Yeah," he continued, "that was about the time I stepped into the motel business with my dad. He needed help, I needed a change. Then he passed on. And then the business sort of did too. And sometimes, like way too often, Jody, I really don't know what the hell I'm doing."

"Oh, Elliot..." She hopped off the counter, landing closely before him. "What can I do to help?"

"Help?" The idea seemed to scare him.

"Maybe it's time someone helped you. Like me. What can I do?"

He shrugged, thought for a moment, then answered, "Just be."

"Be what?"

"You. Here."

"Doesn't seem like much."

"It is."

She smiled at how easy it was. "Okay, I'm me and I'm here."

He smiled back at her. "Thanks."

For some reason his smile, now, felt different than any of the other smiles he'd ever given her. It was like it touched a totally new place in her, and made her feel womanly special rather than on the brink of being tickled or teased or play wrestled.

"So Elliot, if it's so bad with the Treggor, why don't you—"

"What do you mean if?"

"Why don't you dump the motel and do something else with your life? I know you promised your dad that you'd stick with it, but he hadn't known Highway 64 would get rerouted. He'd have wanted you to be happy, Elliot, I'm sure. He wouldn't have expected you to stick with it no matter what."

"I guess you could say I've fallen into something of a rut."

"Ruts. Yeah, tell me about them. I've been in one, Don's been in one. They're not impossible to get out of though. The two of us, we're finding that out. And you can too, Elliot."

"The blame for the way this motel is going," Elliot said, "isn't just Highway 64's fault."

"It doesn't matter where the blame lies. It's still a rut."

He nodded admittedly. "My rut."

He'd helped her with her problem, she wanted to help him with his. "I'm saying that you can get out of your rut, Elliot. You've just got to want to badly enough and…and try hard enough."

He sighed. "I think I'm too old for all that."

"You're not old."

"I've got more than a few gray hairs."

"They're adorable. They don't make you old."

"Maybe being around someone your age makes me feel old."

"Sorry," she apologized.

He laughed. "You don't have to be sorry. It's just the way it is."

"I'm not a kid."

"No," he agreed.

"I'm just a girl…and…and you're a guy…"

"Yeah," he agreed.

"And…and it's raining outside…and…"

"It's coming down pretty hard."

"I know. But I drove out here to…to…"

"Crazy to drive through that storm."

"Crazy," she agreed.

Elliot sighed, getting that scared look again. "I'm really, really glad you're crazy."

Jody seriously agreed. "Me too."

Something was definitely going on between them. Something different from other times. Something that gave Jody a butterfly stomach and a racing pulse.

Elliot straightened away from the file cabinet, cleared his throat as if he were about to give a speech, then saying nothing at all he pulled her into his arms.

Jody had been held by him before. Many times. But never in the way he was holding her right now. He caressed her. Heatedly, sexually. His teddy bear image changed to manly lust. His mouth brushed hers hesitantly, as if giving her a chance to stop him if she wanted to. But she didn't.

They kissed.

It felt kind of scary at first. Then totally awesome. Then kind of like love.

*   *   *   *

Jody got home at six o'clock. Don was on the living room phone. She stood back unnoticed, listening, determining that it was Aunt Marlo, in California, he was talking to. Aunt Marlo.

"I know," Don was saying. "I know the agency has its rules, yeah, but I just thought…I know, I realize that, but isn't there some way you could maybe find out the kid's whereabouts, or at least a phone number Jody could connect with? I don't know if it would be harder or easier for her. I…I just feel like we have to try and do something. Yeah…yeah, you're probably right, Aunt Marlo. I'll try. Okay. Thanks anyway. Bye."

He hung up, and stood slouched over for a long, silent moment.

When he turned and saw Jody, she confessed her eavesdropping by commending him with, "Thanks for trying."

He took no credit. "Thanks for nothing, you mean."

"Maybe it's for the best." She shrugged off her own disappointment with logical excuses. "Maybe I couldn't handle seeing her, knowing I could never get her back. That might really be worse, you know? For her, me, everyone. Maybe it's better keeping the break clean."

Her brother smiled gently. "You're a brave and realistic girl, Jody."

She scrinched her face. "Skip the brave part."

He left his chair to come give her a hug. "I'm sorry, sis."

"I know. Me too."

"So how's Elliot?"

"He's fine. We talked…and we…talked. About Kevin. Also about Elliot's predicament with the motel. He doesn't know what he's going to do about it, Don. I'm worried about him."

"Maybe we can help him."

"You and me?" She was touched by his saying that.

"Yeah," he said simply.

"Like what? How?"

Don began pacing the room. Past the desk, past the window, past her, around the easy chair, over to the doorway. "I don't know," he spoke as he walked, "but there must be a way. We'll find a way, Jody. You and me."

"All right!" she exclaimed, followed by a burst of giggles.

"What's so funny?" he asked, returning to her.

"You."

"I'm not trying to be funny here, Jody." He almost seemed a little offended.

"No, I know. I just mean it's funny, sweet, the way you've changed since first telling Larry to...well, you've just—"

"Larry!" Don grasped his head and moaned. "I treated him so bad that night we ran into each other in Myre."

"Yeah, he told me."

"It's just that he...he seemed like such a threat to me at the time."

"Threat?"

"His wanting to haul me home, right then and there. Like he was the police or something. But he was only my cousin. Cousin."

"And with no handcuffs."

"Think he's home?"

"I don't know. I've tried him a few times since you've been back, but haven't been able to catch him. He doesn't have an answering maching. And he's out of town a lot."

Don grabbed the phone book off a corner of the desk, paged through it, fingered down a column, lifted the receiver, and dialed. As he waited through the rings, he winked at Jody.

Amendment came, when he lucked out reaching him. "Hi, Larry, it's Don. Yeah, man, really. Well, I'm home. Here in Winona. Jody brought me back. I have to admit, it's not half the bad trip I anticipated it to be. Yeah...yeah, I know. That's right. Hey, Larry...I just...wanted to say I'm sorry for treating you like I did in Myre that one night. I'm really sorry. I guess it's about time I, uh...stopped being such an asshole." He paused to laugh. "Okay, for sure. Look, I can't believe how our paths crossed like that. Meant to be, I guess, just meant to be. If it hadn't been for you, Jody'd have never hunted me down. Look, Larry, we'll have to get together for a drink some night." He laughed again. "Well, of course I'm buying. Yeah...yeah, I know..."

Jody walked away happily, leaving Don alone with his phone call.

She went upstairs to her room and over to the window. It was great how Don was making amends in his life. Though she'd made a few of her own, she still had plenty more to deal with, such as now having a complete and settling talk with Kevin. And there was Matthew. Somehow she had to come to terms with Matthew's leaving. And soon she would be needing to look for another job, if Elliot dumped the motel. And where would she go when the house sold? Where would Don go? Would they only end up losing each other again? Amends, so many, toward so much.

She leaned against the window frame, held the curtain aside and stared out at the rain that was falling in but a light mist now. The whole world outside looked like a gigantic gray veil. Despite her romantic moment with Elliot a short while ago, she was starting to feel really down again about her unsolved problems.

Remembering her four-leaf clover, she fetched it out of her shirt pocket and spun it between her fingers. It soon helped to lighten her spirit, renew her hope, and steer her thoughts back solely to Elliot.

It had been quite an afternoon with him. Their having talked to each other as they'd never talked before, looked at each other as they'd never looked before, touched and kissed like lovers rather than friends. Though they hadn't gone as far as making love, their relationship had nevertheless progressed to intimate, intricate, and responsible. It would never again be as casual and carefree as before. Which was okay. Wasn't it? She touched the four leaf clover to her cheek, easily deciding yes.

Chapter 56

On the evening of August tenth, long after Ralph Remeer had left with his signed contract and numerous marketing ideas for the Mitchell house, Jody and Don stood in the front yard staring at the For Sale sign. No matter how much they had talked and planned on selling, the actuality of it hit with unexpected emotions.

"So I guess that's that," Don felt the end of his being needed tagged to an uncertain future.

"Remeer said the house is in such good shape now that it should sell fast and profitably," Jody confirmed, actually sounding more disappointed than pleased by it.

"You okay?" Don asked her.

"Fine. You?"

"Fine."

Neither of them were fine. But as they spoke to one another, they stared steadily at the sign trying to make like they were.

"You did a good job on the house, Don," Jody said.

"We," he corrected her. "You and me both. Plus plenty of help from Rossi, Elliot, and Matthew."

Jody's bottom lip curled. "I'm kind of sorry it's over."

"Yeah…well…things do get over." Don was no more cheerful than she.

"I feel like a deserter. To the house. Don't you?"

He sighed heavily. "Look, Jody, all this has been decided, hasn't it?"

"I know, but when it comes right down to it—"

"I know," he agreed before she could finish her sentence.

"Are we going to be better off, Don?"

He lifted his look from the sign to her. "I hope so."

"New beginnings for us?"

He nodded and smiled. "Brand new."

"I'm going to have to get my talk with Kevin over with now."

Though Don had gotten used to helping her with a lot of stuff, her talk with Kevin was something she'd have to handle strictly on her own. "You'll manage," he told her.

"Kevin was a mistake," she said.

"We've all got past mistakes haunting us, Jody."

"But how do you live them down? How do you ever come to do that, Don?"

Having had very little success at it himself, he could only say with a grin, "If you find out, let me know."

She wasn't letting him off that easily. "Your taking off from everybody and everything, did that really solve anything for you?"

"I thought it did at first."

"Only at first?"

"I guess it solved some problems, created others."

"What sort of others?"

"Regret. Guilt. The need to—"

"To what?"

Don still couldn't get over how Jody had this way of making him say stuff beyond what he wanted to say.

"Tell me," she coaxed. "The need for what?"

"The need to make up for things," he confessed under force.

"Okay, so then why didn't you just—"

"I said the *need* to make up, Jody, not the ability."

"Elliot and I gave you the ability, didn't we?"

He laughed. "Yeah, by way of something like a kick in the butt."

"Your coming back here has made up for a lot of things, Don."

"Yeah…maybe…except…" He stuck his hands in his pockets and turned away from Jody, the sign, and the rest of his sentence.

"Except what?" she asked.

Keeping his back to her made it easier for him to admit, "Except the one thing I most needed to make up for was with Dad. Kind of late for that, wouldn't you say?"

Jody put her hand on his shoulder. "Maybe he knows. Maybe somehow Dad knows that you came back and that you're feeling this way."

Don shook his head with uncertainty. Then he walked away from her and headed out of the yard.

"Where you going?" she called after him.

He didn't say. Didn't know. Except that when he reached the main sidewalk he automatically went to the left.

The next thing he knew he was standing on the Glennon front porch, about to knock on the door but feeling confused as to how he got there. He couldn't remember the walk, not any of it. It felt like he'd been miraculously transcended beyond his consciousness. One moment he'd been with Jody and the next he was here. The whole transition between was missing. Weird, very weird.

The evening was hot and muggy, no let up, how it'd been all day. Nervous and losing whatever confidence he might have started with, Don decided to leave.

Then the door clicked.

Opened.

Krista appeared.

Don wasn't sure if he'd actually knocked or whether she'd just noticed him there on her own. "Hi," he said.

"Hi," she said.

"Can I talk to you?"

"Sure." She stepped back and motioned him inside.

Don entered the living room with her, verifying, "Rossi's working the earlier shift this week, right?"

"Yes. In fact three to eleven might become permanent now."

"That would probably be good, with the baby coming, wouldn't it?"

"Yes." She sat down, motioning for him to do the same.

Though it couldn't have been clear to her why he was there, because it wasn't even that clear to himself, she seemed pleased with his unexpected visit.

"I'm glad you let Rossi help you with the roof," she said.

Don stood beside the wooden rocker, choosing not to sit. This visit was going to be brief. "Rossi gave me no choice. He just showed up and started working one day. I could hardly throw him off the roof, could I?"

"I'm glad you didn't," Krista said with a light laugh. "He's happy that the two of you have put your friendship back on track."

"I didn't come over here to talk about Rossi." Don studied the pretty picture she made. Sitting there in the big chair, a loose-fitting pink blouse topping a print skirt, redness flaming in her hair from the lamp light next to her, a healthy glow in her cheeks, sparkle in her eyes. "I came to apologize to you, Krista. I want to say that I'm sorry."

"For what, Don?"

Her asking threw him like a trick question to what he'd only intended to keep quick and simple. "For everything."

"Everything?" she questioned.

For some reason the immensity of his answer still came up short for her. He nodded, wondering how much better he could say it, cover it. Everything meant everything, didn't it?

Krista, got out of her chair and stuck her hands on her hips, a threatening stance just like Jody's. "You can't just say you're sorry for everything."

"I can't?" Don began to work his foot against the bottom curve of the rocker, setting the chair into a brisk back and forth motion beside him. Swish, swish, swish. "Why not?" Swish, swish, swish.

"Because it's meaningless if you don't specifically label it."

"Label?" He didn't understand. He kept the rocker going. Swish, swish, swish.

"Yes." She stood there, obviously expecting a lot more out of this than what he was so far giving.

He hated how everything he'd ever tried saying or doing with Krista got misconstrued. He didn't know why it'd always been so difficult, only that it was. But times were different now. He could do this. He was older and wiser. And she was married. And it was time for closure.

He stopped the rocker. He stood straight and still, determined to make a strong presentation of his purpose. "Look, it wasn't easy for me in the first place, you know, to—"

"You don't really know what you're saying sorry for, do you, Don?" she said, sounding like a lawyer. "I appreciate your wanting to make things right between us, but simply saying you're sorry for everything doesn't cut it."

Sorry, sorry…he was sorry, at that point, for having ever come there at all. He shoved a hand through his hair. Took a deep breath. Gave Krista a bewildered smile. Surely she had to be putting him on here.

But she was serious and continued in just that way. "I want to hear exactly what it is you're sorry to me about, Don."

He lowered his look from her to the floor. He'd already told her he was sorry about everything, but that wasn't conclusive enough for her. So now what was he supposed to say? He wasn't good at this. Didn't know.

"Are you sorry you ever met me?" she asked. "Or for what we once had? Or lost? For going away? Or coming back? For wrong judgments? For your anger? Tell me what, Don. What does everything mean? Because I'm not sure. And I don't think you are either."

He felt way in over his head with this apology idea.

Krista waited.

Everything. She wanted to hear everything. Not just the word everything, but the list behind it. He resumed eye contact with her, deciding to give it a try. "I'm sorry I had such lousy friends and was too stupid to even know it at the time. I'm sorry that when I did learn the truth about them I couldn't seem to rise above it. I'm sorry I disappointed you so much back then, Krista. More than anything...I'm sorry I ever left and didn't just stay and try to work everything out...with you, with everybody. I'm sorry I...I gave up on you, me, us, everything good I ever had here in Winona."

At last Krista fell satisfied, in her look and in her voice. "Oh, Don..."

"So that's it, everything," he concluded. Except for adding on a whimsical note, "Jody's made me face up to my responsibilities, plus half of hers."

Krista laughed. "She deserves a medal. We've all missed you and worried about you so much, Don."

He knew that now. But for eight years his head had been too thick to ever imagine anyone cared.

"It's not even our having you home that means so much to us, all of us, as it is seeing that you're getting back a real sense of yourself. Your better self. You know what I mean?"

He nodded, finally starting to see it, feel it, believe it. Until Krista came and gave him a hug. Why would she do that? Didn't she think their bodies pressing together would be just enough to knock him off kilter again? That it would only prove how his being sorry didn't necessarily make the agony of losing her vanish?

Before she could catch the hurt in his eyes, he covered it with a fake smile and turned to leave.

He could have gone back for Matthew's car, he'd been given permission to use it whenever. He carried the keys, had full access. But it felt good to walk. Aimlessly. With no particular direction. Except, hopefully, to ease the tension in his head and the ache in his heart. So maybe he'd go have a few drinks somewhere. Damn, it was hot out.

Chapter 57

Jody let Kevin into her house. She'd been so nervous, phoning him earlier, asking him over, waiting for him to arrive, trying to plan what to say. Now he was here and she was hardly feeling any better, any calmer, any more prepared.

Equally uneasy, he made flitting glances in all directions as he entered. "Your brother isn't home, I hope."

"No."

"Good."

They took living room chairs across from one another.

"Kevin, do you want something cold to drink?" she offered.

"No thanks."

"I have iced tea, Coke, water…"

"No, I'm fine."

He didn't look fine. His forehead was beaded with perspiration, his shirt was damp and sticking to him, his hands fidgeted on the arms of the chair, and his eyes shifted about continuously. Jody's own clothes felt clingy, body limp, mind null. It had to be the hottest day of the summer. It was hard enough just to breathe, let alone think. Maybe they should have waited for a cooler day to meet.

"I was surprised when you called me, Jody," Kevin said.

She smiled. "I was surprised, too, that I called."

"But I guess we do need to talk."

"Yes, we do."

"We hardly had a chance the other night."

"No." For this get together being her idea, Jody was doing a bad job of leading. Looking at Kevin, at the directness in his eyes and his resolute sense of seriousness, she realized how much older he was now from back when she'd first met him, dated him. She saw much more maturity in him than in herself.

"What's wrong?" he asked, reading her discomfort.

"Like you don't know."

"I mean, in regards to right now, this minute. You're really edgy."

"Everything that's wrong about right now, this minute, has to do with the past," she said.

"I thought we'd pretty well covered all that with our talk a while back, hadn't we? Come on, Jody..." His voice was softer than his visual image. It helped her to go on.

"In that talk we had a while back," she said, "you...you took it really hard about the baby. Hearing, years later, that you'd fathered a baby and I'd given it away."

He nodded. "It was a jolt, that's for sure."

"When I saw you at Quincy's I didn't know what you were thinking, what you were possibly going to say to me or do. I was scared. Really scared. I guess I deserved it. But...but then one night you came over here to tell me that you forgave me for what I did to you."

A slight grin flickered briefly over Kevin's otherwise taut expression. "Yeah, I guess I did get that much out to you that night before your brother decked me."

"He had it wrong. Don had it wrong. That's why he went so crazy. I...oh, Kevin, I'm sorry, but I was still having so much trouble dealing with having given the baby up that it just seemed easier to...to shift the story a little."

"Shift?" He narrowed his eyes at her.

"What I told my brother was that I'd told you about the baby way back at the beginning and you said you wanted me to get an abortion."

"Abortion?" Kevin leaned forward in his chair, as though surely he wasn't hearing her correctly. "I never even knew you were pregnant back then. How could I have—"

"I know, I know. I said I shifted the blame. I was scared of telling Don the truth. I wanted to make it more your fault than mine. But then when I did tell him the truth he got real sympathetic to you. He was very sorry that you weren't ever told about your own baby right off and that it was given away behind your back. I'm sorry too, Kevin. More than I can ever tell you."

Tears were stinging behind her eyes, but she continued with more long over-due honesty. "I don't know how I could have done such a thing. Except, I guess, that on top of all my own pain at the time, it seemed like a total disconnection from you was the easiest way for me to cope. And maybe it was, all along, until you came back to Winona and wanted to see me again."

"I guess you had your reasons, Jody, for not telling me about the baby, back then." Kevin took his time with his words, putting careful thought ahead of speaking them. "You were young, scared, pressured by your father. But mostly, I'm sure it was because of how I treated you. We went out a few times, risked unprotected sex a couples of times, then I simply said good-bye, I was going out east to stay with my dad and go to college there. I stressed how I wanted to try to make something of myself. Had all these big important goals for myself. I never gave the slightest indication that you could possibly fit into any of them. And so, of course, you sure couldn't see how a baby would."

She nodded. "I was torn over what to do at the time, Kevin. I really was."

He left his chair and came over to stoop down before her. As if with his closeness, and his intense dark eyes, he was going to make doubly sure he got through to her. "I know, Jody. At least, I can imagine. I'm so sorry you had to go through that time all alone. Or at least without the support you should have had from me."

Heavyheartedly, she said, "I guess I didn't even know you well enough to think that you might have been supportive. Or cared."

"I would have cared," he said. "But God, Jody, I honestly don't know what I'd have chosen as the solution to the matter back then. I can't look back now and see myself as a...a father and husband at that time. I'm sorry we messed up. I, more than you, should've been more responsible. I'm just so sorry we messed up," he began again, "but I'm not sorry for what was done about it. I mean, for as difficult as it was for you, giving the baby up, I feel certain that it was the most right thing that couldn've been done for all three of us under the circumstances."

She stood up and moved away from him, feeling an all too familiar onset of uncertainty rising within her. "I don't know," she said.

"Don't know what?" Kevin asked.

"I can never believe that giving her up was the right thing. I wish I could accept it, but I can't. She was beautiful, Kevin. So perfect and sweet. And she had all this really dark hair."

"Jody, Jody." He, too, stood up and came to put his arms around her.

"I could have raised her," she insisted, shaking her head wretchedly. "I could have, with or without your help."

"You say that now because you're older. But back then you...you were only what? Sixteen when you had her? What's done is done. Jody, I've forgiven you…and myself…and accepted what is. That's what you've got to do now, too, you know?"

"I know," she said under force. She broke from his hold, needing to stand on her own strength. "You know what, Kevin?"

"What?" he asked.

"All these years I've tried covering my own guilt by blaming everyone else. I hated that my dad made me go away to have the baby and give her up. I hated that my Aunt Marlo took part in supporting that. I hated that my brother Don wasn't here when I needed him. I hated you for leaving, going away like I meant absolutely nothing to you. It felt like everyone had let me down. But I guess in the back of my mind I knew where the real responsibly lay. I wasn't that young. I could have stood up for myself and for the baby a lot better than I did. But I didn't. I just let everything run right over me. And then, all of a sudden, it was too late."

"I'm glad you didn't feel it was too late to finally tell me all this now," Kevin said.

"I was never able to come to terms with any of this as much as I have lately. It's taken me this long. I just…I wish it had been sooner though, Kevin. A lot sooner."

A smile slipped through his somberness. "Sounds like you've been doing some serious sorting. And that's good. But now you have to let it go, Jody. Can you do that? Because you really need to. You do."

"I know. I can, I will." She stepped away from him and wandered around the living room, gazing at family pictures here and there on table tops. She'd lost her mom, her dad, her baby girl. And her brother, too, for eight years. But now Don, the only family she had left, was back in her life. And that helped. That plus knowing that Kevin wasn't angry with her.

She looked at Kevin, her baby's father, and felt the painful load she'd carried alone for so long now lighten. She took a deep breath and smiled back at him. "I'm going to be okay. How about you?"

He nodded. "Yeah, me too."

Chapter 58

▼

Elliot had been asleep in bed with his clothes on when the motel desk bell woke him with a startle. He jumped to his feet. The book he'd been reading and had dozed off from flew off his chest, and he bumped the dresser lamp, nearly knocking it over.

The desk bell, the desk bell…someone was pounding it incessantly.

He hurriedly unlocked the door to the office. Who would be so impatient? So rude? Who would be so—

It was Don, with some floozy of a girl under his arm, grinning as big as all get out.

"Don! What the hell are you doing here?"

"Renting a room," he said with a loose laugh. "Got any available?"

The couple reeked of liquor and swayed in their standing.

Elliot checked the wall clock. It was 1:30 AM. He rechecked Don. "You're drunk! How could you even drive out here in this condition?"

"We took a cab," Don said. The way he and the girl looked at each other and laughed indicated it'd been something of an adventure. "The driver got lost. Said your motel's a bitch to find."

"Tell me about it," Elliot snapped.

"When he did find it," Don added, "he compared it to the Bates Motel."

"And warned us not to take showers," the girl denoted.

"This is Cleo," Don introduced her to Elliot. "Her and me…we'd like a room, please." He took the pen from the counter and started signing the register book.

Elliot held back, hesitantly. But Don began hitting the service bell again, demanding a key.

Elliot went behind the counter and chose number two off the rack, figuring that would be the closest room for Don to walk to, if in fact he could even make it that far. Then he turned the register around, finding his newest guest had scribbled in the name John Smith.

"Hey—" Don said before Elliot could comment, "isn't that the way it's done?"

"I wouldn't know," Elliot grumbled, reluctantly adding the date and his initials.

Don turned the ledger back to himself to see what Elliot had entered and found it hilarious.

"It's procedure," Elliot said to Don's laughter. "We do have a few procedures, you know. What's so funny?"

"Your initials. E.T.?"

"They are my initials, my official initials. No creativity on my part."

"E.T.?" Don couldn't seem to get over it.

"They would be the initials for Elliot Treggor, now wouldn't they?" Elliot's annoyance grew.

Don continued playing against it. "E.T. Elliot Treggor, E.T. You do know who E.T. is, don't you?"

Elliot knew. "Yeah, sure, the cute little creature in the movie *E.T., The Extra-Terrestrial*."

"Don," Cleo tugged at his arm, as if time were of the essence. She wore a tight purple dress, with a side slit all the way up to her left thigh, and her curly blonde hair toppled freely about her heavily made-up face.

Don got back to his reason for being there. "The key, Elliot. Give me the key."

Elliot resisted. "You sure you want to do this, Don?"

Don gave him an off sided look.

"I mean," Elliot said, "don't feel you have to help out my business here in this such a way, you know?"

Don took some money from his wallet and counted it onto the counter. "Let's see…forty-two, wasn't it?"

"You've been here before?" the girl gathered disappointedly.

"Not like you think," Don told her, opening his hand to Elliot.

Elliot placed the key into it. "Number two. It's just—"

"It must be right after number one," Don smartly beat him to the directions.

The couple left the office and Elliot watched them stagger down two doors. He felt bad over Don's condition. And even worse for having tolerated it.

Elliot stood in the office doorway, wondering what had just happened here? Something surely wasn't right about Don's behavior. Something beyond his obviously having had too much to drink. It was kind of as if he, too, wasn't really sure what was happening. Giving him and that girl a room made Elliot feel like a contributor to a big mistake.

Fifteen minutes later, as he guiltily sat at the office counter still pondering over the situation he'd just dealt with, the door opened and that Cleo girl came bristling in alone.

"Something wrong?" was all he could think to ask.

"Yeah!" she said, holding her head high.

"The room should be in good order."

"The room's fine. Don's not. He passed out."

Elliot had to restrain himself from laughing. "He did have quite a bit to drink, didn't he?"

"I didn't come all the way out here in the boondocks to—"

"Now wait a minute, wait a minute—"

"—to be left in the lurch like this."

"Well, don't look at me," he said when he saw how desperately she was, in fact, looking at him.

"You've got to get me out of here."

Elliot laughed and got off his stool. "Out of here? Lady, I own this place, I'm suppose to get people into here."

"A ride. Can you please just give me a ride back to civilization? Take me home?"

Elliot was getting really tired of cleaning up after Don. "W-well, I don't uh…I uh…"

"A ride," she stressed, as being all she wanted. "I'm not about to spend the rest of the night here with a guy who's completely out of it. And to call a cab…well, it's like out of their normal range or something."

Though Elliot disliked the idea, he felt nudged with obligation. "Yeah, okay, a ride. Let me just go look in on Don first and I'll be right back to drive you."

He took off for number two, leaving Cleo waiting in the office. Good idea, checking on Don. You couldn't be too careful about women you picked up with in bars, he thought, and Jody's brother had hardly been in what you'd call a careful condition. Somebody had to look out for him.

He used his pass key and entered room two. Don was crosswise on the bed, as though it was the way he may have first fallen and since stayed. Elliot walked over, bent down and shook him. "Don. Don. Hey, Don."

"Mmm...wha...?" The body moved some. He seemed okay.

Elliot took Don's wallet out of his back pocket and opened it up. Money and cards were in tact. Good, it looked like the girl hadn't been out to roll him. She'd only wanted sex. Elliot grinned deviously over how this turned out. It was funny. Hilarious. Though probably something of a shame that a woman like Cleo should go to waste.

Walking from number two back to the office, Elliot realized once again how very hot it was. Hot and quiet and boring was how he'd come to read himself to sleep earlier. Though it was no longer quiet and boring, it was still plenty hot. *Jeez*, he thought, wiping his shirt sleeve across his damp brow, *some night*.

Cleo was more than ready to go. He escorted her from the office, she towering way taller than he in her spike heels.

Just as they reached his car, but before they got into it, another car came tooling down the forsaken old Highway 64 toward the Treggor. It turned into the lot, headlights flooding forth, causing Elliot to feel somewhat as if he were being caught in a prison break.

He felt even more caught when it turned out to be Jody jumping out of the surprise car, exclaiming, "What are you doing?"

For a moment everyone just stood gawking at one another.

Then Elliot proceeded to open the passenger door of his car and urge Cleo in. Next, flitting around to the driver's side, he told Jody, "Go wait in the office, I'll be right back and explain everything."

He got in his car and started it. Rolling down his window, he secondly called out to her, "It's not what you think!"

Chapter 59

Jody watched Elliot's car leave, him and that girl. It didn't look good. Whatever this was about, it just didn't look good. She turned off her car lights and pulled the key from the ignition. Then she walked to office, muttering, "How does he know what I think?"

She entered the office, purposely giving the door a hard slam behind her. She'd never seen Elliot with a date, or anything close to a date, before this. But she'd sure caught him now. Well, maybe it was because she'd never been out to the Treggor as late as this before to have ever seen what might go on at this time. It was not pleasant, knowing. She hated knowing. She hated Elliot for being less than she'd credited him with, and she hated herself for having stupidly driven out there. It was just that she'd been so worried about Don, his not coming home, and though she hadn't expected Elliot to have any actual answers for her, she'd at least hoped for his comfort and understanding.

Sadly deluded, she stood at the window staring outward at the parking lot. But all she managed to see was the reflection of herself in the glass. No way did she measure up to the girl Elliot was with. Though she'd barely gotten more than a glimpse of her...blonde, tall and sexy had been easily noticed and remembered. Well, if that was what he wanted, so be it.

Jody left her place at the front window and walked across the office to Elliot's room. Her hand only hesitated a few seconds before turning the doorknob. It was unlocked, good. If he had the right to go out on her, she had the right to go into his room. And on that one-for-one reasoning, she entered.

The first thing she saw was the messed-up state of his bed. It made her sick. Literally sick. Which made her realize, all the more, how very much she'd come to consider Elliot hers, all hers.

"I thought he liked me," she said aloud to herself. "But he's cheating on me."

Her stomach whirled. Her face burned. And the back of her head throbbed. She passed the bed, careful not to touch it, and went into the bathroom. She opened the medicine cabinet, looking for Tylenol or aspirin or…Advil, okay, that would do it. There was a glass on the sink. She ran water into it and washed down two tablets. Then she leaned forth and splashed several handfuls of cold water onto her face.

After blotting herself dry with a towel, and feeling only slightly better so far, she faced the sorry sight of herself in the mirror. She looked every bit as tired and haggard as she felt. That girl Elliot left with probably couldn't look half this bad even if she tried. Jody pretended she didn't care, but the fact was that she did and it hurt.

She was so tired. So dispirited.

She decided to ignore the disgusting rumple of Elliot's bed and lie down on it for a few minutes. Just a few minutes.

Chapter 60

▼

When Elliot got back to the motel he found Jody asleep on his bed. He stood over her, looking down at her, wondering why she'd driven out here this time of night. Wondering why he felt so good that she *was* here. Wondering what he should do about her, if anything. Jody…Jody…her name kept running through his mind, finding no real placement but leaving deep, wide tracks.

She looked so angelic, sleeping like that. And appealing, oh yeah. Blue jeans and tee-shirt. Curled on her side. Breathing slowly. Mouth slightly parted. Dark hair softly tousled.

This girl had come to mean a lot to him. Though precisely what, or how much, seemed beyond his calculation. He only knew it couldn't be love. Jeez no, not love.

A night breeze had picked up and came in small, chilling currents through the open window. Elliot pulled the lightweight quilt up over Jody. Then he sat himself onto the straight chair by the desk and slid far enough down so that he could rest his head against it's back.

He tried settling his mind, but it only kept going around and around in fast, senseless circles. And he wanted to close his eyes, but he couldn't quit staring over at the shadowy, covered form on his bed that was Jody…Jody. The affect this girl had on him was totally disturbing. Stupid. Outrageous. And wonderful.

Eventually the spurts of window air trickling across his bare arms made him reach for his jacket off the desk. He covered his arms and chest with it. Then reshifted himself against his hard chair bed. He supposed he could have taken one of the empty rooms for himself…like number three, four, five, six, seven, eight, nine or ten. But something made him stay right where he was and rough it.

Something like…Jody…Jody. Anyway, he reasoned humorously to himself, he really couldn't afford the forty-two bucks.

Eventually Elliot's mind began to shut down and blend into the quiet serenity of the late night world. No more circles. No more Jody tracks. No more contemplation of what all this meant or where it might be going. Only the simple soothing contentment of here and now, this very moment, and of having someone special close by.

His eyes grew heavy and willing to close. He felt himself drifting…drifting…

CHAPTER 61

▼

Elliot was behind the counter having his third cup of coffee the next morning when Don wandered into the motel office at seven-thirty. "Good-morning," he greeted the guest from number two.

Mussed hair, an overnight stubble on his face, wrinkled shirt half in and half out of his pants, and sulking from something more than a hangover, Don made frantic looks in all directions.

"Lose something?" Elliot asked in a singsong voice.

Don grasped the counter and gave him a surprised eye-to-eye. "You know?"

"That Cleo's gone? Yeah."

"How long ago?"

"About fifteen minutes. *After you checked in last night.*"

Don stood dumbfounded, as though that couldn't possibly be.

With a glint of pleasure, Elliot explained, "She came running to me when you passed out. Wanted me to drive her home."

Don slapped his hip pocket.

"Don't worry," Elliot said, "I checked your wallet before we left."

Don seemed more mad than grateful.

Elliot went to the coffee maker on the end of the counter and filled a mug for him. "Sorry you struck out last night."

"Yeah." Don moaned, one hand holding the top of his head, the other gratefully accepting the coffee Elliot brought him. "Thanks."

"You're welcome. Cleo, she's quite a looker."

"She's not a—"

"Looker," Elliot clarified. "I said looker, not hooker."

"I met her in a bar."

"No kidding."

Don sipped his coffee. "Don't you ever get lonely, Elliot?"

The side door opened and Jody, in her own disheveled look, came out of Elliot's room.

"What the hell are you doing here?" Don's exasperation switched from Elliot to her.

Jody stopped, equally shocked seeing him. "Where'd you disappear to last night?"

"You don't want to know," Elliot advised her.

Her hands went onto her hips as she turned specifically to him. "Who was that girl you were with last night?"

Though Elliot laughed at the impression he'd apparently given, he tried clearing it. "I wasn't with her. Jeez, I was only taking her home."

"And that doesn't count?" she asked.

"You're keeping count on me?"

"Cleo? Are you talking about Cleo?" Don questioned him as well.

"Yeah, yeah, I told you I drove her home."

"*Her name is Cleo?*" Jody scowled, as if she considered name knowing to be an automatic sign of having had sex with the person.

"I want to know what the hell you were doing in his room!" Don demanded of his sister. "Or is it obvious from the way you look and the time of day it is?"

"I was exhausted and fell asleep," she said.

"Exhausted from what?"

"From worrying about you mostly. Then from driving out here late at night and—"

"How'd you even know I was here?"

"I didn't."

Don looked at Elliot. "You phoned and told her."

"No," Elliot said defensively, "I'd never snitch on a customer."

"Customer?" Jody shrieked.

Elliot flagged his hands in the air. "We really, really need to have a talk here."

"We are talking," Jody said. "I'm just not getting it."

"I know, I know," Elliot motioned for her to come around behind the counter and sit on the stool. As she did, he poured her a mug of coffee.

The coffee failed to calm her. Because after drinking some of it she continued just as boisterously, "I want to know what's going on here. With everyone."

"Everyone," Elliot agreed. "Okay, we're going to start at the beginning and get this all straight."

When Jody and Don both began speaking at the same time, he shouted over them, "Take turns! Please!"

Don went first. "I took off last night when I—"

"You're always taking off!" Jody said.

"I don't owe you, or anyone, a minute-to-minute account of my whereabouts!"

"Your problem is that you—"

Elliot whistled through his teeth ahead of saying, "Kids, kids! Give each other a chance here, just give each other a chance! Let's be civil, all right?"

Jody and Don gave each other a silent, yet unsettled look.

Elliot added, "Hey, I know, let's go to Quincy's."

Chapter 62

By eleven o'clock the three of them were eating burgers and fries in Quincy's and laughing over last night's happenings at the motel. Everything had been rationalized and understood for the most part. Yet when Don left their booth to go play the jukebox, Jody had just one more question for Elliot. "It didn't bother you that I was sleeping in your bed when you got back last night?"

He shifted uneasily in his seat. "Like I told you and Don, I slept in the chair."

"I know you slept in the chair, Elliot. I want to know how you felt."

"Felt?" he said with a laugh. "The chair kind of got me in my lower back, so eventually I laid my head over onto the desk, which was better, definitely better."

"That's not what I mean."

"Why do women always dance around what they really mean, trying to make men guess them out?"

"You know what I mean," her voice shortened.

He sighed. "Yeah...okay...it shook me up some, seeing you in my bed like that, Jody."

She grinned. "Really?"

"Yeah, you looked real cute."

She frowned. "Cute?"

"So cute that I was glad you were asleep and I didn't have to make a decision as to what to do about you."

He seemed to be doing a lot of side-stepping of his own, to which Jody kept at him. "This...this restraint of yours...did you feel that way when we shared that room in Duluth?"

"A smidgen," he admitted.

"A smidgen? But last night was more than a smidgen?"

"Probably a smidgen more than a smidgen," he said, chuckling at the sound of their conversation.

Don returned to the booth. The first of his selections began playing out of the ceiling speakers. Something romantically touching by Linda Ronstadt. Jody and Elliot stared across the table at each other as if the song was personally directed at them.

After finishing off the last of his French fries, Don asked Elliot, "So what are you going to do?"

"Huh…? What…?" Elliot answered him vaguely.

"About the Treggor," Don said.

Jody smiled at Elliot and he smiled back. She loved the little crinkles that formed at the sides of his mouth when he smiled.

"The Treggor," Don persisted from the outside world.

Jody and Elliot touched hands across the table, and soon their fingertips were playing together.

"Hey," Don said.

Jody didn't seem to mind the term cute so much now, since she sat there applying it to Elliot's look, manner, and charm, as well. Cute, yes, he too was very cute.

"Hello," Don said.

Elliot blinked himself out of his trance, finally acknowledging the brother. "Oh…uh, I don't know about the motel."

"You don't think it's time to start thinking about it?"

"I think about it a lot," Elliot said.

"Sell it and get out."

"Yeah, right. Like there's millions of buyers just waiting to grab it."

"Then dump it and get out."

"And do what?" Elliot became agitated. "I'm thirty-six. At this point I dread the thought of risking a new failure a whole lot more than I do accepting an old one."

Jody wondered how he rated her. Whether she was considered a new risk or an old acceptance. "You know, Elliot, I'm going to have to look for another job pretty soon. You won't be able to afford me much longer."

"No kidding," he agreed despondently.

"I doubt you'll even be able to afford yourself," she added. "What are you going to do?"

Alternating his look between her and Don, Elliot began grilling them equally, "So what are you two planning to do when the house sells? Where you going to live? Don, you going to get a job down here or go back to Myre?"

"I don't know," Don said.

"See what I mean?" Elliot proved his point.

Don nodded, with nothing more to say.

The effect of too many back-to-back slow songs on the jukebox was beginning to impose too heavy of a mood on everyone.

Elliot came up with a suggestive save. "Hey, what say we get off coffee and onto margaritas?"

Don moaned, still nursing his hangover.

Jody also passed. "We've got to go home and get the house in order. Remeer has a showing at three this afternoon."

"Really? Another one? You've got a good agent."

"We've got a good house," Don stated proudly.

"Wish us luck, Elliot," Jody said.

"Luck," he said, not exactly sounding like he meant it.

* * * *

Appointments to show the Mitchell house came fast and frequent. At least three or four a week. It was, after all, a nice old house in perfect condition now and located in a choice section of town. As Ralph Remeer proudly toured clients through it, Jody and Don spent more and more time next door at Matthew's, drinking hot chocolate and peeking through the curtains at the prospective buyers.

"Ellen will, uh…be here for me next week," Matthew said one chilly afternoon late in September, when they were just so gathered together.

He, Jody and Don watched red maple leaves flittering down past the windows.

"Yeah," Don said, "I guess that time has come."

"Yeah," Jody added, feeling like she owned Matthew and therefore shouldn't have to give him up.

"I'm not sure if leaves ever…ever fall off any trees in Arizona," Matthew said sadly. "It being w-warm there all the time."

"I don't know," Don said.

Me neither," Jody added.

"W-what are you kids going to do when the house sells?" Though Matthew had never outwardly asked them before this, his concern revealed some long wondering. "I'm sure it will one day soon th-the way it...it's getting looked at so much."

Don left his chair near the window and strolled over to the fireplace. He seemed drawn to its flickering glow and crackling warmth. Staring down at the burning logs, he finished his hot chocolate and set the empty mug upon the mantle. "Jody and I, we've been doing a lot of talking, Matthew. And we've decided to go to Myre."

Matthew was surprised. "B-both of you?"

Jody got up from her seat on the ottoman. "Yeah, Matthew, I need a change."

"A change..." Though he gave a nod, it was obvious he didn't understand.

"Don and I want to stick together, and I've decided it's not so bad in Myre."

"Myre," he said, with hardly any more clarity. "Uh...I see..."

"I need some change in my life. Myre seemed to be good for Don, maybe it'll be as good for me."

"Well, uh..." Matthew grinned, as he were trying to visualize it, "sounds kind of adventurous."

"Jody is an adventure," Don quipped.

Matthew raised his cocoa mug. "I'll drink to that."

Though Don was briefly amused, he was soon back to staring solemnly into the fireplace.

Jody exchanged a concerned look with Matthew.

"Well, I'm glad you...you came home for a time like you did, Don," Matthew said to him. "It...it just makes my...my going away a little easier...a...a little more complete now."

"Wish I felt more complete," Don said heavily.

Jody and Matthew exchanged another look.

"Y-you mean about your...dad?" Matthew assumed.

"I never got to tell him I was sorry," Don said, head down and speaking more to the fire than to Matthew, "or that I really did love him. And now it's too late."

Matthew's spindly legs lifted him off the couch. "I know...I know exactly how you feel. I...I'm going to...to tell you kids something now that I've never told you before. Something, in fact, that hardly anyone does know...about me, my life."

Jody couldn't imagine what was coming. And Don looked equally intrigued.

Matthew stood as straight as his aged body would allow, as if conjuring up his deepest courage. "Me and Lydia...we had another child. Besides Ellen and John, we had Leonard."

"I never knew that." Jody felt as if she'd been cheated.

Don shook his head, indicating he never knew either.

"I know..." Matthew said, "hardly anyone did." For whatever his secret was, bringing it forth now seemed very painful, but necessary, to him. "Leonard was the oldest. A...a very indifferent boy, he was. Even...even back in those days kids c-could be indifferent. Oh...he gave me and Lyd a lot of trouble and heartache, which I won't detail you with now. But...but it was just an awful lot, believe me. W-we ran out of ideas on how to help him or...or to handle him, cope with him. Only as a...a last resort we...I, mostly it was I, ordered him out of our house, out of our lives. At least...at least till he could regain some sense of value...in himself, us, life in general. But I...I don't think he ever did."

"Where is he now?" Jody asked.

The tears filling into Matthew's hollowed eyes made her sorry she'd asked.

But he'd been coming to that part anyway. It was, in fact, the point of his story. "Leonard died. In a car accident in Chicago...thirty some years ago. He was...about...probably about your age now, Don. I...I hadn't seen Leonard for many years by then and...and I...never did get another chance with him...to tell him I was s-sorry for...for doing the only thing I could think of doing for both our sakes...or...or to tell him that I loved him...that God, above and beyond everything else, I did love him."

Jody went to give Matthew a hug, while Don stood back absorbing the comparison Matthew was trying to bring out.

"I'm sorry, Matthew," Jody said in their embrace. "I'm just so sorry."

"It's a rough one to...to live with all this time," he concluded. Then he stepped away from her and went over to Don. "We have something in common here...don't we, boy?"

The two of them stood face to face, eye to eye, obviously seeing something a lot more than just each other.

"Yeah," Don replied knowingly.

Matthew laid a hand on Don's shoulder. "I turned my life away from my son, then lost him before we could make up...and you...you turned your life away from your dad and lost him before the two of you could make up."

Though Don was quiet, he was obviously caught up with all that Matthew was saying.

"Maybe..." Matthew suggested hopefully, "maybe we...you and I...could kind of settle this whole thing by...by sort of a proxy. Know what I mean...?"

Don gave a nod.

Matthew placed his other hand on Don's other shoulder. And with deep emotion, he spoke to Leonard through Don. "Son...I'm sorry for all that went wrong between us...for the way things had to come to be. You were a good boy beneath your...your troubled ways and I...I hope I was a good father beneath mine. Life doesn't always go just as we intend it to...expect it to. Lots of...lots of tough and unexpected turns. We...we just do the best we know how, that's all. I...I want to say to you now that I...I never stopped loving you...or missing you. Not once. And I just w-wanted to tell you this now, so as I could finally bear to...to let go...after all this time...and say good-bye." His voice quivered at the last.

While Matthew kept his hands on Don's shoulders, Don put his own hands on Matthew's shoulders. The magical force generating between the guys seemed dredging, hurting, soothing, all at the same time. Jody watched and listened, feeling just as many tugs to her own heart.

"Dad..." Don began, to him through Matthew, "I'm sorry I gave you so much stress. I'm sorry that I couldn't live up to your standards. That I got off onto some wrong paths. You always did okay by me. You had a difficult job, taking care of me and Jody by yourself. Us kids missed Mom so much that I...I guess we never really stopped to think how much you were missing her and hurting over her passing too. When things got so messed up for me, I should have stayed and tried to make them right. But I didn't. I left, and I want to tell you now that I regretted that over and over. I should've come back before this. I wish that I had. I wish that I'd had one more chance to be a good son to you. One more chance to give you a hug and tell you that...that I love you, Dad. I'm sorry for so much. I hope you can hear me now, and forgive me, and know that you'll always be in my heart."

Matthew and Don drew together. And Jody wedged in, making it a three-way embrace.

*   *   *   *

Matthew soon moved away with Ellen. His going weighed sadly on Jody, but she knew he would be happy and well looked after by his daughter, son-in-law, grandchildren and great-grandchildren in Arizona. His nephew came to stay in his house, take care of all the loose ends, and put the house up for sale. Thus two old neighboring houses stood side by side with their signs of forsakenness.

Jody and Don took yellow fall mums to their parents' graves one day. And afterwards took a long walk, involving a long talk about the past, present, and future. The brother and sister were definitely ready to move forward. Together.

They began building a plan. A plan that included Elliot. Except every time they tried discussing it with him, he held back into the limit of his motel world, stubborn and fearful of change and chance.

Jody and Don decided it was going to take some drastic measures to Shaghai him.

Chapter 63

A Sold sign topped the For Sale sign out front of the Mitchell house. The sold part wasn't new. It had been there several weeks, claiming accomplishment, joy, relief and finality. But the realness of it all didn't actually set in until the November afternoon of closing, when what seemed like a million papers got read, shuffled and signed between Jody, Don and the new owners, which were a nice young couple with three kids.

Late that same afternoon, after the entire deal had been wrapped up, done and over with, Jody and Don returned to the house and sat out on the back steps for the last time. They huddled deeply into their jackets, warding off the chilling temperature and the season's first snow flurries.

When they finally gave up staring at their $140,000 check, Don refolded it and stuck it back into the dry safe place of his shirt pocket. They then stared at the desertion both their yard and Matthew's yard seemed to have taken on. Despite the sadness in that, the new goals of everyone involved were undeniably happy and just.

"This wouldn't have happened without you, Don," Jody said dreamily, hugging her knees.

The brother flashed one of his quick grins. "Is that gratitude or blame?"

"I'm definitely ready for this," she stated seriously.

"I hope so." He patted his chest, where through the layers of his jacket and shirt pocket was the house-sale check. "It's funny, isn't it, how a house, a home holding years of existence and meaning, can suddenly be diminished to a little slip of paper."

"That little slip of paper is our transfer out of here," she reminded him. "To something new and different and better."

"None of which holds a guarantee," he reminded her as well.

Jody couldn't bear the idea of him, or herself, slipping at this point. They'd worked hard at overcoming their pasts. They had to stay strong in order to get where they were going. "Who needs guarantees as long as we have each other," she said.

"That has come to be the important thing, hasn't it," he agreed.

"You. Me. And Elliot."

"Elliot. Yeah, let's *hope* Elliot."

Jody stood and clapped her cold hands. "Let's go see Elliot."

"Let's go." Don was ready.

They gave a final walk through the stripped clean and totally empty house. The furniture had been put in storage, clothes packed and put into Jody's car. The rooms had acquired a lonesome feel to the change. But another change was coming, by way of a delightful husband and wife couple, three active young children, and a big running, loping, barking dog.

Jody paused in the front foyer. "Good-bye, old house. You'll love the new owners. They're a neat family. They'll take good care of you."

She could tell from the way Don stood there, before they both went out the door, that he was saying his own unspoken good-bye to the house. And that it was on a much better basis than the other time he'd left it, eight years ago.

They took off in the Reliant, with Don driving. But they were not yet headed for Myre. Not without first stopping by the Treggor Motel for a celebration with Elliot. And certainly not without having a scheme up their sleeves.

* * * *

It was 4:30 PM when they got to the motel. Jody entered the office alone, leaving Don in the parking lot to search the glove compartment of Elliot's car.

"Hi," she said, glad to find Elliot far enough to one end of the counter where he didn't have a view of what was going on out front.

"Well...look who's here." Elliot was notably surprised and delighted for the interruption to his doing nothing.

"Don will be right in," Jody said. "He's grabbing some stuff out of the trunk. Party stuff. We thought we'd throw ourselves a going away party here with you, on our way out of town. Is that okay?"

"The party, yeah," Elliot allowed, "but I'm still not real thrilled about your leaving."

The office door sprung open again, and Don came in carrying a bag. While greeting Elliot, his look to Jody denoted that he hadn't found what he'd hoped to in Elliot's car.

There was an urgent need of plan revision. While trying to maintain a relaxed front to Elliot, and unloading food and drink out of the bag onto the counter, Jody wracked her mind for a new idea. Don, however, at the moment, couldn't wait any longer to take out the house-sale check and show Elliot.

Elliot gave it an eye popping look. "Wow! Hey, that's really something, you guys."

"We've said it before and we're saying it again now," Don coaxed, "come with us to Myre, Elliot."

"Yes, please," Jody pleaded.

Elliot made a quirky little laugh. "No, no…I'm not going anywhere, thank you. Least of all Myre."

"Why not?" Jody could neither understand nor accept his refusal.

Don wasn't letting up on Elliot either. "Our buying that Pinewood Motel up near Myre that I told you about last week sounds like a good deal, doesn't it? When Remeer first told me about the listing, he thought I might be interested since I lived up there for a while. And guess what…I was. He and I checked it out. It looks good, Elliot."

"Hellova deal," Elliot agreed to that much.

"For all of us," Don said. "The three of us as partners. Come on, Elliot. Before someone else snatches it. It's for us. I really think it's for us. Take a chance."

Elliot shook his head at them. "I can't believe the two of *you*, taking this kind of chance."

Jody bounced on her toes a few times. "Believe it, Elliot, because it's true."

He looked back and forth between her and Don, grinning in jest of them. "You guys saw how successful my motel was and just had to go out and buy one for yourselves, didn't you?"

"More like we want you to dump this motel and go in with us on ours," Don said.

"And why would I do that?"

"Because we're friends. And because we need your expertise. And because we want you to be a third owner of the Pinewood."

"And just how do you figure I could financially obtain a third ownership?"

Don waved the house-sale check at him. "Our $140,000 along with whatever you can get for the Treggor and—"

Elliot laughed.

"We're serious," Don said.

"So was that laugh, because I'd get nothing for the Treggor. Nothing."

"You'd get something," Jody said.

Elliot sighed. "A nickel, maybe a nickel."

"That would give us $140,000 and five cents for the down payment," Don said.

Elliot moaned.

Jody stretched across the counter to him, her feet nearly leaving the floor as she did. "We'd be good together, the three of us. You as the manager, me as the desk clerk, and—"

"Don as the bellhop?" Elliot quipped.

Don had no concern for work titles other than, "We'd make a good team, Elliot."

Though Elliot seemed slightly infatuated with the idea for about a minute, he fought it off. "Naw…I'm just a solo type of guy."

Jody didn't want Elliot to be alone. She wanted him to be with her and Don. She'd thought he wanted that too. The three of them, like the three musketeers, taking on a venture together. And besides that, what about the new level she and Elliot had come to in their relationship? Was he going to dismiss that so easily now?

"Well, Elliot, we're sure not going to insist that you come to Myre and buy a motel with us," Don only let him off of that matter in exchange for another, "but we are going to insist on partying before Jody and I leave." He motioned to the two bottles of vodka, a large bag of potato chips and three Subway sandwiches.

"Supper!" Elliot cheered. "Hey, you brought supper! Yes! I'm hungry. Thirsty, too. Let's party! Take your jackets off and stay a while."

Don removed his, but Jody still felt cold and kept hers on.

"Got any music?" Don asked.

"A boom box in my room." Elliot started around the counter.

"I'll get it." Jody stopped him with her quick offer. She was, anyway, nearer to the door of his room than he was.

He nodded for her to go ahead.

The boom box was immediately visible on her entrance to Elliot's room, but there was something else she needed to look for first. It was her chance, her very lucky opportune chance to find the handcuffs. Since Don hadn't found them in Elliot's car, they had to be somewhere in here.

Moving swiftly, but carefully, she began her search. She quietly rooted through one dresser drawer after another. Then the desk drawers.

"Did you find it?" Elliot was soon calling to her. Before she could answer him he called again with, "It's on the floor beside the bed."

"Oh, okay!" she called back, pretending she had just then spied it. Meanwhile her hand struck something hard and cold in the far back of the middle desk drawer. Finally. Yes! The handcuffs, with the key in them. At some time or other Elliot had removed the cuffs from his car and put them in here.

Happy and smug over her detective work, she stuck the cuffs into her jacket pocket, collected the stereo, and left the room.

"Let's party!" she said, returning to the office, tuning in a rock 'n roll station as she walked.

When Don received her mission accomplished signal, which was the nod of her head and a mere twitch of a smile, he too cheered, "Yeah, let's party!"

The three of them stood about bopping up and down to an old Beatles' song as they ate their sandwiches and drank vodka.

"Maybe you shouldn't drink so much," Elliot, at one point, commented to Jody with concern.

She motioned to his own busy glass. "Like you're a good one to give such advice."

"I mean," he said, "it's a little scary seeing that you've graduated to straight vodka now."

Jody lifted her glass, "To my graduation," and took a sip.

"She's okay," Don assured Elliot. "I'm keeping a close eye on her."

"And who's keeping an eye on you?" Elliot asked, which got everyone to laughing.

Later, when Elliot went off to the bathroom, preferring the one in through his own room, Jody pulled the handcuffs out of her pocket to show Don. Their plan was back on track, in that if they couldn't persuade Elliot to go willingly with them to Myre then they would kidnap him. Such a force was, after all, a tried and proven plan of Elliot's own making.

Before Elliot returned, Don and Jody dumped their vodkas into the sink of the office bathroom and refilled their glasses with water from the faucet. As per plan.

Elliot came back none the wiser and continued with his sandwich. "Good party. Good subs. Very good subs."

"Is there any food you don't like?" Though Jody was teasing, she supposed she honestly did wonder.

Amidst his chewing, he gave it some thought and laughingly replied, "I'm not real fond of African Jee-Jee flies, but other than that—"

Jody and Don also burst into laughter. And it seemed like from then on everything struck the three of them as being funny.

Not until the radio music eventually mellowed into something softer and quieter did the three of them, as well, mellow into some shared expressions of closeness that seemed defiant of any break-up.

Elliot wiped his hands on a napkin and approached Jody, asking, "Would you like to dance?"

Totally surprised, it took her a few moments to come around to the answer yes. And when she set her drink down to go with him, he actually seemed more surprised than she at what they were about to do.

Don took to sitting on the stool behind the counter, watching as if never ceasing to wonder about those two.

It was nice, moving to the music with Elliot. They held each other closely, and met looks that were even more intimate. They danced well together. But Jody had to wonder if this dance was Elliot's way of letting her know how much he cared about her, or if he was trying to make this into a memorable good-bye. Maybe both. It caused a sweet, sad ache in her heart.

"Good song," he said of the ballad playing.

"Yes," Jody agreed.

"How come we never danced together before?"

"I don't know."

"Maybe the right song never came along."

"Maybe," she agreed.

"This one's good. Real good."

"Elliot...what about us?"

"Us?" He stopped dancing.

"You're going to miss me, you know," she told him.

They started moving again. "I know."

"So why won't you come with me and Don?" She didn't care that she'd resorted to begging. If that's what it took, that's what it took. "Why won't you come in on that Pinewood Motel deal with us? At least come look at it? Why can't you just take a chance and—"

"Maybe I'm scared, Jody."

They stopped dancing again.

"Scared?" She wasn't sure she could allow him to be.

He laughed lightly. "Pretty scary, wouldn't you say, for a guy my age to not know what the hell he wants."

They resumed dancing. Slowly and tenderly. The mood of the music worked toward lifting the mood of their problem. Almost succeeding, but not quite. The problem wasn't going away, no matter how sweet the guitar notes.

"What about me?" Jody asked, hoping he hadn't changed his mind about wanting her.

"I'm crazy about you, you know that," he whispered in her ear.

"Then don't let me get away."

He chuckled. "I'm not sure I'm up to another one of your adventures."

"If you loved me, you would be."

"Whoa!" He gulped a deep breath. "Nobody ever said anything about *love*. I said I was crazy about you. Crazy."

Jody was sure he was teasing. But she needed more than teasing right now, didn't he know? She looked over at her brother, but all he did was grin, shrug and shake his head, as if far be it for him, either, to figure Elliot.

By the time the dance ended, Jody had at least gotten warm. She took off her jacket and slung it over one end of the counter. The handcuffs inside the pocket clanged against it.

"What was that?" Elliot said.

She thought quickly enough to say, "My car keys."

When he headed for the counter, Jody cringed at the possibility that he might be going to investigate the actual cause of the noise. But he was only after the potato chips. He grabbed a handful, saying, "So Don...you're not sorry then that Jody and I forced you back here...to Winona...like we did? " He also poured another three-way round of vodka.

"Naw, it was the highlight of my life." Don winked at Jody, pleased that Elliot's drinking was on a roll again.

Elliot took more chips. "I'm really glad to hear that, Don." Munch, munch, munch. "I mean...I sure wouldn't want your grudge hanging over me for...for the rest of my life." Munch, munch, munch.

"No way. You're appreciated, Elliot, really."

Elliots' eyes shimmered. "So are you, Don. I...I feel like...I've gained a brother."

Don smiled and nodded, equally moved. "For what we've encountered together, yeah, I suppose you could say it is somewhat like being related."

Chapter 64

A car pulled into the Treggor driveway. Since Don was nearest the window, it caught his attention first and sent a jolt of panic through him. This couldn't be, it just couldn't be. A customer now would surely crimp their plan to take Elliot away with them. He knew he had to intercept with something quick.

Elliot joined him at the window, excited at the sight of a prospective guest. "Dust off the register book, Jody."

"Hey, that looks like my buddy Bill from Menard's," Don said, making up a story to dissuade Elliot's hope. "Good ol' Bill. We got acquainted through my many purchases there. I told him I was leaving town today and would be stopping by here first. He must have wanted to track me down at the last minute about something or other. I'll run out to his car and see what it's about. Be right back." He grabbed his jacket and tore outside into the cold, into his lie.

A stranger, rather than any known Bill to Don, was already stepping out of the car. Wearing a suit and a topcoat, he looked more like an office executive than a store clerk.

Don rushed up to him, knowing Elliot was watching from the office window. "Sorry, Sir, the Treggor's closed."

"Closed?" The guy glanced behind him. "I didn't see a closed sign."

"No, uh…we didn't get one up yet. Family emergency just came up. Sorry."

"Oh, well, uh…no, I'm sorry. Guess one never knows from day to day, huh?"

"Yeah. Thanks."

"I stayed here a couple years ago when I came to Winona on business. Good rates. But it wasn't easy to find this time. It seemed like—"

"They redesigned 64," Don explained. "This is now the old 64."

"Yes, so I found out. Well…okay then…I guess if you're closed you're closed. I'll look for another place."

"Sorry," Don said.

"You need a sign out there on the new 64."

"I know. We will. It's…being made right now."

"Good."

Before the would-be customer got back into his car, Don grabbed his hand and gave it a hardy shake, making a good show for Elliot at the window. "Thanks for coming. Sorry to have to turn you away."

The man gave it up easily enough. "I understand. Hope everything turns out all right for you and your family."

"Yeah, me too."

The car left and Don returned to the warmth of the office. "Bill…that was Bill…" he said about the man he pretended to know. "He just remembered a couple things he…he had to tell me before I left town. Nice guy, that Bill."

"Should've asked him in for a drink," Elliot said, lifting his own drink off the counter.

"Naw…he's working…on his break right now…had to get back…I mean wanted to get back…he's the…actually he's the manager of this one particular Menard's I'd been going to. That's why he, uh…was so dressed up."

"I really like Bill," Jody said, pretending she knew him as well.

As if he felt socially left out, Elliot said, "Huh, wish I could have gotten to meet him."

Chapter 65

▼

As the afternoon progressed into evening, Elliot's intoxication progressed as well. On one of his frequent trips to the bathroom, he bumped hard into the doorway to his bedroom, prompting Jody to ask, "Need some help?"

"No…I…I'm all…right…" he stammered. "It's just…this damn doorway's so damn narrow. Always was…always was." He gave it a hit, as though it might just that easily be altered.

As he clumsily proceeded on his way, Jody and Don shared a quiet secretive laugh between themselves.

"Do you think it's time yet?" she whispered.

"Yeah," Don said, "it's time."

When Elliot came back, staggering and bumping through the doorway to the office, with as much trouble coming this direction as he'd had going the other, he caught the brother and sister doing a strange look on him. "What's up?" he asked. "We out of vodka or something?"

"Jody and I were thinking," Don said, "that we'd kinda like to move our party to Quincy's, listen to some live music, hang out there one last time for a while before leaving. What do you say?"

Jody cheered, "Say yes, Elliot!"

Embracing an edge of the counter, he casually wondered, "Is anybody here in condition to drive?"

"Me," Don said, shaking the car keys in the air. "I'm one experienced alcoholic driver."

The car keys. Jody remembered telling Elliot earlier that they were in her jacket pocket, and now, suddenly, Don had them. Another look at Elliot, however, insured that he was totally unfazed by such detail.

"Okay, I'm game, let's go!" Elliot put on his jacket. But after zipping it up, he headed back to his bedroom, mumbling, "My wallet, where'd I leave my wallet? Can't leave without my wallet. I think it's on my dresser. Be right back."

When he returned, Jody opened the front door, Don turned off the music and lights, and Elliot, with some fumbling, managed to lock up.

The three of them got into the Reliant. Jody and Don in the front, with Don at the wheel, and Elliot in back, between a crowded collection of cartons and clothes.

They drove off. And as they turned out of the lot Jody gave a last look back at the Treggor Motel. Don turned the windshield wipers on just enough for them to swipe back and forth twice. Though the snow was still only falling lightly, it had started a thin accumulation in places such as the grass and the front of the car. Elliot didn't seem to notice that they were taking the opposite direction of Quincy's. He was, in fact, within the next few minutes of car motion, slumped down and passed out.

"As per plan," Jody said to Don, relieved that she no longer had to act stoned and glad to finally be underway.

"All systems go," he said as gratefully.

"Think he'll hate us for this?"

Don glanced over his shoulder at the body on the back seat. "Maybe a little. But at least we'll get him to look at the Pinewood and base a decision on that rather than on just words and long distance speculation."

"The Pinewood is going to be a good thing, isn't it, Don?" She knew it, and felt it, but wanted an extra ounce of assurance.

"It's location, condition and price are all excellent, as far as Remeer and I could determine. Yes!"

"I mean for us...you, me and Elliot personally."

Her brother gave her a look. "We need something. We all desperately need a new focus in our lives, right?"

"Right," Jody agreed.

"So why not this?"

It wasn't much longer before Don stopped the car, took the handcuffs from her and went back to fasten the unbeknownst Elliot's hands together, exclaiming, "Excellent plan. Just excellent. Thanks, Elliot."

Then they drove off again. The snow, floating down before them, sparkled like diamonds in the headlights.

"Are you finally at peace with your past now, Don?" Jody asked.

He looked at her and grinned. "Yeah, I think so. You with yours?"

"I think so. You ready to run a motel?"

Don laughed. "Yeah, I think so. You?"

"Ready."

"Me too," he said.

Still within Winona, and way too early according to plan, Elliot began stirring. Moving, moaning, coming to, he found himself in a cuffed restraint. "Hey! What the hell is this?"

"What do you think, E.T.?" Don answered him. "A dose of your own medicine."

Elliot struggled, trying to sit up better, looking for recognition in the darkness out the windows. "Doesn't look like we're going to Quincy's."

"Myre," Jody said. "Would you believe Myre?"

"No. No way. Come on, you can't—"

"We're taking you to the Pinewood Motel, just beyond Myre," Don informed him.

"It didn't matter to you that I'd said no?" Elliot gave the back of Don's seat a hard kick.

"Ouch!" Don blared.

"Familiar?" Elliot blared back.

"Calm down, Elliot," Jody spoke as soothingly to him as if he were a patient rather than a prisoner.

"Where'd you get these cuffs?" He clanged them together. "You stole them out of my room, didn't you? Stole!"

"Yes, but I—"

"Don, maybe you should warn your little sister about where theft can lead a person. Remind her where your friends wound up."

"We couldn't accept your saying no to this motel venture," Don said. "Not without your giving it a fair shake."

"This is fair?"

Jody looked around at him. "Don't be mad, Elliot. If it was a good enough plan to use on Don, it's good enough to use on you."

"Stop the car," Elliot ordered. "Just stop the car."

"No," Don said.

"Yes," Elliot insisted.

"No."
"I have to get out."
"No, you don't."
"Yes, I do."
"No, you don't."
"Yes, I do. I really, really do."

Jody leaned toward her brother. "Don, maybe he has to…you know."

"Yeah, okay." Don pulled the car over to the edge of the road and stopped. "We're past all gas stations but haven't reached the highway yet. There are bushes just off the road shoulder, Elliot." He got out and opened the back door for him.

But after awkwardly maneuvering out of the back seat, Elliot didn't head for the bushes. He rather walked to the center of the road and kept going beyond the parked car.

"Hey!" Don shouted at him. "Where you going? What do you think you're doing?"

"Elliot, no!" Jody called out her window at him. "Not in the road! Don't do it in the middle of the road! Don, don't let him pee in the middle of the road!" If Elliot was this mad and crazy and spiteful, she at least wasn't going to watch. She covered her eyes with her hands.

But Elliot gleefully shouted back, "I don't have to piss!"

Jody uncovered her eyes, trying to figure him out all over again.

"What then?" Don, standing beside the car, called to him. "Escaping? Is that what you think you're doing, Elliot? Escaping?" He laughed about it, as if he'd have no problem retrieving him. "I'm bigger than you, Elliot, and sober. You don't stand a chance."

Elliot turned in the center of the road, about forty feet ahead of them. "Watch me!"

Holding their attention, he started back their way, fully spotlighted in the car's headlights like an actor in a perplexing role.

Don tensed, ready to nab him.

"Wait!" Elliot said. "Just watch me! Let it register what I'm doing! Just let it register!"

Jody got out of the car to join Don. Together they studied Elliot's approach. There seemed to be a purpose. But what? What?

Elliot paused midway to them, as if allowing them more chance to think. But to their null expressions, he soon proceeded forth again.

Since neither Don nor Jody still didn't have a clue as to what Elliot was doing by the time he reached them, he thus turned and started back up the road to where he'd gone before. Once again, from there, he began another walk toward them. "What am I doing here?" he coaxed. "Watch me. Think."

"You're being ridiculous, that's what," Don said.

Jody was shivering. "It's cold out here. Come on, let's get in the car and go."

Elliot gave up on them. "Okay, okay, I'll tell you, for cryin' out loud! I'm walking a straight line here! The center line of the road! I'm walking it! The straight and narrow! Now do you get it?"

Though snow was blowing and swirling across the pavement and about his feet, the yellow line was clearly visible, clearly the clue.

Jody exchanged a look with Don. "He's not drunk?" Then she looked back at Elliot. "You're not drunk?"

"Congratulations!" he cheered, by then all the way back to them. "You got it, you finally got it! After I so much as told you. I couldn't be drunk, like you thought, and walk the line, like I just did, could I? Surprise!" He stood laughing over what he'd just pulled on them.

"Wait a minute, wait a minute—" Don was still trying to grasp the entirety of it. "You mean, you were onto our plan the whole time?"

Elliot shook his cuffed hands. "I was perfectly aware of your putting these on me."

"So you *were* onto us the whole time," Don verified.

"Not the whole time," Elliot said.

"How long?" Jody asked.

"Well..." he drawled.

"At what point *were* you onto us?" Don demanded.

"Exactly when did you make up your mind that you really wanted to come with?" Jody grilled him for specifics. "When we danced? Was it when we danced, Elliot?"

Though there had been almost no traffic on the road so far, a car now came from the opposite direction, slowed down, and stopped across from them. The driver rolled down his window. "Everything okay, there?"

"Perfect!" Elliot answered, with Jody in front of him hiding the handcuffs.

The car drove on.

"Thank you!" Elliot called after the vanishing car.

"But you drank," Jody said, resuming their conversation. "Don and I dumped drinks you weren't aware of, but you—"

"So did I, kiddo." He burst into another hardy laugh. "You weren't aware that every time I went off to the potty I took my drink along with me? Then you certainly weren't aware that I'd been dumping my vodka and refilling my glass with water same as you guys were supposedly doing, the very same."

"I don't believe this!" Don clutched his head and turned a circle.

"What?" Elliot was highly amused. "That I outsmarted your smartness?"

Jody was still afraid of believing too much, too fast. "Does this mean that you wanted to go with us all along?"

"What it means..." he slowed his speech, promoting his genuiness, "is that yes...I wanted to...but it was really hard for me to admit...to myself as well as to you two. When I got wise to what you were up to...I finally began thinking okay, yeah, why not."

Jody threw her arms around him. "Oh, Elliot!"

"No fair," he said, "I can't hug back."

Don took the cuffs off of him. "Then I guess you're somewhat interested in that three way partnership in the Pinewood?"

"Somewhat?" Elliot shrieked. "You think I'd go through all this if I weren't?"

"You do like to play games," Don said. "I do know you like to play games, Elliot."

Jody hoped it was more than a game. "Elliot, should we go back and pack a bag for you?"

He gave her an astonished look. "You don't have one in the trunk? Jeez, Jody, haven't I taught you anything? I thought you had this stunt down pat. How could you forget to pack a bag for me?"

"I don't know," she admitted sheepishly, "I guess I just never got the chance."

Elliot reached into his right jacket pocket and pulled out a pair of socks and underwear. Then from his left pocket a toothbrush and razor. "One step ahead of you guys, just one step ahead."

The three of them shared a round of laughter. And the bond between them was wonderfully rekindled.

Don gave Elliot a fond slap on the back. "Sounds like you're definitely planning to help us make something of the Pinewood Motel."

"You guys really didn't think, for one minute, that you could ever make a go of it without me, did you?" Elliot boasted.

"Not even for a half a minute," Jody said, misty eyed and happy.

Elliot smiled and kissed her forehead. "You're something, you know that? Really something."

"Like what?" she asked.

"Damned if I know," he said, then gave her a real kiss on the lips.

"Just think of all that vodka we wasted between us," Don said as they got into the car, all three in the front this time, Jody in the middle.

"Hey, whatever works is not wasted," Elliot rationalized.

Don jangled the handcuffs in the air, bringing still more laughs out of everyone.

Elliot reached over to take them. "They come in handy, don't they."

"We've all had our turn with them, that's for sure," Jody said.

"Plus, there are still more ways to use them." Elliot opened the cuffs.

"More ways?" Jody felt a little uneasy.

Click, click…he snapped one cuff around her right wrist. Click, click…the other one around his left wrist.

"Elliot!" she shrieked.

"And this one will undoubtedly prove to be the most interesting," Don said, starting the car and driving off. "Especially since I lost the key on the ground somewhere back there."

Jody supposed he was kidding. But wasn't sure. "No, you didn't. Did you?"

The snow was falling harder now. They passed a sign reading,

> YOU ARE NOW LEAVING WINONA
> BUCKLE UP

Jody and Elliot lifted their handcuffed wrists and smiled at each other.

# # #

Correspondence to the author should be addressed to:

Marilyn DeMars

P.O. Box 28234

Crystal, MN 55428

0-595-29172-4

NORMANDALE COMMUNITY COLLEGE
LIBRARY
9700 FRANCE AVENUE SOUTH
BLOOMINGTON, MN 55431-4399